BEGINNER'S LUCK

BEGINNER'S LUCK

MONSTERS ARE NOT MYTHS VOLUME 1

LES GOULD

FALSTAFF
BOOKS
WWW.FALSTAFFBOOKS.COM

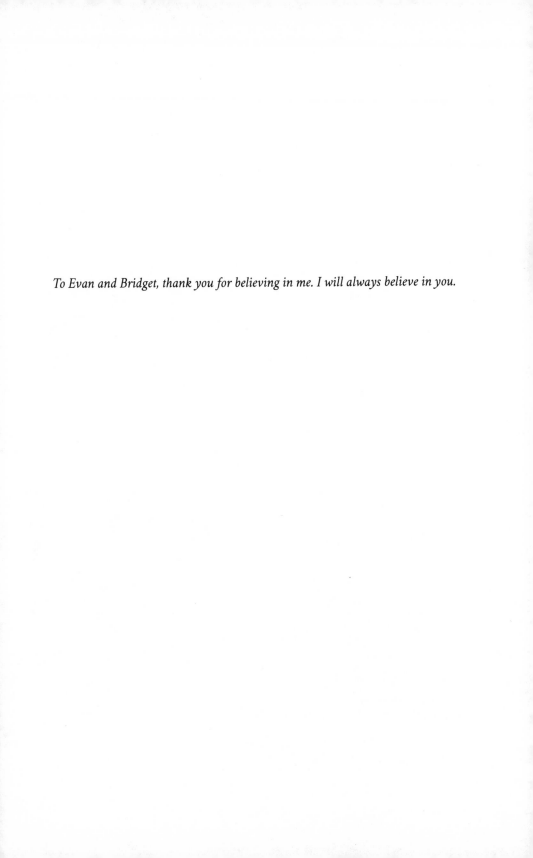

To Evan and Bridget, thank you for believing in me. I will always believe in you.

I

THE LOST PETERSON APOSTLE

1

The air brakes on the Greyhound bus gasped, and a large featureless brick wall overcast by a brooding sky greeted me through the window as if my sullen mood jumped up and painted the picture for me. After four years in the Army, I still loathed my home as much as the day I left. Not that Amsterdam, New York was my hometown, just the last stop on the way.

I hoisted my pack onto my shoulder and trudged down the steps into the beginnings of an early spring rain. The cold drizzle soaked through my high and tight and trickled down my face in runnels. I ran a hand through my hair, casting off water like a thumb over the bristles of a toothbrush, and crushed the cap in my hand, refusing to put it on. The rain felt right.

A ghastly old pickup truck with fender wells made more from rust than metal idled in the parking lot next to the last feeble remains of a gravel-encrusted snow pile; the snow pile looked to be in better condition. Through the cracked windshield I could see the shadowy outline of my old man, Paul Peterson, sitting behind the wheel. I took two long deep breaths weighing my options and almost decided to hike the forty miles to the farm in the rain rather than get into the vehicle with him, but that would only postpone the inevitable fight. Better to get it out of the way now, when my mom and siblings weren't here to witness it.

I climbed into the cab without a word and stood the pack up between us as an ineffectual barrier we both honored. He shifted the truck into gear, and we lurched out of the parking space. Once we passed the city limits, the truck picked up speed along the backcountry roads. The cab remained silent except for the low thrum of knobby wheels rolling on blacktop and the screech-screech of worn-out wiper blades unable to completely clear the windshield.

I watched the trees and telephone poles fly by my window for the first twenty miles or so before the silence finally beat me into looking at my old man. A several day-old beard uncharacteristically shadowed his face, though the sunbaked creases still showed. He wore an unbuttoned worn-out red flannel shirt over a long sleeve waffle-knit with frayed cuffs, and I could see yet another t-shit through the top two undone buttons. Even with all those layers, he still seemed cold.

I felt like I should say something, anything, but for the life of me, I didn't have a clue what to say. Instead, my eyes drifted back out the passenger window searching for inspiration in the passing empty corn-fields, but they spun by unhelpfully. After a few minutes, I chose to be the bigger man and break the wall of silence. Unfortunately, the word came out with the civility of a wrecking ball. "Well?"

"Well, what?" Angry currents carried the deep gravelly voice across the distance between us.

I shook my head and fogged the windshield with a billowing sigh. "Four years. You think we would have something to say to each other by now."

His dark brown eyes broke from the road long enough to glare at me with the same detestable hardness as the day I got on the bus to Basic Training, but I saw something else in them now. Something I never saw there before. Something I could only describe as pain. The deep emotional kind of pain that consumed a man's heart and soul, though I never knew him to own either. It only took my youngest brother, Jonny, committing suicide to bring it out.

It pissed me off. He had no right. You have to care for someone before you can mourn them. And my old man never cared for any of his kids, especially Jonny. I couldn't bear to see it and turned away first. Better the blur of empty cornfields than his feigned pain. "How's Mom holding up?" I asked.

"You'll have to ask her yourself; she's not speaking to me."

I considered about asking after my other siblings, Mark, Luke, and Mary, but the questions wouldn't form, and I'm not sure I wanted to know my old man's thoughts about any of them. Instead, I stared out the window, wondering if I'd stayed and looked after my little brother, would he still be alive? My chest tightened at the pain and I felt tears welling up in my eyes despite trying to will them away.

"It ain't your fault," he said in the no-nonsense, get-over-it tone I always hated.

I spun. It was the closest thing to a kind word I could remember him ever saying to me, and I hated it. "You're right, it ain't my fault. It's yours."

My old man jumped on the brake with both feet. The tires on the truck locked up and skidded along the gravel road, the backend fishtailing as it kicked up stones and mud. Still in gear, the engine sputtered and then stopped with a cough.

His open hand flew across the cab and caught me across the face. "It ain't nobody's fault 'cept Jonny's and you better realize that, son."

"You never gave a rat's ass about Jonny or any one of us, you fucking hypocrite," I spat back at him.

He wiped the spittle from his face with his left hand and took another swing at me with his right. This time, I caught his wrist in an iron grip forged by eighteen years on the farm and four more in Uncle Sam's infantry. I squeezed, feeling the bones in his wrist shift under the pressure. The fire filling his eyes couldn't compare to the inferno burning inside me. "You will not hit me again," I growled. "And you won't strike Mark, Luke, Mary, or Mom again. Do you understand?"

"You best let go my arm, son," he replied in tight, restrained fury. "Let go my arm and get out of my truck. Find yourself someplace else to stay tonight. You're not welcome under my roof."

I threw his hand back at him and snatched my bag from between us. "I'll walk the rest of the way, but you're not going to keep me from seeing my fucking family." I unbuckled and threw open the truck door. Its hinges squawked in protest, but I put enough behind it that the door bounced off its limits and came back at me. I stopped it on the rebound with a stiff arm and slid off the seat. The rain fell in sheets, driving the cold spring air through my uniform. I didn't care.

"You best not show up at the house, son. I shoot trespassers," he growled out the open passenger door. He started the truck and threw it in gear, spitting gravel at me as he drove away. The momentum slamming the door for me.

"Fuck you!" I yelled at the retreating tail lights, flipping him the bird.

The truck disappeared around the corner and left me staring down an empty road with nothing but the cold rain to quench my anger. I turned the other way. The dirt road faded into the mist of rain between fields and trees.

I decided to shelter under a nearby long needle pine tree, trading fine driven rain for large fat drops shaken loose from the canopy above. I rummaged through my pack until I found my parka and threw it on. The light browns of the desert camouflage stood out against the green and dark brown landscape around me, but the parka repelled the rain as well as a duck's back.

After another look up and down the empty road through the shroud of my hood, I still couldn't gain my bearings. The fog of rain hid the Adirondacks, and I felt lost in my own backyard.

Thank God for cell phones.

I pulled out my phone and thumbed the sensor. It blipped to life, but my bargain basement service plan didn't get enough reception in the boondocks of New York to even query the great Google oracle. On a prayer, I opened the maps app and a blue circle about five miles wide covered the map from the last point the phone pinged a tower. The raindrops collecting on the screen smeared as I zoomed out on the map.

"Fuck."

Paul had dropped me off a good ten miles from home.

The long way.

With a growl, I considered the hayfield behind me and the woods beyond it. Less than five miles by the way the crow flies, except I'd be slugging it through heavy grass, underbrush, and woods. Giving the barren road another glance, I weighed hiking through rough terrain against the odds of actually stumbling upon someone willing to give me a ride home in the middle of bumfuck Egypt.

"Shit," I spat into the rain.

Pulling a cheap dollar-store poncho from my pack, I wrapped it over my pack in a life hack my first platoon sergeant taught me years ago. A smirk half-threatened to chase the scowl from my face as I remembered *life-hack day* and the many uses of duct tape, condoms, and tampons that earned my obnoxious hormone-hyped adolescent ass a blistering punishment session I'll never forget.

The pack thumped onto my back and drove the moment of mirth away in a puff of breath. Careful not to catch my clothes on the barbed fence wire, I hopped the fence and started walking through calf-high soaking wet pasture grass without leaving more than the bent grass as a directional marker.

Paul wouldn't send anyone back for me.

Like most of upstate New York, the woods at the other end of the pasture led to a small field, then to another wood and so on. The rain pattered on my parka as my steady monotonous strides swallowed the ground in front of me. It gave me time to cool, and I soon regretted blowing up on Paul like I did. It wouldn't bring my brother back or make his funeral any easier. But I couldn't stand being in the same room with the man, let alone the close confines of a truck cab.

Not too far into the third wood, an itch crept into the space between my shoulder blades, like hungry eyes followed me through the trees. Stealing a glance over my shoulder, I saw nothing in the rainy gloom, but just like Afghanistan, I knew they were there. I could feel them lurking behind the trees or hiding in the branches, getting ready to pounce on me. Veering to the left, I spun around a massive oak tree big enough to be a little brother to a sequoia to check my six.

Nothing moved, and only the sound of rain falling through the canopy above filled the silence. No crunching of leaves. No snapping of twigs. The itch turned into an icy chill running down my back.

I surveyed the ground clutter around me and found a broken limb as big as my arm and hefted it. Too long to wield effectively, I swapped it for one a bit smaller that I could swing one-handed if I needed to. I glanced around the tree once more; the woods remained still. Then I saw a shadow move between the trees. Too low to the ground for a man, but big enough to move the brush two feet to either side. I stepped around the tree, made myself as big as I could and roared a challenge, slapping my improvised club against the tree, trying to make enough noise to scare the beast away. It didn't work.

A black head larger than a basketball lifted into the air, and yellow eyes stared at me from a hundred paces away. I hollered one more time, hoping to convince it to find somewhere else to go. It reared up on its hind legs and I about shit my pants. Granted, I've never seen a black bear other than at the zoo, but I didn't know they could stand ten feet tall.

I turned and ran. By the sound of the crashing brush behind me, I needed to run faster and kicked it up a notch, silently thanking my drill instructors for all those forced marches with hundred-pound rucks they made me do. The ground beside me dropped away to a ravine, and an old survival memory from my teens came to me. Something about bears not

7

running so well downhill and I decided to jump over the edge. I certainly wasn't going to outrun it on flat land.

I splashed across the creek at the bottom and scrambled up the mud hill on the other side. My boots slipped, and I couldn't find anything to grab on to. I fell face first, eating the mud as I slid back down to the bottom.

The bear roared from the top of the ravine behind me before plummeting down the slope after me without any of the promised fumbling on its shorter front legs.

Howling my own war cry, I readied the club in my hands and took the charge full-on, swinging the club into the beast's head. The branch broke in a shower of splinters, and five-hundred pounds of black fur slammed me into the hillside leaving a man-shaped imprint in the mud. As the breath left me, I knew my family would be burying more than one son this week.

2

The creature stuttered back and reared itself onto its hind legs. Frozen in the mud, I received a shower of spittle as it opened its maw nearly large enough to swallow my head whole and roared. My stomach heaved involuntarily at the stench of its breath which smelled worse than a three-day-old road-killed skunk—it's better if I don't admit to how I discovered that particular smell.

The bear lunged forward to remove my arm at the shoulder with its teeth, and I jammed the remnants of my makeshift club into the creature's jaws. It shook its head trying to clear the obstruction, giving me the moment I needed to free myself, but the mud sucked at my pack, holding me in place. I rocked side to side, slipped out of its straps, and started climbing, abandoning the pack in the mud.

My feet struggled for purchase in the muddy hillside as before, but the image of bear teeth sinking into my calves gave me plenty of motivation. I scurried up to a bundle of protruding roots exposed by a recent slide in the creek bank and used them hand-over-hand to pull myself up out of the bear's reach. Who, having cleared the stick from its mouth, charged up the slope, snagging one of my feet with its claws. Four razors skated across my boot cutting deep gouges in the leather I would never be able to buff out. The tips of the claws caught briefly on the boot sole then slipped off leaving my leg relatively unharmed; thank God I traveled in my combats. The attack succeeded in knocking my precarious footing out from under me, and I tumbled back down the bank as the muddy root slipped out of my hands.

I toppled to a stop on my back in the shallow stream. Icy cold water flooded in through the neck and waist of my parka, and I sucked in an involuntary breath as every muscle in my torso suddenly tensed. I forced my head up enough to see the bear charging at me, and I raised my left arm defensively, bracing for the sharp pain of teeth sinking into flesh. Thanks to a bar fight in Afghanistan, I knew how much stab wounds hurt; except the shock of pain never came. Instead, my ears rang with the report of gunfire nearby. The bear let out a cry, and I lowered my arm enough to see the beast receive a second blast, before it turned and ran headlong downstream.

Rolling out of the water and onto the muddy bank, I closed my eyes and tried not to hyperventilate as I slowed my breathing and racing heart. Over the rush of blood pounding in my ears, I heard someone yelling at me. My eyes popped back open for fear the bear changed its mind, but the stream remained undisturbed. Shouts drew my attention to the far bank where a man stood in a wide-brimmed hat. The rain rolled around the brim then dripped down a long duster. He looked more like a character from an old Western than a local farmer. The man held a short rifle, not exactly pointed at me, but not pointed away from me either.

"What?" I hollered back.

He adjusted his grip on the rifle and raised his voice so I could hear, but his tone remained level and firm. "Have you been bitten?"

I fumbled cold hands across my torso searching for open wounds like a cop patting down a hooker for contraband. When my hands collided with my ribs, I winced and whispered a silent prayer that they were only bruised and not broken.

"No. Just banged up a bit," I moaned.

He relaxed and slung the rifle over his shoulder by the strap. The hairs on the back of my neck settled down into place, and the alarm bells I mistook for unspent adrenaline stopped rattling in my skull.

"I've got a bit of rope up here. Think you can climb that or do I need to come down to you?"

I got to my feet, wincing at the ache in my ribs, but surprised to find nothing else hurt. "I can manage."

"Give me a minute to tie it off."

While he found a spot to tie off the rope, I recovered my pack from the wall of mud. It gave a sucking sound as I rocked it back and forth to pull it free. The mud kept a carnivorous hold on the bag's poncho and tore it off. I left the thin plastic beaten into the bank and went to the stream to rinse the larger clods of mud off both me and the bag as best I could. Then cupping my hands, I took a drink of the cool water.

A thin nylon rope slapped against the hillside. "Careful, boy. Drinking untreated water can give you the runs."

After slurping up one more handful of water, I smiled up to the man. "I've been drinking from the streams around here since I was a kid. I'll chance it." Like a four-year-old, I went to dry my hands on my pants, but couldn't find a suitably clean, let alone dry place on them. Reaching under my parka, I settled for wiping them on my undershirt, though it did little to actually dry my hands.

I picked up the end of the rope. It looked strong enough to hold me, but the thin cord would cut mercilessly into my hands which already felt the numbing pinpricks of the cold air. I considered trying the climb with my pack on my back but decided to tie it to the end of the rope instead. Climbing with frozen hands would be hard enough without the additional weight. With memories of the Army's PLDC obstacle course training running through my head, I scaled the slope.

I wrapped the thin rope around my hand to keep my grip and walked up the bank, one boot deep in the mud after the other, rewrapping the rope around my hands with each step. It made slow going, but at least I could hold on to it this way. By the time I reached the top, my raw hands ached from the mixture of cold and rope burns.

Near the top, the man offered his liver-spotted hands to help me up the last yard or so. I reached out, and a grip of iron latched on to pull me up. The stubble of a white beard and deep blue eyes flanked by crow's feet greeted me from below the brim of a broad hat as I crested the ridge.

He gave me a clap on the side of my shoulder. "Damn, Sergeant, you look to be soaked through and as blue as ice. Whatcha doing way out here?" he asked as he hauled on the rope, pulling my bag up the muddy bank.

I tucked my hands under my armpits to force heat back into my fingers, but my voice still stammered. "Hea...hea...heading home."

"Shit, you must be colder than I thought. Here, take off that wet coat and put this on." The man unshouldered his rifle and shrugged out of his duster, revealing a pair of Springfield 1911s nestled into a dual pistol shoulder holster over a red plaid flannel shirt. My old man used a Buck knife nearly identical to the one sheathed between several clip holsters on the man's belt. His clothes seemed to bulge in telltale signs of more concealed weapons. Way more than anyone needed to hunt a bear.

I peeled off my parka and soaked jacket, and after a moment's hesitation, my undershirt too. The cold air still sucked at what little warmth remained in my skin, but not nearly as fast as the wet clothing. Goosebumps sprung out on top of the ugly purple bruises covering most of my chest. The man handed me his duster with a low whistle.

I buttoned the duster closed and stuffed my left hand back into my armpit trying to retain what heat I could, while I extended my right. "Thanks. I'm Matthew."

He clasped my hand with a firm grip that I appreciated. "I'm Jacob. It's a bit wet out here for a fire. Do you have far to go?"

My teeth chattered as I retrieved the phone from my uniform jacket. A mosaic of spiderweb cracks covered the screen. I slipped a thumbnail beneath the edge of the protective tempered glass and peeled it back, the film crackling like a chip bag. The phone's screen survived unscathed, and I blew out a frozen breath of relief; I may actually give it a five-star review, if I ever warmed up. My relief did not last as I thumbed the sensor, and the screen lit only briefly with a flashing zero-battery before fading back to black.

I stuffed my frigid fingers back into my pits in a personal one-man hug as I looked around to get my bearings. The sun had set a while ago, and I couldn't tell north from south in what remained of the last vestiges of twilight.

Jacob sighed, then picked up his rifle and my pack. "Thought as much. Come on, you can warm up in my truck. It's a bit of a walk, but at least I know the way."

He started walking, and I followed with my feet squishing in wet boots and my head down between the lifted lapels of the duster. By the time we got to his F-150, I could barely feel my ears or my toes.

Jacob tossed my duffel into the bed and clicked the button on his key fob to unlock the doors. I hadn't been home in years, but the thunk of door locks sounded more than a bit odd with nothing but trees and grass as far as I could see. Hell, people in the boonies viewed locking your doors about as useful as hiding a light from a blind man. I climbed into the cab, unwilling to let Jacob's paranoia keep me from its shelter.

Jacob jumped in the driver's side and started the truck, turning the heat and the seat warmers to max. Blessed heat began to creep up my back and along the bottoms of my thighs. I sat on my hands to thaw my fingers while I waited for the air coming through the vents to be something other than fast-moving cold air.

"It'll get warmed up here in a minute," Jacob said twisting in his seat to reach into the back of the king cab. He flipped the top off of a Styrofoam cooler and pulled out a string of four Coors cans by the empty rings. He stripped one clear and passed it to me.

I'm not the biggest fan of Coors, but I'm not one to refuse a man who just saved my life either. I thanked him, popped the top and took a sip. It wasn't cold like I expected, but considering the temperature outside, it wasn't warm either.

Jacob opened his own beer and drank the entire thing in one long tilt of the can. He freed a second one, cracked it open, and sipped off the head before placing it in the cupholder. He grabbed a plastic gas station bag from the backseat and tossed it onto my lap.

"I was saving this for later, but I think you could use it more than me right about now."

I opened the bag and saw a prepackaged ham and cheese sandwich, my favorite. I opened it up and took a big bite. "Thanks."

"So, Sergeant, where can I drive you?"

I finished chewing and swallowed. "372 Walker Lane."

"The Petersons' farm?" His voice carried a touch of familiarity.

"Do you know Paul?" I asked, trying to remember if I knew him from before I left for the Army.

He looked me in the eye for a moment. "Not personally, but I know the place." He turned in his seat to face the windshield then dropped the shifter into drive.

T he truck rolled into the drive, gravel crunching beneath its tires, and up to a simple Cape Cod style house. It looked smaller than I remembered, and I remembered it being very small, especially with five kids and only one bathroom. Through the lone kitchen window, I could see my mother, her gray hair pulled up in a hasty bun, walking in and out of view as she prepared dinner. She stopped every few paces to wipe at her eyes with her apron. A knot formed in my own chest in sympathetic pain.

"House or barn?" Jacob asked.

I could hear the vacuum pump still humming from the long two-story barn at the far end of the drive. Mark and Luke were likely finishing up the evening milking and with any luck, my old man would be out there with them.

"House. I want to see my mom first," I replied.

The truck rolled to a stop near the side door. I placed a hand on the door handle, but then turned to Jacob and extended it to him. "Thanks again for the help."

He gave me a crooked grin that blended in with the lines on his face and shook my hand. "Don't mention it."

I opened the door. The cab lights came on and I noticed the pair of Springfield 1911s still hanging in their holsters. "It isn't hunting season, is it?"

He quirked a half-grin at me with something more serious in his eyes. "It is for what I hunt." His attention drifted back to the house illuminated in the truck's headlights and the corners of his eyes tensed. "Are you sure you're going to be alright here?"

I followed his stare to Paul standing in the open doorway to the house with his Winchester 30-30 leveled at the truck. "I'm not sure," I said uncertainly and stepped out of the truck.

"I thought I told you, you're not welcome here, son," Paul hollered.

My mother came out running out of the house and pushed the gun down. "Our son is always welcome in my home," she said in a tight, angry, grief-stricken voice that both broke my heart and made me proud to see her stand up to Paul for the first time ever.

He met the fire in her eyes with a smoldering glare of his own. The gun slowly fell to his side, and I could see the vein pulsing on his forehead like the warning alarms of a nuclear meltdown from thirty-feet away in the dark. His scowl moved to me, and his eyes narrowed to hateful pinpricks before he stormed back into the house without another word. At the moment, I'd rather face the nuclear meltdown, at least then it would be over with merciful speed.

My mother watched the door slam behind him then placed a hand on her hip and waved me in with the other. "Come on in, Matthew, dinner is nearly ready."

"I'll be right there, Mom."

She went back inside while I shrugged out of Jacob's duster and placed it on the empty passenger seat. "I think it'll be alright. I'd ask you in for dinner but…"

"No explanation necessary, Sergeant. I've done a lot of reckless things in my time, but I have no desire to walk into that hornets' nest."

I considered what awaited me inside the house and gave Jacob a wry smile. "Yeah. I kind of wish I didn't need to either. Anyways, thanks again." I shut the door and grabbed my stuff from the back of the truck.

Jacob backed the truck around. Watching his taillights drive away, I realized the rain stopped.

"Who was that?" asked a woman's voice I didn't quite recognize.

I turned to see a teenage girl with black hair flowing down one side of her head to just below her shoulder while the other side sported a half-shaved style I didn't get. At five-foot-three, she still needed to grow into the multiple layers of hand-me-down shirts and sweatshirts whose bulk gave her a deceptively fluffy exterior. On top of it all, she wore a layer of cow shit and grime, which made me wonder what she left in the barn. But beneath it all, I recognized the green eyes of my fourteen-year-old little sister.

"Mary? Damn girl, you got big."

"You better not let momma hear talk like that," she scolded before jumping into my arms and giving me my first hug since I came home. "Where's your shirt? You've got to be freezing."

I put her back down. "Ah, I fell in a creek and it got a little wet, so I just took it off."

"Was this before or after Daddy threw you out of the truck?"

I shrugged my shoulders dismissively. "After."

The sound of the house door slamming drew our attention. Paul stomped to the old farm truck and tossed a small duffel into the back. The fan belt squealed as he started the engine and pumped the gas pedal. He backed up then shifted into first and our eyes met just before the engine roared and the rear tires spewed gravel. If looks could kill, the one he gave me as he drove by would have obliterated me where I stood.

"I see he hasn't changed much in four years," I said dryly.

My sister stared after the truck rumbling down the dirt road then spat into the dirt. "Oh, he has. He's gotten worse."

"I'm sorry…" I began, but she cut me off.

"Come on, Mark and Luke will be finished with the milking soon, and you look like you need a hot shower before they use up all the water." She grabbed my bag, only grunting a little at its weight, and carried it into the house, not waiting for me.

I shook my head and sighed, mad at myself for staying away so long. I could only imagine what Paul had put Mary and my brothers through in my absence. The goosebumps sprouting on my arms had nothing to do with the night's chill. I tried to rub warmth back into my flesh as I jogged into the house after her.

The vestibule door banged closed behind me. Rows of wooden pegs jammed into the exposed studs in the wall sat mostly empty, except for a few barn shirts and Mary's encrusted sweatshirt. Her tall rubber boots lay on their sides relatively beneath it. My mother's boots stood neatly near the kitchen door, and her tattered brown barn jacket hung on the peg above it. The clothes washer, dryer, and chest freezer filling out the room gave new meaning to the term, scratch-and-dent specials.

I couldn't help but peek into the family freezer as I passed. Spring meant that only remnants of the butchered bull remained, and after a quick survey of the white packages, I found the heart and liver, but not the tongue. I gulped with dread as I finally identified the aroma coming through the kitchen door.

Resigned, I sat on the small step leading to the kitchen and unlaced my boots then pulled them off and upturned them next to my mother's, letting the water run out onto the concrete floor. I peeled off my socks, wringing them out and adding to the puddle forming on the floor then draped them over my boots to dry. The cold of the concrete sank into my feet as I stood up and quickly danced my way through the kitchen door.

My mother stood by the stove stirring a pot of green beans. With worn blue jeans, a gray sweater starting to tatter at the cuffs, and an apron tied around her waist, she looked much the same as the day I left.

She raised her head at the sound of the door clicking closed. Her brown eyes grew at the sight of my shirtless bruised body, but not as large as mine when I saw the rough shape of an angry red handprint on her left cheek. My blood boiled chasing away the cold, I would have hunted down my no-good old man and gave him one to match if I only knew where he ran off to. Instead, I moved to comfort her, making it a whole two steps before my mother, with eyes hardened by the aftermath of his strike, pointed toward the bathroom with her wooden spoon.

"Don't you worry about that now. Go take a shower and get some dry clothes on." The mix of pain and anger in her voice stopped me in my tracks.

I stared at her for a moment, locked in a battle of wills which she eventually won. "Yes, ma'am."

In the hall just outside the bathroom, I met Mary carrying a clothes basket heaped to almost overflowing. Her eyes widened and her mouth dropped open as she nearly collided with my purple chest. Before she could voice the question, I forced a smile and shook my head. "You should see the other guy." When her gaze refused to rise from my bruised chest, I grabbed the dark blue garment off the top of the basket to cover it. "I'll tell you about it later," I said before recognizing the coat protecting my dignity as my class A jacket. Upon closer inspection, the basket she held contained every bit of clothing I packed. "What do you think you're doing with my stuff?"

"Your shi…" she began, then paused when I raised an eyebrow and whispered *"momma"* with a brief nod over my shoulder. She looked past me then amended what she started to say. "Your *stuff* was all wet and covered in mud, so I thought I'd wash them for you like the loving sister that I am." She flashed me a sardonic smile.

I always felt close to my sister. She'd follow me around, liked the things I liked, and let me complain about our old man when I needed to. In turn, I sheltered her on the school bus, watched out for her at school, and protected her from Paul's worst. Up until the day I got on Uncle Sam's bus. I regretted leaving her behind the most. My mind struggled for the right words, but I only managed a mumbled, "thanks," as we squeezed by each other.

She nodded her acknowledgment. "You'll have to wear some of Mark's clothes for now. I put some in the bathroom for you." She rolled her eyes at my involuntary groan. Mark's idea of fashion differed from mine by miles. "Don't worry it's only a pair of sweats and a plain black tee."

"Thanks again."

She shrugged and moved off toward the washer. "Thank me after he sees you wear it. It's his only one." I smiled as she walked away, the instigator as always.

I took a long shower, letting the heat of the water thaw me out. It's funny how you don't realize how cold you are until you start warming yourself up, and then even lukewarm water can be as excruciating as sticking your hands in a fire. Once the pain of pinpricks in my skin subsided and I felt normal once again, I finally turned the water off.

I pulled back the curtain and grabbed my towel when Mark began hammering on the door. "Come on, you don't need that long of a shower, I don't care how long you've been gone."

"Ah, quit your hammering, you little turd-fart. I'll be out as soon as I get my clothes on," I hollered back through the closed door.

I slipped the t-shirt Mary gave me over my head and grabbed the pair of sweatpants. I put them on commando, shuddering at the thought of wearing my brother's underwear.

Mark began to tap, tap, tap on the door again, and I yanked it open. Fortunately, I stood far enough back that his overswing with an actual hammer missed me as he tried to stop it.

I snatched the hammer out of his hands. "Geez, Mark. I didn't come home to have you bash my head in with a hammer. The Army gives me plenty of opportunities to get killed, I don't need you helping them out." I regretted the words as soon as they left my mouth and the playful grin on Mark's face disappeared.

He shouldered past me and shoved me out of the room and into Luke, who gave me a stunned look as he put up his hands to catch me.

I spun to apologize, "Mark, I'm sorry. I didn't mean..." but the door slammed closed in my face.

"Yeah. I know." The sound of the shower drowned out any other words between us.

"Don't worry about him. He'll get over it soon enough. He's just taking Jonny's death a little harder than the rest of us," Luke said placing a hand on my shoulder.

I turned back to my...now youngest brother. His blue eyes seemed older than any high school senior's should be. The gravity of our loss slammed into me like a Mack truck, and the tears I refused to shed welled up in my eyes. Jonny wasn't here to greet me. Jonny would never be here again. The tears fell and I wrapped Luke in a fierce hug, not caring that he still wore his filthy barn clothes.

4

O ver the next few days, I caught up with the family and made up with Mark. Paul didn't return and while I wouldn't say I missed him; his absence did leave us a bit shorthanded around the barn. At the continuous whining of my brothers, which to me sounded more like fornicating feral cats, my mother kindly reminded me that four years couldn't possibly be long enough to forget how to push a broom or use a shovel, so I picked up the slack where I could.

On the day of Jonny's funeral, we rushed solemnly through the morning chores then filed into the shower one after the other. As last of five, I shivered through the cold water raining on my head and made it a two-minute quickie. After toweling off, I laid out my class A uniform, straightened my name tag, and pinned on my rack of medals. Not just the ribbons, not for Jonny, but the actual medals, including the Purple Heart he always asked me about in his letters. I tried not to think about how I never told him how I earned it, but when the jacket settled on my shoulders, it felt heavier than ever.

At the funeral home, my mother clung to my arm with one hand and mopped at her eyes with a handkerchief in the other as I led her into the building. We walked through the broad double doors to an auditorium large enough to hold a couple hundred people, though the attendees filled little more than the first couple of rows.

I escorted my mother at the head of the family procession to the front of the room where Jonny's casket stood closed between two modest floral arrangements. An eight by ten of his junior year high school photo stood in a cheap plastic frame propped up on a velvet cloth draped over his casket.

I clenched my fists in anger, in rage, but at what I didn't know. I wanted to scream. To howl at the wind. To say goodbye. To tell him I love him. To ask him why. But I could do none of those things, so I held my mother's arm in the crook of mine and let the tears run down my face.

Mark stepped up beside us, running a hand along the wooden top of the casket while pressing the forefinger and thumb of his other against the bridge of his nose, though the tears still found their way to the lacquered wood. I wrapped my spare arm around his shoulders, half-expecting him to shake me off, but he leaned in, shaking softly beneath my arm instead.

As I held onto him, the unbidden memory of when I asked him about finding Jonny in the woods filled my blurred vision. Replayed upon my tears, I watched his eyes grow distant and the blood drain from his face as if Jonny's ghost walked into the room. I tried to banish the memory, but I could still hear his hollow stutter, "I followed the buzzards."

Luke pressed in from the other side, adding his arm around Mark's waist for support. The two of them jostled into me as Mary added her weight to Luke's other side. We settled together, arms around each other, as a wall of grief, staring at a picture on a wooden box.

Eventually, we crumbled apart. My siblings drifted back into the crowd, searching for solace amongst their friends. Like me, my own friends fled town the day after graduation intent on never coming back, so I settled in the front row next to my mother and endured the parade of nervous church-Bettys. They offered their condolences to my mother then chatted about me as if I were a ten-year-old incapable of caring for myself. I reached my limit after the tenth lady in a row felt the need to hug my grief away. I stood, trying to separate myself from the gaggle, and saw Paul hovering near the back of the room. His red eyes met mine in an unspoken truce, and I moved away from my mother and her friends to give my parents their space. Neither of us wanted to cause a scene; at least not today.

I surveyed the room for someone to help me get my mind off of who lay in the box at the front of the room. Mark stood off to one side with three of his friends from high school who never left town either. Half of Luke's basketball team showed up for him. Mary, looking more than a little awkward in a dress, sat knee-to-knee with her childhood friend Beth, who held Mary's hands in hers. I thought about offering my own comfort, but Beth could give her more than I could at the moment. The corner of my mouth curled in a wry almost-jealous expression as I found myself with no one to lean on.

In the back row, I saw an unexpected familiar face. Aside from his duster folded over the chair in front of him and his shoulder holster missing, Jacob looked little different than before. The Buck knife still hung from his belt and he still wore a flannel shirt, albeit a different color. His eyes roamed the room, never staying too long on any one person until they met mine. He tilted his head in a slight nod and a comforting smile touched his lips as I approached.

I reached out a hand to him. "Jacob, I didn't know you knew Jonny?"

He shook my hand. "Not as well as I would have liked. We corresponded a few times."

The way he said *corresponded* filled my mind with ridiculous images of Jonny, the computer nerd, hand-writing calligraphic letters with a quill and ink. I quirked a lopsided grin as the more I thought about it, the more I could see him doing it, but for the life of me, I couldn't imagine what the two of them could have talked about. Weathered and hard, Jacob appeared to be approaching his late sixties. While Jonny, more nerd than outdoorsman, had one of those birthdays that made him the youngest student in eleventh-grade. He played *Dungeons and Dragons* behind Paul's back under the ruse of participating in the chess club. All of which made him the favorite target of bullies, at least until Mark and I put an end to it years ago, before either of us graduated high school. I chewed my lower lip at the memory and felt, not for the first time, more than a bit responsible for Jonny putting himself at the wrong end of our old man's 30-30.

"If you don't mind me asking?" I began then paused to swallow. "What did you and Jonny talk about?"

Jacob stared at me a moment like a drill instructor sizing up a new recruit, then nodded toward the door. "I need a smoke."

I followed him outside into the unseasonably warm air, a stark difference from our first meeting. Jacob produced a pack of Black and Milds as he walked to the corner of the building. He pulled one of the thin cigars from the package and held it out to me then placed it between his lips when I refused. In a practiced flip and slap motion of a silver-plated lighter, he lit the cigar. The scent of cherry smoke curling from the tip reminded me of my grandpa, back when he owned the farm and life was good.

I could just see the pipe clenched between Grandpa's teeth as he welcomed Jonny with open arms, right before the two of them started raising hell in Heaven. I almost pitied poor Saint Peter.

Jacob raised an eyebrow. "Something amusing?"

Reality wiped the broad grin from my face. "No. Your cigars remind me of my grandpa's pipe. I just hadn't thought of him in a long time."

Jacob puffed on his cigar, letting the smoke roll out of his mouth. "Funny how things like that bring people back."

"Yeah," I said weakly. "So, what did you want to tell me about Jonny that you couldn't tell me inside?"

Jacob took another puff of his cigar. "I'm not sure how Jonny found out about me or what I do, but he had some specific questions pertaining to my work and I tried to answer them as best I could."

I rolled my eyes at his evasive answer. I didn't have time for shit I spent my whole life putting up with. Not today, when I should be inside mourning Jonny with my family. My feet made for the doors, but stopped halfway at the thought of having to watch Paul feign emotions he wasn't capable of feeling. Better I wasted my time out here with this old man than in there with the other one.

With a heavy sigh, I spun back around and gave Jacob a *cut-the-shit-and-give-me-a-real-answer* look. "And what is it you do, Mister…"

"No Mister, just Jacob. And I'm a hunter." He puffed on his cigar, as if it said it all.

"You mean, a professional hunter? Like a field guide or a safari?"

Jacob choked on his cigar, barking out billowing clouds of smoke worse than Paul's back-firing truck. "Not exactly. I hunt the shit that no one talks about anymore. The things that are almost more legend than reality."

My eyebrows knitted together in confusion.

"I hunt the stuff that goes bump in the night: werewolves, ghouls, vampires, and other things. There's a real beast behind every legend you can think of, and I hunt them on the behalf of the Holy Roman Church."

Naturally, I didn't believe him, but he said it like one says the sky is blue or the grass is green. I've seen enough crazies in the Army to know better than follow them down their rabbit hole or outright argue with them. Those kinds of arguments had a habit of going sideways. I took a step back to get out of the reach of his knife, just in case. I tried to play it off as a shift in my stance, but he noticed, I saw it in his eyes. Still, he didn't move closer, he simply puffed on his cigar.

"And what does that have to do with my brother?" I asked.

"Well, I wasn't in those woods hunting that werebear for the hell of it."

"You mean that black bear that attacked me?"

Jacob coughed a laugh. "Well, I can't say all that noise you made would have been a great idea even if it was a black bear, but I can tell you, bears don't get as big as a microbus. Well, Kodiaks maybe, but not black bears." He tossed the last bit of his cigar on the ground and crushed it with the heel of his boot. "Look, Matthew, I don't expect you to believe me, but you asked what your brother and I discussed. He asked about werebears. Their strengths. Their weaknesses. How they're made. How to recognize them. And of course, how to kill one. I thought he was just another enthusiast until I got his latest message."

Jacob pulled out his phone and pressed his forefinger to the biometric scanner. He then opened an email before handing it to me.

Jacob,

I'm afraid that the werebear I've been writing you about is all too real. And I have been unsuccessful in killing it. I've tracked it to its den in the woods near my family's hunting cabin, but it attacked me and bit me before I shot it in the leg and it ran off.

I write this to you as I feel the effects of the were-venom spreading through me. I don't dare tell my family, they won't understand and they'll try to hunt the bear without the proper ammunition.

Please do what I couldn't and protect my family. I will do what I must.

Thanks,

Jonny Peterson

"What he must?" I mumbled.

Jacob plucked his phone out of my numb hands. "I'm sorry, Matthew, but your brother took his life before he became a werebear."

His words hit me like a sucker punch to the gut and I couldn't breathe. I bent over bracing myself on my knees and gulped for air. "No." I shook my head and pushed myself upright. "No. He left us a note. He said he couldn't live with himself anymore." Tears streamed down my face. He committed suicide, I didn't like it, but I could accept it. I could be angry I wasn't here to see the warning signs and get him the help he needed. I could hate myself for my guilty part in his death. Now this man, someone

I hardly knew, told me I was wrong. That my brother lied. That he died to protect us from some imaginary beast. I wished I could believe my brother died a tragic hero, it would be so much nicer than the truth, but I couldn't let myself accept the lie. Anger boiled inside of me and I clenched my fist in illogical rage. My panting turned to growls of fury.

Jacob adjusted his stance and raised a tentative hand. "Whoa. Buck up, Sergeant. Get a hold of yourself."

It was more than I could stand to hear, and I threw a windmill right at Jacob. He stepped to the side, pushing my fist past him, letting my momentum carry me into the holly bushes at the base of the funeral home. I clambered out of the bushes and glared at him. Between the blind rage and tears welling in my eyes, I could barely see him.

He held his hands up in front of him, and I couldn't tell if he held his knife or not. "Easy boy, I only told you the truth."

I spat in the ground. "You filled my brother's head with a bunch of crap, and he killed himself for it." My chest heaved in large panting breaths as hot blood roared in my ears.

I rushed at him, but instead of wrapping him in the grappling move I intended, he somehow swung me around, hooking one of my arms then the other in a full nelson hold. He applied pressure to the back of my head, wrenching back my shoulders and making my neck hurt. I fought, trying to wriggle out of the hold, but he applied more pressure.

"Calm down," he said in an even tone which just pissed me off even more.

When I realized I couldn't escape, I stopped fighting him. He held on a moment longer then let me go with a shove, putting a couple paces between us.

I whirled around to face him, blind with hate and tears. "Get your ass out of here. Leave!"

The form in front of me backed away a few steps before he turned toward the parking lot. I wiped at my eyes and watched him get in his truck and drive away. The blind heat of anger faded as his taillights disappeared from view, leaving only the hollow loss of my brother behind.

I waited for my breathing to normalize then went to the restroom and washed my face before going back into the chapel. When I eased back in through the doors, Reverend Thomas stood behind the pulpit, already well into his sermon. I found a seat in the back row and tried to keep the tears from returning to my eyes.

5

I've been to more funerals than anyone my age ever should, my grandfather a few years before I left for the Army, two battle-buddies who never made it out of Afghanistan, but there was something different about my little brother's. The knife in my heart felt sharper and cut deeper, removing something I knew I would never get back. When the service moved to the gravesite, Mark, Luke, Mary, and I, along with a pair of funeral home employees, carried the casket. Jonny weighed a buck forty soaking wet, yet I had never carried anything heavier.

Reverend Thomas opened the gravesite service with a prayer. When he lifted his head, he turned his sympathetic eyes on me, then to Mark, and finally to Luke before he began, "Today we return to God, the youngest of the Peterson Apostles." We each let out an uneasy chuckle. I only ever remember him calling us the bloody Peterson Horsemen, especially that time we added a bottle of Aristocrat to the punch for the best church Christmas party of my childhood.

He kept the remainder of the gravesite service extremely short, just a scripture reading before entrusting Jonny's soul to God's care. My mother sat in her chair beneath the green tent and cried through it all. Paul sat stiffly next to her, pointedly not holding her hand, so my mother cried on my sister's shoulder with the hands of her remaining sons resting comfortingly on her back.

As the reverend finished the closing prayer, Paul got up, placed a hand on the casket, mumbled something I couldn't hear, then a single tear fell from his iron face. He lifted his head and shook the preacher's hand before leaving without so much as a glance at the rest of us. The tear glistened on the enameled surface of the coffin, a solitary pool of emotion from a lifetime of drought.

I shared a look of disbelief with my brothers, not because he didn't spare us a glance, but because we didn't think he could actually cry. The very sight of it brought the surreal day to a crashing reality.

I rose from my seat and ran my hand along the glass-like surface, trying unsuccessfully to hold back my own tears. I reached for the Purple Heart pinned to my chest and with trembling fingers, I undid the clasps and pulled it free.

"Jonny, you've always been prouder of me than I deserved." I sniffed back my tears then wiped them away with a thumb. "I earned this for surviving. For being the lucky one. But I never knew how lucky I was. I had you for my brother. I'm sorry I failed..." I swallowed the softball lump in my throat and tried to breathe, but couldn't.

I felt a hand against my back and turned to see Mark through my blurred vision. Then another hand and Luke stood beside me as well. Mary wedged herself in between Mark and me with an arm around us both.

I searched the heavens above for the words to say, then placed my Purple Heart on the casket pressing the tines into its surface. "I would have given anything to keep you here. I love you, little brother." My brothers and my sister crowded into me then, and we stood huddled together in tears unable to speak.

After we all said our final farewells, my mother stood, pressing herself up wearily from the arms of her chair. She leaned over Jonny's casket and kissed it just above the Purple Heart. When she straightened, she seemed ten years older than this morning. She wiped away her tears with an embroidered handkerchief, then slipped a hand into the crook of my elbow and we walked to the station wagon, now parked alone on the paved drive.

When we got back to the farm, I scoffed at the empty driveway. I should have known better than to expect Paul to put our feud behind him and come home to mourn with his family. My mother shot me a look and I instantly regretted the derisive gesture; I was as much at fault as him.

"Sorry," I mumbled, the somberness in the car eating the word before it could echo off the glass.

The car crunched to a halt, we piled out, changed our clothes, and went about our evening chores in virtual silence except for the incessant mooing of cows with udders too full to care about our grief. We completed our chores then walked numbly back to the house under the dark clouds of a new storm consuming the peaks of the Adirondack mountains, as if the sky itself mourned the passing of our brother.

Mrs. Kirkpatrick from the church's ladies club greeted us at the kitchen door. She shooed us back to the bathroom to wash up and change out of our barn clothes, barely giving us the opportunity to smell the casserole baking in the oven. While I never cared much for a church that condoned the way Paul treated his children, their ladies club knew how to take care of each other. Mrs. Kirkpatrick would be the first of several visits over the next couple weeks, providing meals and cleaning up, while my mother grieved. Small blessings like this made me almost miss being home, if not for how infrequently they came.

Washed and in fresh clothes, we sat at the table and let Mrs. Kirkpatrick wait on us while our mother stared out the kitchen window to the vanishing mountains. She picked at the plate in front of her, pushing the food around with her fork and ignoring Mrs. Kirkpatrick's urgings to eat.

Then out of the blue, she said, "I thought he would have come home by now." The words brought the silent clatter of forks on dishes to a stop like a crack of thunder, it drew the attention of every head in the room.

"Who?" I asked.

She looked up at me, her eyes lonely, scared, and full of grief. "Your father. He's never been gone this long." My siblings all turned to me, troubled expressions marking their faces.

Mark placed a hand on her arm, but her eyes didn't leave mine. "Mom, we just saw him at Jonny's funeral."

"He should have come home by now." Her voice shook as she spoke. "Could you check on him, Matthew? Get him to come home. Please."

Suddenly losing my appetite, I let the forkful of casserole in my hand return to the plate. I could not refuse the hurt in those eyes and I bit back the thing I wanted to say for, "Yes, ma'am."

Mark's gaze shifted from our mother to me. "He should be up at the cabin. I'll drive you."

I wasn't sure if he volunteered to drive me because he didn't want me driving his Bronco, the only vehicle besides a tractor that could make it up the hill to the cabin, or because he wanted to witness what would happen when I got there. Come to think of it, having a witness may be a good thing.

"Thanks," I mumbled as I went out to the vestibule to slide on my work boots and dirty jacket.

I climbed into Mark's old Bronco, careful to not step on the rusted-out door sill for fear my foot would break through. Mark turned the key on the old truck and the engine cranked weakly until it finally roared to life. He put the shifter in reverse and pulled out the knob to turn on the lights. The low beams lit up the side of the house as Luke came out carrying a pair of shotguns.

"Wait for me," he yelled.

"What the hell does he think he's doing with those?" I asked.

"My guess? Keeping you alive," Mark replied with the first hint of a smile I'd seen from him in days.

I sighed and got out of the truck to let Luke climb up into the back. I forgot to watch where I put my foot as I got back in and added another floor-vent with the crunch of disintegrating rust.

"Hey, take it easy or old Betsy here may just leave you at the cabin," Mark said caressing the dashboard like a passionate lover.

I looked at him with a raised eyebrow and slammed the door harder than I needed to. "What, this rolling tetanus shot waiting to happen? She'll probably leave us all with a long walk home."

"If you two udder wankers are finished screwing around, can we get going? My dinner's getting cold." Luke harassed from the backseat.

"What did you call us?" Mark and I asked in unison as we both moved to swat him. He dodged out of the way and we ended up knocking knuckles together instead and just like that, the tension of the day suddenly evaporated and we all burst into much-needed laughter. It didn't stop me from leaning over the seat to slug Luke in the arm. Mark put the truck in gear and grunted in satisfaction at Luke, who rubbed at his arm still laughing.

The dirt trail to the cabin rounded a twenty-acre cornfield, crossed a creek, and climbed a thirty-degree incline nearly straight up into the backwoods. We locked the front hubs, engaging the four-wheel drive to keep the truck moving through deep ruts and slick mud from the snowmelt and early spring rains. At the top of the hill, the trail turned right and crested a ridge to reveal Paul's rusted-out pickup parked by the family hunting cabin.

Calling the thing standing in front of us a "cabin" was much like calling a one-eyed three-legged old mutt a shoo-in for the Westminster Dog Show. Propped up on cinder blocks and two by fours, the old gray and white 1968 Sunline pickup truck camper did little more than keep the rain off your head while you slept. From the looks of it, I doubted it could still do that anymore.

The Bronco's engine coughed to a stop as Mark turned it off and killed the headlights plunging the cabin and the world back into the darkness of the stormy night.

"Mark, do you have a flashlight in this rust bucket?" I asked, not at all pleased to be sitting blind in a truck, outside a hunting cabin occupied by a man who had threatened to kill me the last time I showed up at his place unwanted.

"Should be one in the glovebox."

I opened the glovebox to a burned-out light and rummaged through its contents blindly, trying not to give too much thought to what Mark kept in it. My hand came across something cold and hard. I pulled it out and stared at the 9mm pistol in my hands.

"When did you get this? And why do you have it?"

Mark snatched it out of my hands and stuffed it into the small of his back behind his belt. "It's for protection," he said in a hard voice.

I slapped the glovebox door closed and stared at him a moment but could barely see more than his outline in the dark. "I can't find your flashlight."

Luke reached over the back of the front seat with his phone. "Here, use this." He thumbed on the flashlight app, and its bright light nearly blinded me.

Instead of taking Luke's phone, I pulled mine out of my pocket and turned on its flashlight feature. "Thanks, I have my own."

"Then quit whining and let me out. This backseat smells like ass."

"Then, you better check yourself. You're the only one who ever sits back there," Mark quipped and got a face full of blinding light from Luke in response.

I pushed down Luke's phone. "Stop horsing around," I said. My voice quivered more than I liked. Paul could be aiming his 30-30 at me right now.

The Bronco's door creaked loudly as I opened it; at least we wouldn't surprise him. My boot sunk into the muddy forest floor which sucked at my feet with each step. Luke climbed out behind me awkwardly trying to manage both his phone and a shotgun. Mark rummaged around in the cab a moment longer before emerging from the driver side with the other shotgun and a flashlight in his hands.

"Where did you find that?" I whispered harshly over the hood of the Bronco.

Mark matched my volume, but with considerably more sass. "In the glovebox, like I said."

"Whatever," I scoffed then lifted my phone to blind my old man, should he actually be aiming at me. "Paul!" I called. "Mom sent me to see how you're doing."

No one answered.

"Dad?" Luke called and still no one answered.

I nodded for my brothers to follow and walked slowly around the camper to the other side where the door was. I flashed my light along the ground as I walked, not wanting to trip over a tree root hiding beneath the coating of damp leaves covering the majority of the ground. When I got to the edge of the cabin, I lifted my light and flashed it around the corner at eye level before I stepped around it myself, just in case. My old man wasn't there. Neither was the door to the camper. It lay in the mud a few steps away.

"What the?" Luke asked as he turned the corner. The metal door frame bent awkwardly to the sides as though something too large for it forced its way through; presumably whatever decided to remove the door in the first place.

Mark rushed into the camper calling Paul's name. He stuck his head back out the broken doorway a moment later. "He's not here."

"Luke, go check the truck. See if the engine's still hot," I said in that sergeant voice the Army taught me. To my surprise, Luke moved without objection to do what I asked.

Mark knelt beside the bulge in the door frame examining it, so I began to search the ground looking for footprints. We both said, "Hey, look at this," at nearly the same time. I went to see what Mark found first.

His light shined on a piece of jagged metal with a patch of black fur stuck to its sharp edges. I pulled the fur free. Coarse and only a couple inches long, it could only be one thing.

"Bear," I said. Then I pointed my light at the footprints I had seen in the mud. Huge paw prints with clearly defined edges and claws partially obscured the boot prints entering the camper. Man, then beast had passed through here. A second set of paw prints left the cabin, half-obscured by

31

drag marks. I heard Mark swallow as his light followed the skid marks into the darkness.

"The engine's still warm," Luke said coming back around the corner. "Hey, what are you two gawking at?"

"Bear," I said. "Looks like it broke into the cabin and drug something away."

"Or someone," Mark said, voicing what I didn't want to.

"Mark, give me your nine. I might need it."

"Why?" asked Luke timidly.

"We're going to go see what this bear took."

Mark handed me his 9mm. I popped out the magazine to check the load. In the poor light, I couldn't tell for sure, but it looked to have only five bullets in the clip. I pulled the slide back, hoping he didn't actually keep a round in the chamber, and snatched the ejected round out of the air. I glared disapprovingly at Mark.

He shrugged his shoulder. "Like I said, protection."

I pressed the bullet back into the magazine and reinserted it into the pistol. I racked the slide and readied the gun with my finger resting against the guard, well away from the trigger. "Come on."

I followed the tracks away from the camper.

6

My boots slipped in the mud softened by the early spring rains as I raced after the tracks deeper into the woods. The breadth of each paw print testified to the size of the beast we followed. While my heart trembled the indiscriminate ruination of shrubs and small trees broken and bent by what the bear hauled with it drove urgency into my every step.

After the first mile, Mark tapped me on the shoulder. "I think it's taking him up to Thor's cave."

My gaze followed Mark's light up the mountain. I could see the overgrown path we took as kids winding up the steep grade like a slithering snake. The beaten shrubs of the bear's trail sliced a straight line up the slope, bisecting the serpentine path, but clearly heading to the same destination. Thor's cave.

"Shit," I muttered, still staring into the distance beyond the reach of his flashlight. About a half-mile further up, the rock face split as if Thor himself struck it with his hammer. At least that's what it looked like to the comic-book fueled imaginations of a bunch of kids. As kids, we went adventuring in the cave whenever we could and found a couple rooms a few hundred feet in, either of which would make a perfect bear den. If the bear took Paul into the cave, we wouldn't be able to just scare it away. We would need to kill it to get him out. "What are you loaded with?"

"I've got the twenty-gauge, so birdshot. Luke's carrying the twelve," Mark replied.

"Luke, what kind of shells do you have?"

I heard Luke pump the shotgun. His light dropped to the ground as he located the expelled shell. "Birdshot."

"Alright," I said, trying to think the scenario through. "If it's gone into the cave, I'll lead. Birdshot won't do more than piss a bear off. Not that a nine will do much better, but it should make it think twice." I didn't get any objections from either of them.

I took a doubtful look at the nine in my hand before setting my shoulders, then scrambled up the newly blazed trail despite the incline, using the vegetation as handholds. Halfway up a sapling pulled free, and I nearly lost my balance. I caught myself with my other hand on another tree, but not before I dropped the pistol into the mud. I cursed and tossed the root ball behind me like a dirt grenade.

The victim of friendly fire, Mark sputtered then shone his light up into my eyes. "Hey, what the hell?"

"Sorry. The damn thing pulled free and I almost fell."

Mark swatted the dirt from his hair. "So. That's no reason to hit me with it, shithead."

"Well, douchebag, next time I'll just fall on your sorry ass," I grumbled, retrieving my weapon.

Luke pushed past us both with a shoulder. "Quit your bitching. Dad needs our help."

Mark and I shared an apologetic glare for letting the stress get to us then continued to scale the mountain behind Luke.

Like Mark guessed, the tracks lead straight to the cave entrance. The markings at the mouth of the cave showed the animal turning around to drag Paul in backwards. Scuff marks from Paul's boots marred the green slime covering the rock face of the opening. I prayed that it meant he still lived; more for my mom's sake than for his.

"Stay back at least 50 feet so I have room to run if I need to," I said shining my light into the cave, but I could only see about 20 feet or so into it. "On second thought, just stay here. If I need to run, I want to be able to run all the way back out without tripping over either of you."

Mark looked up at the sky. The dark of night made it hard to tell when the clouds would open up, but it smelled like rain. "Just be quick. We'll wait for you over by those pine trees," he said pointing to a copse of trees about a hundred feet away. They wouldn't offer much protection from the rain, but it would be better than none.

"Fine. If I don't come back out in twenty minutes, go home and get help. Do NOT come in after me."

They both bobbed their heads and moved off to the trees. I checked my phone. Eight thirty and fifty-percent battery.

I glanced over my shoulder one more time. "Save your batteries," I said, then went into the cave.

In my left hand, I held my phone in front of me, lighting the hard walls of the cave. In my right, I carried the pistol down by my side with my finger on the guard to keep from accidentally discharging it.

After a few dozen feet into the cave, the slime disappeared and with it the tracks. I raised my head and stared deeper into the darkness beyond the feeble limits of my phone's flashlight app. I thought I could hear something. Sweat beaded on my forehead despite the coolness of the cave.

Pulling up the settings on the flashlight app, I changed it from the camera flash to the front screen where I set the light to a low red that barely lit more than a yard or so in front of my feet. I tucked the phone behind my belt and partially into the pocket of my pants to free up both of my hands for a clammy two-handed grip on the pistol.

I stepped forward softly, rolling my feet as quietly as I could, but the gravel crunched beneath my boots like popping bubble wrap with each step. I cringed, but the sounds coming from the depths of the cave did not change. As I inched closer to the first room, the noises began to fade, receding deeper into the depths of the mountain.

I rounded the last corner of the cave and stooped behind a rock that protruded into the path at the opening to the room. The smell of earthy mildew and something more fetid filled my nostrils. I took out my phone and changed the settings back to the camera flash, covering up the light with a forefinger to not give myself away. Taking a one-knee shooter's stance I propped my right hand on the rock, ready to shoot, and held the phone out with my left.

With a last steadying breath, I slipped my finger from the flash, flooding the room in bright white light. Ancient stalagmites rose out of the floor like giant stone teeth casting long shadows across the small room, but the ceiling rose well out of reach of my light. I scanned the uneven floor searching for the beast and found Paul lying in a bloody heap at the far end of the room near the mouth of another cave diving deeper into the mountain.

I darted from one stone formation to another, rescanning the room each time, paying special attention to the other cave mouth. Nothing moved, and I eventually reached Paul's torn body.

Several rending claw marks slashed open his coat, shirt, and chest. Blood soaked into the frayed fabric. A large bite ruined one of his shoulders. I felt at his neck for a pulse, counting out several seconds in my head, until I found it. I hung my head and let out the breath I didn't realize I held. He was still alive.

I looked him over and decided I couldn't move him on my own. Not while holding the gun and the light, and I didn't dare leave either without knowing where the bear ran off to. I tried calling my brothers, but I couldn't get a signal through the mountain of rock, so I raced back to the cave opening as fast as I could, abandoning the precautions I used earlier.

I stopped at the cave entrance, breathing hard. Peering through the cold wind-driven mist of a steady rain, I found my brothers huddled close to the trunks of the pine trees in a feeble effort to shelter themselves from the wind and rain. I whistled a sharp shrill that cut through the forest sounds and saw Mark's head snap up.

Mark tapped Luke on the shoulder, who jumped with a start, and they rushed over to me when I waved.

"Did you find Dad?" asked Luke still ten feet away. The rain matted his hair to his head, which amplified the misery on his face.

I shushed him with a finger across my lips. "Quiet, there's a bear in there somewhere. I found Paul, but he's in a real bad way and I can't move him on my own."

"Is the bear with him?" The shake in Luke's voice could have been mistaken for a shiver in the cold wind, but I'd seen that particular look of fear on the faces of soldiers I've been to hell with.

"You just left him with the bear?" Mark asked right on top of him.

"I didn't see the bear. I think it's deeper in. Now, come on, you two can carry him while I cover your backs." I turned and headed back into the cave. I made it past the slime before I heard the two of them following me.

"Let me go! I'm coming," Luke said, his voice now more annoyed than scared.

I prayed the bear wouldn't be there when we got back to Paul, or Luke might just run for it. He never cared much for animals, especially the dangerous kind, not like Jonny. Jonny would have led the way into the bear's den spouting all sorts of useless facts along the way.

If he were still here.

I pushed the pained thought from my mind and moved deeper into the cave.

The lights of our phones, each in flash mode, illuminated the cave like those bright lights they use for nighttime road work. They cast hard pulsating shadows along the walls in front of us and deep into the cave. Not that we gave it much thought as we hurried along making more noise than pigs hunting truffles, but if we did happen upon the bear, we'd probably blind it long enough to get away. I knew we should be more careful, but Paul didn't have the time, and while I didn't know why, I needed to get him out alive.

I stopped us just before the last bend in the cave. "I'll go make sure he's still alone. Stay here until I signal for you," I whispered more to calm my own racing heart than for stealth; if the bear was still in the cave, it should have heard us coming long ago. Mark and Luke nodded. "And keep your lights pointed the other way for now," I added before partially covering my light and moving up to the rock I hid behind before.

I listened but didn't hear anything from the room in front of me. So, I readied my pistol and lit the room with my phone. It remained empty except for Paul. I turned my light back up the cave and flashed it several times with a finger.

Mark and Luke scurried up to my position, and I shined the light on Paul. One of them gasped and the other croaked on a mouthful of bile.

"I'm going over there behind that stalagmite to watch the back cave. You two go get Paul and get out of here."

Mark held out his twenty-gauge. "You better take this. I can't carry him and the shotgun."

I took his shotgun and slung it over my shoulder by the leather strap. Luke handed me his as well, but the twelve-gauge lacked a shoulder strap, so I pushed the pistol into the waist of my jeans at small of my back. I half-pumped the shotgun and checked the breach. A long red shell sat ready in the chamber. I slammed the pump forward and fingered the safety on, then hustled into position.

I propped the wooden grip of the pump over the back of my left wrist so that I could still aim the light on my phone. I shined it to one side of the entrance to keep the beam from directly illuminating the cave and used only the spill to watch for anything coming out. If by some miracle the bear didn't know we were here, I didn't want the light to give us away.

Mark and Luke made their way to Paul. Luke convulsed again but kept his dinner down.

"Take his legs," Mark said, trying to find a way to pick up Paul's torso without grabbing some injured part. He settled for slipping his hands under the armpits and clutched a fistful of coat in each hand.

Luke picked up Paul's legs, and they lifted him from the floor. Paul's head arched back slamming into Mark's shoulder as he let out a terrible moan and they almost dropped him.

"Turn around and grab him the other way, so we can both see where we're going," Mark said in a harsh whisper.

Luke turned and dropped one of Paul's legs in the process. The sudden shift in weight made Mark grunt as he tried to compensate, and Paul screamed in pain.

"Shit," I said through clenched teeth. "Get going."

They rushed as fast as they could carrying the body between them, but it was too late. I could hear something coming up the other cave.

7

I waited for the sound of approaching footsteps to get closer then adjusted my phone to shine the light straight down the cave mouth, hoping to blind the bear. However, the light didn't land on a bear, but rather a stocky, naked woman with muscles that would make the She-Hulk feel small. Thick black hair shot through with streaks of white hung over her shoulders. Little ornaments tied to the ends of the white strands swung like silver monkeys swinging on vines as they bounced across her pale bare chest. She growled at the light and raised an arm in front of her face to protect her eyes but continued to walk forward.

"Stop or I'll shoot."

She didn't stop. I released the safety and pointed the shotgun in her general direction, at this range, with birdshot, aiming was only a formality. She dropped her arm and roared at me like a wild beast.

I stepped backward toward the exit and into a stalagmite. My right shoulder took the brunt of the impact knocking my aim to the left. The jolt of the sudden stop made my finger slip onto the trigger and the shotgun boomed in the small room. The echo rung in my ears and the muzzle flash made me lose sight of the woman. I blinked to clear the ghost image from my vision and found her a few steps farther back into her cave, still standing. The bulk of the shot had missed, but blood still oozed from a dozen tiny holes in her skin.

Her eyes flared, and she flexed her arms as if gathering the darkness around her and roared another challenge. She leaned forward and fell to all fours. Her shoulders thickened while her arms grew shorter, absorbing their length into thick muscle. Her white flesh disappeared into black fur and her head grew round like a black pumpkin. Her nose and mouth morphed into a long snout between large round eyes which glowed inhumanly in the light of my phone.

I stood paralyzed, unable to believe what I was seeing. In my hesitation, the werebear charged, her claws scraping across the stone floor like nails on a chalkboard. The noise snapped me out of my stupor and I blindly aimed the shotgun in her general directions, pumping and pulling the trigger as fast as I could until the hammer clacked onto an empty chamber.

The bear lowered her head against the barrage but did not slow. I retreated around the stalagmite, dropping the shotgun to pull out the 9mm, moving to keep the stalagmite between me and my adversary.

I let loose with two shots to center mass. The werebear hardly flinched at the impact but slowed her advance. Her head swept from one side to the other as she considered the best route around the stone barrier. I moved to another rock, putting several more feet between us while at the same time working my way closer to the cave mouth and the passage to freedom.

I knew the 9mm didn't have the penetration I needed, so I shifted my aim for the creature's head in a vain hope to confuse her enough to get away by rapping her in the skull with my last few rounds. With no more stalagmites to hide behind and my heart pounding, I steadied my breath and put the last four shots dead center between her eyes. I took off running down the cave, not waiting to see if they did any real damage.

I holstered the pistol behind my belt as I ran and took the twenty-gauge off my shoulder, releasing the safety one-handed, ready to fire back into the cave. I didn't hear the werebear behind me, not that I could hear anything above the ringing in my ears but I didn't slow down, either. I kept my legs pumping as fast as they would move while half-looking over my shoulder as I ran.

Halfway back to the cave opening my phone died, and I nearly tripped over the uneven rock floor. I jammed the phone into my pocket so I could hold the shotgun properly then continued to move toward the exit. Fortunately, my brothers were only a few dozen yards in front of me and I could follow their silhouettes out of the cave.

Outside the cave, Mark and Luke sat Paul up against the rock face and leaned on their knees to catch their breath.

I rushed out of the cave yelling, "Keep moving!"

"What? Didn't you kill it?" Luke asked but I only caught half of what he said through my deafened ears.

"I doubt anything I have can kill it. We need to run."

Mark open and closed his fingers to work out the cramp in his hands. "I'm not sure how fast we can carry him."

I tossed him the shotgun. "Then cover my back."

Bending down on one knee, I lifted Paul's arm to tuck my shoulder under his chest, hoisted him to his feet, then dropped to get him leaning over my back. It took another bounce to work him into a fireman's carry. He groaned plaintively, but I didn't care or have time to worry about it. I began stumbling and running down the mountain as fast as I could, praying we would somehow make it to the bottom alive.

Luke soon passed me to light the pathway with his phone, and I could sense more than hear Mark crashing through the brush behind me. We made it down the initial steep slope, somehow keeping our feet under us when the werebear unleashed a chilling roar behind us, as if we needed more motivation.

Mark fired blindly up the mountain. The crack of gunfire echoed in the wet night, and I prayed the bear couldn't tell the difference between the 9mm and the shotgun and would think twice about chasing us. Because if it could tell the difference...well, I didn't need to finish that thought.

By the time we made it back to Mark's truck, my legs felt like rubber and I stumbled the last few feet, finally falling and dropping Paul into the mud with a moan. Mark and Luke picked him up and put him in the front seat of the Bronco, propping him up as best they could and buckling him in. I got up out of the mud and climbed into the back through the driver's side. Luke jumped in behind me.

Mark pushed the driver's seat back into position, jumped in and started turning the truck engine over in one swift move. The engine cranked and coughed to life. He dropped it in reverse and turned on the headlights. We didn't see the werebear, but he floored the pedal just the same.

The engine groaned at the sudden call to action, but the truck lurched in reverse. Mark backed straight into a tree jolting our heads with whiplash. He moved the shifter to drive and raced down the dirt track far faster than was safe, but much slower than any of us wanted to move.

We hit the hard-top road and flung mud more than a mile before Mark stopped to unlock the front hubs. I took the opportunity to check on Paul's pulse and couldn't find it at first. When I did, I gave Luke a worried look. I doubted Paul would survive the forty minutes to the nearest hospital without medical care.

"Call 911, I'm not sure we're going to make it to the hospital in time."

Luke called, frantically exchanging our location with the operator and explaining our situation. Mark drove like a madman, and I held Paul in his seat against the curves.

Fifteen minutes later we met the ambulance on the side of the two-lane county road. We stayed out of the paramedics' way as they transferred Paul to a stretcher and began treating his wounds while moving him into the back of the ambulance. He still breathed, but barely.

I felt sick in the backseat as Mark chased after the ambulance and Luke called our mother. I couldn't remember the last time I considered the man clinging to life in the vehicle in front of us as my father, but as we drove on, I kept reliving my last words to him and prayed I'd be able to apologize for accusing him of Jonny's death.

At the hospital the ambulance veered off toward the ambulance entrance while we found a place to park. We rushed in through the main entrance and, after some mis-navigation, we eventually found our way to the emergency room waiting area. The ceiling vaulted high into a skylight lit from below by large bowl-shaped chandeliers. The fine finishes of the room made me uncomfortable in my ratty farm jacket smeared with Paul's blood. I shrugged out of the coat, electing to wear only my sweatshirt. With fewer holes, it only made me feel slightly better. Mark and Luke either didn't share my compunctions or simply didn't notice the décor as they strode straight to the reception desk.

If the nurse behind the desk thought anything of our attire, she kept it to herself as she patiently took Paul's information. Mark dug out his well-worn leather wallet and handed the nurse his copy of the farm's health insurance. It barely met the minimum Obamacare requirements, which meant this would cost way more than the already cash-strapped family farm could afford.

The nurse finished taking down the pertinent information then asked us to find a seat to wait for the doctor. We turned from her station to the waiting room. Short wood-clad walls divided the space into several small, open waiting areas each with chairs for six, but most of the alcoves contained clusters of people in small anxious groups with only a scattering of empty chairs between them.

I couldn't sit and wait. I needed to move, to clear my head. As I considered my options, the exterior door slid open, admitting a mother with dark sleep-deprived bags beneath her eyes and a bawling child cradled in her arms. In no mood to deal with a screaming child rattling my brains, I stalked past them searching for enough space to stretch my legs.

Mark followed me a couple steps before checking his hands as if noticing the dried blood from carrying Paul out of the cave for the first time. "I need to go wash," he said heading toward the restrooms instead.

Luke glanced nervously between us, his shoulders and hands shaking with small tremors. I knew he needed someone to comfort him. To help him rationalize the night, but I didn't have it in me. Besides, I had spent his most formative years in the Army and didn't have the emotional credibility to be the rock he needed. He took one more look at me then turned to follow Mark.

Watching them leave, I shook my head as my mouth curled in a regretful frown. The knife of wasted years dug into my soul as I stepped out into the cool night air. With my jacket draped over my arm, the breeze cut through my sweatshirt and chilled my skin. I crumpled the jacket in my hands, refusing to put it on, and shivered as I paced the sidewalk searching for distractions or answers, but the night air offered neither and the pacing only served to burn off my worried energy. I reached the end of the short walk and did an about-face, letting the precision of military drill work my body automatically.

With each cadenced stride, my mind replayed the transformation of woman into bear, like watching Bumblebee change from a robot into a VW bug in slow motion. My stubborn disbelief shattered and I realized that Jacob had been right, Jonny really had died a hero.

I staggered to a panic-stricken stop as the memory of Jacob, ready with his rifle, flooded my mind. He had asked if the bear had bit me.

I ran back into the waiting room and collided with Luke coming the other way. We stumbled a step or two as we both tried to keep the other from falling.

"Mom and Mary are here," he said once we stopped dancing.

I looked into the room. Our mother stood in her overcoat with a shawl still wrapped over her head, next to Mark and Mary. Another man in a long white doctor's coat stood with them. The badge pinned to his coat showed a picture of a much younger man with a full head of hair and trimmed beard. The resemblance was close enough to the clean-shaven, half-bald man wearing it that I didn't doubt he was Doctor Sheffield as it claimed. They all waited patiently as Luke and I strode across the room to join them.

My mother took in a deep breath, straightened her back and nodded to the doctor. "You were saying, doctor?"

"Yes, ma'am. Animal wounds are extremely dangerous, especially large wild animals like the one that attacked your husband. Your sons did a remarkable job getting him here as fast as they did, but he lost a considerable amount of blood. We gave him a blood transfusion but couldn't get ahead of the infection. I'm afraid…"

My mother fell into Mark's shoulder crying loudly before the doctor could even finish his sentence. Mary and Luke joined the group-hug clinging together for mutual support.

"Are you sure? He's dead?" I asked, stunned, and hoping it didn't work like I feared.

"I'm sorry, son," Doctor Sheffield answered.

I didn't like it when Paul called me son, I certainly didn't like hearing from this man now. Heat rose in my cheeks, but I checked my anger, unsure of who or what I was actually mad at. I looked at my family huddled together and somehow felt apart from them.

The doctor touched me on the shoulder in a fatherly gesture I never received from Paul, then moved to leave.

"May I see the body?" I asked, needing to be sure Paul was actually dead.

He kept his voice low and I could see the caution in his eyes, but he nodded toward the back doors. "Of course. Follow me."

Before following the doctor, I pushed my coat into Mark's hand, whose fingers closed around it without letting go of our mother.

8

Doctor Sheffield led me down a wide hall lined with patient rooms on one side and a long nurse's station on the other. Heavy curtains, drawn across the patient rooms, muffled the noise of TVs that offered their occupants a small distraction over the chirps and beeps of the medical equipment. The air smelled of antiseptic and felt pregnant with a half-distracted urgency one heartbeat away from a catastrophe, putting my already frayed nerves on edge.

He walked up to a tall blond nurse in scrubs pushing a blue folder into a slotted wall. "Joan, has the patient in room 107 been transferred yet?"

The nurse turned. Beneath narrow-set eyes, her thin lips flashed a quick smile at the doctor. Her smile slipped when she saw me beside him. "Um, yes. Just a moment ago."

"Well, aren't they just Johnny-on-the-spot tonight," The doctor said not quite under his breath. His tired frustrated eyes met mine and betrayed his practiced apologetic smile. "I'm sorry, Mr. Peterson. I'm afraid your father has already been transferred to the morgue."

I took a half-step toward the waiting room before stopping, unable to get the feeling of dread out of the pit of my stomach. I needed to be sure. "Doctor Sheffield, I really need to see him. Please."

"Ah," he sighed. "Well, if you still wish to see the body, I'm going to have to get someone else to escort you. I have other patients I need to see to."

Joan looked at me, her face melting with sympathy. "I can take him."

He nodded with an acquiescent grimace. "Thank you, Joan." The doctor turned back to me. His lips curled in that awkward way people do when they want to be comforting but know they can't. "I am truly sorry for your loss, Mr. Peterson."

I dipped my head in acknowledgment as he walked away. For a reason I could barely understand, I felt bitter watching him leave.

The nurse gently touched my arm and pointed toward another pair of doors. "This way, Mr. Peterson."

We walked in silence as we moved past people and beds, both of which became more sporadic as we approached the morgue. My escort held a brief conversation with the technician at the door before he let us in.

The technician walked up to a bank of what appeared to be old freezer doors stacked along a stainless-steel wall three high and twenty across. He opened the middle door, third from the left and pulled out the drawer inside. He folded back a white sheet then stepped aside for me to see.

Paul's body lay on the cold metal surface, the color already beginning to seep from his skin. I sighed in audible relief and drew a suspicious glance from the nurse, but I didn't care. He was clearly dead.

"Thanks. That's...um, that's him," I mumbled as guilt replaced my moment of relief.

The tech lowered the sheet back over Paul's head. As it fell, I saw an eyelid move in a flutter of reanimation. I rubbed at my own eyes trying to suppress my imagination as the tech pushed the drawer back into the wall and closed the door.

"That looks pretty robust," I said, nodding to the door, unable to keep the words from leaving my mouth. "I'd hate to get put in one on accident. Still alive, I mean."

"No worries there." The tech's flat voice gave me the impression he answered stupid questions like that on a daily basis. "We make sure the bodies are good and dead before they go in." I gave him an uneasy smile, and he let out a mollifying chuckle. "Besides, there's a release installed on the inside of the freezer, just in case."

We all walked back to the door where he flipped the light off and let the door close behind us. We made it another two steps before we heard the bang like a sledgehammer on steel from back inside the morgue. "What the hell?" the tech said, turning back to the door.

"No, wait," I said too late.

A large black werebear reared up on his hind legs as the door swung just shy of his nose. The tech froze in his steps as the bear opened his maw and roared, only inches from the man's face.

"Run," I yelled, grabbing the technician's coat and yanking him back away from the door. I threw him in the general direction of the nurse already sprinting down the hall.

The morgue door swung on its double-action hinges back through the door frame. The Paul-werebear dropped onto all fours and started nosing his way out of the room. I kicked the door the other way, smashing the metal door into his snout. He stumbled back, shaking his head from side to side, then reared up and threw his full weight against the door, returning the favor. The door slammed into me with enough force to drive me into the neighboring wall. I collapsed to the floor, struggling to draw air into my lungs.

The werebear stumbled out of the room as if uncertain of how to walk on four feet. Concealed where I lay behind the door, he wandered past me after the nurse and retreating technician. I watched in horror as the werebear became more sure-footed and started to amble after them.

My lungs finally began to work again, and I drew in a gulp of the precious air I needed. "Hey!" I croaked, trying to get the werebear's attention as I tried to get back on my feet. "Hey, Paul, you fucking piece of shit! I'm over here!"

The werebear slowed and turned. I could feel sweat forming on my hands as I instantly regretted drawing its attention. Paul, no—the werebear, better I thought of him as a werebear than Paul. The werebear walked toward me, sizing me up as it came. I eased myself backward into the morgue, holding the doors open so that the werebear never lost sight of me.

I stole a glance over my shoulder, scanning the room for the door they used to load bodies into the hearses when the funeral homes came to collect. Set into a wall at the far end of the room, a large plate window looked into a sally port of sorts with a rollup door in the opposite wall. That had to be it. I mentally mapped my run through the handful of gurneys between me and the door to the room. I took another backward step, stretching my fingertips to keep the morgue door open. The werebear, only a few feet away, stalked another step forward.

"Come on. Come on, I'm right here," I taunted ready to release the door and bolt for the sally port, when I heard Mark call from the other end of the hall.

"Matt, you back here? What the...how did a bear get in here?"

The werebear twisted his massive head back to peer over his shoulder at the new voice.

"Shit! Mark, run!"

Without thinking, I lunged forward and kicked the werebear in the shoulder. His head snapped back around and nearly caught my foot in his teeth.

I sprinted toward the sally port room with the werebear nipping at my heels. I considered my options as I ran. The door or the window? I didn't have time to open a door, so I dove through the window crossing my forearms in front of my head. The glass resisted at first then shattered as the full weight of my body followed. I landed with a combat roll through the shards of tempered glass. The fragments bit into my arms and hands. I sprung back to my feet and kept running as the werebear crashed into the wall, breaking through it in a shower of concrete. The metal frame of the window twisted and fell onto the dazed beast, tangling him up.

I slapped the controls and the overhead door began coiling up toward the ceiling. It inched open slowly while the werebear struggled to free itself of the frame. I rolled beneath the door as soon as I could fit. The werebear's claws raked my back before I got out of reach. I could feel them tear through my sweatshirt, t-shirt, and skin. The gravel on the pavement chewed painfully into the gashes as I rolled away.

I pressed myself up onto my feet. The door behind me rattled in its frame. I spared a quick look and groaned. The werebear's head gnashed through the rising door as he swiped wildly with a forepaw. I sucked in a large gulp of air and forced my feet to start moving again, gathering speed as they pounded away at the pavement. Within moments, I heard the scratching of claws chasing after me.

The road wrapped around the corner of the hospital then squeezed between the hospital and the employee parking lot. I reached the front corner of the hospital where the drive slipped by the main parking lot on its way to State Street. A pair of security guards rushed down the sidewalk from the hospital's main entrance, and I could see the flashing blue lights against the glow of Gloversville in the distance. This late at night, cars only half filled the parking lot, but people still milled between them.

The werebear grunted and snorted behind me like an animal freight train trying to run me down. I felt him gaining on me but didn't dare spare the time to glance over my shoulder. With the parking lot and the hospital entrance to my right and Gloversville ahead of me, I considered my options, knowing I needed to lead the beast away from both before he became interested in easier prey.

I dodged left through the employee lot past the first row of vehicles then slipped between a new Mercedes SUV and a 1980-something Oldsmo-Buick. In a crash of metal and screeching tires, the werebear slammed into the Mercedes, almost trapping me against the other vehicle. I bounced off the rear fender and popped out of the gap like the cork from a champagne bottle. I stumbled the last few yards to the tree line, favoring my bruised hip and fearing I would not survive the night.

When I didn't hear the animal crashing through the underbrush after me, I hooked a hand around a tree to slingshot myself in the other direction back toward the hospital. I ducked behind a thick maple tree at the edge of the woods. While not as well-lit as the main parking lot, I spotted the werebear engaged in a one-sided fight with the Mercedes.

With both front paws, the beast delivered a hammering blow to the SUV and finished ravaging the offending Mercedes, silencing its car alarm with one final squawk. The werebear sniffed at the ruined hood of the vehicle as if making sure it would not breathe again. Satisfied, he lifted his massive head, nose flaring as he tested the air. His ears twitched at the wail of sirens growing closer. I prayed they would get here soon.

"Shoo! Get out of here!" hollered a voice closer to the hospital.

I looked up. The guards stalked across the drive with their weapons drawn. The huskier rent-a-cop raised his pistol and fired two warning shots into the air. "I said shoo!"

The werebear ambled slowly around tilting his head as if deciding whether the new intruders were food or threat; if any part of Paul remained in that bear, it wouldn't matter as he'd chew them up out of spite. True to form, the werebear reared back onto his hind legs, grunting with the effort and swaying awkwardly for a moment. He steadied himself and issued a challenging roar.

"Dan, I don't think he likes taking orders," said the other guard, the point of his pistol shaking as much as his voice.

The werebear bellowed another roar which drowned out the police sirens. Then it fell down onto all fours and charged, billowing a raspy huffing breath with each galloping step.

Dan broke with a scream and ran up the drive, leaving his companion in frozen shock.

The raging werebear shouldered the Miata between him and the petrified guard out of his way like a bale of straw. The crash of crushing metal snapped the now lone guard back to his senses, and his pistol erupted in muzzle flashes. At point-blank range, each round found its mark in the beast's center mass with little effect. The werebear bowled into the guard locking his jaws around the man's throat and ripping it out as he barreled past.

Police cars screamed up the drive. Their strobing blue lights cast the werebear in an otherworldly glow as he continued after the fleeing guard.

Dan fired blindly behind him, missing the werebear and hitting more than one police car. They swerved to avoid his wild fire. Several of the shots ripped through the foliage near me, and I dropped to the ground for safety.

I watched through the low underbrush as the werebear tackled Dan from behind, landing on his back with a sickening crunch of breaking bones. The creature's mouth engulfed the man's head then twisted violently and tore it completely off of his body.

A police car slammed into the side of the werebear, and Paul rolled off of the vehicle's brush guard. A second car swerved around the first and screeched to a halt. Officers opened fire on the beast before their doors finished swinging open. The boom of shotguns punctuated the staccato of pistol fire.

With a wail, the injured werebear staggered back to his feet and rushed off into the woods, thankfully not in my direction.

9

More emergency vehicles arrived, turning the access road into a three-ring circus without a ringmaster. I eased back deeper into the tree line. With my cuts and tattered clothing, I didn't want to get caught up in the expanding police scene having to field questions to which the answers would likely land me in the loony bin. I took the long way around the hospital through the woods then wound my way back to the emergency room.

The ER buzzed with uncertain excitement from nervous clusters of whispering people gesturing out the windows where blue lights strobed from vehicles just out of view. Others looked about the room as if worried the roof would cave in at any moment. My mother waited in one of those groups with Mary and Luke. When she saw me squeezing through the crowd, her worried face relaxed slightly and she nodded me toward the reception desk where a few of the bolder individuals harried the poor nurses for answers.

Mark stood at one end of the counter interrogating a shorter nurse with brunette hair and an iron face that did not appear at all pleased with the tone of his voice. "Damn it, I want to know what the..."

I tapped him on the shoulder to keep him from cursing at the nurse further. He spun at the interruption, and I pointed with my chin toward our family huddled nervously in one of the seating alcoves. "Mark, why don't you get everybody ready to go home."

"Matt, where the hell have you been?" he asked, throwing his arms around me in a crushing hug and slapping his hands into the open wounds on my back.

"Ow," I said in a tight groan.

He let me go in worry. "Are you all right?"

"Yeah, I'll be fine. Just a little scratched up is all."

"Oh good. I saw that bear and I thought…wait, how the hell did a bear get into the hospital?" He swung a sour face in the direction of the nurse about to go off on her again like a teakettle.

I grabbed his shoulders and twisted him to face me, saving the poor nurse from one of his red-tempered explosions. "I'll explain later. Now, go get Mom ready to go home." His eyes narrowed for a moment before he stalked off in the direction of our mother.

After he left, I gave the nurse the best apologetic smile I could manage. "I'm sorry, ma'am. We've had a very rough night."

"I understand," she said with an *I'm-used-to-it* expression.

"Sorry," I said one more time then turned to join my family.

The nurse spoke up in alarm. "Sir, your back!"

I grimaced. I needed to go home and figure out how to get in touch with Jacob, not tend to flesh wounds that didn't hurt that bad. I peeked over my shoulder nonchalantly. "Oh, it's nothing, I'll be fine."

Unconvinced, she stepped around the desk to get a better look. "Sir, you're dripping blood on my floor. Now come here and let me see." She took me by the arm and pulled me after her.

I tried to pull my arm free, but she held my arm in an iron vise of a grip. "Thanks, but I'll clean them out when I get home. I don't have time…"

She cut me off with a *don't-argue-with-me* stare. "No one leaves my emergency room still bleeding. Besides, I'll be quick."

The numbness of adrenaline wore off as we talked about my injuries, and my back blossomed in the fire of pain. Besides, I didn't know what kind of nasties werebear claws held, not that I thought she could do much for the supernatural kind, but she could at least keep me from getting a very real infection. I flashed Mark a five-minute hand signal then reluctantly followed her to one of the open examination bays.

Thanks to the thorough ministrations of the chief nurse, I emerged from the exam room a full two hours later and carrying a mountain of paperwork. At least with Uncle Sam's insurance, my bill wouldn't be going to the farm.

Only Mark waited for me, sprawled out in one of the chairs and using my jacket as a blanket. The five-year-old in the chair beside him kept shooting him dirty looks every time Mark rasped a particularly hoarse snore. At seeing him comatose, an urge to tie the laces of his boots together tugged at my mind, but my own exhaustion kept it at bay. I settled for nudging his shoulder a bit harder than necessary. He woke with a jolt and a half-annoyed half-confused glare around the room.

"Where did everyone go?"

Mark roughly rubbed his hands over his face, making a gurgling noise that chased the kid into the arms of his sleeping mother. He then handed me my jacket and struggled to his feet. "Luke and Mary took Mom home. They're going to try to get some rest before the morning milking. But seeing as they're the ones doing the morning chores, I think I got the better end of that deal," Mark said with a weak smile. He got up from his chair and began walking.

His words filled the emptiness between us, but I couldn't muster more than a grunt in response as I threw on my jacket and shrugged my shoulders. No one won tonight and he knew it. After the aborted attempt to break the fetid mood, we walked to his truck in silence.

The doors creaked open as we climbed inside. I put my seatbelt on and waited, but Mark didn't start the truck. He sat in the driver's seat staring at me like a dog waiting for a bone.

"What? We need to go."

"I'm waiting for you to tell me what the hell is going on," he said holding the keys in his right hand and nowhere near the ignition.

"Just drive. I'll tell you on the way."

He squinted at me as if debating whether or not to trust me, then pushed the key into the ignition and started the truck with a screech of the fan belt. He backed out of the parking spot, then slammed the truck in drive and smashed the gas pedal at the same time. The wheels squealed, and I tried not to curse as the momentum slammed my injured back into the seat.

We pulled out of the hospital parking lot and rounded the curve in the road. The rearview mirror flashed with the blue lights of police cars. Mark twisted to see the lights over his shoulder. I didn't bother.

"I'm not sure where to begin," I said after we drove through Gloversville.

"Try starting with why there was a bear in the hospital and what the hell you were doing with it."

I ran a hand through the bristles of hair on my head. "Ah…you're not going to believe me."

He flashed a hard scowl at me then turned his attention back on the road. "I'll keep my mind open. Now spill."

"Okay. That bear was Paul. I think he's a werebear or something like that."

Mark spared a quick disbelieving look in my direction. "What the hell are you talking about?"

"Damn, Mark, I don't think I've ever heard you swear so much."

"Dad's gone; I'm trying something new. Now, what the hell are you talking about?"

"You remember that bear we ran from tonight in the woods?"

"I didn't get a good look at him, but yeah."

"Well, for starters it wasn't a boy, it was a girl."

Mark scoffed. "You got close enough to check?"

"No. In the cave, she was still a very naked woman. I watched her transform, um, change into that bear. It must have given Paul that nasty bite mark on his shoulder and, well, I guess it works something like all those werewolf stories Jonny loved." I swallowed the sudden lump in my throat and wondered how long it would keep coming back at every thought of him.

"You're bullshitting me."

"I wish," I said as we rolled through Johnstown and past the all-night Miss Johnstown Diner. I twisted in my seat at the sight of a truck I'd seen too much of lately. "Turn around!"

"What? Why?" Mark asked.

"I think that's Jacob's truck back at the diner."

Mark lifted his foot off the accelerator and found an empty parking lot to turn the truck around. "The guy who gave you a ride home?"

"Yeah. He's also a monster hunter…or…something. He'll know what to do."

The truck rolled back down Main Street then rumbled to a stop a few spaces back from Jacob's truck. I peeked into the windows as I walked past. Jacob lay sprawled across the backseat, his duster draped across him like a blanket. I pounded on his window to wake him up.

He rolled over onto his back and lifted his head. It took him a moment to focus on me, but his eyes grew in recognition. "Hold on, I'm up. Just give me a minute." He sat up and rubbed at his eyes then reached over and unlocked the back-passenger side door.

When he didn't make a move to get out, I pulled open the door. "Jacob, thank God I found you."

"Yes, thank God," he grumbled.

"This is Jacob?" Mark asked, looking over my shoulder.

"Yeah, I'm Jacob. Who are you?"

"This is my brother, Mark."

"Oh, another of the Peterson Apostles."

"Or the red horseman, depending on who you ask," Mark said with a grin. He always preferred the horsemen of the apocalypse moniker over the apostles.

Jacob squinted at Mark, then smiled with a snort of a laugh at seeing the red tinge to his beard. He then turned his smirk to me. "Guess that makes you the white rider of conquest?"

"Only by birth order," Mark answered for me.

I gestured over my shoulder to the Miss Johnstown Diner. "Jacob, can I buy you a cup of coffee? I have some bear questions."

His mouth opened in a wide yawn he didn't try to stifle. "Sure. Go get us a table, I'll be right there. I've got to use the head first."

The diner itself didn't look like much. An open kitchen with a counter and a row of stools ran the length of the long, narrow room. A handful of laminate tables and padded metal chairs lined the other wall, leaving only a narrow aisle between them. The smell of bitter coffee cut through the grease-laden air of fried meats.

"Seat yourselves," said the lone waitress at the sound of the ringing bell above the door.

This late at night the restaurant remained mostly empty except for the two other patrons sitting at the counter where they could talk with the cook. At the back of the room, Mark and I found a table far enough away from everyone else to give us some privacy and still comfortably seat the three of us.

I glanced at the chalkboard touting the daily special but didn't feel hungry. Mark, on the other hand, studied it like he didn't eat here every Friday night after the high school football games.

Jacob joined us a few minutes later, his face dripping with water. He took the napkin from under his silverware and dried his face. "I didn't realize they were out of towels in the bathroom until after I splashed water on my face."

"I'm sorry, sir. I'll bring you some more napkins," the waitress said, coming up behind him with a fresh pot of coffee and a set of mugs. Blue

LES GOULD

highlights tipped the ends of her blond bob, complementing her remarkable green eyes. She tucked a lock of bright blue behind an ear before
filling the mugs.

Jacob gave her an easy smile. "No worries, ma'am. Not as long as you
keep my cup full and the coffee strong."

She pursed her red lips. "Please, you look about as old as my granddad,
just call me Sophie."

His smile grew wider. "That's a pretty name. Who were you named
after?"

Sophie rolled her eyes but let a pleasant smile crease her face. "Well,
thank you. I'm named after my great-grandmother on my dad's side.
Now, what can I get for you gentlemen?" Jacob and I ordered only coffee,
but Mark ordered the breakfast special with extra everything.

"I didn't realize you're ex-Navy," I said after she left. He raised a questioning eyebrow. "You called the restroom a 'head' earlier."

"So I did. How very perceptive for an Army grunt," He said concealing
a grin behind a sip from his mug. I took the slur for the endearing term
between servicemen it was.

"Well, we're not all as slow on the uptake as you squids," I retorted.

Jacob grunted a laugh. "And that's why you're here asking me about
bears. Last I recall, you and I had a distinct difference of opinion about
the topic."

Mark seemed confused, but I didn't bother enlightening him. "Yeah,
I'm sorry about that. After tonight, I fully believe in werebears."

Jacob took another sip of coffee then warmed his hands by curling his
fingers around the mug. "What happened?"

Mark's late-night dinner came and disappeared as I explained to Jacob
what all happened tonight in as much detail as I could remember. I had
plenty of practice with after-action reports. He sipped his coffee as I
talked, and mine remained forgotten on the table. Despite not touching
my coffee, my foot bounced nervously on the floor and my hands were
shaking by the time I finished.

"So, you know where the first werebear's den is and your Pa is now a
werebear?"

Calling Paul my Pa dredged up the usual unhelpful spite in my stomach, but I shoved it down. "Yeah, that's about right."

"You said he killed two men at the hospital?"

"Yeah."

56

"And he tore up Matt's back too," Mark added before I could stop him. I didn't know if being clawed by a werebear meant anything, and I was too afraid to find out. But by the way Jacob's eyes flared open, it couldn't mean anything good.

"Let me see," he said in a stern voice that brooked no argument. I slipped my arms out of the jacket, pulled up my tattered sweatshirt, and showed my bare back to him. Jacob leaned forward and picked at the dressings to get a better look. "You're damn lucky, boy."

"He's not going to turn into one of them, is he?" Mark asked, and I could feel him shy away from me like I had just finished cleaning the manure pit.

"Nah, you can't be turned by claws. They can give you a nasty infection, though if not cared for properly. But you should be fine, whoever bandaged you up knew what they were doing. If you start noticing any hot spots or any kind of pain other than raw wound pain, you let me know."

"Sure," I agreed.

"So, what do we do about Dad? How do we get him back?" Mark asked.

Jacob's stone-cold eyes shifted to Mark. Carved out of a face of granite, his expression held no sympathy, no quarter, no doubt about the truth he was about to lay down. Jacob waited for Mark to swallow hard then said in a voice of iron, "You don't. Your father died in that cave before you ever found him. Do you understand?"

Mark studied his empty plate unable to answer him.

Jacob's icy gaze swung to me. "Do you understand?"

I didn't need to see the force behind his eyes to convince me; I had decided the truth of it back at the hospital. I dipped my head in an acquiescent nod.

"Now that it's tasted man, this can end in only one way. The sooner you accept that the creature using his body is not him, the easier it'll be."

The last glimmer of hope shattered in Mark's eyes, and they became misty in a way mine never would for Paul's death. I put a hand on his shoulder to comfort him, but he shook it off. He pushed back from the table and shot me a daggered stare. "You knew about the werebear. You could have saved him."

"I didn't—"

Mark stormed out of the diner before I could finish. His truck squealed then roared to life. The backend of his Bronco fishtailed as he turned it around in the middle of Main Street then gunned it down the highway.

I watched the taillight disappear from view then shook my head with a sigh of frustration. "There goes my ride—again."

10

J acob grunted a laugh. "That's okay, he's going the wrong way anyways."

Confused, I mentally double checked the direction my brother ran off in. "No, I'm pretty sure he's heading home?"

"Yeah, but we're heading back to the hospital. We need to deal with the new cub before we can handle the momma bear."

"You keep saying we. I figured you hunter types were more of a solo act."

"Not when I can help it, and if you're the kind of man I think you are, you're going to want to see this through. Am I reading you wrong?"

I shook my head. "No, you're not. I also don't like going into action without a plan."

"Me neither."

"Good." I leaned forward in my chair, ready to get to business. "Now, what do I need to know about werebears? I've seen plenty of movies about werewolves, but I don't think I've ever seen one about a werebear."

"Well, first of all, forget everything you ever heard about werewolves. Most of it's wrong and what is right doesn't apply to werebears anyways."

I took a sip of my still-warm coffee. Somehow, I had missed Sophie freshening it up. "Okay," I said, taking another longer slurp of coffee to chase away the fingers of exhaustion from a long night without sleep.

"First off, bears aren't pack animals like wolves and neither are their counterparts. However, werebears are fiercely defensive of their families. Now I don't think the werebear you found meant to turn your...uh, Paul." Jacob paused over a sip of his coffee and waved to the waitress at the far end of the kitchen. "You know what, this may take a bit of time to explain. I think we better get something to eat; we've got a long day ahead of us."

The waitress stepped up to the table with a smile and topped off both of our coffee mugs without asking.

"Sophie, dear, I think I would like to order after all."

She reached into her apron and pulled out a menu. "Certainly, hon. What can I get you?"

Jacob passed the menu to me without looking at it. "I'll take the breakfast special with my eggs over easy and tell Georgie to make the bacon extra crispy this time."

"Georgie's off today, but I'll let Keith know."

Jacob squinted at the man working the grill and his face turned sour. I could almost hear him growl in disappointment. "Thanks."

I glanced at the menu then gave it back to Sophie. "I'll have the same, thank you. But make my bacon regular."

"Two specials, one with bark, the other regular, coming up," she said with a wink before heading back to the kitchen.

"As I was saying," Jacob continued after she walked out of earshot, "I don't think our momma bear intended to turn Paul. It's possible, but considering we're just coming out of winter, my guess is she woke up early from hibernation and needed to eat." He finished his cup of coffee and placed it on the edge of the table. "The best time to kill a werebear is when they're asleep in their den—if you can find it. The next best time is to hunt them when they're nearly full and starting to get lethargic. The absolute worst time to go hunting werebears," he said with a grimace, "is right after they wake up and they're starving."

Sophie came back carrying four plates stacked up an arm and a fresh pot of coffee in her other hand. She put the first large plate with a trio of eggs and a stack of pancakes dripping with butter in front of Jacob. Then gave me one of the same. I plucked a strip of bacon off my plate, it sagged in a gentle arc of fried perfection right on the edge of done and too crispy. Jacob's, on the other hand, looked almost black.

He picked up one of the over-fried pieces and bit into it. It snapped and crumbled in his hand. "Mm. Perfect. Tell Keith he's my new favorite chef."

She snorted as she topped off both of our coffee mugs. "I'll be sure to let him know. If there's nothing else, I'll leave this with you. No rush, though." She placed the check face down on the table between us and walked away.

Jacob picked up the syrup from the rack of condiments and drowned his pancakes before handing the bottle to me. "Where was I?" he asked, cutting through the stack of pancakes with the side of his fork and then stuffing it in his mouth.

I poured a healthy amount of syrup on my own cakes, but not nearly as much as he did. "The worst time to hunt werebears."

"Right, right. Normally, now that I know where our werebear's den is, I would set a trap and try to take it unawares. She'll need to heal from the gunshot wounds you gave her before she'll go out looking to replace the dinner you interrupted."

"So, we have time?" I asked, stacking pancake and egg together on my fork and running them through the mixing syrup and egg yolk.

"Not much. They heal quick. Maybe a day if we're lucky. But she's not the only werebear we have to worry about."

"Okay. So, we go after Paul first then?"

"You're catching on quick, Grunt. Being newly turned, he's the biggest threat right now. He needs to eat and bulk up to sustain the transformation, and he already has a taste for man. We have a small window where he'll still be confused by the transformation and not fully aware of what he is."

Jacob finished off the last of his bacon. "Plus, once the other werebear figures out Paul's been turned, she'll try to find him and defend him as a cub. We can't let that happen. A momma werebear defending her cub and starving from hibernation, I can't imagine a worse werebear scenario."

The way he said *werebear scenario* made it sound like just another really bad Tuesday and not the end of the world it felt like to me. Then it dawned on me, if werebears and werewolves existed, how many other monsters were there? I studied the man across the table and saw him with a whole new appreciation.

Jacob glanced at the bill, pulled out his wallet and tossed down a pair of twenties then handed me the check with a smirk. "I think this is for you."

I glanced down at the scrawled phone number and message, "Call me —Sophie." I looked up to find the waitress refreshing the coffee mug of one of the regulars. When she noticed me watching her, she shot me a flirtatious wink from across the room. Despite my miserable day and lack of sleep, a boyish grin twisted my lips as I folded the paper and slipped it into my pants pocket.

Jacob shook his head and got up from his chair. "Come on, Grunt. You can call her after this is all over."

I followed him out to his truck. The door opened easily without screeching like a night owl and, unlike Mark's rust-bucket, the floorboard seemed solid enough to keep me from having to Flintstone it. Jacob pressed the push-button start, a feature none of the farm vehicles had, and the engine roared to life.

The first rays of sunlight broke over the horizon to our right as we made our way back up Route 30A. Turning left onto State Street, the image of the werebear attacking the guards flashed through my mind again, much the same way as some of my worst days in Afghanistan revisited me at times, especially when I was punchy from lack of sleep. I shuddered with the violent memory.

"You alright, son?"

Reeling from the shock of the memory, I didn't object to the diminutive nickname. "Yeah, just remembering how the werebear ripped..." A sudden thought slammed into me and my anxiety doubled. "Hey, what about the guards? Paul bit both of them, won't they become werebears too?"

"Not the decapitated guard, for sure. The other shouldn't have lived long enough for the were-venom to take effect. We'll have to make sure, though." Jacob's voice trailed off as he slowed to pass the crowd of vehicles and flashing lights blocking the side drive. A pair of dark environmental conservation officer SUVs and several state police vehicles joined the throng of black and white Gloversville police cars. A large command tent stood to one side, officers milling in and out of it while small pop-up tents sheltered the bodies from view.

"Shit, we'll have to check on that body later." Jacob's drawn-out slur expressed a considerable amount of frustration. "Sheriff, State Police, Gloversville Police, and EOC. If the FBI and DEMON were here, we'd have a full ensemble."

My head snapped back around to Jacob. "There's demons too?"

Jacob choked back a laugh. "I didn't say demons, though yes, they are real. I said DEMON. They're a supernatural government black ops division. And when they're not fucking up, they're usually cleaning up shit like this. They must not know it's a werebear yet."

Jacob drove past the commotion with one last look over his shoulder. "That's way too many cooks in the kitchen, and not one of them knows what they're really up against. Put that many uniformed officers in the woods with a werebear cub and it'll eat them alive. Then we'll have a whole new mess to clean up tomorrow. Damn it!"

Jacob turned right onto a road paralleling the woods behind the hospital. The speakers in the car chimed when he touched the phone button on his steering wheel. "Call Gracie."

The phone rang once before a high-pitched voice said, "Hey, old man, how you holding up?"

"Better than the local authorities," Jacob answered in a voice a little lower and more gruff than usual.

"How bad?"

"They've got two locals dead and are about to walk straight into a momma bear and her cub and there's no black Suburbans in sight. Would you please give the kind folks at DEMON a heads up for me?"

"Afraid to call them yourself?"

"After the last time? Hell yeah, I am."

The voice on the phone broke out in a laugh cutting off with a snort. "I'll take care of it. Anything else you need, Gramps?"

"Not at the moment," he said then clicked the phone off.

"Who's that, Gramps?" I asked.

"My guardian angel. And, son, you don't get to call me Gramps."

I put my hands up defensively. "So long as you don't call me son anymore."

He smiled. "Deal. Now, do you know what's around these woods?"

I pulled out my phone, but it didn't respond to my touch. "No, and my phone's dead."

He fished out a cable from the console compartment between us and tossed it on my lap. "See if this works."

The cable fit my phone, and I leaned forward to plug it into the port below the radio. When I sat back in my seat, Jacob slapped me with a thick folded piece of paper which read Rand McNally across the top. "Here. Use this for now and tell me where these woods go."

I unfolded the map to its full size and turned it around to get my bearings. "Where'd you get this? I didn't even know they made paper maps anymore."

"Just tell me you know how to use it."

"Yeah, they still teach land-nav in the Army." The map felt almost frail in my hands and fresh clear tape layered over old yellowed tape struggled to hold most of the folds together. I held it as gingerly as I could. "How old is this thing?"

"A few years, I don't remember exactly."

I found the copyright at the bottom of the legend. "I think 1999 was more than a few years ago."

"Maybe, but it's working better than your phone, now ain't it?"

He had a point; just not one I intended to acknowledge. "Well, presuming nothing's changed in the last twenty years, it looks like they go about three miles to the northeast to where Route 30A and...Phelps Street meet."

Jacob sighed. "Good. We may still have a chance to find him before the authorities do."

"That's a lot of woods. Any ideas on how to find a werebear in all that?"

Jacob smirked and shot me a wink. "Yes I do." He touched the phone button on the steering wheel again.

"Miss me so soon?" asked Gracie.

"Need a little help finding a needle in a haystack. Think you can give me a hand?"

"Probably. What's the needle and where's the haystack?"

"The needle is a werebear cub about..." Jacob's eyebrow rose questioningly in my direction.

I shrugged my shoulders. "I don't know. I was running away from the damn thing the last time I saw it. Probably about as big as the first one, maybe a hair larger."

"Who's that?" Gracie asked, her voice jumping two octaves with a crack.

"Oh sorry. I have a local running shotgun on this. The first Peterson Apostle."

"Oh," she said weakly.

"Now Gracie, I don't need you gettin' all bashful on me just because some boy is listening in. I need your help. I'm trying to find a thousand-pound werebear in some dense looking woods."

She gulped audibly over the speakerphone, but when she spoke, I could barely hear her. "Where?"

"Between Route 30A and Phelps Street, just north of Gloversville."

"I'll get back to you," she whispered before the phone cut out.

Jacob pulled off the road into what may have once been a hayfield before the weeds and shrubs moved back in. "Good girl, but damn, she's shy," he said, bringing the truck to a stop.

J acob walked to the back of his truck, extended the bumper step, dropped the tailgate, then climbed up into the bed with a groan. He opened the diamond plate toolbox and pulled out a collapsible camp stool. Lowering himself onto the stool, his knees gave a crackling pop as if full of gravel.

"Used to not need one of these, back when my knees were better." He said rubbing the offending joints. He looked about until he saw me leaning against the sidewall. "Well, come on. Climb up here and I'll get you properly fitted out for hunting."

With no geriatric assistant-step on the passenger side, I hoisted my foot onto the raised bumper and nearly impaled myself on my knee. I placed a hand on the sidewall of the truck bed and half-pulled, half-leapt into the back with a groan as much against the pain lancing across my back as with the effort of climbing into the bed.

I peered over Jacob's shoulder at the neatly arrayed weapons cache. He pushed the trays of stakes, knives, machetes, and enough ammunition to start a world war to one side where they nested together revealing an assortment of firearms on the bottom.

"Damn. Are you sure you got enough shit in there?"

He surveyed the stash. "Hm. You'd think so, but I always seem to be missing the one thing that'll make the hunt easy."

"And what's that?"

He gave me an incredulous grin. "Now if I knew what it was, I'd have it, but I can't prepare for everything." He pulled out a blaze orange vest and handed it to me. "Here, we'll look like hunters and hopefully the police won't shoot us."

I took the vest with a raised eyebrow. "Um…I thought I saw conservation officers with the police, and I think we're a little early for spring turkey season. It'll probably be best if we don't look like hunters."

He snatched the vest from my hands and tossed it back into the toolbox. "I suppose that means no rifles either. Shit, we need something small but with penetration." He let out an exhaustive sigh as he considered his options. "Argh, and there it is. The one thing I needed. Told you there was always something. What I wouldn't give for one of those Desert Eagle hand cannons that southern redneck uses. It'd be good for taking down a werebear."

Jacob rummaged through the selection of pistols and handed me a Smith and Wesson 327 TRR8 revolver and a box of .357 Magnum ammo. "Wish I had something with better stopping power, but short of a rifle or my 1911s, this is the best I have. Just make sure you aim for a soft point. Shooting a werebear straight into the chest or the head won't do shit."

I dropped the cylinder to the side, surprised to see eight chambers for bullets. "At least I won't run out too fast."

Jacob laughed. "Boy, I thought you've seen combat. There ain't no gun that can hold enough bullets once the shooting starts."

I raised my eyebrows and nodded in agreement. "That's for damn sure." I popped open the box of ammo and pulled out the first of the long cylinders and furrowed my brows at the silver hollow point pressed into its end. "Silver? Really?"

"At the core of every myth is a kernel of truth." Jacob pushed the tray of ammunition to the side and pulled out a short double-barrel shotgun with a pistol grip. "I only have iron loads for this, so use it as a last resort. It won't kill the werebear, but it will make it think twice about chasing after you." He handed me another box of ammunition. "Use two hands or it'll rip your arm off."

I dropped a pair of three-inch shells into the breach and slung the shotgun's shoulder strap over my right shoulder, then tucked a handful of extra shells into my pocket. I loaded the TRR8 and adjusted it in the belt holster Jacob gave me. It rode considerably higher than my Army-issued leg holster. I tried a few quick draws and needed to re-adjust the holster twice until I could draw the weapon comfortably. With a pouch for two loaded moon clips, I felt like a walking arsenal. I just wished the look on Jacob's face didn't seem so doubtful.

Jacob slipped into his double holster then checked the load on his Springfield 1911s before slipping them and several spare mags into position. He patted down his shirt and pants pockets then checked his Buck knife in its sheath. "That's about everything. Anything else you need?"

"Do you have a spare knife?"

He reached back into the cache, detached a longish blade with a sheath from the side of the box, and tossed it to me. I pulled it from its sheath. The knife's worn wooden handle fit well in my hand with a perfect balance despite its fat heavy blade.

"That's my pa's old Bowie knife. I plated it in silver years ago but it's grown a bit too heavy for my old hands, I'm afraid."

"It's beautiful."

He stared at the silver-clad blade, and the emotions flashing across his face reminded me of what I endured every time someone mentioned Paul. Eventually, his dark eyes turned away. "If you say so." He folded up the camp stool and dropped it into the box. His hand rested a moment longer on the lid, considering, then he shook his head and slammed it closed.

Back on the ground, Jacob reached into one of his pockets and pulled out a small bottle of pills. He shook two into his hand and tossed them back dry.

"Any chance those are caffeine pills or aspirin? I could use a dose." I could feel the pick-me-up from the diner's coffee beginning to wear off and needed one or the other before a sleep deprivation headache kicked in.

"No, these are for my heart. I keep some Excedrin in the glovebox, though. Help yourself."

I found the bottle and took a double dose. I didn't double down often, but I wanted the extra caffeine to keep me alert. I tossed the bottle back into the glovebox then checked the charge on my phone. Fifty percent, good enough for now. I pulled the cord out of the bottom and slid it into my back pocket.

Jacob's phone rang with a classic bell ringer from some 1950s black and white movie. He pulled it from his shirt pocket and slid the answer button to the side. He placed the phone on the hood of his truck and touched the speaker's control. "Speak to me, Angel."

"I've found your bear. Sending it to your phone now." The screen of his phone changed to a map app with a blue dot near Phelps Street and a flashing red dot in the woods just to the northwest. "I've also been monitoring the activities of your smokies and they're preparing to move out on their own hunt soon."

"Shit. Hasn't DEMON reined them in yet?"

"They've got no one in the area and, quite frankly, they didn't sound too pleased that I called."

Jacob's face creased in a sour expression. "I'm sure."

"You're on your own, Gramps, but I'll keep my eye on you." The phone went silent for a moment then Gracie came back on. "You best hurry; they're moving out now."

"Thank you, darling," Jacob said then handed me the phone. "Here, you navigate."

A synthetic 3-D rendered map of the local terrain filled the screen on the phone. I spun until I faced the red flashing dot then nodded up a squat hill toward the woods. "About a mile that way."

The red dot on the map meandered around, as if the werebear didn't know where to go. Helpful, considering how much the uncut field and the underbrush at the edge of the woods slowed us down. Still, we gained ground and closed to a few hundred yards of the beast within the hour.

We slowed as we crested the next hill and Jacob pulled out both of his 1911s, checked the chambered round in each, then slid one back into its holster. I followed his lead and drew my TRR8.

The woods thinned near the bottom of the rise, and the sun reflected off the meandering creek. The wind blew gently into my face, and I could catch the hint of something foul on the air. The way it clung to my tongue made me want to gag.

Jacob sniffed at the air then pulled a red bandana from his shirt pocket and unfolded it, careful not to snap the cloth. "We're in the right place. The longer it goes without eating the worse it smells," he whispered so quietly I barely heard the words drift across the breeze.

He leaned up against a thick beech tree and pulled out a monocular and glassed the edge of the woods to find the werebear. He panned left then stopped, pointing with his pistol. "About 200 yards that way."

With eyes on the werebear, I slid Jacob's phone into the front pocket of my jeans and took a two-handed grip on my pistol. I slipped to the tree on my right and advanced down the slope with my pistol ready. Jacob shifted left, putting twenty yards between us in an unspoken plan to pin the werebear between us and the creek.

Near the bottom of the rise, I ducked behind a fallen tree caught up in the lower limbs of a neighboring maple. Jacob glanced around the trunk of the tree he'd backed up against and signaled in direction of the werebear.

As I peered over the fallen trunk the werebear stomped in the dirt and pawed at its head, growling and nipping at the air like a swarm of hornets buzzed around between its ears. I looked back to Jacob, and he gave me a hand signal to move in.

I crawled under the leaning tree, popped up on the other side and bolted to the next biggest tree between me and the werebear. Even turned sideways, I could barely conceal myself behind the girth of the tree. Jacob's duster rustled out from behind the even smaller oak while the brim of his hat and his pistol stuck out from behind the other side.

The werebear stopped pawing the ground and lifted its head sniffing the air. Jacob rolled around the tree, his pistol at arm's length taking slow encroaching steps to improve his shot when the phone in my rear pocket screamed: *"What does the fox say?"*

I nearly jumped out of my skin and cursed Luke for changing my ring tone again, especially to that fucking song. I contorted myself trying to reach around to my vibrating ass with my pistol in the wrong hand. The werebear's head snapped in my direction and it charged at full speed before I could fish the phone out of my pocket. I panicked and pulled the trigger, firing blindly into the stampeding beast as my ass yipped away like a mad chihuahua. I unloaded my pistol into the werebear's face, and it shook the shots off like I did nothing more than spit at it.

I dropped the cylinder to the side, dumped the spent shells and dropped in another moon clip, but before I could get the pistol pointed back on target, the werebear leapt through the air. Its maw opened wide enough to engulf my head. I moved to the side as fast as I could. Its jaws snapped at the empty air, but its shoulder slammed into my chest and sent me sailing like a beach ball.

I heard the staccato report of Jacob's .45s. All ten rounds discharged in less than two seconds. The werebear whirled on its new attacker. Jacob pulled his other 1911, taking time to aim now that the werebear stalked toward him.

I scrambled back to my feet and searched for the pistol I lost in the impact. As I whirled, the shotgun swung on its strap and slapped new stingers into my back. Stifling a moan, I abandoned my pistol and ripped the shotgun off my shoulder. I leveled it, ready to unload both barrels, but only the thick hide of the werebear's back filled my sights.

Meanwhile, Jacob methodically plugged one shot after the other into the creature, but nothing punched through the beast. It crept forward grunting chuffing growls with each impact.

I let the shotgun drop back to my side and drew the Bowie knife instead. My chest hurt as I sucked in a huge breath of air through broken or at least bruised ribs. Pushing the pain to the back of my mind, I waited for Jacob to pause and reload.

Bang. Bang. Click.

I charged, screaming my head off.

The werebear ignored me and kept its focus completely on Jacob.

I leaped onto its back and plunged my knife into its neck. The flesh resisted and the knife skated across the thick fur shaving a few hairs off its coat until the edge finally bit into skin. It didn't cut deep enough to do any real damage, so I pulled back and drove it in again. This time I found the soft spot just behind the jaw, and the knife sunk in to the guard.

The werebear staggered forward a step or two then dropped to the ground with a thud. In the impact, I lost my grip and fell from its back.

Jacob strode up, releasing the slide on his reloaded pistol. He pulled the trigger twice more, shooting the beast through the eyes.

1 2

J acob pulled his buck knife from its sheath and knelt beside the werebear. "Come on, we don't have much time," he said cutting through the hair and flesh of the creature's neck.

"What are you doing?" I asked panting for breath.

"Removing its head and making sure it doesn't come back."

I popped back to my feet, my heart racing again. "You mean it's not dead?"

"Oh, it is. I'd just rather not be surprised again."

"Oh," I said with a very audible and confused sigh of relief. My knife came loose with a sucking sound as I pulled it free from the werebear's chin and began working on the other side.

Jacob looked up with a crooked smile. "Bravest damn fool thing I've ever seen anyone do and get away with. Charging a werebear like that."

"I didn't see where I had any options. Our pistols only pissed the thing off."

Jacob grunted and began cutting through the thick muscles holding the head in place until he finally hit bone about the same time I did. He drove the slender Buck knife blade between two vertebrae and severed the spinal column. The head rolled free and Jacob kicked it away watching it roll like a fumbled football.

Jacob's phone in my front pocket rang. I fished it out with a bloody hand and passed it to him. He wiped the blood from his own hand on the werebear's thick coat then thumbed the answer button.

"You two need to skedaddle, the posse is almost on you," Gracie said. A touch of urgency tainted the playful tone from earlier.

"Thanks," Jacob said, sliding the phone into his own pocket.

Jacob sheathed his knife, holstered his pistols then ran at a right angle to the way we came in, away from the police and conservation officers. They would certainly have questions we didn't want to answer.

I collected my things and followed after him.

It took nearly an hour to get to Phelps Street moving through the woods as silently as we could, then a half hour more to walk back to the truck.

We hopped into the cab. Jacob turned the engine over and put the truck into gear in one fluid motion. He backed out onto the road then turned North to Route 30A and away from the hunting party.

Once the field faded from the rearview mirror, Jacob asked, "What the hell was that on your phone back there, anyways?"

I pulled the offending phone from my back pocket. Cracks spider-webbed across the dark screen, but it still lit up at my touch. "Sorry, that would be my younger brother Luke. He thinks it's funny to change my ringtone. I plan on beating him with it when I get home."

"I can hold him down if you want."

Almost as if on cue my phone started barking again. Jacob and I burst into laughter, the kind of mirth you share with someone who miraculously survived hell with you.

Through my fractured screen, I could make out the word *Home*. I suppressed my laughter as best I could and swiped the answer button.

"Luke, I'm going to kill you," I said trying to sound serious, but choked on another burst of laughter.

"Matt, where are you?" Mary's panicked voice shocked me back to reality like the snapping of a rubber band.

"Almost to Johnstown. Why?"

Jacob's laughter cut off abruptly at my sudden change in tone. I could see him trying to watch me and the road at the same time.

"Mom says Mark came home, grabbed Dad's 30-30, and took off in his truck muttering something about where a bear is. Says she tried to call you, but it went to voice mail."

"Shit," I muttered. At Jacob's raised eyebrow I added, "Mark's gone after the other bear. By himself."

Jacob shook his head and pressed down on the accelerator, flying through town at twice the speed limit. "Stupid kid."

While I hadn't considered Mark a kid in a long time, I agreed with Jacob about his stupidity.

"What's that?" Mary asked then I heard her yell to someone else. "Luke, wait up! I've got Matt on the phone. He's on his way home now." Then back to me, "You are on your way home, right?"

"Yeah. We'll get there as fast as we can."

"We?"

"I'll explain later. Don't let Luke go after Mark until I get there."

"Hurry," she said followed by an aggravated, "Luke, wait!" as she hung up the phone.

We cruised out of Johnstown and raced down the road to the farm. Jacob drove the F-150 on the curvy back roads like a Camaro. The backend fishtailed with each turn, but he managed to keep the truck under control and cut a thirty-minute trip down to twenty.

Mary ran out of the house as soon as we pulled in. With one arm through her barn coat, she gathered her sweatshirt sleeve in her other fist and stuffed it through the flapping arm of her coat.

"Where's Luke?" I asked, jumping out of the truck to meet her.

"He went after Mark, hoping to catch him before he got too far. Said he'd meet you at the hunting cabin."

I spun around to jump back into the truck when Jacob rushed by. "Where are you going?"

"I have to use the head. I'm too old to not go when I have a chance," he said as he practically danced into the house.

Suddenly I needed to go as well and ran into the house right behind him only to draw up short as the closing door reminded me we only had one bathroom. While I waited, I turned to Mary's incessant tapping foot. Keeping my two hot-head brothers from getting their throats ripped out by the fucking werebear would be hard enough without having to keep track of my fourteen-year-old sister. "I need you to stay here with Mom and call me if they come back."

She gave me a cross look. "Like hell. I'm going with you."

"No, you're not. You don't understand what we're up against here. This isn't a normal bear."

"No, shit. It killed Dad, and it's likely to kill the three of you too." Her voice cracked and jumped two octaves. She already lost one brother and her father; at fourteen that was a lot to handle all at once.

If I let myself admit it, it was a lot to lose at twenty-two as well. My chest tightened with a pain much deeper than claw marks or broken ribs and I wrapped my arms around her, pulling her in tight. She resisted at first then let me hold her. "We're going to be all right. I'll bring both of those idiots back safe and sound, but I can't do that while I'm keeping an eye out for you." I pushed her back enough so I could meet her watering eyes. "I've never said this enough, but I love you, Sis. Can you stay here, for me?"

"Fine," she said in a defeated whisper. She wiped her eyes with a dirty sleeve and sniffed the snot running from her nose. Jacob reached over my shoulder and offered her a handkerchief.

Mary took it and blew her nose loudly. "Thanks."

I rushed into the bathroom to relieve myself. When I came back out, Jacob held a travel mug of coffee in one hand and screwed on the lid with the other. Mary handed me my own mug of coffee. She didn't say anything, she didn't need to, her dry but still red eyes did the talking for her. I saw the fear, the worry, and the challenge in them.

"I'll bring them back. I promise," I said accepting the cup.

"You better," she said before running upstairs. I watched her boots disappear and heard the crash of her bedroom door.

Jacob took a sip of his coffee, then sucked in a breath of cool air through his teeth. "We better get going."

I took one more look up through the ceiling in the direction of my sister's room, then followed him out the door. Jacob tossed me the keys. "You drive. You know the way better than I do."

I climbed in behind the wheel and pushed the start button. The engine roared to life as I pumped the gas generously. "Sorry, I'm used to vehicles that need a little more persuasion."

"No worries, but let's get it in gear."

I put it in drive. "Right."

Once I figured which button enabled the four-wheel drive, the beast of a truck handled the muddy hill up to the cabin without any troubles. I parked the truck between Mark's Bronco and the family station wagon.

Luke leaned against the driver's side door of the wagon, waiting for us, but I didn't see Mark.

I came around the front of the truck. "Damn, Luke, how did you get the wagon up here?"

"Give her enough gas and she gets you where you need to go."

"So, where's Mark?"

"Don't know. He wasn't here when I got here. I followed his trail about halfway up the hill before Mary called and said you were on your way. So, I came back here to wait for you."

Jacob shut the passenger door and joined us. "I see one. Where's the other Peterson Apostle?"

"Who's this?" Luke asked.

"Oh, sorry. Luke, this is Jacob. He's a bit of an expert. Jacob, this is my other brother, Luke."

Jacob laughed. "Are you the one responsible for teaching your brother what a fox says?"

Luke's apprehensive look broke into a mischievous grin. "Yip, yip, yip."

I gave Luke an *I'll-kill-you-later* glare to which both he and Jacob laughed. Too tired, hurt and angry to put up with the bullshit I snarled, "If you two are finished hamming it up, we need to go get Mark before he gets himself into something we can't get him out of."

Luke opened the car door and pulled out the 12-gauge shotgun. "Mark has Dad's 30-30 so I brought the next best thing."

"You're not going with us," I said in a no-nonsense tone I used when talking to a new Army recruit. I reached for the shotgun. "I need you to go home and help Mary with the evening milking."

Luke yanked the shotgun out of my hand. His eyes drew down angrily. "Fuck that, the cows can burst for all I care. And fuck you, I'm not going back. I only came back here because I need you to get Mark, but if you're going to be like that, I'll go get him myself." Luke started to stomp away.

Jacob grabbed Luke's sleeve and my brother turned ready to hit him with the butt of the shotgun. "Son, if you're going with us, you're going to need something better than that. We all are."

I glanced from my brother to the meaningful look Jacob gave me. "Fine," I growled under my breath.

Jacob nodded toward the back of his truck. "I've got a couple rifles in the toolbox."

With the truck keys in hand, I hopped up into the bed of the truck and unlocked the toolbox. Jacob came to the side of the truck and leaned over the side rail. "They're on the bottom."

I slid the series of trays to the side exposing a pair of rifles sitting in the padded bottom of the chest. A bolt action Ruger Hawkeye Alaskan with a scope and a semiautomatic Browning BAR with a shorter barrel. I pulled them both out and handed them over the side of the truck to Jacob.

"Give one to Luke, he's a better shot than I am." While not necessarily true, I already knew what a werebear could do and damn if I would let Luke get any closer to the creature than a 300-yard shot. Jacob quirked an eyebrow but seemed to understand what I meant.

"Here. You take the Hawkeye, I'm too old to carry something so heavy." Jacob said as he handed the longer rifle to Luke.

I reached back into the bottom of the toolbox and pulled out an ammo can tucked into the corner and handed it over the side. Shifting the trays around, I found the box of .357 Magnum ammo and pulled a tray to reload the TRR8 I still carried.

Jacob set himself up on the hood of his truck pushing silver-tipped .308 Winchester shells into the 10-round clip. "Hey, Matthew, grab me a box of .45 too."

Luke put the Hawkeye down beside Jacob, who handed him a box of .375. Luke opened the cardboard box, took out the first shell and stared at the silver bullet glinting in the afternoon sun. "What the hell kind of bullets are these?"

13

I placed the box of .45 ammo next to Jacob, then plucked the round out of Luke's hand to examine the silver hollow point. "It's what you use for werebear. When you can get the penetration, that is," I said handing it back to him.

Jacob gave me a sideways grin. "No worries there, this baby has plenty of penetration," he said, patting the side of his Browning BAR. Then with a nod to the rifle in Luke's bewildered hands, he added, "or the Hawkeye."

"I hope so," I said, not fully convinced. "By the way, do you have any flashlights? I didn't see any in the toolbox."

"Like my knife, I always keep one on me." Jacob pulled a small LED light from his pocket, clicked it on to verify it worked, then clicked it off again. "There should be a spare in the glovebox, though."

Luke stared dumbly at both of us. "Wait, what kind of bear did you say we're hunting?"

Jacob dropped the clips from his 1911s and started loading them. "Werebear," he answered in as flat a conversational tone as I had ever heard. Like he hunted werebears every spring, nothing special. Perhaps he did, but Luke's eyes flared wide just the same.

"What? How?" Luke couldn't quite complete his questions despite his mouth working up and down.

Jacob placed his weapons on the hood of the truck and gave Luke a fatherly smile that neither of us had ever seen from Paul. I felt the pang of loss, but I wasn't sure what for, certainly not for Paul's death; at least I didn't think so.

I rummaged through the glovebox for the other flashlight half listening while Jacob gave Luke the broad strokes on werebears. My fingers fumbled across the bottle of Excedrin and I decided to go well over the maximum daily allowance with yet another dose. I only knew a handful of ways to get through a firefight on no sleep and an aching body, and I didn't have anything else at hand.

Beneath a mountain of napkins from a half dozen different fast food joints, I finally found the flashlight. I checked to make sure it worked. It emitted a blindingly bright light that dimmed through successive clicks of the button until it eventually turned off and I slipped it into my pocket. Shutting the passenger door with a bang, I rejoined them. "You two ready?"

Luke, with his face flushed whiter than usual, looked anything but ready. *Good, then he believes us,* I thought and then prayed it would keep him from doing anything stupid.

"Does...Mark know?" Luke asked after swallowing dry air to get his mouth working.

"We told him. I'm not sure if he believed us though. You can still go back and take care of the milking if you want," I suggested, half-hoping he would go, but he didn't. Instead, he picked up his rifle and chambered the first round dramatically. I took the remaining box of .375 ammo and slid it into his sweatshirt pocket. "Then let's go. And put the damn safety on."

I led the way in a low force-march stride I had learned in the Army. It chewed up the distance, like a woodchipper eating through tree limbs. A little more than a hundred feet from the cave mouth, I paused to wait for Luke and Jacob to catch up. While I waited, I scanned the available terrain around Thor's cave with a military eye searching for an optimum place to have Luke set up overwatch.

A few yards to my right stood the copse of trees where Luke and Mark had sheltered from the rain a few days ago. *Or, shit, was that only yesterday?* Either way, the trees offered little cover and an even poorer firing position with limited up-hill lines of fire.

Less than a dozen yards from the cave, a large boulder sat half submerged in the forest floor, as if cleaved from the rock face above, then stomped into the mud by some ancient giant. However, with a bolt action, I doubted Luke could get a second shot off before the werebear closed the short distance.

Lastly, I considered a thick fallen pine tree about a hundred yards to the left and on even ground with the entrance. From there, he could keep an eye on the cave and have enough time to get off a handful of shots before the werebear could close the distance. With any luck, he might actually kill it. With better luck, Jacob and I will have already done the job for him.

Luke crashed to the ground at my feet breathing hard. Jacob found a tree to lean against while he rubbed his knees and back.

"You didn't need to run up here like that," Jacob complained in a hoarse whisper.

In my haste, I had neither considered Jacob's age nor Luke's unfamiliarity with military pace, but I didn't apologize. The hike up the mountain took a lot out of my already tired body too, but without knowing how much trouble Mark managed to dig himself into, we didn't have time to waste. So, like I did on every other force march, I shoved the part of me wanting to bitch about it to the back of my mind and told it to shut the hell up.

"Luke, I need you to set up behind that tree over there," I whispered loud enough to be heard over his panting. "Set yourself up in a semi-prone position and use the tree for support. If that bear comes out before the rest of us, kill it and then make sure it's dead. Don't check it for a pulse, just put another two in its head. You hear me?"

He gave me an *I'm-not-stupid* eyeroll. "Yeah, I hear you," he said before getting to his feet and moving to the tree.

Why Luke followed my orders without the usual sibling quibbling or why Jacob continued to let me lead this party, I didn't know nor did I care. I had a mission and at the moment I needed to be Sergeant Peterson and keep my mind focused on saving Mark. I readied my pistol, tested my flashlight, and then checked my nerves.

Luke found a spot to sit against one of the thick branches which allowed him to sit up and keep watch without straining his back or knees. He propped his rifle in the crook of a broken branch on the fallen trunk then scoped the cave entrance, keeping his fingers well away from both the trigger and the safety. Satisfied, he whistled and gave us a move forward hand signal.

Jacob clapped a hand on my back. "I wouldn't worry about him. We're the ones going into a werebear's den."

Still, I gave my brother one last worried glance. He sat crouched over the rifle like a disciplined hunter waiting for his prey, cooler than most soldiers I'd been with in combat. I never gave Luke enough credit. If I made it back out of the werebear's den, I'd have to let him know.

Jacob and I took up positions at opposite sides of the cave mouth. We looked at each other like a pair of SWAT officers ready to break into a meth lab. He held his Browning BAR in two hands and nodded for me to lead. Adjusting the hold on my flashlight and pistol to a cross-grip, I held them in a low ready-fire position as I rolled around the edge of the rock and I slipped into the cold stone maw of the cave.

Like reentering a haunted house that scared the shit out of me the first time, a déjà vu of complex emotions, similar but different at the same time, roiled in a pressure cooker threatening to explode with each step. Like a shot of nitro straight to my imagination, the dark recesses of the cave came alive with my worst fears. Every shadow, every bend, hid were-bears ready to pounce or Mark laying in a bloody heap about to die, or even worse, just bitten like I found Paul. I stopped dead at the sudden troublesome thought.

If he's bitten, can I really do what I would need to?

Jacob walked into my back, and we staggered a step before we both regained our balance. "What's up?"

I took a settling breath to banish the haunting image of Mark from my mind; I would cross that bridge when I came to it. "Nothing. Sorry."

Forcing my feet to move forward again, I chastised myself, *Suck it up, Buttercup.* The contempt boiling in my chest at Paul's favorite saying filling my mind broke me out of my rut, and I finally compartmentalized my emotions.

We continued deeper into the cavern, the gravel crunching beneath our feet with every step. Just shy of the last curve, I stopped and waited for Jacob to draw in close. "The first room is around the next corner. There's a decent shooting position, behind a rock jutting into the path a bit on the right. Set up there to cover the room. I'm going to go left and take a position behind a stalagmite. There's a bunch of them, so be careful of blind spots."

Jacob nodded in understanding.

"The last time I was here the werebear was deeper in the cave but who knows, so be careful." The age perfected *I'm-not-stupid* eyeroll Jacob gave me put Luke's to shame, except I wasn't in the mood to admire it. Instead, I returned it with a glower. "Just making sure we're on the same page."

His cheek twitched, softening the edges of his frown. "Sorry." He pulled out his flashlight, clicked it on and took a modified grip on the rifle to keep the light and his rifle pointed at the same place. "On your count."

I held up three fingers, then two, then one, then we both hustled forward. I rushed to the first column of rock stretching up from the ground and used it to shield my back while we cleared the room. I rolled around to the left and scanned the room. Empty except for the light from Jacob's flashlight. I twisted to the right, still nothing. No sign of the were-bear or Mark.

I flashed my light just in front of Jacob to get his attention then deeper into the room to not blind him. His light shifted, keeping me in the outer fringes of its glow. I hovered my hand above my head in a cover-me gesture, then pointed at myself before signaling moving forward. He gave me the okay sign.

I spun around the stalagmite away from Jacob and ran to the furthest rock pillar in the room, almost directly opposite of the back entrance. I quickly scanned left then right again, making sure not to shine my light down the other cave as I cleared the room.

Jacob's light waited a moment longer before it found me. I gave him the *come-here* hand sign, and he moved up to a stalagmite a few feet away, checking behind and around each of the others as he moved.

"There's another cave and another room that way," I mouthed more than whispered while I pointed in the general direction of the back entrance.

Jacob looked to where I indicated then nodded. When his eyes returned to mine, I mimed and mouthed twenty-five yards then gave him the *cover-me* signal again.

He leaned against the stalagmite with his rifle ready and nodded. I took a steadying breath before moving around the rock pillar toward the slim opening. Raising my flashlight, I shone it down the cave somewhere between bear and human eye-level while Jacob's light silhouetted me from behind in an effort to blind and confuse the beast, but the light faded into the depths of the empty cave.

With a slow breath, I double-checked the door on my mental vault. Miraculously it still held my emotions at bay. I took one more determined breath then moved forward. About fifteen yards into the cave, the floor started to slope deeper into the mountain. The walls glistened damply as if the rocks themselves were sweating as much as me. The water oozed out of the rock face and collected into runnels along the side of the walking surface to flow deeper into the heart of the mountain.

As the cave sank even lower, the floor narrowed, sharing the small space with a crevasse which dropped dramatically deeper into the ground. The trickle of water disappeared into its depths, but I couldn't hear where it hit below. As kids, we lost more than one of Jonny's GI Joe figures into the chasm along with the baler twine rope used to lower such sacrifices in an attempt to find its bottom.

A few yards from the next room, the crevasse widened enough for a man to fall in and the path shrunk to only a foot or so wide. I edged past it sideways as my heart tried beating its way out of my chest in anticipation of the rushing impact of the werebear to carry me into the abyss.

At the mouth to the next room, I laid flat against the cave wall, making myself as small as possible. I checked back the way I came, planning my escape route, then shined the light into the room. Much larger than the first, the room spanned roughly twenty feet across and more than twice that in length. A large multi-spired stalagmite rose from the center of the room. Smaller ones crowded along the walls.

At one side of the room, a tattered old upholstered chair sat next to a makeshift pallet of blankets strewn on the floor where it rose enough to remain dry. Women's clothes, heaped in barely organized piles of tops and bottoms, completed the makeshift bedroom.

I took my time clearing the remainder of the room but again found neither the werebear nor Mark. By the time I made it back to the main entrance, Jacob finished easing past the fissure, shooting a wary eye into its depths.

"They're not here, but this is definitely her den," I said to his raised eyebrows. I shined my flashlight on the pallet and mounds of clothes. "She has a place to sleep over there and piles of clothes there."

Jacob scanned the room then shook his head. "I'm not so sure, I don't see a bathroom anywhere."

"She probably uses that hole back at the entrance," I said pointing back the way we came. "She could live here for decades and never fill it up."

He gulped visibly. "True. I didn't see a bottom. Any idea how deep it is?"

"More than a hundred feet," I said then added to his questioning look, "It was all the rope we had."

Jacob tore his eyes away from the black pit with a shiver. "Could she be hiding, deeper in, then?"

"You'd know better than me. There's a couple of much smaller branches in the back, but squeezing by that hole scared us too much to explore them as kids. You don't think she took Mark down one of those do you?"

Jacob surveyed the cavern once more, the corners of his mouth turning down in consternation. "No. I doubt it. I'm more concerned she may have decided to move her den after your last visit. Either way, we need to regroup. Come on. Let's go get Luke."

14

With the focused, nervous energy of our assault mostly spent, my mind drifted distractingly to my brother Mark as Jacob and I worked our way back up through the cave. I couldn't decide if I felt more worried or relieved that we hadn't found him.

I wound my way through the maze of stalagmites in the first room mentally retracing our steps from Mark's truck at the cabin to Thor's cave and realized I had never looked for his tracks. After Luke said he had followed them halfway up the mountain, I just assumed. *And you know what assuming makes you?* I asked myself rhetorically. Though, I couldn't help but voice the answer bitterly, "A dumbass."

"What did you just call me?" Jacob asked with a critically raised eyebrow.

"No, not you. Me. I…" The echoing crack of gunfire cut my explanation short.

The shot echoed and reverberated in the acoustics of the stone chamber like the inside of a drum. Thoughts of Mark and my foolishness evaporated in fresh terror for Luke. I charged up the cave, the gravel floor crunching and shifting beneath my feet. Jacob hollered after me to wait for him, but I ran on, leaving him behind.

I made the last turn, the illuminated cave mouth less than a dozen yards in front of me when another shot rang down the tunnel. *Crack!* I poured everything I could into pumping my legs as fast as they would go.

Bursting into the open air, I skidded to a stop just outside of the cave entrance, frantically searching for the werebear.

Crack!

Luke cast furtive glances over the tree trunk he hid behind as he pressed another round into the magazine then rammed the bolt forward. He leaned back into his firing position, propped the arm of the gun on top of his closed fist for elevation and scoped the hill above my head. I turned, following his aim up the slope. The afternoon sun cut through the sparse trees and blinded me for only a moment before something large blotted out the light.

A heavy body slammed into me carrying me to the ground. I felt like the icing between a pair of sumo wrestlers trying to make a cookie sandwich. The impact drove the breath from my lungs and sent my pistol and flashlight sailing from my hands. I struggled to throw the body off, punching with a free hand.

"Umph." I heard in my ear, then, "Matt, stop it's me." Mark rolled off and clawed his way across the dirt to retrieve the 30-30. He spun around on one knee and raised the rifle to his shoulder squinting into the sunlight. "Where the hell is it? It was right behind me."

Crack! Luke's rifle answered. Then in the span of a few heartbeats, it answered again. *Crack!* Then silence.

I struggled to catch my breath as I groped along the ground for my pistol.

Jacob ran out of the cave, panting. He brought his rifle up and scanned the area. "Where is it?"

"It went back over the hill," Luke yelled from behind his tree. He scoped the hillside once more then rose and ran over to join the group.

Mark sagged back onto his heels. "I thought it had me for sure."

Jacob lowered his rifle, then grabbed Mark roughly by the shoulder and tossed him around inspecting him for injuries. "Did it bite you, boy?"

Mark threw an arm to break Jacob's grasp of his jacket. "No. It didn't," he spat. "I put six shots into it from a hundred yards and it barely flinched." His eyes found mine and a pleading, incredulous expression ghosted over his face. "I know I hit it in the heart, but it just growled and then charged at me. And I...I just ran for my life."

My lungs began working again and my worry turned to a blaze of anger. I holstered my pistol and snatched my flashlight from the ground so fiercely I almost lost my grip on it. "I guess, lucky for you, I broke your fall. You could have broken your leg and the damn thing would have eaten you for sure. What the hell do you think you were doing, going after it all by yourself?"

Jacob collected the 30-30 from Mark's numb hands. He levered the handle, but nothing came out. "I told you it was a werebear. What made you think a conventional 30-30 would do anything to it?"

Mark's eyes softened in confusion. "Why wouldn't it? What the hell are you guys using?"

Luke pulled a shell from his pocket and tossed it to him. "Silver."

"Shit," Mark said with a mixture of awe and embarrassment.

"Yeah, shit," Jacob said as he threw the rifle back to Mark, who, on his knees, barely managed to get his hands up in time to catch it. Jacob paced back to the cave entrance looking up over the hill. "That damn werebear ain't coming back here now."

"So, what do we do?" I asked.

"We go home," Luke volunteered, but I ignored him and kept my eyes on Jacob.

Jacob turned back with a sigh. "We do it the old-fashioned way. We go hunting." He stalked over to Mark and reached an arm out to help him up. "Where did you say you saw it?"

Mark took the offered hand and let Jacob pull him to his feet. "At the pond, next to the ruins."

Jacob raised an eyebrow. "Where's that?"

"About a half-mile that way." I pointed over the hill.

"Anything there that she can turn into her new den?" he asked hopefully.

"The cabin's not much more than a stone chimney anymore, but there's an old root cellar. It's pretty deep, like they widened another cave to make it."

Jacob scanned the cliff and then started to work his way to the left. I tapped him on the shoulder and nodded to the right. "The climb is easier on this side." I walked toward the saddle in the hill, leading the way.

"Where are you two going?" Mark asked, with more shake to his voice than I ever heard before.

Luke didn't sound any steadier. "Yeah, we found Mark. Now, let's go back home."

They both knew the truth about werebears now, and it scared the shit out of them. I admit it scared me too. I'd already wrestled one of these beasts, twice, and barely got away alive. Then again, I'd seen combat and knew how to suppress my fear.

I pushed the part of me screaming to run deep down inside until it no longer rattled my brain, then turned to my brothers. "We can't let it live. It'll kill someone else, or worse, change them like it did Paul."

I weighed my visibly shaken brothers in the same way every NCO weighs a battle-shaken new recruit. Do you put them in the front to burn away their fear and show them they have the courage they need, or do you put them in the rear, out of the way of those that do? Unlike the Army, I didn't have to use them and they didn't have to come, so I gave them the choice. "Look, I've got to go back to my unit in a few days and I can't take the chance it fucking gets either of you, or Mom, or Mary. I'd never be able to live with myself. Jacob and I are going to put an end to that thing, but if you want to go back to the farm and help Mary with the evening milking, I understand, but this will be a lot easier with you than without you."

They glanced at each other, unwilling to meet my gaze, but I could see the uncertainty on their faces.

"But... it's a..." Luke began.

In only a few strides, I crossed the ground between us and grabbed the rifle Luke held on to like a lifeline. "Go home and take care of the chores, but I'm taking this."

Luke tightened his grip until his knuckles grew white, his eyes meeting my challenging stare. Then, I watched him push his own fear aside. "Fine, I'm coming."

I let the rifle go and turned to Mark, "What about you?"

His wide eyes flicked from mine to Luke as if we were crazy. He was probably right. "Depends. Do you have anything better than this?" he asked holding up his 30-30. "I'm not going to just be bait."

Jacob held out the Browning BAR to him. "Here."

Mark swallowed hard, slung Paul's old rifle over his shoulder, and took the BAR. "Okay, I'm in."

"Great," I said, letting the word drip with sarcasm as I strode up the hill.

We found a break in the trees at the top of the hill which gave us a clear view of the ruins near the bottom of a small ravine. Jacob took out his monocular and glassed the area. Luke also scanned the area through the scope on his rifle.

"There it is," Luke said. I followed his rifle but couldn't see anything at this distance besides boulders and trees. "She's about fifty yards from the ruins, up by that rock outcropping. Wait! Where did she go?"

"Let me see?" I asked with a hand on the rifle. He let me take it. I found the outcropping but couldn't see the werebear.

Jacob scanned it as well. "Must be another cave entrance or that root cellar."

"You don't suppose it's connected to the other cave, do you?" Mark asked.

I tried to imagine the layout of the caves beneath us. They stretched in the general direction of the ruins, but with the twists and turns of the cavern, I couldn't envision the second room quite reaching the ruins. "It might if one of those little branches was long enough."

"So, it could double back through the cave if it wanted to, while we try to chase it from this end." Jacob's voice rumbled like a building thunderhead.

I handed the rifle back to Luke. "Only one way to find out. Luke and I will double back to the other entrance, while you and Mark push it through."

Jacob considered it for a moment. "I don't like splitting up," he said, eying Mark and Luke much the same way I sized them up earlier. Not as if he thought he needed their extra firepower but as if he didn't like letting a bunch of newbies out of his sight in a dangerous situation. When his eyes met mine, they took on more of a look between equals: sergeant to sergeant.

"Me neither, but we need to finish this. I'll text Mark when we're in position." I tugged on Luke's sleeve and double-timed it back over the hill.

At the cave entrance, Luke moved back to his overwatch position while I crouched behind the boulder. It gave me a decent close shot with my pistol should the werebear suddenly emerge from the cave and would protect me from a stray bullet should Luke miss.

I drew my pistol and waited for Luke to settle into position before I sent the text to Mark. *Ready.*

A moment later Mark replied. *Moving in on the outcropping now.*

After a couple minutes, *It's a cave, but it's too small for us with the rifle. Jacob says you need to push.*

Okay.

I took a deep breath and waved at Luke then signaled I was going in. He lifted his hand but didn't wave back. The evening sun glinted off the phone in his hand just before mine buzzed with a new message from him.

What?

The other cave is too small. I need to push.

89

On my way.

No. Stay put, in case it comes out past me. I hoped he didn't read into how the werebear could get past me.

He crouched back down into position. *K*

I pulled out my flashlight and clicked it on. I heaved my shoulders to release the building tension then took a deep breath before entering the cave once more.

15

I walked into the werebear's den alone knowing that this time I would not come back out unscathed.

The algae-covered entrance gave way to loose gravel, but I knew the footing well enough to keep my flashlight aimed down the rock tunnel with my pistol braced across the back of my left wrist. Without trying to conceal my approach, I worked my way down to the first room in half the time as before. I needed to keep moving quickly and not let my mind dwell on how stupidly crazy this was. I rushed up behind the rock Jacob used for a shooting position and scanned the empty room. Then, I worked across the room pillar-to-pillar, hiding behind the stalagmites, still nothing.

At the last stalagmite, I pressed my back into the stone, closed my eyes, and inhaled deeply. This close to the second room, the danger felt much more real and my suppressed fear tried to claw its way up my throat. I exhaled slowly and steadily, beating it back down into the depths of my being. My eyes popped open, and I spun around the rock pillar. I moved forward, placing one foot in front of the other. My pistol floated on the back of the flashlight with my finger on the side of the trigger guard ready at any moment to squeeze off a shot.

The crevasse opened up in front of me, and I sidestepped along the narrow shelf of rock, careful to not cross my feet and risk getting caught off balance. I didn't want to find out how deep it really was. At the mouth of the room I paused, back against the wall, and shined my light to the left then right, clearing my immediate flanks. I slowly passed the light from the makeshift bed to the piles of clothes. My light landed on the brilliantly white full moon of a woman's stark-naked backside. Bathed in sudden illumination, she rose seductively and calmly turned to face me. Her eyes flared in the light like a cat's at night.

She sniffed at the stale air. "So, you're the one who'd been here before. Do you like what you see?" She took a swaying step toward me. The silver ornaments in her hair swung teasingly over breasts which played peek-a-boo through her thick mane. "Do you want me?" she asked, taking another provocative step closer.

I stood my ground, keeping her centered in my light and trying to keep the point of my pistol aimed at her chest. If not for the barely controlled fear already beating at my heart like a bass drum in a rock concert, the lust welling up between my legs would have started it racing.

"Stop right there," my voice squeaked.

She took another step.

"I said, stay right there. I know what you are, and I'll shoot." My voice didn't crack this time, but it still lacked authority.

Another step and she closed to half the original distance. "It's been a long cold winter and I could use a mate to keep me warm. I want you in my bed. Will you help keep me warm?" She swept her hair over her shoulders giving me a full view of her womanly lures.

Had she done the same with Paul? No, the tracks showed that the werebear attacked and then drug him out of the hunting cabin. But Jonny...at sixteen and full of hormones...wouldn't have stood a chance.

The thought of her tempting Jonny broke the spell and my finger slipped onto the trigger. The muzzle flash momentarily lit the whole room and the ground near her feet erupted from my stray shot. Aiming at a werebear was one thing, but aiming at a naked, unarmed woman was quite another.

She gave me a frown. "Now that wasn't very nice. If you won't be my lover, then you will be my dinner." She lunged forward, changing as she fell.

I pulled the trigger again and again, aiming true this time. The first caught her mid-transition in the chest, too low for her heart. The second sunk into her shoulder. The third round bit harmlessly into the flesh of a werebear only slightly smaller than Paul. The remaining four shots did little to her, then the hammer clicked on an already spent shell. I dropped the pistol and pulled the Bowie knife.

She roared and the hard stone walls amplified the sound, making my bones hurt. The next time her front foot hit the floor it failed to support her, and she staggered a step. The first two silver bullets, now embedded within her flesh, ate at her arm, rendering it nearly useless.

I bellowed my own war cry and charged forward with the knife. She turned to run, hobbling on three legs, unable to move faster than me. I pumped my legs trying to catch her before she could escape down one of the back caves.

When she reached the piles of clothes, she collapsed and changed back into a woman. Blood oozed from the multiple gunshot wounds. I saw her change in front of me this time and would not let her cast her spell on me again.

She sprawled on the clothes, her good hand flailing in the garments, but she didn't move forward. I reversed my grip on the knife as I ran. Fighting for your life is never a time for modesty or for honor. You fight to win. I didn't hesitate to jump on her, intent on plunging the knife into her back.

She rolled over as I descended through the air. The light from my flashlight glinted off a pistol in her good hand. Falling through the air, I could do nothing to evade her shot. She pulled the trigger. The bullet bit into my left shoulder and I nearly lost my grip on the flashlight.

My momentum carried me down upon her, but the gunshot wound twisted me and I missed my mark, cutting into her shoulder with the knife instead. She screamed at the impact and the pistol discharged beside my ear, deafening me, but the bullet went wide.

I slashed at her gun hand with the knife, but she twisted in an attempt to bite my wounded left arm. In a panic, I yanked my hand away from her teeth and fell unsupported onto her. She turned back the other way, teeth snapping at my neck. I scrambled to leverage myself up, pushing off her bosom. Thanks to the military's sexual harassment training and years in the Baptist church, I jolted back from the unintentional full hand grope of her breasts and almost apologized. In the impulsive effort to empty my hands of the forbidden fruit, I sent my flashlight skittering across the floor.

Recovering my wits, I gave the flashlight little mind and readied my knife to finish the task when the slender waist I straddled suddenly grew into a fury belly whose girth threatened to split me in two at the groin.

The werebear's thick paw relieved me of that worry as it slammed into the side of my wounded shoulder and sent me sailing through the air. I rolled across the stone floor and popped back up to my feet. My left arm hung limply at my side. I could feel trails of blood trickle from the burning bullet wound. Gritting my teeth against the pain, I tossed the knife in my right hand to change my grip then set my feet and braced for the impact of the werebear.

She didn't charge, though. She paced sideways in the dim light of the poorly aimed flashlight, circling me. She still favored her shoulder, unwilling to put much weight on it. The werebear huffed and growled challengingly.

I yelled back at her, pacing in the opposite direction. We circled each other, neither of us committing to the attack. Time, however, was not on my side. With each step, more blood seeped down my arm, casting weights onto the anchor of my fatigue. I couldn't wait for the perfect opening.

I lunged.

The werebear hopped back, then swiped at me with a massive paw. I dodged and claws swept through the air nearly catching my outstretched arm.

We now paced in the other direction. She moved against my injured arm, me against her good arm. I waited for her weight to land on her bad leg and then slashed. Caught on her injured leg, she couldn't retreat fast enough and the Bowie cut deep into her flesh.

The bear reared back in anger. Fully erect on her hindquarters, she stood more than a head taller than me.

I rushed in, sinking the knife into her soft underbelly.

She wrapped her arms around me, then twisted, throwing me across the room.

My knife wrenched in my hand and I lost my grip in the toss. It remained impaled in the werebear as I skated across the floor until my body wrapped backward around the large stalagmite growing from the center of the room. Pain flared in my back, matched by the pain in my bruised chest, but the pain in my arm eclipsed them both. I howled in agony.

Dazed, I struggled to get back to my feet empty-handed. My flashlight lay on the floor several feet away. The beam of light pointed back toward the main entrance where I could see the dark shadow of my pistol; much too far away. This was it then, but damn if I would let the bear just eat me. I turned to face my opponent.

The werebear, still on two feet, roared, then pawed at the knife trying to remove it with a clawed hand. After several swipes, the knife came free and danced across the floor away from me. The werebear dropped back down to all fours. The lust of hunger filled her eyes and her snout curled in what I can only describe as a smile of satisfaction. She knew she had me.

"Come on!" I yelled. Anger and fury keeping me upright. "What are you waiting for?"

The werebear roared in response. She took a stalking step forward. I set my feet and clenched my fists, then from the corner of my eye I saw a muzzle flash only moments before the chamber boomed with the rifle shot.

Crack!

The impact of the rifle bullet at such close range shifted the werebear's weight, making her sidestep to keep her balance.

Crack!

A second shot rang out and I could almost see the surprise in the werebear's brown eyes as she fell to the floor.

"Is it dead?" asked Luke. I could hardly hear him over the ringing in my ears.

"Put another in her head to be sure," I yelled back, covering my ears.

Crack!

The head snapped violently from the impact and a chunk of skull broke away from the far side.

"Man, am I glad to see you," I said venturing to retrieve my flashlight. I then found my knife and set to work at removing the werebear's head as Jacob had done to the other werebear.

Luke stepped up beside me with the barrel of his rifle pointed at the werebear's blistered melon of a head as if it would jump up and bite him. "I couldn't just wait for you. Not against that." He poked the werebear's head with the tip of the barrel. She didn't move.

"She's dead."

"Then what are you doing?"

"Making sure she stays that way."

Luke turned his head away. "Oh."

After I finished, I wiped my bloody hands and knife on the werebear's black fur before sheathing the blade. Stumbling in the numb aftershock of the fight, I collected my pistol and holstered it as I joined Luke at the wall. I found a patch of smooth stone to lean against and breathed while the cold granite leached away the remaining heat of my emotions.

Luke came up beside me. "Are you going to be okay?"

"Yeah. I just need something to eat and to sleep for two days straight."

He clapped a hand on my shoulder, and I flinched with pain. He pulled his hand back as if he'd been burned. "Are you bit?" his voice cracked in panic.

"No," I groaned. "She shot me."

"Who? The bear?"

"She wasn't a bear at the time, but yeah, the bear."

"Damn, bro. Only you would get shot by a werebear." I could hear the laughter in his voice.

I shook my head, too worn out to find it as funny as he did. "Just get me out of here."

Once we passed the crevasse, Luke put my good arm over his shoulder and he half-supported me the rest of the way out of the cave. Outside, he propped me up against the cliff face. The cool spring breeze smelled of gathering rain. I breathed it in deeply as Luke texted Mark. He slipped the phone into his pocket then sat down beside me to wait.

A few minutes later Mark and Jacob stood over us.

"Are you sure it's dead?" asked Mark.

I showed him my blood-stained hands in answer.

"Are you hurt?" asked Jacob. Though I knew he meant, "Did it bite you?"

I gave a slight shake to my head, which felt much harder to move than it should have. "Nah. Nothing worse than before."

"When have you ever been shot before?" asked Luke.

I raised an eyebrow, but in no mood to share my war stories, I didn't answer the question. Not today. Maybe not ever.

Jacob examined my shoulder. "It's a through and through. I can stitch it up for you if you want?"

I gave him a wan grin, "I would, but my commander is likely to ask questions and I better have a medical report to back up my answers. 'Cause they sure as shit won't believe what really happened."

"Suit yourself. Why don't you boys get him to that hospital he wants while I go...check on things."

I opened my mouth to tell him I already ensured the werebear's death remained permanent, but he disappeared into the cave before I could muster the energy to speak.

Mark and Luke helped me to my feet. I tried to take a few steps on my own but nearly fell. Thanks to exhaustion and blood loss my head swam from the effort and my brothers carried me down the mountain.

16

After a few days of sleep and rolls of bandages that made me feel more mummy than human, the local sheriff paid me a visit with some government stiff in a suit on his heels. My short one-word answers did little to satisfy the officer, but after sharing a few uncomfortable glances over his shoulder with the suit he eventually stopped asking the same reworded question.

"Have a...good day, Mr. Peterson," the sheriff said with enough tension in his voice to play the fiddle. He then turned on his heel, shot the suit a less than pleased glare, and strode from the room. From the look he gave the sliding glass door, it should have slammed closed and shattered to a million little pieces in dramatic fashion.

The suit remained where she stood through the entire interview, her eyes never leaving my face.

I coughed to clear my throat, and she raised a questioning eyebrow. "Ma'am, I didn't get your name."

"I didn't give it," she answered in a clipped manner I've come to expect from government officials.

"Of course. And, what's the official story I'm to tell my CO?"

"You mean you don't remember? Your brother accidentally shot you in the arm while trying to clear a misfire. As far as your bruises, well, I hear farming is a hazardous occupation."

"Ah, now I remember. Thank you," I said with as much bland sarcasm as she gave me. I swear I saw the corners of her mouth twitched upward, but they retreated so quickly I may have imagined it.

"No, thank you for your service, Sergeant." She stepped softly to the door, the combat boots peeking out the bottom of her trousers didn't make a sound. She paused just shy of the opener's sensor range. "If you should see your squid friend, tell him we appreciate his assistance, but next time leave the matter to us." The door opened and she left without waiting for my response.

Not wanting to push my government-sanctioned luck with the sheriff, I waited for Luke to fill me in on the happenings since I had become Sleeping Beauty.

The police had recovered Paul's body nearly four hours after Jacob and I had left the scene. Sufficiently long enough for the discovered corpse to revert back to its natural human form. The police gave my mother their condolences but offered her no explanation as to why the body snatchers removed his head nor why they shot a corpse full of holes. Mark walked in during this part of Luke's story and immediately ran to the toilet with a hand over his mouth.

"He had to identify the remains. Mom couldn't do it," Luke explained, turning a bit green-faced as well.

As if summoning her, Mary escorted my mother into the room. When my mother saw me sitting upright, she rushed over to the bed, wiping away her tears both before and after we exchanged hugs. Mary, on the other hand, punched me playfully in my good arm and I made a show that earned a weak grin before she helped Mom to the soft armchair near the window.

When Mark returned, our mother sat upright and sucked back her tears and sobs. Her sharp red eyes took each of us in one at a time. "I only know half of what you all have been up to over the last few days." I opened my mouth, but she held up a hand and I closed it. "Don't try to explain. I can't bear the lies. It's best I don't know what really happened to your father, or why you are lying in a hospital bed with a gunshot wound."

Her eyes dared us to repeat the lies we told the police. None of us did. After a moment, she wiped a handkerchief she pulled from her purse across her nose and continued. "We don't have the money for another proper funeral. I know you all never had the best relationship with your father, but he deserves better than he got. Still, I am going to have him cremated." She paused, waiting for one of us to object. None of us did.

I mustered the energy to swing my legs over the side of my bed and stand. I reached for the IV and my mother glared at me. "Don't you dare. Sit your ASS back down in that bed. I'll come to you."

In all my life, I never heard my mother swear and her words sent me back to bed faster than any drill sergeant I ever had. She got up from her chair, shuffled over to me and wrapped me in a hug tight enough to make my bruises hurt, but I didn't mind. Mary, Luke, and Mark all joined in, circling me in the ring of love I'd forgotten my family was capable of.

The embrace ended all too soon as Mark let go first, "Well, we have to get back to the farm, there's chores to do."

Luke and Mary also let go and then finally Mom. As her arms fell away, I couldn't stop the tears from welling up in my eyes. My mother wiped them away for me.

Before she left the room, she looked back to me. "You need to call your unit, son."

As ordered, I called my company commander and received a begrudging extension to my leave to attend Paul's funeral. I wouldn't have bothered except for my mother's sake.

Two days later, we sat together in chairs at the foot of Jonny's grave staring at a plain black urn sitting in the grass beside his temporary marker. The attendance at the graveside-only affair exceeded my expectations. Though to be fair, the other attendees consisted mostly of church parishioners who never missed one of Reverend Thomas' sermons, regardless of the occasion.

After an interminable hour, the preacher finally said, "Amen," and I got up to follow my family past the urn, watching them as they said their teary goodbyes. When my turn came, I mutely laid down my rose with neither a tear nor a kind word to spare for my old man, other than perhaps, *I wish it hadn't ended the way it did.* However, I kept the thought to myself and tried to banish the memory of blood on my hands.

I searched for Jacob among the attendees but didn't see him. He never came by the hospital or the farm, either. In the rush to the hospital, Mark and Luke left their loaned rifles in the bed of his truck, but I figured he would have come by for the pistol and Bowie knife. But when the time came for me to catch my bus back to my unit and they still sat in the top of my pack, I figured he must have gone back to wherever he came from. As I said my goodbyes to my family at the bus stop, I tried to not let my disappointment show.

My mother kissed me on the cheek and made me promise to not wait another four years before coming home again.

Mary flung her arms around me. I wrapped her in mine and gave her a fitting bear hug. When I let her go, she punched me in my bad shoulder, lightly, but it still hurt like hell. I mussed her hair with my good hand in turn. She gave me a deserving teenager glare as she flipped her hair back in place.

I reached out to shake Luke's hand, but he slapped my phone in my outstretched palm instead. Unsure of when he had taken it from me, I looked at it askance, unable to figure out what he might have done to it other than possibly add a few more cracks to the screen. "Something to remember me by," he said with a smile before giving me a quick brotherly hug.

Last, Mark stood before me and took my hand in a firm grip. "Safe travels, Matt, and seriously, don't make it another four years."

"I won't and good luck with the farm," I said with a smile, still thanking my lucky stars that he actually liked farming and the whole family had agreed to gift the farm, and all its debt, to him. He nodded, then opened the driver's side door of the family station wagon. With one last nod and a determined grin, he got in, and I watched them drive away. Somehow, I managed to stay dry-eyed until I could no longer see their tail lights.

My bus wouldn't arrive for a few more minutes, so I found a seat on the concrete block outside the Ace Hardware store next to the bus stop. The door to the store swung open with a chime, and a moment later, I nearly jumped out of my skin when a hand grabbed my shoulder from behind.

"Easy, Matthew," Jacob said with a smile.

I let the shock go with a slow breath. "Oh, it's you."

"I'm glad to see you're moving around better."

I rolled my left shoulder as much as I could without the pain becoming excruciating. "Thanks. Still hurts like a bitch, though, even with the help of my little friends." I rattled the bottle of painkillers in my pocket. Then remembering why I'd been looking for him, I opened up my bag and pulled out Jacob's Bowie knife along with his TRR8. "My brothers missed these when they dropped your guns into your truck. I kind of hoped to return them to you sooner, but you never stopped by."

He took the pistol and its holsters but put his hands up in refusal when I pushed the knife toward him. "Keep it. Call it a memento of your first real hunt, or a gift, or whatever. Damn, I suck at goodbyes." He pulled out a pack of Black and Milds and lit one up.

I pushed the knife back into my bag, grateful he didn't want it back. "Thanks. So, why are you here then?"

He blew out a puff of gray smoke. "I was hoping to catch you before you headed back to Georgia."

Confused and a little creeped out, I asked, "How did you know where I was stationed?"

He laughed. "Same way I knew when your bus was supposed to leave. Gracie."

"Oh. I didn't think she could hack…"

"Oh, it's illegal, but there's not a computer she can't hack. Still, she didn't need to. Getting info on bus tickets isn't that hard to get if you know the rider's name."

"Hmm. Well, I am glad you stopped by to see me off." I reached out my hand.

He shook my hand with a firm grip, and I could feel something between our palms. When he let go, I pulled my hand back and gawked at the card. It read: Jacob McGinnis, M.H.

"M.H. Is that some sort of degree?" I asked.

He laughed. "It's a degree in badass. Like I told you, I'm the New York/New England Regional Monster Hunter for the Holy Roman Catholic Church. And in case you haven't noticed, I'm getting old. Older than any hunter has the right to be." His mouth turned up in a wry smile. "I'm looking for a replacement. Someone I can train. You showed me something out there a lot of people don't have: moxie."

I chuckled. "Moxie? Damn, you are old."

"Boy, don't mock an old man," he said, though his voice held no scorn. "As I was saying. If you're interested, give me a ring after your term is up."

"But I'm not Catholic."

"No one's perfect and that can be remedied. Or not. One hunter still talks to her rabbi."

A bus pulled into the lot and the air brakes gasped as it slowed to a stop. The front end lowered to the ground and the door opened. Two people got off, followed by the driver, who called out my bus number.

I got up and slid the card into my pants pocket. "I've got almost a year left. Will that be a problem?"

"Not at all. And, oh, I have one more thing for you." Jacob handed me a tattered leather journal. "Found this while cleaning up the den, and I thought you might like to have it."

The bus driver called *all aboard* before I could really look at it. I picked up my bag and slung it over my shoulder. "Thanks, and I'll think about it," I said shaking his hand one last time. I boarded the bus, tossed my bag in the overhead bin and settled into a seat halfway to the rear. As the bus lurched forward, I cracked open the journal. Scrawled on the first page in Jonny's familiar hand was *Monsters Are Not Myths*.

THE END
The Story of the Peterson Apostles will continue in
Solo Op, coming soon from Falstaff Books.
Read on for a sample!

II

SOLO OP

1

The barrack's door opened, and a blast of hot Georgian summer bitch-slapped me across the face with humidity so thick I could practically swim in it. Not even two steps outside and sweat erupted from my forehead, ran down my body, and worked a knot in my underwear tight enough to cut off circulation. Sucking in a breath of hot soupy air, I shook a leg, trying to free things up, but only managed to make matters worse. Days like this made me wish for the comforts of a snowy New York winter where I could at least adjust my layers. Here all I could do was choose how to sweat my balls off, clothes on or clothes off, except Army regs even took that choice away from me.

The heat did help loosen up my muscles, and I gave my left arm a test swing. It moved with only a hint of pain, which was likely more psychosomatic than real. After months of physical therapy, the werebear inflicted gunshot wound had healed nicely, and I had finally been released for full duty. In fact, my arm felt so good, I was actually looking forward to this morning's PT despite the dreaded company run through a virtual sauna.

We formed up in our unit area, faced right, and stepped off at double time, which, as it was a company run, meant I could walk faster. We left barracks behind and hustled along the streets of the post echoing First Sarge's bellowing call. He led us past the golf course then turned down a street lined with manicured lawns, tall trees, and some of the older homes on post. Why? Because as my old man used to put it, there's absolutely no reason anyone should sleep past oh-seven-thirty. And in general, I found the army to second that doctrine by shepherding a hundred and twenty of the US's finest in semi-perfect step, chanting a ridiculous marching song with a strong dose of misery loves company. All-in-all we did it in good fun, and we kept the cadences to bastardized versions of nursery rhymes like *Old King Cole*.

We didn't even make it to the first side street before First Sarge called out in perfect time, "I wanna hear from someone new. I wanna laugh and giggle too." He waited for the company to reply the response. It came out as a hoarse half-chuckle from most of us as our minds tried to process the image of the man giggling. Carved from obsidian, First Sarge would only show emotion if hell froze over, and even then, it would only be a small tight satisfied smile because it did so at his command.

"Better not be shy; better be bold. Better sound-off like you're told. Sound-off. Sergeant. Sound-off. Pete-r-son."

I took the beat during the response and carried the call. "Left. Left. Left—Right," I hollered, running through the myriad of cadences I'd learned over the years for something comedic and uplifting. As the unit called back the lefts and rights, I caught an odd-looking black dog just staring at me further down the street. My eyes locked with his, and my mind suddenly went blank of every cadence I had ever learned except one. A sexist innuendo-filled song that you only sang deep in the woods where even the animals could scurry away in shame.

We trotted passed the family homes of the post's highest-ranking brass, and my inability to recall *any other* cadence began to twist my stomach into a knot. In a desperate hope to shake something more appropriate loose with a little more time, I took the company on one more round of *left-rights*. However, nothing budged, and as the company echoed, "Right," one last time, an energetic preschooler emerged from a front door dragging a sleepy mother behind him. Then to my horror, my chest filled with air, and my mouth bellowed of its own accord. "Don't let your dingle-dangle dangle in the dirt. Pick up your dingle-dangle and tie it to your shirt."

The entire column of soldiers next to me stared straight ahead in disbelief. Other than a few half-muffled responses, most refused to chorus my insolence back at me.

First Sarge screamed, "What the hell, Sergeant Peterson? Clean it up. Now!"

I tried to will my mouth closed, to swallow the words in my throat, but they continued to flow unbidden. "Don't let your dingle-dangle wobble to and fro. Pick up your dingle-dangle and tie it in a bow."

"Damn it, Sergeant Peterson, I better not hear another word come from your mouth." First Sarge's New Orleans accent thickened with each word.

The soldier running beside me, Private First Class Steven, gave me a confused *what-the-hell-are-you-doing* look.

In response, I clapped a hand over my mouth and shook my head in denial, but then my teeth bit into the flesh of my hand like a rabid dog, and I withdrew it in bloody pain. My mind cried, *please make me stop*, but my voice said, "Don't let your dingle-dangle dangle in the mud. Pick up your dingle-dangle and hand it to your bud."

First Sarge stormed through the unit's formation, soldiers parting around him like the Red Sea. "Somebody shut him up!"

Private Stevens' eyes darted from mine to First Sarge's, and without a second glance, he sucker-punched me in the stomach. A fist the size of a cannonball and powered by a body Mike Tyson would envy drove the air from me. I doubled over and collapsed to the ground, unable to pull in a breath even though my mouth continued to work the next line, thankfully in silence.

The soles of a hundred shoes shuffled pass, and I faintly heard one of the other sergeants pick up the cadence. "Old King Cole was a merry ole soul, and a merry ole soul was he. Uh-huh."

A pair of size thirteen running shoes stopped an inch from my nose as the company moved beyond my blurred vision and earshot of First Sarge's fury. He squatted down, his breath heaving and not from the run. "Sergeant Peterson, I do not know what cockamamy, fool-brained stunt you think you were trying to pull with that despicable display of lack of self-control. But you and I are going to have a long conversation about propriety and respect. Do you understand me, Sergeant?"

I blinked up at him, my chest burning with the lack of air, tears streaming from my eyes, and my mouth still moving to *Don't Let Your Dingle-Dangle*. I shook my head side-to-side as blackness started moving in around the edges of my vision. The angry storm in his eyes melted into something akin to worry before the press of unconsciousness eclipsed the bright morning sun.

I woke to a splash of water and the rhythmic beat of an elephant doing power squats on my chest. After a second or two, my vision cleared, and my lungs began to move once more on their own. The elephant finally disappeared to the ether from which it came as First Sarge relaxed back onto his heels, washing me in the hot sunlight.

A new shadow moved in and mercifully blotted out the sun from my eyes. After a few blinks to remove the phantom sunspots, I saw PFC Stevens fitfully wringing a crushed paper cup in his hands.

"I...I didn't mean to hit him that hard, First Sarge. I swear."

"That's alright son; you were following my orders." First Sarge diverted his gaze back to me in an unreadable expression. "Go help Private Pagan with the paramedics."

PFC Stevens snapped his heels together and barely stopped his hand half-raised in a salute. "Yes, First Sarge."

First Sarge watched him about-face and run off. "I swear it takes all types, but if he makes corporal, I'm out. I meant that water for you to drink."

I tried to sit up, but he placed a hand of tented fingers on my chest and pressed me back down without a look. "You stay right there, Sergeant." His dark eyes dropped to mine. "I would really like to know what the hell happened this morning." I opened my mouth, searching for an explanation that even I would believe, but before I could utter a word, he broke in. "Shut it before you say something stupid."

He sized me up with a stare that weighed every part of my being as if tallying my worth, and I could see my career evaporating under his scrutiny. The silence stretching out between us only made my anxiety worse. Eventually, sirens sounded off in the distance, and the pressure of First Sarge's hand on my chest eased a bit.

"The paramedics are on their way. We'll make sure you didn't damage something permanently, then we'll get you the help you need."

I could have sworn I misheard him, and my eyebrows rose one on top of the other. "What?" I asked thickly, though I didn't get an answer.

Flashing lights of the ambulance contested with the blazing sun as it rolled up the street. First Sarge stood to greet the paramedics as they piled out of the vehicle. I knew better than to move and remained where I lay—on the street feeling helpless.

First Sarge relayed the events of the morning to the medics in short, succinct sentences. He painted my physical condition in broad brush strokes, which thankfully didn't include my rendition of that stupid song. I almost sat up in shock when he got to the part about me not breathing for four minutes. Though it did explain the elephant bruise developing on my chest.

The medics loaded me onto a backboard and then hoisted me onto a gurney before wheeling me to the back of the vehicle. First Sarge placed a steady hand on one of the medic's shoulders, and they paused, giving him a moment.

"When they release you, come see me. Before you report to the CO," First Sarge said.

"Yes, First Sarge." I cut the last word off with a grunt as the gurney shook, clattered, and collapsed into its traveling position as the medics shoved me into the back of the ambulance.

One of them climbed in behind me and, as he cleared the door, I thought I saw a shaggy black dog sitting in the shade of one of the houses lock eyes with me before the ambulance doors slammed closed.

The medic prepped an IV and reached down for my hand. "What the? Who bit you?" he asked, taking a closer look at the matched set of teeth marks gouging the meat of my right hand.

"Uh, I think I did?"

"Damn. Better give me the other one." He let my hand go and reached for the other to put in the IV.

At the post hospital, a nurse took their report then helped them transfer me to a hospital bed, before pulling a curtain across my new room. Other than a brief interruption when she returned to clean my bite wound, she left me alone with nothing more than my thoughts for the better part of two hours.

My doctor finally walked in. The end of a long shift pulled at the edges of her eyes, and she rubbed at her forehead curtained beneath dark bangs. "So," she drew the first word out into a yawn, stretching her red lips to their limits before she hid it behind a fist. "Why are you here today, uh…" she checked her clipboard, "Sergeant Peterson?"

"I…" I didn't know where to begin, despite how long they gave me to come up with a half-decent story. "I had an episode."

"Hm. Well, your first sergeant says you collapsed during morning PT panting for breath until you passed out. He then performed CPR to resuscitate you. Perhaps you could tell me what happened just before you passed out?"

With a hundred and twenty witnesses, lies can be a bit tricky, but sometimes you don't have any other option. Of course, if you weave in a good bit of truth, they're a lot more believable. "I don't exactly remember, ma'am. Today is company run day, and we may have gone a mile or two when First Sarge called on me to lead the cadence. I'd done it a hundred times before, but…ah, I don't know, I guess I just panicked."

"Must have been one hell of a panic attack to leave a fist-shaped bruise on your stomach."

"Well, I did wake up to First Sarge performing CPR on me, but I probably hit something when I fell."

Her eye roll complemented her sigh in an *I'm-too-tired-to-drag-the-truth-out-of-you*, kind of way. "And I suppose your hand just happened to find its way into your mouth when you fell?"

"Oh no, ma'am. I felt the attack coming on, and I put my hand in my mouth to keep from biting my tongue."

She scoffed and shook her head. "Of course. Let me see it." I extended my hand to her. "You broke the skin, but it's not so bad that you need stitches." She rummaged through one of the cabinet drawers and pulled out a small tube of surgical glue. "This will hold it together for now, so long as you don't stress the skin for a few days."

She glued the wound back together, then wrapped my hand in a mile of gauze before taping the bandage closed and pushing back from the exam bed with the efficiency of a sniper reassembling his weapon. Her eyes then drew down, and the corner of her mouth quirked in a tired, frustrated expression. "Sergeant Peterson, I'm not comfortable prescribing you any anti-anxiety medications without a psychiatric consultation. I'm going to order you a referral, but until then, I'm going to hold you overnight for observation. A nurse will be by shortly to move you to a room for the night."

That gave me another day before facing First Sarge, and I almost sighed in relief over the stay of execution, except I hated waiting.

2

I spent the better part of the following day with nothing better to do than twiddle my thumbs and watch the snow on the failing TV in my room. Except for a handful of brief visits by the nursing staff to draw fluids for testing or the slightly more pleasant deliveries of hospital chow, the day passed with about as much excitement as watching ice melt on the fourth of July.

It did give me time to think, and the more of it I did, the more confused and the more suspicious I grew. By the time the psychiatrist paid me a visit, shortly before evening retreat, I seriously doubted any natural cause to my sudden predilection for dingle-dangle, and I certainly didn't want to discuss it with the one person who could place me in a psych ward for the remainder of my military career. Of course, it was probably just my little brother Jonny's blasted journal of monsters ravaging my brain. I hadn't been able to put the damn thing down since I returned to post after slaying the werebear that killed him. My fingers itched for it now like a hypochondriac needs WebMD, but I had left it in the best hiding place I knew—the second shelf of the bookcase in my room, third book from the right.

The psychiatrist walked into my room, giving me a welcome distraction from the machinations of my imagination. I didn't need to look any further than the mirror shine on the dress shoes clicking on the terrazzo floor beneath starched pressed trousers to smell West Point on him.

However, the major tabs on his shoulders deserved respect, so I swallowed the groan before it could escape my lips and tried to sit up a little straighter in the bed.

The major came to a stop beside my bed with the military precision of years of marching parade at the Point. He gave his portfolio the briefest consultation before hazarding, "Sergeant Peterson?"

I cleared my throat. "Yes, sir."

"Good. Then I didn't get it wrong for a third time." He tossed a manufactured chuckle through the slightest of smiles. I returned the gesture hoping it fulfilled whatever prerequisite icebreaker they taught head doctors like him. "I'm Major Daniels. Do you mind if I have a seat?"

"No, sir."

He pulled the lone chair from beneath the window over next to the bed then descended into it with a razor straight back. "Thank you." His voice came out soft, but everything else about him was strung tighter than a violin. "I understand you had a panic attack yesterday; would you care to tell me about it?"

Not just no, but hell no, I thought, but voicing that opinion wasn't really an option. "Well, sir, as best as I recall, it began shortly after we started our company run yesterday. First Sarge called on me to sing cadence, and shortly after I started, I couldn't breathe. After that, it's a bit hazy, to be honest."

Major Daniels' blank, emotionless eyes never left mine as I spoke. "Have you felt any symptoms since then? Unexplained anxiety? Shortness of breath? Racing heart? Things like that."

"No, sir. None of that."

"Have you felt any of those symptoms before yesterday?"

I sighed as I tried to think, but damn, who hasn't felt a racing heart or shortness of breath at one time or another. "Maybe once or twice," I admitted.

"As best you can remember, were you under any unusual stress when you've had those symptoms?"

You mean like going toe-to-toe with a werebear? Then hell yeah. I thought, but settled for a simple, "Yes, sir."

The interview dragged on for another thirty minutes or so while he asked about the recent loss of my brother and my old man. About my upbringing, life on the farm, and even my tours in Afghanistan. I kept my answers simple and short, and thankfully he didn't press; I really didn't feel like doing a deep dive into my personal life at the moment.

Major Daniels finished jotting down the last of his notes in his portfolio, then closed it with a snap and stood. He pulled out a phone from one of his pockets and began dancing his fingers across the screen as he spoke. "Well, Sergeant Peterson, on the surface your symptoms certainly appear to be a panic attack, but an isolated incident is not a disorder, and it could be something else entirely. We'll take a look at your bloodwork to rule out any medical conditions. In the meantime, I'm going to schedule a regular appointment for you and me to address any outstanding symptoms, starting with fourteen hundred hours four weeks from today." He glanced up from his phone with a detached mechanical smile.

"Thank you, sir," I said, internalizing an eyeroll.

His head bobbed in a short nod, then he pushed the chair back to its place beneath the window and strode out of the room.

A cacophony of colliding bodies sounded just outside my room, followed by an "Excuse me, sir," in a voice that tickled my memory. A moment later, a shorter soldier dressed in combats rounded the door frame. His whip of a frame swam in his uniform, and his high-and-tight looked more like someone had run an orange highlighter over his head than a hairstyle choice. His freckled face split into a wide grin as he saw me leveraging myself out of bed.

"Leaving already? I thought you'd be locked up in the loony bin by now."

"Sergeant Sweeney, I wish I could say I'm glad to see you."

"Figured as much, but don't fret it. First Sarge just got a little concerned when you didn't show up for evening formation." Sweeney spoke in a clipped staccato like an M249 on full auto.

"I'm sure. He probably has the CO breathing down his neck, ready to bring me in for a court-martial."

Sweeney shrugged his shoulders. "Hah, well yeah. You know I love that cadence, but your timing couldn't have been worse. We were two houses up from the garrison commander's, and his kids were just getting ready for school."

I closed my eyes and rolled my head back. "Shit."

"That's a bit of an understatement, but yeah, shit."

"All right, no point in putting it off. Just give me a second to get dressed." I felt defeated before it even began.

I pulled my PT shirt over my head and heard, "Just where the hell do you think you are going, Sergeant Peterson?"

"Huh, what?" I asked, popping my head through the neck of the shirt like a bunny peeking out of his hole to see who's about to shoot him. "Uh…what's up, Doc?"

The ER doctor who admitted me yesterday didn't even crack a smile, and her eyes narrowed threateningly. "Sergeant, you have not been released. Please sit back down."

"But you said I could go after the psych eval, and Major Daniels just left."

"I said you must have a psychiatric consultation before I would prescribe you any anti-anxiety medications."

I felt like a deer caught in the high beams of a Mack Truck. I glanced at Sergeant Sweeney, who gave me an *I'm-not-getting-involved* shrug of his shoulders and took a sideways step toward the door. His hand fumbled in a blind reach for the door, jittering the handle noisily.

The doctor turned to face him. "Sergeant, what are you still doing here? Perhaps you would like to join Sergeant Peterson for his examination."

"Um, no ma'am. First Sarge sent me to check on him is all."

"Well, you can tell your first sergeant that I'll release Sergeant Peterson only after I am satisfied that he won't collapse between here and barracks. Is that understood?"

"Yes, ma'am," Sweeney said, frozen next to the door.

"Well move along then, soldier," the doctor said, and Sweeney leapt through the door like she had cracked a whip. When she turned back to me, the corner of her mouth curled up slightly. "You all jump so easily." Her smile disappeared, and she ordered, "Now get back in bed and take your shirt back off."

I flew through the air, landed on the bed, with my shirt half over my head before I even processed what she had said, earning another rare smile.

She checked my breathing, my eyes, my ears, my throat, my blood pressure, and even had me turn my head and cough before she made me wait another half-hour for a nurse to draw more vials of blood. Only then did she let me put my shirt back on and release me from the hospital.

I made my way through the lobby and out the front doors, feeling drained of both fluids and spirit. The hot summer sun sat low in a painted sky, nearly kissing the tops of the trees and casting long shadows along the ground. Few people milled about in the late evening heat, and the silhouette of a man and a dog watching me from beneath the large tree caught my attention. As I approached, the apparition materialized into the familiar face of my childhood best friend, Craig Flannigan.

I'd known him my whole life. His dad owned the farm next to ours, and we even went to the same church. But where my old man was a bastard who treated his cattle better than his children, his father was an angel of grace, and I spent as much time as I could in that sanctuary. No one knew the shit I went through with my old man better than Craig; he helped me get through some tough years, which eventually led to us joining the army together through the buddy program.

We were inseparable and thicker than blood until he married Teressa, the woman we both loved, just before our first deployment to Afghanistan, and I let jealousy drive a wedge between us. Then his perfect life began to crumble, his father died, and his mother lost the farm. It drove him to drinking, brawling, and women, not necessarily in that order and certainly not independently. I tried to help and even took a knife in the gut rescuing him from a bar fight he started—because that's what friends do. But somehow, the incident got him stripped of his rank with two months of half-pay while putting me on the fast-track to promotion for exemplary *esprit de corps* in coming to the aid of an embattled fellow soldier. By the time I got out of the hospital, I had a new stack of chevrons on my chest and he'd been transferred to another unit. At that point, the fires of jealousy burned both ways, and only Teressa kept them from consuming us.

I stopped in my tracks, staring at his shadowed form. "Craig, is that you?"

"Hello, Matthew." His voice sounded dry and raspy. "Funny running into you here. Visiting someone?" His tone declared it as anything but a coincidence.

"No, not visiting."

"Well, I hope it's nothing too serious," he said, though the statement lacked any real sincerity.

"I thought you were still in Afghanistan. When did you get back? And when did you get a dog?"

"Recently," he replied, though to which question I couldn't be sure. Then he abruptly turned, let out a short whistle, and walked away, the black dog trotting after him.

Bewildered, I watched him walk away into the setting sun. "Well, all righty then. That was weird." I made a mental note to call Teressa when I got a chance and check in, but that would have to wait until later. I needed to report to First Sarge.

The lights in the company area were off except for a few egress lights buzzing in the ceiling. *Everyone has gone home for the night.* My heart lifted at the thought until I saw light spilling out from beneath a door at the end of the hall. *Everyone except First Sarge that is.*

I stopped at his door and adjusted my PT uniform before taking a settling breath and raising my hand to knock.

"Get in here, Sergeant Peterson." I heard First Sarge holler before my knuckles even connected. Any settling effects from my breathing exercise evaporated, and my heart began to race. *Maybe I really do have an anxiety issue.* I swallowed hard and opened the door.

3

The behemoth of a metal desk First Sarge sat behind looked as if it should have been surplussed and replaced decades ago. Stacks of paperwork stuffed into neat brown folders adorned the desk's corners and a single five-by-seven picture frame I'd never seen the front of stood front and center. An assortment of accolades, merits, and the usual regalia of an *I-love-me* wall gained from a long and exemplary military career adorned the rest of the office.

"Take a seat, sergeant," First Sarge ordered as he stood up and strode around the desk. He shifted the picture to the other side of a stack of folders and half-sat on the front edge. "I don't like to get involved with my soldiers' personal lives, but when it affects their performance, I don't have much choice. Now I need to be sure you are taking your medical situation seriously." He leaned forward and handed me a sticky note with a phone number. "I'm sure whoever the VA assigned you is a capable psychiatrist, but Doctor Swartz is independent and has helped hundreds of soldiers deal with what the hell-of-war leaves behind."

He stood up and returned to his seat behind the desk. "I'm not saying you have to call that number, but you need to either continue with the VA psychiatrist or seek a private doctor, the choice is yours. I will be meeting with the CO in the morning, and she will ask me about you. I'd like to be able to tell her you are taking your mental health seriously."

I stared at the number in my hand, and the memory of Major

Daniels flashed through my mind with his awkward icebreakers, and a pole shoved so far up his ass I couldn't imagine how he tied his shoes. "I'll call first thing in the morning," I said, slipping the paper into my pocket.

"Good to know. Now get out of here and get some sleep. You have your own appointment with the CO tomorrow, and I'm pretty sure you're not going to enjoy that conversation."

I gulped and stood. "Yes, First Sarge."

"Go on. I'll see you in the morning."

I spun on my heel and left his office feeling the storm clouds building, praying I'd survive the hurricane when they broke. Absorbed in those particularly unpleasant thoughts, I made it up the barrack's stair and down the hall to my room on autopilot, not really noticing the doors creaking open as I passed. As I reached to insert my room key into the door's card reader, I came face to face with more rubber dingle-dangles than a bachelorette party.

The hall broke out in a hiss of suppressed mirth.

I reached up and grabbed the central ornament by the tip of the shaft and tore it off the door, wielding it balls out like a mace. "All right. Ha, ha. Really fucking mature. But I'm warning all-y'all, if I see another fucking shlong, I'm going to tear it off and beat someone with it."

I spun around, nearly connecting the pink bulge with my neighbor, Sergeant Perez. At five-foot four, her dark eyes stared at the bulk of the improvised club swaying only inches from her damp face. Apparently, I had interrupted her shower as the robe she wore clung to her chest in ever-widening and darkening pools of damp, cream-colored silk.

She ran her tongue across her plump lips and reached up to stroke the shaft between a thumb and a pair of manicured fingers. Her eyes rose up the rubber rod, sizing it up before locking with me. "Now, Matthew, don't make promises you don't intend to keep."

The entire hall collected itself in an orgasmic gasp, and I could feel the blood rush to my face. I yanked the rubber mace out of her fingers and clutched it to my chest as if violated, and the hall exploded in billowing bouts of laughter. I fumbled for the door handle, eventually working the door open, and retreated into my room. Then slammed the wooden barrier closed to the rising chorus of catcalls.

I sagged back against the door, trying to breathe through the anger, when I realized what I still clasped in my hands. I pitched it across the room, and it bounced off the wall in a spastic rebound. When it rolled to a stop at my feet, I pushed it under my bed and out of sight with the tip of my shoe.

I fell onto my bed and buried my face into my pillow. "Tomorrow is going to be one *hell* of a long day."

My phone buzzed beside me on the nightstand. I rolled over to pick it up and saw a new message from my sister, Mary. We'd been talking more since my recent visit, but I couldn't say I felt much like talking at the moment, so I skimmed the message and jotted back a short reply before tossing the phone back down.

I laid on the bed staring at the ceiling for a moment, then ran my hands over my face, digging my fingers into my scalp. The ruckus on the other side of the door simmered down to a low hum, but I knew I would never live this down. I needed to vent, to scream, but settled for growling through clenched teeth instead. *What the hell is wrong with me?*

After a good five minutes of self-pity, I sat up and glared at the back of the door. I couldn't talk with any of them about what really happened. Not my fellow soldiers, not First Sarge, and certainly not Major Daniels. I pulled out the paper with Doctor Schwartz's number on it and placed it by my phone, uncertain if I could even talk with him about it.

I shifted my gaze to the phone and debated talking with Mary, or one of my brothers. They'd at least listen. They all knew about the werebear that killed Jonny and our old man, Paul, but this wasn't the same. This was in my head; still, it felt wrong. Not that I could imagine how it could feel right, but still, it felt—unnatural.

I kicked off my shoes and went to my bookcase. Jonny's leather-bound journal stood where I had left it, sandwiched between a mint condition *King James Bible* and a tattered copy of *Starship Troopers*. I pulled it out and unwrapped the leather thong as I sat in my desk chair.

The imitation leather cover cracked as it opened. My fingers traced the smudged words in Jonny's familiar scrawl; *Monsters Are Not Myths*. I turned the pages, searching through the newspaper clippings and short handwritten passages, which filled about half the pages. Most sections like *Dokkaebi—Korean Goblins* contained little more than the title and a few words followed by several blank pages, while others like vampires contained pages upon pages of material. Sometimes his notes contradicted each other with huge question marks, other times, he scratched through whole sections with the word "myth" written in the margin. I could hardly call the work definitive as most of it appeared to come from sources like Wiki-lie-to-ya, which made deciphering the truth from legend near impossible. Still, it was Jonny in my hands, and I would never be able to get any closer to him.

About a month ago, I had finally added a few pages of notes to his *Werebear* section, based on my run-in with the one that killed him. Somehow, it felt wrong to leave the section incomplete.

I'd read every page at least a dozen times and even bought some sticky tabs and indexed the damn thing like a textbook. I admit I was more than a little obsessed about it. *But knowing is half the battle, right?*

I settled into the search and quickly got lost in re-reading passages I could quote by heart. About halfway through the section on vampires, which left me more confused than certain of anything, my phone sounded with a new text message. I placed the journal face down on my desk and tried to rub some moisture back into my eyes.

My chair creaked as I stood, the sound sharp in the otherwise silence. That drew my attention as barracks didn't normally fall this quiet until well after midnight.

"What time is it?" I asked myself as a yawn stretched my mouth open. The bright green numbers glowing on my alarm clock showed two twenty-three. "Oh shit. I need to get some sleep."

I killed the overhead lights and stumbled to my bed under the half-muted glow of my phone on the nightstand. I set my alarm for oh-five-hundred then crawled into bed on top of the covers. I reached over to put my phone to sleep and saw the name on the text message: Teressa Flannigan.

I pinched the sleep from the bridge of my nose and threw my legs over the side of the bed. The message opened with the touch of my finger on the sensor.

Call me ASAP!

I switched to the phone app and touched Teressa's smiling face on my favorites screen. The phone rang once.

"Matthew?" Teressa's voice came through the phone in a hoarse whisper.

"Tee, it's late; what's up?"

"It's Craig. He's back." I could hear the stress in her muted voice; a steel guitar held less tension.

"I know. I ran into him earlier."

"You did? And?" Curiosity eased the strain a touch.

"And nothing. We exchanged hellos, and then he left."

"Did he...Did he seem normal to you?"

"Normal? Craig hasn't been normal since his dad passed."

"I know, but this time…he's different. I don't know how to explain it." The panicked stress tightening her voice raised the small hairs on the back of my neck.

"Tee, what did he do?"

"I'm sorry, Matthew. This was a mistake. I shouldn't have called."

"Wait. Tee, wait. What's going on?"

"I'm sorry, Matthew, I just don't know what to do." She made several indecisive noises, and I could almost see her chewing on her lower lip. "The first time the two of you went to the desert, I lost the man I married. He came back to me bitter and angry at the world. This time I…I don't even recognize the man that came back."

I knew exactly what she meant. I watched in person as pain and loss ate away at my friend until I didn't recognize what remained. "Tee, I'm not sure how I can help."

"I know. I'm just worried it might be PTSD or something. I was hoping you might talk to him? Maybe try to see if he'll get some help?"

"Uh…" I didn't know how to answer that.

"I'm sorry, Matthew. I know it's an impossible ask. Just forget it." I could hear her tears through the phone.

"No. No, Tee, it's not." I tried to keep my voice level, but in truth, it was the last thing I wanted to do. "I'll give him a call. Maybe go out for a beer and catch up on old times. We'll have to see where it goes from there."

"Oh, I love you, Matthew. Thank you." Hearing her voice utter those words lifted my spirit even though I knew she didn't mean it the way my heart wanted her to.

"I…" the words almost slipped from my lips, but I managed to stop myself before she could hear the truth. "You're welcome, Tee." I held the phone to my ear, trying to figure out how to keep the promise I just made while mentally replaying my earlier run-in with Craig. "Tee, when did you and Craig get a dog?"

"Uh, we don't have a dog."

4

The following morning, I stood at parade rest beside the olive drab door to Captain Holland's office—waiting for the last twenty minutes. Waiting was a huge part of military life, and it didn't take long to learn how to use all that extra time to catch up on a poor night's sleep regardless of what position you might find yourself in, including standing. The trick was actually learning when not to sleep, like while you're about to be ripped a new asshole. Still, my eyelids continued to droop as if anchored to the floor by lead weights. Forcing them open took a strength my meager three hours of rest the night before hadn't given me. I'd prop them open with toothpicks like Wile E. Coyote waiting for the roadrunner if I had any. Instead, I settled for trying to decipher the voices slipping out of the room beneath the door.

Captain Holland's higher-pitched female voice occasionally broke into the low rumble of a heated argument between two men. Not necessarily a shouting match, unless you could tell the nuances of the chain of command. In this case, I could hear the hint of New Orleans in First Sarge's tightly controlled voice; a sure sign of frustration. The other man's gravel-infused baritone, however, sounded more like a trail boss in one of those old westerns my grandpa used to love. No yelling meant the voice didn't belong to anyone with a rank higher than captain, but not lower than first sergeant, considering how tightly First Sarge reined in his own temper. My face blanched as the fog of sleep deprivation cleared enough for me to identify the voice a fraction of a second before Captain Holland ordered me into the room.

I opened the door to find First Sarge standing just behind my CO, stiff as a statue. To the captain's other side stood none other than the battalion sergeant major, Sergeant Major Gunnerson. The man looked to be a mirror image of First Sarge except instead of being carved from obsidian, he was chiseled from a solid piece of marble roughly twice the size. I took a step into the room and three sets of eyes locked onto me like laser-guided missiles. I felt my knees buckle and transferred the slip into another step, finally stumbling to a stop a few feet from Captain Holland's desk.

I brought my heels together with enough force to make the rubber soles of my boots click as my hand snapped an unsteady salute that nearly poked me in the eye. "Sergeant Peterson, reporting as ordered, ma'am."

The captain returned my salute from her chair, and I lowered my hand to my side. Sweat dampened my fist as I held the position of attention and tried not to divert my eyes from the captain's despite the weight of the twin glares of icy blue and stone-cold brown that made my spine wilt. I wanted to run back out the door, but I forced my feet to remain rooted to the floor.

Captain Holland turned her head slightly in First Sarge's direction. "First sergeant, read the charges."

"Sergeant Peterson, you are hereby charged with violation of Article One Thirty-Four. You are accused of bringing a discredit upon the US Army and the armed forces by your conduct while on the company run through a residential neighborhood." First Sarge read out the charge in a formal tone, stripped of any emotion. I couldn't help but cut my eyes up to him; his face showed just as little.

"Sergeant Peterson," Captain Holland said, drawing my attention back to her. "You will be tried under Article Fifteen of the UCMJ. You are not entitled to a defense attorney; however, you have the right to refuse an Article Fifteen in lieu of a special court-martial. Do you wish to exercise this right?"

I have the right to what? I glanced up, confused. The sergeant major was unreadable, but there appeared to be a hint of hunger in his eyes. First Sarge gave me the barest shake of his head.

I gulped. "No, ma'am."

"Then the charges have been read; do you understand the charges?"

"Yes, ma'am."

"How do you plead?"

"Guilty, ma'am."

"Do you have anything to add prior to judgment?"

I took a moment trying to form a reasonable defense or at least an explanation, but I couldn't even believe monsters made me do it. "Ma'am, I apologize for the inappropriateness of my behavior, but no, I have nothing further to add."

"I see. Well, sergeant, fortunately for you the crudeness of your cadence was lost on the garrison commander's six-year-old. However," Captain Holland glanced over her shoulder to the sergeant major before casting her scowl back on me, "the commander's wife has expressed her displeasure to the colonel, who then let the battalion commander know that those types of cadences no longer have a place in today's army, which I happen to agree with. I'm sure you can imagine my dismay when the battalion commander stepped into my office yesterday to personally inform me of this."

She paused, and I couldn't tell if it was to take a breath or if she wanted me to say something. I erred on the virtue of silence, not wanting to trigger a worse tirade, and kept my back straight while I stared at a patch of wall just over the CO's head and between First Sarge and the sergeant major. However, from my peripheral I could see her eyes never left mine.

"First Sergeant has suggested your lapse in judgement may be the result of residual stress from your time in Afghanistan." She paused again, this time letting the statement hang in the air like an accusation waiting for a response. But as it wasn't a question, I kept my mouth shut and my eyes focused on the wall. "However, this is a fighting unit and I am not inclined to humor such lapses in judgment. I expect nothing less than the utmost professionalism from my NCOs as a shining example to the soldiers they lead. Can you be that kind of example, Sergeant Peterson?"

There was no avoiding a direct question; there was also no other answer than, "Yes, ma'am."

The bluster in her sails ebbed slightly as she continued. "I understand you are seeking professional help in dealing with the lingering stress from Afghanistan. Is that correct?"

"Yes, ma'am."

"As you have taken initiative prior to this Article Fifteen hearing, I will not take your pay, but you will serve fourteen days extra duty." The sergeant major's eyes narrowed disappointingly at the captain's verdict while First Sarge remained stone-faced. The argument I overheard through the door became clear, and I owed First Sarge for sticking his neck out for me. I only hoped I wouldn't disappoint him. "Sergeant, be thankful my rank does not entitle me to give you more. Do not abuse my leniency."

"Yes, ma'am."

With the bulk of the formalities over, she sat back in her chair. "Extra duty will be served at the sergeant major's discretion."

The corner of the sergeant major's mouth bent imperceptibly upward with the equivalent effect of a wolf licking its lips at a cornered rabbit, and I swallowed the sudden lump in my throat. I fled home four years ago to avoid my old man's ire but found myself suddenly missing his brute force and lack of imagination; somehow it seemed more merciful at the moment.

A fter two weeks of the most mind-numbing tasks imaginable, I could vouch for the sergeant major's imagination. Within the first week alone, the blisters on my forefinger and thumb bred new blisters quicker than a pair of mating rabbits, but I managed to scissor-cut every blade of grass surrounding the flagpoles at battalion headquarters to a precise two-inch length. Of course, it left me a whole week to paint and repaint each stone in the river-rock border until every one of them had doubled in size.

By the end of my fourteen-day sentence, my brain felt blistered by the sun and the knot in my back managed to creep up my spine, between my shoulders, and seize my neck in place. I could spend the next month beneath the ministrations of the best masseuse in the world and still not be able to walk right.

Fatigued in more ways than one, I finished my last round of painting under the feeble glow from the light over the building's door and the scrutiny of the sergeant major himself. I placed the last rock back into its place and rose to my feet. His eyes narrowed in a disapproving glare as he waited for me to assume the position of parade rest. I muffled a groan against the pain of making muscles which forgot how to function move again.

His eyes slowly dropped from mine to survey my uniform, and I watched his scowl deepen. "Sergeant Peterson, your uniform is a disgrace," he said, just like he had every other night. That made fourteen ruined combats in fourteen days; a sergeant major's fine and we both knew it. "You will report back here tomorrow morning at oh-four-hundred in a clean uniform for personal inspection. At which time you better impress upon me that you are capable of representing this great nation's army to the highest of standards. Am I understood?"

I kept my eyes facing forward, where a rouge gray hair curled out from beneath the sergeant major's cap just over his left ear in the direction the sun retreated hours ago. Twice as long as the remainder, the meager light highlighted it like a fishing line glinting in the twilight. Through the loop, the shadows in the distance played games with my vision, as I could have sworn I saw a black dog watching us, but it disappeared in the blink of an eye.

I refocused my attention on the sergeant major, replaying his statements in my head. "Oh-four-hundred? Yes, Sergeant Major!" I couldn't begin to guess the time, but I doubted four in the morning was more than four hours away.

The expression on his face hardened as if deciding whether or not my attitude warranted insubordination. He stood there for a long moment, and I could feel my body waver, crying for sleep. Then finally, he said, "Dismissed."

I trudged back to barracks and made it up to my room, thankful to find my door un-adorned by prosthetic genitalia. A fresh uniform lay folded on my bed, and I reminded myself to buy Sergeant Sweeney a case of beer for keeping me in uniform.

I ripped off my name tape and insignia in a satisfying scratch of releasing Velcro and transferred them to the new uniform. Thank God I kept at least one set of the hook-and-loop fasteners just in case; I'd have been up shit's creek these past two weeks without them. I draped the replacement uniform, ready-to-wear, over my desk chair, then collapsed unconscious into bed.

5

The following day, the sergeant major sent me back to barracks three times to address minor flaws in my uniform. Eventually, I found and removed all the Irish pennants, and he released me just in time for First Sarge to smoke my ass in morning PT. The tag-team effect left me functioning on an almost animalistic level that no amount of pick-me-up pills could pull me out of.

At least the day's training schedule would keep my body moving with a ten-mile road march followed by weapons quals. Apparently, in Captain Holland's opinion, an infantry unit should be able to march ten miles and still shoot expert. The whole thing put the entire company in a dour mood, but I didn't really care. I just thanked God for muscle memory and added another achievement to my military career—sleep-marching.

"Halt." A hundred and twenty pairs of boots stomped to a stop at First Sarge's command but, still half-asleep, I took an additional step. I asked PFC Stevens to march behind me for just such an occasion, and his meaty hand reached out, grabbed the back of my combats, and hauled me back into position.

"Thanks," I whispered through the side of my mouth. He grunted in reply.

"Left—face." The company turned in unison, but my sleep-deprived brain struggled to process the command, and I turned a half-beat later. I hoped no one noticed, but I caught a twitch in First Sarge's eye as I met his gaze.

"Third platoon, you have the honor of going first and showing us how it's done. I want to see some sharp shooting today. Second platoon, you're on deck. First platoon, you get to take up the rear. First platoon, second squad, report to the ammo shack for reload and brass duty." An inaudible groan emanated from the soldiers beside me as ten sets of eyes stared at me without actually looking; they all knew why we pulled the shit assignment. "Fall out for the safety briefing."

I followed the slumped heads of my squad into the ammo shack. I knew I should say something, but getting my brain to come up with something motivating was like trying to slog through a swamp in concrete boots. Not like anything I could have said would have made a difference. In the army, you get used to shit rolling downhill, and my soldiers just happened to be a little further down the slope from me.

I broke the squad into teams, and we started loading the bins of magazines waiting for us. I joined PFC Stevens at the pile of blue magazines and ripped open a case of 5.56 ammunition. I pulled a box out and pried the cardboard flap open with a forefinger. The edge sliced through the blisters on my finger, and clear fluid oozed out of the wound. An aggravated growl rumbled in my throat as I pushed out the excess fluid and wiped my finger on my new combat trousers, leaving behind a dark smear.

I spilled the box of rounds into the case, then began pressing them into the magazine one at a time. The lingering drainage dripping down my finger made the round slip as I forced them against the heavy spring, and the slide slammed up, pinching the forefinger of my left hand.

"Son of a bitch." I stuck my finger into my mouth to suck away the pain. My squad let out a nearly uniform cackle which, while I couldn't deny deserving, I certainly didn't appreciate considering my lack of sleep. I scooped up a handful of bullets and slammed them into the magazine until it held the required twenty rounds, only managing to pinch my fingers twice more. Each time, the laughter built as I grunted with the pain, but I didn't take my hand off the magazine until I tossed it in a box with two others. "Ha. Ha. Now shut it."

The laughter stopped, though a few of their shoulders still bobbed. I grabbed another magazine and pinched my finger again with the very next round. I growled through gritted teeth but managed to choke back the swear word. *Today is going to be one really—long—shit-day.*

The first members of third platoon collected their magazines and took to the range. The tat—tat—tat staccato of gunfire set off an avalanche of a headache that, while it kept me awake, made it hard to see. The pain pulsed with each of the twenty rounds by twenty soldiers pounding away at my skull like a woodpecker at a tree.

I reached in my pocket and shoved a double-dose of Excedrin into my mouth, chewing two of the pills to expedite the effects. I grimaced at the bitter taste, and PFC Stevens offered me his canteen. I thanked him and took a swig of water to wash the mess down.

The range broke for lunch after third platoon finished, but instead of chowing down our MREs like the rest of the company, I ordered my squad onto the range to police up the brass. They each shot me a wary eye as they each grabbed an empty ammo can and made their way onto the range.

My assistant squad leader, Corporal Henderson, picked up a pair of ammo cans and handed one to me. He glanced over his shoulder and waited for the last soldier to disappear out the doorway before he turned back to me. "Sarge, you doing all right?"

I sluggishly swung my head in his direction in an effort to keep my brain from bouncing around in my skull like a raquetball in a doubles match. "Um...yeah, I'll be fine."

"You sure? You don't look so well. Maybe you should sit here and get some water. I can wrangle up the loose brass."

I stared at the bright light slipping in through the open door. Even from here, it seared into my eyeballs like a hot poker. I closed my eyes in a vain attempt to block out the light and licked my dry lips to steady my voice. "No, I'll be fine."

Outside, the sun burning through a cloudless sky turned my helmet into an improvised oven, and the mixture of light and lingering gunpowder burned my eyes, taking my headache to a level I'd never felt before. I ambled up to the first shooting position and bent over to pick up a spent shell. The blood rushing to my head threatened to topple me to the ground. I dropped to a knee and caught myself with a hand in the sand. Corporal Henderson scoffed as I made a futile effort to disguise the slip by grabbing the nearest shell casing.

I finished collecting my brass without ever getting up off my knees and somehow still managed to be the first to dump my load of shells into the fifty-five-gallon drum. The sound of brass clinking on steel walls pecked at the inside of my skull like tiny hammers. Corporal Henderson and two others dumped their loads in after me, adding to the assault on my sanity.

Out of the corner of my eye, I saw First Sarge storming onto the range. "Sergeant Peterson!" The heat in his voice drew the attention of every one of my squad members. Their heads snapped up then back down with such speed they should all have whiplash.

I swallowed hard; this was not going to be pleasant. With a nod to Corporal Henderson to oversee the collection of brass, I stepped off to intercept First Sarge. At a pace away, I snapped to parade rest, and a bout of nausea nearly took me off balance. Fortunately, my MRE remained safely in its plastic wrapper and not in my stomach, or it would have been a shower that neither First Sarge nor I would have appreciated, though breakfast did come dangerously close.

I swallowed back the bile and said, "Yes, First Sarge?"

"Sergeant, what kind of bullshit are you trying to pull? Have you been deliberately shorting the loads, or do you really expect me to believe that you can't count to twenty?"

My headache threatened to pummel its way out of my skull at the volume of his voice, but it didn't help me understand what he meant. "Shorting? What? No, First Sarge, I would never."

"Well, sergeant, you better double-check each and every magazine coming out of your ammo shack. Cause someone hasn't been putting in full loads. I've had several requests for re-shoots, and Jeeters, Sumpter, and Cole haven't shot less than expert since basic training."

"Yes, First Sarge. I'll see to it personally."

First Sarge jabbed a knife hand in my direction, stopping only an inch from my chest. "You better. I don't care if you have to take your boots off and count on your toes."

"Yes, First Sarge," I shouted enthusiastically despite the echo of pain it caused.

His hand hovered a moment longer before he turned and stomped off in the direction of the range tower.

I waited four pounding beats in my head before I turned to my squad, who were trying hard to look busy dumping shells into the barrel very slowly. "Shit," I muttered under my breath. "Corporal Henderson, get 'em back inside. We need to recheck all our loads."

They upended the last can into the barrel and filed back into the ammo shack without so much as a glance in my direction. No soldier wants to make eye-contact with their NCO right after a chewing like I had just received, and for the devil beating away at the back of my eyes, it's just as well they didn't.

With one hand, I rubbed at my aching temples, and with the other, I pulled out another dose of Excedrin and downed the pills dry. I'd been exhausted before, but I never had a heavy metal band pounding away at the bass drum between my ears like this. I didn't know what was wrong with me, but at the moment, the day couldn't be over soon enough.

I dropped my hand to my side and squinted down range to get my bearings, buying a moment's hesitation before dealing with the recount. My subconscious tried to make some joke about Florida and chads, but in my current state, I couldn't grasp it.

A shadow of a dog dodged across the range, pausing for just an instant on the two-hundred-meter manmade dune in front of me before disappearing over the backstop. It moved too fast to be anything more than my imagination, and I rubbed my eyes to clear my vision before ducking back into the shack.

It took the better part of the lunch break to verify the load in the hundred magazines we prepared. Not one of the ten-shot magazines was off, but nearly a third of the twenties required additional rounds. I kept my tongue silent as I was fairly certain I had loaded each of the short magazines.

When second platoon took to the range, I broke my squad into two, setting half of them to eating their MREs while the rest of us continued to load. The entire squad soon found something to joke and laugh at like the good soldiers they were. I, however, stared solemnly at the rounds I pressed into the magazine in my hand, my vision blurring.

I tapped Corporal Henderson on the shoulder with my completed magazine. "I'm seeing double, and First Sarge will have my ass if I send out another short magazine. I need you to double-check my loads for me." I choked on the words as they left my lips. I hated asking for help, and Corporal Henderson's arched eyebrow was one of the main reasons why, but I couldn't afford another mistake.

He took the proffered magazine and pressed down on the top round. It gave only slightly under his pressure. "You're good, Sarge. I got your back."

The daylight burned on, and we managed to get through the remainder of qualifications without another short magazine, though my headache never lessened. Finally, we each gathered our weapons, collected a set of magazines, and stepped onto the range for our own qualifications.

The sun hung low in the sky, casting long shadows across the range. I laid down on the ground and adjusted the sandbags in front of me until they supported my rifle comfortably. Then resisted the urge to let my eyes close and sleep as I waited for further instructions from the range tower.

The tower cleared the range and made it hot then gave the order I'd been waiting for. "Soldiers, load your twenty-round magazine, and ready your weapon."

I slapped the magazine into the rifle, pulled the charging handle, and tapped the forward assist. I lowered my cheek to the stock and switched the selector switch from safe to semi. A moment later, targets began popping up behind the dunes, and despite my headache, I soon found my rhythm. Identify—aim—breathe out—squeeze—fire.

Twelve shots in, and I hadn't missed yet. The three-hundred-meter target popped up. I aimed and fired, but instead of falling back down, it leapt over the dune. Mid-stride down the hill, it fell to all fours, nearly doubling in size as its head morphed into a melon with menacing inhuman eyes.

My finger froze on the trigger as pain and alarm flared in my skull. The two-fifty-meter target leapt over its own dune, charging in stride with the first werebear. I tried to scream out a warning, but my throat locked in fear. *How did they find me here?*

I regained my presence of mind as the two-hundred-meter target morphed into another werebear and joined the charge. I fired, shifting between the bears. My bullets kicked up dust but didn't even make the werebears flinch. Crack—crack—crack—click. I pressed the release button, and the empty magazine clattered into the sand. My fingers snatched up one of the ten-round magazines, and I slammed it into place.

"Sergeant Peterson, what are you doing?" asked Sergeant Perez from behind me.

I cut my eyes back in her direction. She took a hesitant step up the shallow hill toward my shooting position, half-lifting her range safety paddle. "Matthew, you're not supposed to load until the tower orders you to. Now safe your weapon and put it down." She kept her voice low though she could have shouted and no one except me could have heard her over the echo of gunfire.

"Don't tell me you don't see them," I growled, pressing the bolt release and chambering another round.

"See what? You just blew half your load in the dirt!"

If she couldn't see the pack of werebears charging us, I didn't have time to point them out to her. The thought nagged at my subconscious, but I rolled back onto my elbows and sighted in the werebear now only fifty meters away. I placed the front sight post on the werebears head, trying to track its eye as it ran. *Maybe, just maybe if I shot it through the eye.* My mind raced, though my comprehension lagged. My finger slipped off the guard and dropped to the trigger. My target raced in, only twenty meters away, and as I prepared to shoot, I mentally organized my firing order to the four more behind it. *So many werebears, why aren't the others shooting them?*

Finally, my subconscious screamed through the fog in my brain. *Werebears don't pack!* I forced my finger off the trigger and switched the weapon to safe. *They're just in my imagination.*

Ten meters then five meters.

I put my weapon down and closed my eyes.

Two, one, then…nothing.

I opened my eyes and watched my fifty-meter target drop back down as it timed out. The range became quiet as the other shooters all placed their weapons on safe and put them down.

Boots crunched on gravel as Sergeant Perez knelt beside me. "You all right, Matthew?" Real concern etched her voice.

"Yeah, just a flashback. I'm good now."

Her eyes didn't believe me.

"Seriously. I'm good."

She breathed heavily through her nose, then shook her head as she rose back to her feet. I waited, wondering what she would do, then sighed in relief when she showed the tower the go-side of her paddle.

"Soldiers, load one of your ten-round magazines and ready your weapon," the tower speakers announced.

I pushed the sandbags out of my way and assumed the unsupported prone position. I dropped my sights onto the range and saw a black dog staring back at me from on top of the bullet trap. *What the hell?* The thought barely crossed my mind before the shooting started and the werebears returned.

6

I stormed back into my room and slammed the door as hard as the closer would let me, which meant it bounced off an invisible air cushion and drifted closed with a soft *click*. My closet door, however, jerked open with a more agreeable crash against the stops. I yanked my Class As off the hanger and stripped off the expert qualification badge, losing the pin-backs in the process. I had never scored so poorly in my life. Twenty-five out of forty may have met the Army's minimum standard, but it was well below the company's or mine, and it pissed me off, ghosts of werebears or not.

I tossed the defrocked garment back into the closet and tried not to engage myself in an internal debate of what ghostly werebears said about my sanity; that could wait till morning. My bed called to me with a siren's song that seduced my weary muscles and lulled my aching head. I peeled off my combats and crawled in under the covers, but before I reached my pillow, my phone rang.

I turned the phone over intent on swiping ignore, but Teressa Flannigan's name filled the screen. My head dipped with a moan as I swung my legs over the side of the bed and swiped "answer."

"Hi, Tee." I couldn't keep the exhaustion from my voice.

"Matthew, have you...are you okay? You sound exhausted."

"That's the understatement of the century."

"But it's only eight."

"That's twenty-hundred, military time." She never could make the conversion, and I couldn't help correcting, I always have. "I've had a rough couple of weeks."

"Oh. I'm sorry." Her tone carried a level of shyness to it like she didn't want to impose. "Um…"

"It's fine, Tee. I always have time for you." I forced a little more life into my voice.

"Um. Have you had a chance to talk with Craig yet?"

The heel of my palm slapped into my forehead hard enough to double the pain behind my eyes. "I'm sorry, Tee. I totally forgot." In my defense, I hadn't had time to sleep over the last two weeks, let alone talk Craig into seeing a psychiatrist. The thought reminded me of my own appointment tomorrow afternoon. "My schedule just opened up. I'll give him a call tomorrow and see if we can get some drinks this Saturday."

"Thank you, Matthew," she said, though I could still feel the tension through the phone.

"Tee, how bad is it?" I wanted to know what I was getting myself into. Soldiers could be a finicky lot, especially when you started talking about what's going on between their ears. I should know.

A muted sniffle answered me.

"Tee, are you okay?"

"I don't know. He's hardly been home since he got back. And when he is…it's like he's not really here. He won't talk to me, and some of the other wives say I should call his CO, but…"

"Don't do that. Not yet. Let me try to talk to him first." I swallowed, trying to figure out a better way to ask my next question, but couldn't think of one. "Has he hit you, Tee?"

"No. No. He's never done that."

My lips scrunched together in a consoling grimace. "All right then. I'll do what I can."

I didn't know what else to say, but at the same time, I didn't know how to say goodbye, so I listened to her breathing. It broke my heart to hear it shudder with tears. I let the silence drag on until it became awkward then racked my sleep-deprived brain for something consoling to say.

"Tee…I…" I began, but she cut in.

"Thank you, Matthew," she sobbed then hung up before I could reply.

My hand with the phone dropped to my lap, and I stared at her name until the screen faded to black. I debated calling Craig before I forgot, but

I didn't have the mental capacity to deal with him directly at the moment. Instead, I settled for negotiations by text message.

You up for drinks Saturday?

His reply came back before I could put my phone back on the charger. *You buying?*

I shrugged my shoulders then typed back, *Sure.*

Then I'm in—McNamara's?

The heavy groan rumbling deep in my throat sounded more like a growl. I could never figure out what Craig saw in the place. It tended to cater to a few too many locals with a penchant for picking fights with military personal than I liked. But on the other hand, they had darts and offered two-dollar drafts for happy hour; or at least they had a few years ago when Craig and I found the place.

Savannah was my biggest problem with McNamara's. I loved the city, but not the forty-five-minute drive, especially since I didn't have a car. Though, finding someone to bum a ride with shouldn't be a problem; there was always someone going to the city on a weekend who could use a few extra bucks for gas. Getting back, on the other hand...well, it wouldn't be the first time I took an Uber that far.

Why not. Happy Hour.

10-4.

"There you go, Tee. I just hope it doesn't turn into a clusterfuck of a shouting match like last time," I muttered, placing my phone on the wireless charging pad. I rubbed my temples and blew out the ball of frustration churning in my gut.

In my peripheral vision, I could see my pillow illuminated in the fading light of my phone. "You know what, Craig? You're a problem for Saturday." I maneuvered myself beneath the sheets once more and found blessed sleep within moments.

The following morning, I woke five minutes before my alarm went off and stretched stiff muscles with a smile. Slept in till oh-five-hundred, no sergeant major's inspection, and I'd still make PT. It was shaping up to be a fabulous day.

The tightness eventually left my limbs over the course of the five-mile run, and I managed to finish without uttering a single lyrical double entendre. After a hardy breakfast, we cleaned our weapons from yesterday's qualifications, and I remained in high spirits. No headaches and no phantom werebear attacks; it was amazing what a full night's rest could do for the mind.

The only cloud of the day came at fifteen hundred hours when I stood immobile in front of a heavy wooden door bearing a brass placard reading "Doctor Swartz, MD Psychiatrist." Something about that last word deflated my sails, and I halted my hand only inches from the doorknob. I couldn't quite figure out what kept me from opening the door because if it went as well as I hoped, I could cancel my appointment with Major Daniels.

While I still tried to convince my fingers to grasp the handle, the door opened, and a woman with dark hair in a smart business suit walked into me.

She dropped her purse and stumbled in her heels at the impact. Instinctually, I reached out and caught her to keep her from falling. In that instant, my mind flashed back to a wrestling match with a werebear in a poorly lit cave as it shifted back to human form, and I got an unintentional handful of breast. I snatched my hand back from the woman in front of me as if burned.

She made a startled noise and placed a hand on her chest, breathing a little hard.

"Um. I'm sorry, ma'am. Excuse me."

Her free hand moved to my arm, gripping it for stability as she took a few more settling breaths to regain her composure. "Oh, you scared me." Her voice reminded me of my sister.

I reached down and picked up her oversized leather purse. It felt heavier than I expected, but she slung it easily over her shoulder when I handed it back to her. "Again, I'm sorry about running into you."

Her lips curled in a polite smile, but she still sounded a bit winded when she spoke. "Thanks. Um…I really need to get going."

I looked over my shoulder to the empty hallway behind me. "Oh, I'm sorry," I said, taking a quick step back from the door to clear her way.

The carpet muffled the sound of her heels as she walked briskly down the hall, while I tried to suppress the memories of a very alluring and very deadly werebear playing at the edges of my mind. The doctor's door clicked closed, snapping me back to the present with a jolt. I lifted a hand to the doorknob and stared as my fingertips vibrated inches from the chrome handle. *Maybe I really do need to talk to someone,* I thought, though I doubted Doctor Swartz would find my fascination with werebears anything less than a justifiable reason to commit me. I needed to discuss it with someone who knew the truth. I needed to find that monster hunter,

Jacob McGinnis's, phone number when I got back to barracks and give him a ring.

With an effort of will, I pushed the door open and balled my hands into fists to stop their shaking as I entered the office. The small waiting room contained a pair of leather chairs with a side table beneath an over-flowing selection of outdated magazines between them. A taller table topped with a large touch-screen computer stood adjacent to the open door on the opposite side of the room. A laminated sign taped to the wall above it read, "Please sign in."

The door closed behind me, and the balding man sitting behind a desk in the adjoining room looked up. A smile bunched his cheeks in stacks of wrinkles. "Ah, Sergeant Peterson, please sign in and have a seat. I'll be with you in a moment." The man returned to the notebook in front of him and scribbled away feverishly.

I signed in on the computer, electronically acknowledging the half dozen forms and detailing my family history of mental illness as best as I could attest to. Which pretty much amounted to a hill of beans, as I never did find the checkbox for crazy son-of-a-bitch father.

Finished, I waited only a few minutes before the doorway to the inner office darkened with a short man in khakis and a sweater-vest over a long-sleeve plaid button-up shirt. I couldn't see how he could wear so many layers while beads of sweat rolled down my back in the warmth of his under-performing office AC. Then again, dressed in my combat uniform with the sleeves buttoned around my wrists, I couldn't really judge.

He extended his hand as he approached. "Sergeant Peterson, I'm Dexter Swartz."

I stood and pumped his hand. "Doctor."

"No. Please, in my office, it's just Dexter. I like to keep our discussions a bit less formal than I'm sure you're normally used to."

"Uh...okay, Dexter." The lack of an honorific made his name feel thick like molasses on my tongue.

"Please, come in my office," he said, leading the way back into the inner room. He waited by the door for me to enter before closing it. "Please, sit wherever is comfortable."

The seating options varied from a chaise lounge in one corner to an oversized stuffed armchair, to a rocker, to even an old gothic stiff-backed wooden chair. For some reason I couldn't really explain, the gothic torture seat called to me, and I sat with my back rigidly pressed into the ornate carvings.

Doctor Swartz gave me another friendly smile as he sat in the rocker and crossed his right leg over his left before folding his hands in his lap. If he grew a half a foot, gained another hundred pounds, and started smoking a pipe, he'd be the spitting image of my grandfather. However, despite the lack of physical resemblance, his gentle rocking brought back fond memories of a man I sorely missed.

"Now, please. Tell me how I can help you?" he asked, and the bubbles of warm memories evaporated in an instant.

I swore if he said *please* one more time, I'd reconsider Major Daniels. "Could you please…ah…just not use so many pleases."

"Certainly. Sorry about that." A firmer expression replaced the smile on his face. Not so much in displeasure, but more like he couldn't smile without saying that damn word. "So, what brings you into my office?"

7

My extended two-hour soul-baring session with Doctor Swartz brought more tears to my eyes than a Barbara Walters interview. Except this interview wouldn't see prime-time and left me with a battery of follow-up appointments intent on ruining every free weekend I had. They started with *Coping with Grief and Loss* this Sunday, followed by *Adult Survivors of Child Abuse* the following Sunday, and then *Veterans with PTSD* the one after that.

I was just beginning to accept having my free time reduced to nights and a single weekend a month when Doctor Swartz cut it in half yet again with a three-month plan of personal one-on-one sessions to work through any lingering issues. I stumbled to the door clutching a stack of brochures and papers, feeling overwhelmed and drained.

Doctor Swartz held the door for me and placed a hand on my shoulder as I passed by. It carried a warmth I've rarely experienced in my life. That alone convinced me to cancel my appointment with Major Daniels.

My lips curled in a weak smile, which he returned with confidence and understanding. "Thanks."

"Certainly, Matthew. It was my pleasure. Now, don't lose my phone number. You can call me anytime, day or night."

I nodded and stepped through the door before a thought occurred to me. "Doc, I got a battle buddy of mine who lost his dad a couple of years ago. Would it be all right if I brought him along with me to the…uh?" I flipped through the handful of pamphlets looking for the right title.

His eyebrow shot up when I called him Doc but quickly dropped as a broad grin scrunched up his face. *"Coping with Grief and Loss*, or just G-and-L if it's easier. But, *please*, feel free to bring him along. It's open to all vets."

He stressed the word *please*, teasingly pointing out how he hadn't used the word since I asked him to stop. It cut through the quagmire of emotions boiling inside me and brought out a chuckle. "Point taken, *Dexter*. I'll see you there." I shook his proffered hand and headed back to post.

By the time I got back to post, my unit had been released for the weekend, and I headed straight up to my barracks room. The load of paperwork made a sloppy pile as I dumped it onto the corner of my desk and pulled Jonny's journal off the bookshelf. I flipped open the cover and retrieved Jacob McGinnis's business card from one of the slots inside.

My thumb hovered over the keypad to my phone as I stared at the card in my other hand. I hadn't mentioned the visions or werebears to Doctor Swartz, but even so, he almost had me convinced werebears and monsters were nothing more than figments of my imagination.

I spent a few minutes considering the M.H. following Jacob's name while I relived the confrontation with the werebears we had taken down together. Absently my hand drifted to the now healed bullet wound I took fighting one. No, I would never be able to believe they didn't exist again.

I dialed his number and placed the phone to my ear. It rang twice before I heard the sweet soprano of a young female voice instead of the gruff old man I had expected.

"Hello, Mr. McGinnis's phone."

"Um, can I speak to Jacob, please?"

"He is currently unavailable. How may I help you?"

Something in my brain finally clicked, and I recognized the voice. "Gracie?"

She hesitated, and I could hear the caution in her tone. "Who is this?"

"Gracie, it's Matthew Peterson. Jacob helped me with a werebear problem a few months ago in upstate New York."

Her words came back in a shy whisper. "Matthew? The Peterson Apostle?"

"Well, I can't say I'm a huge fan of that nickname, but yeah, it's me."

"Um, sorry. It's just what Gramps calls you." Her voice gained a little more strength as she spoke. "So, have you called to let him know about the offer?"

I'm not sure what caught me off-guard more, her calling Jacob *Gramps,* or the fact he'd told her about asking me to take over his monster hunter reigns. Either way, it took me a second to remember what I called for.

"No. No, I haven't made my mind up about that yet. Though, there is something else I really need to talk to him about. Do you know when he might be available?"

"Not really. He's off with the Cardinal on some church thing. I'm just manning his phone until he comes home."

"Shit." The word slipped out of my mouth before I could bite it back.

"It's that important, eh?"

I blew out a heavy sigh. "I had a question about werebears."

The shyness left her voice completely. "What's your question? Maybe I can help?"

"Well, since I don't have anyone else to ask, is it possible that the were-bear I wrestled with did something to my brain? Like...I don't know. Poison it or something?"

"Poison? No, werebears can't do that. Why do you ask?"

I rubbed at the tension building in my forehead and told her about the vision of werebears at the range.

I heard some clicking on a keyboard before she said, "No. There's no record of werebears ever being able to mess with someone's mind. Not like that. Um...it could be stress. Maybe PTSD?" She floated the sugges-tion with a huge heaping of caution like she was skating on thin ice and could see the cracks spiderwebbing across the pond.

It made me laugh, not the ha-ha funny kind, but the ironic burst of noise like a farm animal kind. "I'm already seeing a doctor about that."

"Oh, sorry." Her voice wore an apology I could hear through the phone.

"No. No. Don't worry about it. A couple weeks ago, I...um..." For some reason, I couldn't quite tell Gracie about the dingle-dangle incident. My mouth just wouldn't form the words. She waited silently, the gentle sighs of her breathing the only sound in my phone. As the seconds ticked by, the more uncomfortable it got until I couldn't take it anymore. "Let's just say I got caught up in a cadence and couldn't stop singing it. Even after I was ordered to."

"Why would they order you to?"

"We were running in a residential area, and it wasn't exactly an appropriate kind of cadence for small ears."

"Oh." The way she drew the word out made it sound more dismissive than understanding. "I see."

I suddenly felt defensive. "I didn't mean to sing it. It just came out, and I couldn't stop."

"Hmm."

"What?"

"Did anything else seem out of place? Maybe something that happened both times."

"Ahh…" I dragged the word out, racking my brain. "Well—there was this black dog. I saw it at the cadence thing and then again at the rifle range. Why?"

"A hunch, but I want to check on some stuff first. It may be nothing, but there are a few creatures with some mind-bending powers. It might be one of them or nothing at all. It's hard to tell. I've got your number; I'll call you if I figure anything out. Call me if something happens again or if you find out whose dog that is."

"You want me to call you on Jacob's phone?" I asked.

She snorted into the phone, and then her voice dropped back to just more than a whisper. "No. I pushed my phone number into your contacts. Later," she said before the phone fell silent.

I pulled the phone away from my ear and scrolled through my contacts. A dozen M-names drifted up the page until "McGinnis, Gracie" appeared. I opened the contact, but while the call icon lit up, the word *unlisted* showed in the phone number field. I didn't even know my phone could do that. Then again, I shouldn't have been too surprised considering how it got there. I scrolled further down and found Jacob listed in my contacts as well, though I never entered his information. While I appreciated the help, the digital insertion made my skin crawl. I got more than enough of that kind of big brother help in the army.

Werebears plagued my dreams as I slept, or, more specifically, a particular werebear. Large and dark, circling me in a cave looking for the perfect time to strike. Derived from memory, the dream-werebear lacked the shadow and mysticism of the attack on the range. This beast came with very real fear and adrenaline, and I woke up drenched in sweat.

With the memories still fresh in my mind, I reconsidered the incident on the range. The whole thing made me uneasy in a way I couldn't quite put my finger on. Perhaps it was the stress of spending two weeks under the sergeant major's thumb tainting my recollection, but something about it felt...manufactured.

Sweat dripped from my nose, and I snapped my towel off the back of my closet door. However, with the towel still wet from my earlier shower, running it over my face did little more than smear the sweat and make room for additional droplets to bead up in their place. Disgusted, I threw the towel against the closet door with a splat and settled for turning down the thermostat instead. As the AC strained to control the heat of the midsummer night, I crawled back into bed and closed my eyes. I had no intention of wasting my first opportunity, in two weeks, to sleep in on a Saturday morning worrying over the origin of phantom werebears.

I spent the remainder of the night and half the following morning in a comatose state from which not even the beginning of Armageddon could wake me. A large lunch and a lazy afternoon left me feeling almost like a new man or, at the very least, the closest to normal as I'd felt in ages. That was until the time came for me to meet up with Craig and a sense of foreboding dampened my mood.

M y ride pulled up to a one-story wooden building with dark alleyways to either side that made its neighbors appear to shy away in an effort to avoid catching the urban plague. I passed a ten to the driver for gas and slid out of the back seat of a Chevy Geo packed fuller than a clown car. Not exactly the bummed ride I hoped for, but it got me here. The car pulled away as I looked up at McNamara's neon sign dangling at a precarious angle from a single chain. It swung in the gentle breeze, and a faulty electrical connection made the flickering green light cast fluttering shadows across the peeling paint.

The passing hands of customers wore a muted shine into the dark patina of age adorning the brass pull on the honey-colored oak front door. My own hand buffed the handle as I pulled the door open with a jingle of the bells hung above it. The vintage smell of beer and greasy food greeted me with the cool embrace of air conditioning. The door slapped the bells a second time as it closed behind me, and the bartender looked up to give me a wave with the mostly white cloth he used to shine the glasses. I nodded a greeting back at him, and he returned to the glass in his hand, his mop of greasy salt-and-pepper hair swaying to his efforts.

I worked my way through the scattering of tables filling the room in front of the horseshoe bar dominating the better part of the east wall. Navigating the haphazard placement of the tables actually got easier the drunker you were, and I intended to achieve that particular state of being as quickly as possible. In my haste to find the bottom of a glass, I banged my knee hard on the seat of a chair someone left turned around backward.

"Son of a bitch," I growled through gritted teeth in a vulgar attempt to banish away the pain. I lifted my glower from the offending chair in search of witnesses to my stupidity.

With the exception of a handful of regulars too engrossed with the drinks in their hands to have noticed, the majority of the room was deserted. *I'm not early, am I?* I thought with a glance at my watch, which read seventeen-ten. I did the conversion to civilian time in my head as I checked the blackboard above the register. Happy hour started ten minutes ago, at five p.m.—yesterday.

"So much for the cheap beers," I grumbled while mentally deducting my recent investment in uniforms from my paltry bank account. "Good thing I brought the Visa."

I rounded the end of the bar to the dart lanes. Two cork dartboards hung on the far burlap-covered wall. A pair of high-top tables crowded the fragmented scraps of white paint on the floor marking the throw line about a foot short of regulation distance.

I selected the high-top table closest to the wall. "Still there," I said with a grin at seeing Craig and my names etched into the surface along with the dozens of others.

My hand slipped into my pocket in search of my dart tin but found nothing but bits of pocket fuzz. I emptied my other pockets but only came up with my phone, room key, and wallet.

"Shit," I said, realizing exactly where I left them. Back on my desk, in barracks. I let out a resigned sigh. At least I still had my wallet; otherwise, tonight would have been awkward.

A practiced hand slid a bowl of peanuts across a marred tabletop. "Whatcha say, Honey? I didn't quite catch that."

My eyes rose from the peanuts to a pair of skin-tight blue jeans then up to a white button-up straining so hard to remain closed over an ample chest that the black tank top beneath was the only thing keeping it modest. Further up, my eyes found a stern face that didn't quite go with the body wearing it.

"Uh...nothing. Just pissed I forgot my darts at home."

Her features softened in a pleasant smile. "No worries, Hun. We rent them if you want."

"Yes, please, and a round of drafts for me and my friend. He should be here shortly."

"You got it, Hun."

She returned a moment later with four glasses of beer on a tray. "Didn't want to keep you waiting for a refill," she said with a wink, then placed the beers and a set of house darts on the table.

"Thanks," I drawled with a raised eyebrow and a questioning glance around the vacant room. She just gave me a wink and sashayed away.

I forced my eyes away and perused the table tent while nursing a beer and waiting for Craig. My eyes drifted over the weekend specials to the picture of a bronze dart filling the lower half of the tent. Tucked up in the crook of the dart, as if hiding from view, the price read fifteen dollars an hour.

I exchanged the table tent for a dart with a bent point. The teeth marks ruining the plastic flight only needed a good set of dental records for a positive identification. "Fifteen dollars an hour—for this?"

Well shit, I'm not going to waste fifteen dollars an hour waiting for Craig. I tilted back my glass in a salute to the thought and drained the amber liquid in one long fluid chug. I crushed a thumb painfully to the side of the dart's point until it shifted into something resembling alignment with the barrel. Satisfied, my arm snapped out, and the dart hit the board with a gratifying thunk.

Playing right versus left, I managed to beat myself four games out of five by the time Craig strolled across the room in a pair of bedazzled skinny jeans and a half-buttoned paisley shirt. An onyx encrusted dog-shaped medallion dangled from an ornate gold chain and danced through his exposed chest hair like a pup running through tall pasture grass. The whole getup looked so ridiculous on him that I suspiciously examined the half-empty glass in my hand. Though, considering the two empty glasses already collecting suds on the table, it could only be blamed for the beginnings of a good buzz and not my friend's fashion tastes.

Finishing off the beer, I raised the empty glass in a mock salute. "Craig, good to see you. Even if you are a hair late." The glass clinked with the others as I placed it on the table.

He raised an eyebrow at the collection of empties. "Couldn't wait for me, could ya?"

"I drink when I throw and at fifteen dollars an hour? Hell, no. I wasn't going to wait for you." The darts rattled as I dropped them on the table in a manner I never would have handled my own, but then again, mine actually fly true. I gave him a lopsided grin and pushed the remaining full glass in his direction. "But I'm pretty sure you'll have no trouble catching up."

8

Craig shrugged his shoulders and lifted the corner of his mouth in a mischievous grin. He lifted the glass in a toast. "I'll do my best." Tipping the beer back, he drained it in one long, smooth go. As the last drops disappeared, he waved the empty glass at the waitress across the room. She gave him an acknowledging nod, and he added the glass to the others.

He picked up one of the battered darts and crinkled his nose as if catching a whiff of some foul stench. The sneer grew as he straightened the crumpled flight. "So, Matthew, it's been a while. I'm guessing my lovely wife sent you." His tone remained level and flat, with only a snap of his arm toward the dartboard to punctuate his statement. The dart left his fingers and sailed across the room, landing with a thump that pulled at my attention, but I kept my eyes locked on his.

"I suppose she asked you to convince me to see a shrink." Another snap of the arm, without looking, and another thump. "I suppose you thought beer would mollify me to your charmed life." Thump!

Only after he threw the third dart did I break eye contact and check the board. Buried up to their shafts, all three darts shared the tiny red bullseye. Any other day my jaw would have been on the floor, but he came out swinging, and while we both knew the truth of the first two statements, the third one touched a nerve. We'd been down this road before, and I couldn't believe he still had the audacity to call my life blessed, just because my abusive old man outlived his loving father.

A furnace ignited in my chest and flushed my face with a heat I couldn't stomp back down. I turned slowly, letting the embers come to life in my eyes. "Charmed? Fuck you. By the way, Paul's dead, not that his passing brought me a whole lot of grief, but Jonny's suicide certainly did." I spat the words accusingly at him, like darts aiming for his heart.

Something broke in his stone-hard expression, and I could almost see sympathy in his eyes as his hand drifted to my forearm. "I'm sorry. I didn't know."

The empty glasses wobbled as I snatched my arm back and grazed them with an elbow. "How the hell would you? You weren't...Damnit. I could have used my best friend." The venom I began the statement with didn't make it to the end as the ice of a lost friendship cooled the fire within to forgotten embers. I strode to the board where I yanked the darts free.

His beady eyes watched me stalk back to the table, and I thought I saw the flicker of something cross them. Regret—possibly, but they narrowed back to black wells too deep to read before I made it back to the table.

"Matthew, we haven't been friends for a long time."

My head swung in bitter remorse; he was right, but hell if it was my fault.

"Boy's night out?" The waitress flashed us both an infectious smile as she dropped off a pair of fresh beers and loaded the empties onto her tray. "Can I get y'all anything else?"

"Nope. Just keep these coming," I said, raising one of the new glasses to my lips.

"Sure enough, Honey," She said with a wink before she turned to go.

I watched her sculpted jeans walk away until the weight of the glass in my hand drew my attention back to the table. I pushed the other glass to Craig, breaking the spell-lock on his own eyes. "Look, the beer is flowing, and we have the dart lanes to ourselves. Let's forget everything else and just play like old times."

He took the glass and drained half of it without touching it to mine. "Fine, let's play," he said, taking the darts from my hand and throwing them into the center of the bull's eye once more. At least this time, he looked at the board first.

"I see you've been practicing."

"The sandbox gave me plenty of time."

"Well, I guess it's a good thing I'm already buying the drinks then," I said with an uncomfortable chuckle.

As promised, the drinks flowed, and we played darts like old times, except he beat me nine times out of ten instead of the other way around. After my latest loss, I drained my beer and added it to the stack of spent glasses, which momentarily doubled in my vision.

"I'm not sure how you talked me into a..." A belch erupted from my throat and cut off my slurred words turning more than a few heads. "Sorry, but why did I ever agree to a drinking game?"

I didn't catch Craig's response as my attention drifted to a giant of a man with a Hooter's-inspired style and a chest big enough to charge *Custom Iron—Gym and Fitness* billboard rates for advertising. Explosions of muscles threatened to split his scandalously tight shorts in two as they roped their way down his legs. He mopped at the sweat flowing from his bald head with a towel as if he only just stopped pumping iron long enough to walk into McNamara's.

The man's every step shook the floor beneath my feet, and I clutched the table for support. Craig, however, apparently couldn't feel the quaking earth and shot me a bemused look. He then followed my gaze over his shoulder. His eyes doubled in size, and his lips moved silently, forming the word, *damn*. I swallowed hard and bobbed my head in drunken agreement.

A second man dressed in chinos and a loose-fitting linen shirt rounded the bulk of the first to join him at the table beside us. His broad shoulders and thick arms would have been imposing on their own, if not for Paul Bunyan standing next to him. Unlike the gym rat, whose mass forced him to move in stiff sweeping motions, the other man moved in the fluid economy and grace of a stalking mountain lion. A small gold hoop in his left ear peeked out through wavy black hair, and his neat beard ended in a braid. He had the appearance of a man you don't forget meeting, but for the life of me, I couldn't place where I'd seen him before.

The smaller man, well, smaller like a super-duty king cab was smaller than a Peterbilt, pulled out a dart tin with calligraphic artwork inspired by the Kama Sutra. He opened the lid, and either it had a holographic film or all those beers gave me one hell of a pair of beer goggles, but I swear the multi-armed characters on the lid gyrated to the music coming from the jukebox across the room. He tipped the tin, and my mouth dropped open as he showed off the set of emerald embedded golden darts to Bunyan.

"I've got to hit the latrine," Craig said, but when I didn't acknowledge him, he socked me in the arm, and I teetered unsteadily. "Hey, Matthew, I'm gonna take a piss, order me another beer."

Still gripping the table, I recovered my balance and gave him a confused look as my inebriated mind processed what he said. "Huh? Oh, yeah. Sure." I watched him walk away sure-footed and re-evaluated my share of the stack of empty glasses on the table. It tallied to more beers than I had in the last few months. *And when did we do shots? I think it's about time I cut myself off before I end up in the hospital with alcohol poisoning —again.*

I caught the waitress's attention after she took Bunyan's and Beard-braid's order.

"Can I get you another round, Hun?" she asked, spinning around to my table.

"Um...no. Just another for my friend." I struggled to keep my words from slurring. "I think I need to switch to coffee."

She propped the edge of her tray on the table and transferred the forest of glasses to it. "Of course, Hun."

She left, and a moment later, a shadow stretched across my table. I looked to the lamp overhead, figuring the bulb had blown, but saw Bunyan's noggin instead. Startled, I stepped back into the wall.

The big man dominated my vision, and I didn't notice Beard-braid stepping up beside me until he spoke. "Hello, friend. I am Nadeem." He lifted a manicured hand to his chest and dipped his head. His voice carried a hint of a middle-eastern accent that made me wonder what he was doing in a hillbilly bar in Georgia. "And this is Bobby." A bracelet dangled from the wrist of the hand he lifted toward Bunyan. A lone golden dog charm bejeweled in black gems caught the light before his sleeve fell back over it.

Neither of them offered their hand to me, and I didn't offer them mine. My mind struggled to sober up in response to something about the way they stood. "What can I do for you gentlemen?" I managed to keep my words and my stance solid.

Bunyan leaned a bit further over the table aggressively. "I didn't like the way you were gawking at me, boy."

My rage bubbled at being called boy, but I forced it back down. For all his muscles, the caveman in front of me didn't have the first clue on how to fight; otherwise he wouldn't have presented his throat as such an easy target. Still, I lightened my grip on the table, ready to act, as his threat beat away at my inebriation. Keeping one eye on the standing hormone, I directed my question to Nadeem. "And you, sir? Was I gawking at you as well?"

"No, friend. I simply saw you noticed these darts I have for sale." He placed the dart case on the table. The characters adorning the lid twisted into a sexual position that even a contortionist would find difficult.

My eyes rested on the case, and I had never wanted anything more. Lust pulled my hand toward the box.

"Hey, those are mine," Bunyan chimed in a childish outburst. His meaty hand reached out to my shoulder.

Between his sudden movement and my excited drunken state, I reacted without thinking. Instead of reaching for the box, I knife-handed the thug in the throat. He stumbled back from the table and clawed at his neck as he bent over, wheezing for air.

Chairs scuffed back as customers from several of the neighboring tables rose to their feet. I turned in their direction and recognized the same gym logo stretched thinly across many of their barrel chests.

"Shit," I said, searching for the best way out as a handful of them took a step forward. Behind the wall of steroid-inflated human flesh, I watched the remaining patrons, and even the waitress and bartender, scurry out the front door. I glanced in the direction of the bathrooms hoping for a little help from Craig, but only found a neon-green shamrock flickering on the wall.

Bunyan's brute-squad halted at his raised hand. "Mine," he croaked.

Nadeem stepped back, leaving the box of copulating creatures on the table in front of me. His own hands raised defensively. "Hey, I don't want any trouble. You keep them." His voice trembled, but I could see a slight smile teasing up the corners of his mouth, and the whites of his eyes disappeared behind growing irises that caught the light much like an animal's.

The box on the table glowed in the cheap fluorescent lighting of the bar, drawing the attention of myself and everyone else. The characters on the cover ground against each other, humping faster than any porn I'd ever seen. The sight of it filled me with a sense of animalistic desire.

What the hell is wrong with me? I thought, reaching a longing hand out for the box. My phone rang, dancing on the table as it vibrated. The bell tone broke the spell, and I looked up to a wall of muscle stepping across the floor, closing in like a gate on a massive human cage. Their eyes flicked jealously between me and the case. Even Bunyan managed to stop coughing and brought himself erect, greed and hatred filling his eyes.

The ringing of my phone changed mid-ring to the yipping chorus of "What Does a Fox Say?" Startled by the sudden change in ringtone, I picked the phone up and held it to my ear without taking my eyes off Bunyan and his brood.

"What?"

Gracie's voice filled the other end. "Matthew? Oh, thank God. I thought I might be too late. I'm not exactly sure, but I think that dog you keep seeing may be a djinn or maybe a…"

I cut her off. "Gracie? I really don't have time right now. Some asshole just left me a box of gold darts, and the whole bar is looking at me like I stole their baby."

9

I heard Gracie beat away at her keyboard faster than tornado driven hail on a tin roof. With each heartbeat, I waited as the press of steroid-fueled muscle closed in like the walls of a trash compactor.

"I...I...he must have enchanted it."

"Probably," I said in a strained voice that leapt an octave as Bruno, the frontman of the brute-squad tossed the stools out of his way. Murderous wouldn't even begin to describe the look he gave me. Despite the odds, my body moved of its own accord, and my hand reached out to keep the box from him.

"Whatever you do, don't touch it!" Gracie shouted through the phone as if she saw me move.

In a conditioned response to a direct order, my fingers wrapped around the table's edge to halt their advance. Then taking a cue from Bruno, I leaned my weight into heaving the high-top into him and his compatriots, or at least I tried to. The damn thing was bolted to the floor, and I managed to strain my shoulder with the effort. Worse, I hurled myself back toward Bunyan rather than flinging the table at his friends.

A meaty hand seized me by the shoulder, and Bunyan's thick sausage fingers dug painfully into my flesh as if he intended to rip my arm out of its socket.

I swung my opposite leg and connected with the side of the brute's knee. It gave a pop as something dislocated, and he let out a holler. His grip on my shoulder changed from malicious to a desperate grasp for support, not that it mattered as his bulk pulled us both to the floor. I rolled with the momentum to land on top of him, adding my weight to his as his ruined knee collided with the concrete floor.

He screamed, and his posse surged forward. Some part of the back of my drunken brain laughed, *Cry havoc and release the dogs of war!*

I rolled off Bunyan's writhing form and sprung back to my feet. Somehow, I kept the phone in my hand but didn't have time to put it in my pocket before the first sledgehammer of a fist came flying at my head. I ducked under the blow and slammed my right fist, phone and all, into the guy's solar plexus. He stumbled to the side, gasping for breath. The impact shattered the phone's screen, and the edges of the glass cut into my fingers.

A pair of python arms wrapped around me, pinning my own to my sides. Between the jolt and my blood-slicked fingers, my phone slipped from my grasp as the arms lifted me off my feet and crushed the air from my lungs.

I drove my heel back and up. My first strike caught his thigh and the pressure trying to introduce my spine to my chest doubled. My second strike rang the twin knockers with enough force that even his steroid-shriveled jewels cracked.

He let out a yelp worthy of a position on a children's choir in the soprano section. His arms slackened, and I drove my head back into his nose with a satisfying crunch. Though I didn't find the pain flaring in my skull all that delightful.

With three of their number on the floor, the rest of the muscle held back, re-evaluating their strategy. Just like Bunyan, they all counted on their size to intimidate, but not one of them actually knew how to fight. They looked from one another to me, to the box and then back to me. Unwilling to give up the prize, but also not sure how to deal with the rabid badger in front of them.

I pulled in precious gulps of air as I surveyed my working space. Bunyan lay to my right, clutching at his knee. I doubted he'd be leaving in anything less than a wheelchair. *Neutralized, just don't trip over him.* I noted in my head.

Solar Plexus worked his way back to an upright position and appeared to be regaining his breath. He looked pissed and dumb enough to believe I only got lucky the first time. *Roid-Rage-One back in action.*

Blood spilled from Choir Boy's broken nose as he crawled away from the fight. That left four Mr. Universe wannabes and one inebriated moron. I only hoped the moron could outwit the cavemen.

Solar Plexus was the first to attack. He bellowed out a war cry and charged, but didn't see the prone Bunyan between us. Bunyan yelped and rolled beneath the other bodybuilder's weight. I stepped to the side as the unstable footing sent Solar Plexus careening past me and into the wall headfirst. His eyes rolled back into his head, and he crashed to the floor, motionless.

Make that three cavemen.

The next thug moved in, rolling his shoulders and popping his pecs as if it would scare me. He took wide waddling steps, swinging tree trunk sized thighs around each other.

I hopped over Bunyan toward the dartboards, evaluating the approaching hulk's weak spots. It doesn't matter how much iron someone can press; every person has their weak points, and the big guys are usually too full of themselves to see them. Hulk wasn't any different. He kept his hands low, protecting his groin and his solar plexus like I would go for the same target twice. Well, I would if he was dumb enough to leave them exposed, but he already forgot how I took Bunyan down the first time.

He took a lumbering step over Bunyan, dropping his eyes to the floor to place his foot, and I sprung. What looked to be more than four feet between us evaporated in a moment, and my hand snapped at his throat.

He reacted instinctually, flinching back and bringing an arm up to defend. His foot came down on Bunyan, and the other man slashed an arm out under the pain.

With my assailant's balance thrown, I threw a kick at his gut, but I was too close for full extension and too far away to connect with a knee. The blow did little more than drive him stumbling back as he disentangled himself from Bunyan.

A crashing sound came from the direction of the remaining two, and I saw them both holding remnants of chairs in their hands.

So much for fighting fair, not that a fight ever is. I retreated to the dart-board and retrieved my tattered darts. *Three darts, three opponents.*

I made a feint at one of the brutes. The one on the left made a wild defensive swing with his new club, and his friend barely ducked under it in time. When he stood back up, he shoved his reckless companion to the other side of the narrow dart ally. Once they gave each other some swinging room, hungry smiles broke across their faces. They had my back against the wall—literally—and they knew it.

I needed to think, but my head pounded from using it as a battering ram, and my side ached in the familiar pain of several cracked ribs.

The unarmed hulk searched about for a weapon. Apparently, he didn't want to be the only one to have to get within arm's length to beat the hell out of me.

The barbarian to my right swept a hand across Craig's and my table, throwing the contents at me. I raised a hand to shield my face, but the glass salt and pepper shakers still stung as they bounced off my chest before clattering to the floor along with the table tent. The glowing dart box, however, sailed a bit further to my left and smacked into the wall with a muted thud. It drew our eyes like moths to a flame.

The characters pounded away raucously in time with the pulsing light that now appeared to come from the box itself. Desire welled up inside of me, and I took a covetous step in its direction. I sensed more than saw the others do the same. Even Bunyan squirmed along the floor toward it.

Somewhere beyond the rushing beat of blood flowing through my ears, I heard my phone cry out once more with "What Does a Fox Say?" The ringtone wedged its way into my brain and pried my mind free of the trance. Then my phone died under the crushing weight of a two-ton diesel giant with a yip and a squawk of a dying dog.

The siren song of the box immediately tried to pull me back in. But before I lost myself to its enchanting call, I stepped up and kicked it. The box skated across the floor, spinning like a hockey puck and pulling the diesel giant's and the barbarian's head as if connected by leads hooked through their noses.

The shot sailed cleanly between the hulk's feet, ricocheted off the wall behind him, then slipped beneath a table. The hulk bent in two, turned clumsily, and chased after the box like an oversized toddler running down his favorite toy.

I resisted the urge to chase after it myself and used the distraction to work my escape. I leapt over Bunyan, and his meaty hand reached out and hooked my leg. I pitched forward, and my head snapped back as it collided with the edge of the table. Stars momentarily clouded my vision.

Bunyan scaled my leg hand over hand with a grip that could have crushed rocks. Each clasp sent bolts of lancing pain up my leg. I kicked at him with my free foot, but he batted it away and reached for my knee.

I tried to pull his hand away, but it felt like grappling with a mountain. In desperation, I reached for one of the bolted table legs to keep from being eaten by his arms. I swung with my free foot again. This time I

159

connected with his head, but it had the same effect as punting a boulder, and pain shot up my foot.

The darts, still in my hand, pinched the flesh of my palm against the table leg. I abandoned my hold of the table leg, sat up, and rammed the full set of darts into his shoulder. I pulled them free and took a second stab at his hands. Bunyan let go before I could connect, and I stuck myself in the leg instead. I shuffled away from him, the darts planted into my leg like little flags.

Finally out of Bunyan's reach, I pulled the darts free, letting them fall to the floor, and stood. I searched the bar for Craig, Nadeem, or anyone to help, but except for my grizzly friends, the bar was empty.

Bunyan groaned on the floor, the agony of his ruined knee making him immobile once more. Solar Plexus remained unconscious where he fell. The other three fought in a scrum for the dart case, looking like a herd of pigs fighting over the last ear of corn.

Distance lessened the mesmerizing effect of the box, and I hurried from the bar before the sirens and blue lights could arrive. As I pushed through the wooden door, a fleeting thought crossed my mind. *Where did Choir Boy go?*

10

I barged through the front door, sending two regulars jumping back out of the way, miraculously managing not to spill the contents of the glasses they fled the bar with. The closer at the top of the door arrested the door's momentum before it could bounce off its hinges then pulled it closed, clipping my heels on the return swing and sending me sprawling into the crowd of onlookers. Rough hands caught me, spun me around, and tried to throw me back into the fight like some schoolyard brawl, but I leveraged myself out of their grasp before they could succeed.

I scanned the crowd for threats or friends, and they took a collective step away from my glower as if I intended to spin up a fresh twister of mayhem on anyone within arm's reach, like the Tasmanian Devil himself. With a pounding head, bleeding leg, and still riding the heat of fight-or-flight adrenaline, if my face showed half of what I felt, I couldn't fault them.

The parting crowd allowed my probing glare to penetrate through their ranks to where the bartender stood half-out in the street with his cellphone pressed to his ear beneath his greasy hair. I found Choir Boy crumpled up against the side of the building with the waitress kneeling beside him. She held a rag to his bloody nose and shot me an admonishing glare. I returned it with an apologetic shrug of my shoulders. It did little more than magnify her scorn, but I didn't have time to defend myself now.

My quick once over of the crowd didn't turn up that beard-braided-bastard, Nadeem, or my old friend, Craig. Whose noticeable absence reignited the furnace of betrayal simmering in my soul. The fires touched my eyes, driving the crowd back another step. On the plus side, it also fended off any Samaritan hands bold enough to try to stop a man from leaving a bar fight before the police arrived. Sirens echoed in the distance, and I limped-stormed up the street, figuring I'd look less suspicious heading toward the sirens than running away.

Two sets of blinding headlights greeted me as I rounded the corner. The police cars rolled past in a scream of noise and flashing red and blue lights, shooting arrows of midnight shadows back the way they came. Through the fading strobe light, a pair of yellow eyes glared at me from an alley across the street. A familiar sense of trepidation twisted my stomach and scaled my spine like a poisonous spider. I stumbled back as the eyes advanced from the shadows into the light of a streetlamp. Like coalescing smoke, the darkness collected about the golden globes to materialize into the black, shaggy fur of a hound.

I turned and limped away woodenly on my wounded leg. At the next street lamp, I spared a glance over my shoulder. The dog trotted up to a pole two lamps back and paused within the cryptic shadows of a tree. Its head tilted to the left, then to the right, and I could feel myself being weighed and measured. Normally, I would describe myself as a dog person. I even had one growing up until it disappeared in the middle of hunting season, but something about the mutt staring me down now made me quicken my steps. I stretched out my stride as long as I could make it without collapsing. Each impact of my heel sent shards of pain through my leg, forcing out a series of grunts through clenched teeth that sounded like a steam locomotive charging up a hill.

I turned randomly at corners, navigating the streets of Savannah haphazardly until I no longer saw the dog following me nor knew where I was. With my adrenaline spent and my leg in sheer agony, I slowed and found a streetlight to lean my weight against while I stuffed a hand into my jeans' pocket to retrieve my phone and call an Uber.

My hand hit the bottom of my pocket, and my heart leapt in a panic. Frantically, I rummaged through my other pockets and only turned up my wallet. Then, like an echo from the past, I heard the dying cries of my phone beneath a mass of muscle that would make Hercules jealous. My head dropped back in a violent groan before rebounding painfully off the metal light pole.

While I massaged the rising bump on the back of my head, I scanned the street, looking for a payphone. Trees and lamp posts decorated the sidewalks fronting unfamiliar buildings, but not a single blue-box relic. Not that I should have expected anything else. I couldn't remember the last time I ever saw one off of post.

"Well, shit." Resigning myself to trudging on, I searched the night sky for Polaris and the way toward the river and Savannah's nightlife and scoffed at a dark sky full of pregnant clouds in disgust. "Of course. Well, nothing for it except to keep moving." I gritted my teeth, sucking in a hissing breath against the anticipation of pain, and made my legs move again.

The memory of an overenthusiastic drill sergeant flashed in my mind, and I challenged the night with his favorite mantra. "Inaction is the first step to defeat, and I ain't done yet." The night, however, ate my words, chewed them up, and spat them back at me in a spittle of misty rain without the shot of motivation I hoped for. I scowled up at the clouds and muttered, "Fuck you, too."

My progress over the next few blocks came in slow, jerky movements complete with a string of curses to give the pain and misery someplace else to go. Eventually, the rain faded away, leaving my clothes clinging to my skin and sodden clumps. Still unsure of where I was, I took advantage of a streetlight to relieve the aching pressure in my injured leg while I took off my shirt and wrung out as much moisture as I could. In the still of the night, I could hear the thumping bass beat of a rock anthem drifting upon the air. Music meant people and people meant phones. I slipped my shirt back over my head and followed the beat.

Two blocks later, I found a sea of people dressed in vibrant colors of neon green, yellow, and pink milling about the open door of a club with a gray cloud of cigarette smoke drifting over their heads. Despite the neon kaleidoscope assault on my eyes, I hobbled across the street and through the door.

Inside, garish lighting nearly matched the throng of people facing a low stage where a longhaired band rocked to Bohemian Rhapsody. Behind the mass of bouncing flesh stood several tables and an incongruous couch strained to capacity.

I limped past the couch and along the long bar, searching for a vacant stool to climb onto. About halfway to the back of the room, I found one between a woman wearing leg warmers and a pair of heels that rivaled the height of her hair and a man with the popped collars of no less than three polo shirts. I situated myself on the stool and propped my feet on the brass rail while I hailed the bartender.

The bartender poured the contents of his shaker into a martini glass, garnished it with an orange slice, and slid the drink to the woman beside me. In contrast to the crowd, his all-black attire stood out, but then again, my T-shirt and jeans didn't exactly match the rest of his clientele either. He slapped a cocktail napkin on the bar in front of me then sized me up with a little more interest than I felt comfortable with. His lips creased in a leering smile. "I appreciate the effort, but we don't have a wet T-shirt contest."

I gave myself a quick once over as if I didn't realize that even my boxers were spongy with rain and glanced back at him in shock. "Damn, I got the wrong place again."

He snorted a laugh. "Cute and funny. You're precious."

I don't know if I just don't have the right look for it, but I don't usually draw this kind of flirtatious attention from members of the same sex, and I couldn't decide precisely how best to respond. "Uh, thanks? But I'm not..."

He brushed the comment aside with a wave of his hand and spared me the trouble of finishing it. "No worries, man. Not everyone's perfect, but some come close."

My cheeks burned with the complement. Damn, I really wasn't used this kind of flirting. I changed the subject with a gesture over my shoulder. "What's all this?"

His toothy smile faded, and his voice sounded almost bored. "Eighty's dance party night. Dollar off the drinks if you come in costume. Though, to be honest, I expect most of them would have dressed up even without the discount."

With a new context, I surveyed the crowd and felt the time warp sweep me away to a decade I only knew through movies. A lopsided grin crept across my face as I turned back to the barkeep. "I see what you mean."

"So, what'll ya have?"

"Whatever's on tap and a phone if you have one."

"Local or distance?"

It took me a moment to think about it. I wasn't even sure who to call. I couldn't get an Uber without my own phone, and I didn't know many people willing to drive more than a half-hour to pick my dumb ass up. "Distance," I said, finally deciding who to call.

"Sorry, house phone is for local calls only. You still want that beer?"

I let out a deflated sigh. "Sure."

The bartender filled a tall glass and placed it in front of me before disappearing to service another customer. I took a long sip from the glass, letting the beer head gift my upper lip with a mustache I couldn't properly grow in the military.

A light hand with fluorescent pink fingernails landed gently on mine. I followed the fingers as they drifted up my arm. When they stopped at my bicep, my gaze followed the arm up to a metallic hot pink leotard and then to the brown eyes beneath bright blue eyeshadow of the woman seated next to me.

Her red lips split in a friendly smile. "You sound a little down and out, soldier."

I glanced at my plain black tee and the stain of blood on my jeans, which the rain thankfully washed out to a less noticeable pink. Regardless, I shifted a hand to conceal the wound before raising a questioning eyebrow.

"What makes you say that?"

She plucked the orange slice off the edge of her glass. "You look the type," she said before lifting her cosmopolitan to her lips.

I shrugged my shoulders with an acquiescent grunt and sipped my beer. "I suppose I do."

She studied me from behind her glass, waiting for me to say more, but I didn't. I lowered my glass back to the pool of condensation collecting on the bar top and lost myself in it as I tried to figure out how to get back to post.

The woman leaned forward companionably. "Well, now, don't go talking my ear off." Her voice teased on the edge of flirting, but I didn't have the mental capacity to spare sparring with her.

"Sorry, ma'am, but it's been a rough night."

"Oh, I can see that. And please call me Molly, not ma'am. You wanna talk about it?"

"Not really."

"Okay." She took another sip from her glass, then put it down with a sigh and began digging through her sequined clutch. She pulled out a blue-cased phone and thumbed it on before sliding it over to me. "Here. My daddy would be pissed if I didn't help a soldier out."

"Thanks, but who's your daddy?"

Her eyes brightened, and lips pursed in a barely constrained laugh.

"Shit, no…" I could feel my cheeks turn hot. "That's not what I meant."

The dam broke at my linguistic fumble, and she burst out in a choking snort of a laugh, which she quickly covered with the back of her hand. I buried myself in beer, and her laughter only grew stronger, making my ears hot.

"It's not that funny," I muttered into my brew.

She raised a placating hand, and the shake in her shoulders slowed. "No, I know, but with my father, it kinda is. I'm sorry." She lowered her hand and looked to the ceiling as she drew in a deep breath. She blew it out heavily, banishing all signs of amusement from her face except for a lingering twinkle in her eyes. "Oh, I haven't laughed like that in ages."

"So glad I could amuse you," I said dryly.

"I'm sorry," she apologized again. "My *father* is Major Harland."

I racked my brain, trying to place the name and then breathed a sigh of relief. "Oh, thank God, he's not in my chain of command." I picked up the phone and chuckled at the grinning Stitch in a hula skirt staring back at me.

Molly's lips pursed, and her eyebrows knitted together. "Hey, don't judge."

It was my turn to apologize. "Oh, I'm not. This is the best thing I've seen all day. My sister loves Stitch."

Mollified, she returned to her cosmopolitan while I tried to remember the number I needed. I couldn't recall the last time I actually dialed a phone number, and it took me a moment to mentally visualize the contact entry in my phone. Praying I remembered it right, I punched in the numbers. The phone rang twice before it sent me to voicemail.

"Hi, this is Teressa Flannigan's phone. I'm on my honeymoon, and I'm not available right now. Please leave a message." Teressa's bubbly voice sounded happier in her greeting than I'd heard her in years.

"Tee, it's me, Matthew. I lost my phone. Can you call me back at this number as soon as possible?"

I busied myself with another drink of beer while I waited for the phone to ring. By the time I reached the bottom of the glass, I lost hope she would call back tonight and slid the phone back to Molly.

She took the phone back with an apologetic smile. "I'm sorry, Matthew." She stressed my name, and I realized I never introduced myself.

"Geeze, I'm sorry. I'm Matthew," I said, extending a hand to her.

Molly shifted the phone from her right to her left, then gave my outstretched hand a cordial pump. "Pleased to meet you." She released my hand in a sudden jump as her phone buzzed and slipped from her fingers. Her hand flew to her chest with a sharp breath. "Oh, my," she said as Stitch shimmied along the bar to Elvis Presley singing *Hound Dog*. She flashed me a lopsided smile, then picked up the phone and answered it.

The single side of the conversation I heard came in short bursts of words. "Hello?—Yes, he did—Yes, he is— Sure."

Molly handed the phone to me. "It's for you."

"Thanks," I mouthed before placing the phone to my ear. "Hello, Tee?"

"Matthew? Is everything all right?" Teressa's sleepy voice contained a note of alarm.

"Yeah. Everything is fine." Though, mentally I added, *I only just got in a bar fight, lost your husband, and stabbed myself in the leg. Everything is just peachy.* But I didn't need to worry her with all that. "I just lost my phone and really need a ride back to barracks."

"Um...Annabelle is sleeping. Have Craig drive you back."

"I would, but Craig left before I lost my phone."

"Left? What happened?" Now she just sounded annoyed.

"I'm not exactly sure. Things were going pretty well; then he ran off to the bathroom just before a bar fight broke out, and I haven't seen him since." My anger at his abandonment built with each word, and I stamped it down with some effort.

"Figures." I could hear the eye roll in her voice. "Fine! Give me a moment to get Annabelle suited up, and we'll be on our way. Where are you?"

Now that was a good question. I glanced up at my new friend and asked, "Um, where are we?"

She shook her head with a snicker. "The Wormhole."

I relayed the bar's name to Teressa.

"Where's that?"

"Savannah."

The sigh echoing through the phone said more than words. I hated making her drive the hour and a half round trip this late at night. Come to think of it, I didn't even know the time. I pulled the phone back from my ear and gulped; it wasn't even Saturday anymore.

"Never mind. I'll just Google it." Her voice carried an unmistakable quality of irritation.

"Thanks, Tee. I owe you."

"I'll see you in a bit." The phone clipped silent, biting off the end of her last word.

"Just peachy," I said, handing the phone back to Molly.

"So, is your wife coming to get you?" She asked, placing it back in her clutch.

The comment dug up emotions I usually kept safely locked away. It took an effort to beat them back into their pit and bolt the iron door closed despite how pissed Teressa was at having to come get me. *I'd rather have her pissed and in my arms than...whatever we were,* I thought dreamily.

"Yeah, but she's not my wife; just a friend." Molly's face brightened, and I thought, *what the hell, I could use some fun tonight.* Besides, my buzz from early was seriously fading. "Looks like I have some time to waste until she gets here. Can I buy you another cosmo?"

She smiled as she finished her pink cocktail. "That would be wonderful."

I lifted a hand to hail the bartender.

11

I maintained a more reasonable level of inebriation while Molly and I filled the time with pleasant conversation until her phone danced along the bar with Teressa's text that she had arrived. I settled the tab as Molly snatched a cocktail napkin to write down her number. She slipped it into my hand and whispered, "call me," into my ear before bidding me farewell with a peck on the cheek.

A horn blurted out in the street, but I barely heard it over the band's rendition of White Snake's *Here I Go Again*. I hopped off my stool and winced at the stab of pain in my injured leg. Molly's hand reached out to catch mine, but I flashed her a toothy grin and made a show of slipping her number into my pocket as a distraction. However, I quickly withdrew it, deciding to carry it rather than lose the number to the damp fabric.

I managed to hide the limp in my step until I made it out of the bar. From there, it only took me a moment to find Teressa's car parked beneath a light further up the street. The spot-like glow of the streetlight made the white and rust-colored Civic look like the haunted before-shot in a body shop commercial.

My limp became more pronounced with each step as my leg rebelled at the forced action. I reached for the passenger side door handle with a glance over the top of the car, and a shiver ran down my back that had little to do with my wet clothes. Nearly hidden in the shadows across the street, a familiar set of glowing eyes peered back at me.

They didn't move, and neither did I until I heard the door lock cycle closed and back open again. I pulled the door open and slid into the torn vinyl seat, losing sight of the black dog for only an instant as the car's roof obscured my vision, but when I searched the shadows from inside the car, the beast was gone.

"The door wasn't locked," Teressa said with more than a fair share of annoyance in her voice. She glimpsed my face then turned to follow my spooked gaze. "What is it?"

"I'm not sure."

"Well, stop it, you're scaring me."

I brought my attention back to her nervous eyes. "Sorry, let's just go."

Teressa put the car in gear and lurched away from the curb. She never could drive a stick worth a damn.

Annabelle made a startled, sleepy noise from the back seat at the sudden jolt of action. An empty smacking sound followed, and I checked the back seat. Her binky had fallen into her lap. I returned it to her lips, where she gave it a few wet sucks then cooed as the rumble of tires on pavement lulled her back to sleep.

I smiled at the satisfied way her face relaxed and brushed a dark curl from her forehead. With an effort of will, I pushed away thoughts of what could have been and turned back around. "She's getting big," I said, buckling in.

Teressa shot a glance over her shoulder, and a motherly expression of worry and pleasure spread across her face. "Yes, she is."

We rode on in silence for a while until we passed the city limits, and I couldn't take the tension in the air any longer. "I'm sorry."

She sniffed at my apology. "Well, you were only out here because I asked you to. Giving you a ride home is the least I could do."

I felt the heavy weight of failure sit on my shoulders, and I shook my head. "Yeah, I'm sorry for that too. I didn't get a chance to ask him."

Her eyes broke from the road to me in a worried glance. When she returned her attention to the road, I could see her eyes mist in the glow of the car's dash lights. "I don't know what I'm going to do, Matthew. He's barely been home since coming back, and when he is, he won't talk to me."

I reached out and wiped away a tear cascading down her cheek with my thumb. She leaned ever-so-slightly into my touch, and it took all I had to pull my hand back. With my hand out of the way, she dried her tears on the shoulders of her shirt while she drove.

"I'll try talking to him again," I said, and the corner of Teressa's mouth turned up in a thankful expression that rose to her eyes as she glanced at me. "I had intended to invite him to a grief group therapy meeting tomor-row...well, I guess it's later today now...either way, we got interrupted before I got the chance." The last few words came out in a strained groan as I retrieved my wallet and a spasm of pain shot through my leg at the effort. The dampened edge of a folded piece of paper stuck out of the worn leather. I pulled it out and placed it on the dash. "In case I don't get the chance, here's the time and address."

"Thanks, but are you okay?" Her eyes dropped to my leg as I tried to get more comfortable in my seat.

I scoffed in self-deprecation. "Yeah, I just managed to stab myself in the leg with the darts tonight and walking around in the rain didn't help."

"And why the hell didn't you stay put and call me from there?"

I raised an eyebrow. "Because, the first rule about bar fights is, you don't stick around and wait for the cops. Well, actually, that's more like the second rule."

She scoffed. "Okay, and what's the first rule? Don't get in one to start with?"

"No...well, actually yes. So, it's the third rule then."

"Ah, and then the second would be?"

My eyes narrowed. "Don't leave your buddy to fight alone." The words came out more bitter than I intended.

"Oh," Teressa said in recognition.

"Yeah, it's something else I intend to talk with Craig about."

We rode in silence once again for a handful of miles, until Teressa turned on the local country station. I don't really have an opinion about country music. Half the time, it sounds more like pop than anything I would call country, but Johnny Cash came through the speakers in his rumbling, deep voice, which soon put me to sleep in the passenger seat.

I woke to Teressa's soft prodding of my arm.

"Matthew, we're here."

I blinked my eyes a few times to lubricate the sandpaper. When they adjusted to seeing again, I opened the door and got out of the car. Keeping my wounded leg as straight as I could, I rose on my good one. The door squeaked closed before I realized we weren't parked in front of my barracks. Instead, a squat row of two-story townhomes stretched for several units in both directions. Even in the dark, I could tell the one in front of me was in desperate need of some maintenance. "Why are we at your apartment?"

Teressa wrangled the half-asleep Annabelle from the back of the car, clutching the two-year-old to her small frame. "Because you're soaked, that leg needs some tending, and I don't trust you to take care of it properly."

"What? This? It's just a flesh wound. I've suffered worse," I said in a horrible imitation of a British accent. Teressa rolled her eyes. She never did appreciate Monty Python like Craig and I.

"You're about to get worse if you don't get inside and let me take a look at it."

I took a hobbling step toward the front door. "Yes, ma'am."

Once Teressa had Annabelle back in her bed, she took my clothes, minus my boxers, and threw them in the dryer while a pot of coffee brewed. Making myself at home, I sat in a seat at the kitchen table and propped my leg up on an adjacent chair. I examined my wound and started the blood oozing again from three small holes with puckered edges. "I think the Predator shot me with his targeting laser."

"Stop playing with it," Teressa scolded as she dropped off a pair of bottles and an assortment of bandages. She then filled a mug with coffee and handed it to me black.

"Thanks," I said, warming my hands on the mug while I waited for it to cool enough to drink. Even in the midst of a southern summer, walking around in wet clothes at night saps the heat out of you, and Teressa had the air conditioner turned up.

She knelt on the floor in front of me and began exploring my wounds with a cotton swab. "Damn, Matthew, how deep did you stick yourself."

"A dart's tip is about an inch and a half, so...I'd say about an inch and a half."

Her face turned serious. "You're lucky you didn't hit an artery."

I sighed. "Yeah, I know."

She uncapped a bottle of rubbing alcohol. "This might hurt a bit," she said then poured it onto the wound before I could voice my objection. I clenched my hands into fists and sucked in a harsh breath as the liquid fire burned its way into my wound.

Neither of us realized the front door had opened until it slammed closed. Craig stared at me in nothing but my boxers with his wife on her knees in front of me. Daggers couldn't describe the fury boiling in his eyes. "What the hell?"

"It's not the way it looks," I yelled, but Teressa jumped back like a child caught with her hand in the cookie jar.

Craig mistook her surprised-worry expression as something else and charged me.

I scrambled to get to my feet, but he dove, tackling me before my wounded leg hit the floor. The chair rocked backward, then collapsed under our combined weight. The sharp edges of broken wood bit into my bare skin and I would have yelped if not for Craig's body knocking the breath out of me.

He straddled me UFC style and started throwing punches. Innocent misunderstanding or not, I don't take getting hit very well.

I bucked my hips and knocked him off balance, though he managed to continue riding me like a bronc. I got my left arm up in time to take the brunt of his next punch, then shot the heel of my palm upward, catching him in the chin. His head snapped back, and I threw a right into his unprotected ribs.

He rolled off me and spun up to his feet in a fairly fluid motion. "You son of a bitch. I knew you were fucking my wife."

I rolled in the opposite direction and got less nimbly to my feet with my hands up in a guarded, defensive position. "Craig, nothing happened."

"Craig, stop this," cried Teressa.

He gave her an evil glare then turned it to me. His nose flared, and his feet shifted like a bull pawing the ground before a charge. He lifted a knee in a feint, and I dodged back, but my leg didn't push like I wanted it to. His lead foot then dropped back to the ground, and his rear foot flew forward in a roundhouse kick. It landed on my upper arm with enough force to send me the handful of feet into the wall.

"That's it," I growled. "You don't get to abandon me in a bar fight and then beat the hell out of me later." The surge of adrenaline pumping through my veins gave me the strength I needed to ignore my wounded leg. I rushed in with a jab and then a hook.

He blocked the punches, but not the knee I brought up into his groin. I learned a long time ago; there's no such thing as a fair fight.

He grunted with the impact, using the involuntary forward momentum of doubling over to drive his forehead into my nose in response. I heard a nasty crunch, and my eyes welled instantly in tears as the pain flared. Blood gushed from my nose as I took a few steps back. I tried to keep an eye on Craig through the mist clouding my vision.

Craig braced himself with one hand on the table and the other to his groin. Deep heavy breaths steamed out of him like a bull clearing its head. His dark eyes glared at me as he straightened back up and brought up his guard.

I wiped at my eyes, briefly clearing my vision. *Shit, he's not done yet,* I thought, readying myself for another round.

He took a step forward.

Water returned to my eyes, and the blood made it hard to breathe.

He took another step, still out of range. On his next step, I lunged while his foot was still in the air. I dove under his guard and wrapped my arms around his waist. Off-balance, he stumbled back and tripped on the remains of the broken chair, and we fell into the table as one.

The table broke in the crash, tilting up like a sinking ship over its central leg and seesawing my cup of coffee up into the air. We landed on the floor, and hot coffee rained over us both along with the medical supplies Teressa gathered to care for my wound.

We both rolled away from each other, groaning in pain. Craig rolled over the bottle of alcohol, and it burst under his weight. The fragrant scent of antiseptic blended with the smell of fresh-brewed coffee.

We heard Annabelle crying over our moans. Teressa huffed and stomped out of the room, leaving us alone in our wreckage.

"You need to leave," Craig growled.

I lulled my head to the side and considered him for a moment. He looked tired and wounded in a way I hadn't seen since his father died. In that expression, I saw the friend I missed so much. I wanted to help, to mend the rift between us, but at the moment, I didn't know how. "Craig, I'm..."

His eyes closed, and he rocked his head side to side. "No, I don't want to hear it. Just get the fuck out of my house."

I worked myself up to my feet with a considerable amount of pain. Grabbing my shoes in one hand, I pinched the bridge of my nose with the other to staunch the flow of blood, then stumbled out the door in nothing but my boxers.

12

Sunday morning came, and I woke up much later than usual with a splitting headache and a pair of raccoon eyes. I went to the mirror and examined the spectacular shades of purple coloring my bruises. At least the bright red, inflamed nose between them looked mostly straight.

"Oh, don't you look beautiful," I told the man in the mirror. My voice sounded hollow and nasally with the pair of tampons I rammed up my nostrils the night before still in place. Tampons are great for arresting nose bleeds as well as other deep bleeding wounds like those caused by speeding jacketed lead projectiles. So, I always carry a small handful of tampons and condoms in my battle bag, just like every other soldier I know. One of these days, I'm fairly sure some ex-military geek is going to get their big break writing the book on the thousand and one uses of tampons and condoms.

I carefully pulled the tampons out of my swollen nose, hoping I wouldn't start a new fountain of blood. They came free, and I resisted the temptation to massage my aching nose. Instead, I took a couple of soft test breaths. Air leaked into my lungs, but not enough, and I resumed sucking in air through my open mouth.

"First night off restrictions, and I let Craig use my face as a punching bag. Oh yeah, First Sarge is going to have a field day with me tomorrow."

I abandoned the disgrace in the mirror and flipped on the shower.

Turning the valve to full hot, I let the steam soak into my muscles for a luxurious five minutes. To be honest, I don't think I know how to take a longer shower. Afterward, I got dressed and sat down with my laptop, trying to decide the best way to burn the handful of hours I had until my first group therapy session.

I logged in and pulled up my internet browser, but before I could remember what Gracie said the black dog was, a text messenger window popped up. The string of letters and numbers meant nothing to me, and I moved to close the window when the first message appeared.

Matthew?

Who's this? I wrote back.

Gracie :)

I let out a troubled sigh of relief. On the one hand, it was Gracie, and I could really use her help figuring out what happened last night. On the other hand, she had hacked my computer, and the intrusion kind-of pissed me off. The irritation quickly slipped into embarrassed anxiety with a prayer she hadn't gone looking through my internet history. A hot flush rushed to my cheeks, adding yet another shade of red to the kaleidoscope already decorating my face.

You need to stop hacking my shit!

Sorry :(Just wanted to make sure you were alright.

I tried to cool my anger; she helped me out last night, and I owed her. My fingers moved across the keyboard to tell her thanks when another text popped up.

Ouch, what happened to your face? You didn't look that bad when you left the bar last night.

"What the hell," I cursed then slid the privacy aperture closed over my laptop's camera.

Oops. Sorry :$ Can't help myself sometimes.

Aggravated, I closed the laptop, pushed it away, and debated the value of taking up an entirely unplugged lifestyle. No sooner had I considered it than I could feel the itch in my hand for my phone. Unplugged wasn't an option, and neither was shutting out Gracie. I needed information, and she was the only one I could talk to about it. Well, okay, I could have talked to my brothers or my sister, but they didn't know anything more about monsters than I did. Gracie, on the other hand, was better than Google.

I pulled the laptop closer and opened the screen, though I left the privacy slide closed over the camera.

How'd you know what I looked like last night?

Security cameras ;) McNamara's might be a POS bar, but at least they're digital.

"Crap!" I never thought about there being a camera at the bar. If the cops got ahold of the footage from last night, I could be in some real deep shit. I quickly replayed the events of the night in my mind trying to remember how it all began. My head fell as I remembered who struck first. They would never believe that knife hand was a defensive move.

*Don't suppose...*I started typing then deleted it. I couldn't believe what I was about to ask her. *Can you do something about the recording?*

What recording? She typed back. *McNamara's cameras were out last night.* >;)

I breathed a heavy sigh of relief then typed back, *Thanks. I owe you one.*

Don't mention it :|

So, do you have any idea what happened?

Djinn.

What?

I think you may have caught the attention of a djinn :-/

The word fluttered in the back of my brain like something I should know, but I couldn't place where I ran across it before. *What's a djinn?*

Think genie.

Like the one in Aladdin?

:D Not exactly, but close enough. They're tricksters and have access to all sorts of powers like shapeshifting; especially into dogs. It would explain the dog you've been seeing and your hallucinations.

I ran a hand through my hair, massaging my scalp to jostle my brain into action, as I drew in a heavy breath through my aching nose to get a handle on what she said.

But why me? Aren't they from the middle east or something?

:-/ You're in the army, haven't you been there?

Memories of Afghanistan floated through my vision, but I pushed them away. *Yeah, more than a year ago. Shouldn't it have been haunting me before now?*

Probably :(Do you know anyone else who may have been there more recently?

I knew one person in particular who had just gotten back when all this started.

Yeah, I do. Craig. I wrote back.

Any chance he has a grudge against you, seeing as how the djinn seems to be fixated on you =L

The throbbing in my nose punctuated her message more than her silly emoticon. *We have our differences,* I replied.

The djinn is probably feeding on that. It has Craig trapped, but he probably thinks it's the other way around.

OK then, it's a badass genie feeding on my friend. How do I free it?

D=< You don't unless you want your friend dead.

OK then, how do I kill it?

Between its shapeshifting and invisibility? `:/ With a lot of luck. It's easier to just take it away from him. If the djinn is still harassing you, then it must still be bound to the object he picked up. It's how they're connected. You need to figure out what it is and take it away from him.

So, I'm looking for an oil lamp. That shouldn't be too hard. I rolled my eyes as I typed, and I missed having my phone to relay the concept in a text message. The lack of emojis made my half of the conversation seem more than a little flat.

Oil lamps are only in the movies :J It's probably a piece of jewelry or something else he keeps on him at all times.

That would make it a little tougher, considering my one-on-one with Craig resulted in more injuries than my brawl with a whole gang of gorillas. I shoved the worry aside for the moment. Mission parameters first.

OK. Objective one: get djinn possessed jewelry from Craig. Then, what do I do with it when I get it?

Good question. I'll have to get back to you. But whatever you do, don't use the djinn yourself >:O

Right then. All I had to do is confront a man who commanded a genie with *phenomenal cosmic powers,* get him to hand over…whatever it was that gave him control of the genie, and then not use the genie myself. Had I missed anything there? Oh yeah, after last night, I was pretty sure the man in question wanted nothing more than to kick the living shit out of me—again. "Piece of cake," I muttered.

Gracie texted, *Gotta go. Don't forget to open your camera back up.*

I flicked the privacy screen back open and realized I'd never seen what Gracie looked like.

Wait, since you've seen me, I think it's only fair I get to see you.

Maybe next time :P The text flashed in the window for only a moment before the app closed itself.

My derisive snort flared painfully in my nose. "Somehow, I doubt that," I said nasally.

After my conversation with Gracie, I fell down a fruitless rabbit-hole looking into djinn online. A complaintive gurgle from my stomach pulled me back to reality, and while I pondered what to eat, I glanced at the time and leapt out of my chair. If I hurried, I might just be able to make it to my group session on time.

With a quick finger dance across the keyboard, I locked my laptop then buzzed around my room like a mad bee trying to find my room key and wallet. At the door, I did a double check, then rushed back to the bookcase and snatched up my brother's journal; if I was going to talk about him, I wanted him with me. Finally ready to go, I started making my way down the hall knocking on doors in search of someone with a cellphone to call a cab.

Lady Luck still refused to smile on me as the only person to answer their door was Sergeant Perez. She wore a pair of legless shorts and a tight tank top with a neckline that thankfully didn't plunge all the way down to her belly button. Though it hugged her curves and the laces holding it together did little to conceal her cleavage. In a way, it was almost worse. I averted my gaze up from her chest before she could get on a high horse about me staring at her bosom and met her eyes. A moment of shocked horror spread across her face before she broke down into raucous laughter. I let out a heavy sigh and rolled my hand in a *get-on-with-it* gesture, which only made her laugh harder.

"Damn, Peterson, you look like a raccoon butted heads with a baboon."

"Ha, ha, very funny. Can I borrow your phone?"

"My phone? Oh, that's a great idea. Stay right there." She rushed back into her room while I waited impatiently, bracing the door open with a foot. She came back around the corner, and her phone flashed before I realized what she was up to. "I'm going to want to remember this."

I reached up to rub the phantom flash from my eyes and succeeded in only making them hurt more. "Damnit, Perez. You had your fun; now can I borrow your phone?"

She held it close to her chest. "But why?"

"Because I need to call a cab, and I lost mine."

"Where are you going on a Sunday afternoon?"

"That is none of your damn business."

"It is if you want to use my phone. I'm not about to let you use it for a booty call." She teased, moving the phone to reveal a bit more of her cleavage.

I only just managed to stop my hand from rubbing the stress from the bridge of my nose. I swear God put her in my life to make up for all the shit I pulled on my brothers. "Fine. I need to call a cab to get a ride to the group therapy session my psychologist recommended."

She straightened at the confession, and her eyes grew serious. "If you need a ride, I can take you. I'm not doing anything right now."

The one-eighty flip in attitude left my head spinning. "Huh?"

She pushed her phone in her back pocket and snatched her purse off a hook on the wall. "Come on. I'll drive you." The level no-nonsense tone she used with her soldiers replaced the teasing tone I'd become accustomed to.

I followed in her wake, still more than a bit dazed by her sudden change of disposition. She led me out the back of the barracks to a lavender-colored VW Beetle, where she climbed in and started the car. I lowered myself into the passenger seat, making my wounded leg bend more than it wanted to, then buckled my seat belt and waited for her to put the car in gear. After a moment, I gave her a *why-aren't-we-moving* look.

Her eyebrows shot up halfway to her hairline. "I said, where to?" she repeated.

Reality finally came back to me as I sat in the car staring at the one person who had made it her mission in life to antagonize me. "Um, why are you doing this for me?"

Her eyebrows dropped back into place, and the pain in her eyes made me regret asking the question. "Matthew, it takes a lot for one of us to admit we need help, and I'm not going to give you or anyone else the excuse they need to not get it. I did that once. I'll never do it again. Now, where am I driving you?"

I gave her the address and stared silently out the window as she drove. Questions I didn't dare ask mulled in my head. We never had more than a teasing-sibling kind of relationship, and her soberness now felt...well, I couldn't describe how it felt, only that it made me respect her in a way I never did before.

She rolled up to the community hall building just outside of the post. The white brick building resembled every other governmental building built in the seventies—utilitarian and without much flare.

I unbuckled and opened the door, but Perez's hand touched mine before I could swing my wounded leg to the pavement. "You want me to come in with you? It can help sometimes."

I glanced from her to the glass doors fronting the building and could see a handful of people milling about in the entryway. "No. I think I got it. But thanks."

"Sure. If you want, I can come back and give you a ride home?"

My eyes dropped to my lap, shying away from her generosity. "I appreciate it, but I think I'll walk."

She reached into the center console of the car and pulled out a pen and a small notebook, then jotted down her number and handed it to me. "If you change your mind, give me a call."

I took the sheet of paper with a bob of my head and got out of the car. It didn't exactly feel like a push, but she didn't leave until I entered the building.

13

I eventually found conference room 214 after two wrong turns and an embarrassingly awkward conversation with a freckled face youth with red, stringy hair and crooked teeth. The conference room door was unadorned except for a simple brown plaque with the room number on the adjacent wall. The door, however, opened onto a small gathering of people engaged in about a half dozen little groups of sober conversation.

I scanned the crowd looking for a familiar face but didn't find one until Doctor Swartz's head popped up from behind the back of a man with broad shoulders. He flashed me a congenial smile then said a few more words to the man before rising and patting him gently on the shoulder.

He crossed the room and drew me the rest of the way through the door as he reached out and shook my hand. "Matthew, I'm glad you could make it. Though you look a bit rougher than the last time I saw you."

I pumped his hand and shrugged my shoulders. "It hasn't been my weekend, Dah—exter."

He cracked a half-smile at my last-minute catch of his name. "Why don't you help yourself to a cup of coffee? We'll get started in a few minutes."

My damaged nose followed the sweep of his hand to the refreshments bar, where the scent of coffee practically lifted my feet from the ground and pulled me across the room like a cartoon character. A commercial-grade coffeemaker with a stack of foam cups stood to one end of the table, and an assortment of homemade cookies and mini-muffins crowded the other end. I took one of the cups, not even half the size of what I really wanted, and filled it to the rim. Then, like any good field-hardened soldier, I proceeded to pour it down my throat while sucking in large quantities of cool air until even the grinds were gone.

I refilled the cup and brought it back to my lips when someone touched my elbow. I took a more modest sip and turned. As my eyes locked onto the man beside me, the coffee in my mouth solidified into a lump of hot coal with ragged edges that scoured my throat as I swallowed hard.

"Craig," I said in a rasp. "What are you doing here?"

He held out a plastic grocery bag. "I brought you your clothes. Teressa said I'd find you here." His words came out in a forced, barely audible, rumble. "I...I over..."

"Alright, folks. Let's get to our seats." Doctor Swartz's voice interrupted Craig, who snapped his mouth closed as if he swallowed something bitter.

Craig let the bag fall to the floor then wandered around the edge of the circle in search of a seat like a kid playing duck—duck—goose. He settled on an empty chair between a man in a three-piece suit and an elderly lady whose large purse looked amiss without a little yippy dog poking its head over the side.

An irritated growl rumbled deep in my chest as I stuffed Jonny's journal under an arm and collected the bag from the floor. I took my clothes, my coffee, and a complicated stew of emotions to an empty chair as directly opposite from Craig as I could. It also happened to be right next to Doctor Swartz, who waited for me to sit down before beginning with a smile.

"Thank you all for coming. We have a few new people joining us today, so I'll briefly go over the group rules." Doctor Swartz's voice held a grandfatherly tone that made the entire group both relax and listen up at the same time. It even captured Craig's attention, and he pulled his sullen eyes off of me.

"First off, this is a safe place where we can help each other deal with our loss. Everyone is free to share, regardless of who or what we have lost. And just like your momma should have taught you, if you don't have anything encouraging to add, don't say anything at all.

"Secondly, while this is not A.A., whatever is said here is expected to stay here. By sharing, we open ourselves up to the trust and faith of those around us. If you are not capable of honoring that trust, I invite you to leave now. I'll be more than happy to help you on a more intimate one-on-one basis."

Doctor Swartz paused and let the silence draw out awkwardly as he passed his gaze across the room. No one moved to leave, though Craig shifted uneasily in his seat when the doctor's eyes met his as if the seat suddenly became uncomfortable.

I slouched lower in my chair in silent criticism. *Like the army didn't teach us how to make a rock comfortable enough to sleep on.* Then the doctor's eyes met mine, and I sat up, leaning forward respectfully.

"Good. Now, like I said, this isn't A.A., but I find it's easier to all be friends if we know each other's names. So, we'll go around the room and introduce ourselves, just a first name is fine. Then I'll open it up to sharing.

"Alright, I'll get us started. I am Dexter."

Doctor Swartz nodded to the dark-haired woman with sunken eyes on his right. She sucked in a shuddering breath. "I'm Natalie." She sniffled and wiped at her dripping nose. Doctor Swartz handed her a box of tissues. She took one and blew her nose harshly as the next person along the circle introduced themselves.

The gentlemen to Natalie's right gave his name in a barely audible mutter I didn't catch before the freckle-faced boy next to him chimed in, "I'm Eric, and I lost my grandfather a year and a half ago."

"Eric," Doctor Swartz interrupted with a firm voice. "Please wait to share until everyone else has had a chance to introduce themselves."

Eric slumped back in his chair with his bottom lip pushed out like a child who just got his hand slapped for sneaking into the cookie jar.

After the remainder of the group gave their names, Doctor Swartz leaned forward with his elbows on his knees and his hands open. "It's been a few weeks since we met last, and I'm sure we all have something to share, but please let everyone have a turn and wait for me to acknowledge you before you start. Thank you." While his eyes didn't linger any longer on Eric than the rest of us, we all knew who he was addressing.

"Now, for those of you who don't know, I am more than your facilitator. Three years ago, today, I lost my wife Esther to breast cancer. I have been where many of you are now. I have gone through the stages of grief, and I still miss her and grieve for her every day. She is why I started this group, so please trust me when I say I understand. I also know how hard it is to share, but more importantly, I *know* how critical discussing your loss is to the healing process. So, please try to find the strength to open up and share; we are all here to support you."

Doctor Swartz gave Natalie a gentle, encouraging smile. "Perhaps you would like to get us started, Natalie."

Eric stomped his feet and crossed his arms in a tantrum. The majority of the group cast less than charitable glares at him. However, Natalie continued to stare at her fidgeting hands.

"I...I lost my baby boy..." Tears rolled down her cheeks, and she mopped at her face with the crushed tissue in her hands. "I can't," She sobbed.

"It's okay, Natalie. Maybe next time." Doctor Swartz laid a hand on her back as one of the other women in the group got up from their seat, knelt in front of Natalie, and pulled her into a hug. Doctor Swartz scanned the room and then, with a sigh, nodded to Eric, who was bouncing impatiently in his seat. "Okay, Eric, but please keep it shorter than last time."

I tried to pay attention as Eric spoke about losing his grandfather to cancer, but it was hard to ignore the eye rolls from the regulars as he droned on about how he helped everyone and their brother, to include the attending nurses and doctor, cope with the loss of a great man. The story felt worn-out, like even Eric had said it so often he spoke more from repetition now than with any real emotion.

I found my mind kept drifting back to Craig. Something about him didn't add up, and I couldn't puzzle it out. Only yesterday, he had tried to kick the shit out of me, and then he returned my clothes with what I could have sworn was going to be an apology. And then the man who wouldn't even talk to the chaplain about his father dying decided to stay for group therapy.

Craig, what the hell are you up to? His eyes locked on mine as if I had spoken the thought out loud. I worried I may have done just that as most of the room stared expectantly at me.

Doctor Swartz touched my arm. "Matthew, would you care to share?" His words held the familiar ring of a repeated phrase.

"I'm sorry, what was that?"

"I asked if you would like to share?"

My worried thoughts of Craig evaporated. The air in the room turned thick as concrete, and my tongue stuck to the roof my mouth. "I...um... sure." I worked some moisture into my mouth and dropped my eyes to the floor. The corner of Jonny's journal poked out the top of the plastic bag at my feet. I pulled it out slowly. The simple leather cover felt familiar in my hand as my throat relaxed, and words began to form on their own.

"I grew up on a dairy farm—the eldest of five with a...less than kind father. I learned to protect my mom and siblings at a fairly young age. To keep my old man from harming them as best I could, which is what I did until I was eighteen. Then I couldn't take his bullshit anymore. That's when I talked a friend of mine into joining the army with me. I convinced him to leave his loving family just so I could run away from mine. I left them when I should have been there for them.

"When I left, I thought I was hard. That after my old man, nothing could harm me. But I was wrong. I lost friends in Afghanistan. Friends I didn't cry for because I was too hard, too much of a man." Tears came now—tears for every one of them. In the mist clouding my vision, the faces of the group dissolved and reformed into my lost brothers-in-arms. Into faces I would never forget.

"A little more than a year ago, I saw my best friend lose his father. A man who was more of a father to me than my own, and I was too hard to help even my best friend. I couldn't break through the walls I built over a lifetime to give him the support he needed." I looked in Craig's general direction, but I couldn't see him any better than anyone else, and I refused to wipe away my tears. It hurt to remember the day Craig's mother told him about his dad's heart attack. It hurt more now than it ever did then.

The tears falling from my nose splattered and slid across the worn leather of Jonny's journal. I held it tight in my fingers as I felt Doctor Swartz warm hand land on my right shoulder and another more feminine hand land on my left. "I didn't understand what my friend had lost until a few months ago when I buried my youngest brother, Jonny." My voice gave out at Jonny's name and with it all the strength I had left in my body.

Wrung out and weary, I endured the kind words and gentle hands as those around me tried to give me the support I needed to stay upright in my seat. Then a pair of strong arms wrapped around me and pulled my head to their shoulder. Their hand braced the back of my head and told me I could cry. Through the fog of pain, my brain slowly registered the voice as Craig's.

14

While a handful of others shared stories that broke our hearts as much as they drew showers of tears, Craig never shared his own. After consoling me, he returned to his seat and spent the remainder of the session sitting in cool silence, staring at the tops of his shoes. When Doctor Swartz dismissed us with one last admonishment about faith and trust, Craig got out of his chair and crossed the intervening distance between us with a sense of purpose.

I opened my mouth to say thank you or...at least something of the kind, but he pulled Jonny's journal from my fingers and stuffed it into the bag at my feet before I could. Still numb from publicly baring my soul, I remained in my chair and watched him as he hefted the bag and strode out the door.

People shuffled about moving chairs and rearranging the room per Doctor Swartz's direction. I drifted up out of my chair and carried it to the side of the room when the door cracked back open, and Craig stuck his head in. "Matthew, come on."

I followed him out of the room, not because I didn't want to help put the chairs away, but Craig was my best chance for a ride home and...well, yeah, I didn't want to help put the chairs away.

Say what you want about how hot a midsummer Georgian afternoon can get, but when I walked out of the over-air-conditioned community hall, I closed my eyes and lifted my face to the sky, letting the sun bake away the clammy chill. With the sun turning from comforting warmth to the front steps of hell once again, I ran into the parking lot chasing after Craig.

A few steps back from his pickup truck, Craig tossed my bag of clothes into the bed. The bag fluttered through the air and then landed with a thunk from Jonny's journal hitting the metal bed.

"Hey, be careful with that." I jumped into the bed of the truck and checked the journal before pushing it back into the bag and tying the handles closed. With my things protectively in hand, I stood to find Craig staring blankly just over my shoulder. "Craig, you okay?"

His dark eyes moved sluggishly as they focused on me. "Yeah, I'm fine. Teressa wanted me to invite you over for dinner." His words came out wooden and hollow, like from an old speaker box. He moved toward the driver's side door with the thick actions of a drunk trying to act sober.

His sudden, deadened demeanor worried me. "Um...dinner sounds great, but do you mind if I drive?"

"Sure," he said, tossing the keys in my direction.

I watched the keys sail over my head, and I knew something was seriously wrong. Even when we were on the best of terms, Craig never let me drive his truck. I hopped out of the bed to retrieve the keys, but as my feet hit the ground, the small hairs on the back of my neck rose. At the far edge of the community center, peering around the corner, I could just make out a black head with pointy ears watching us. I swallowed as its lips pulled back in a toothy grin, which, coming from a dog that looked more like an emaciated wolf, made me feel like dinner.

Oh, what big teeth you have. The thought popped in my mind, and before I could fully process it, I'd chucked my bag back into the truck bed, and my legs began pumping in an adrenaline-fueled charge. When my fight-or-flight kicks in, I tend to move on instinct, and I've never been much of a flight person, even before the army.

The dog's lips dropped, and its eyes grew two sizes. *Oh, what big eyes you have.* I bared my teeth in a wicked grin as the dog spooked and fled around the corner of the building with a yelp. "You're not getting away from me that easy, Nadeem," I said, pushing my legs harder and forcing them to move faster.

A pair of very human hands grabbed my shoulders and twisted me as I rounded the corner and tripped over an extended foot. My momentum sent me sailing, and I combat rolled along the concrete walk, though it still grated my elbows and knees like sandpaper. I sprung to my feet and crouched in a fighting stance.

"I'm getting really fucking tired of shapeshifters," I growled.

Nadeem's lips curled back. "You are absolutely adorable." The djinn's thickened middle-eastern accent pierced my temples like a pair of ice picks prying into my brain.

I gritted my teeth against the lance of pain and stumbled a step as I lost sight of the ground beneath my feet. The afternoon sun intensified, blinding me as if I just emerged from a salacious night in the gentlemen's club into the bright light of noon. I threw an arm across my eyes to blot out the light and pushed one foot in front of the other. Murderous fury built with the pain of each step as I inched closer to Nadeem.

"Now, Matthew, that is no way to think of a friend."

"Get out of my head!"

Nadeem chuckled, and I could suddenly feel something crawling in the depths of my leg wound. I looked down, and my jeans wavered as something moved beneath the fabric. I slammed a hammer fist into my leg to kill it and instead drove a new spike of pain into my thigh. My leg collapsed under the shock of it, and I fell to all fours. I crawled a few more feet before the weight of his mental attack drove me completely to the ground. I wrapped my arms around my legs and retreated into a fetal position.

Nadeem drew a manicured fingernail across my trembling cheek. "Matthew, you have been so much fun, but unfortunately, my new master wishes me to no longer harm you."

The sun returned to normal, and the ice picks pulled free from my skull. My breath returned in short, ragged drags of air. The bright edges of pain receded from my vision, and I watched the black blur of a long tail disappear only moments before Craig came cautiously around the corner of the building.

He stared off in in the direction Nadeem had fled for a long minute. Relieved fear touched his eyes as he blew out a heavy breath. When he lowered his gaze to me, he extended a helping hand.

I slapped it away. "What the hell are you playing at?"

He took a couple of cautious steps back. "I'm not playing at anything," He grumbled, keeping his head up in wary surveillance of our surroundings. He looked like he expected an ambush.

I spared a glance at the empty sidewalk where Nadeem had disappeared around the back of the building. I didn't see the djinn, but that didn't mean it wasn't watching us from the shadows. It also didn't mean it wasn't playing with my mind, but at the moment, I didn't care. My rage burned, and the humiliation of not even laying a finger on the djinn didn't help.

I got my feet under me and rose, brushing the dirt from my pants. I winced as my hands contacted my skinned knees and last night's leg wound with a bit more violence than I intended. My anger consumed the pain as fuel for the fire. "Don't feed me that bullshit. Your djinn has spent the last few weeks screwing with me like a cat with a new toy."

His eyes snapped to mine. They grew wide in surprise then narrowed in suspicion. "You knew." The words came out more like an accusation than an admission.

"I'm catching on. Even if I don't know why."

He thrust out an open hand and took a threatening step forward. "Give it back to me," he demanded.

I dropped back a step and set my feet. "I don't know what you're talking about."

The muscle in the side of his jaw twitched as he clenched his teeth and spoke moving only his lips. "Give it back to me. Now!"

"I—don't—know—what—you're—talking—about." I spoke slowly, punctuating each word with a spit of breath as if it would beat the words into him.

Craig reached up and pulled his shirt apart, showing a patch of curly red hair on white skin that hadn't seen as much sun as this in years. The top three buttons snapped free and bounced along the concrete. "Give me back my necklace!"

Even in the heat of my anger, my mind processed recent events, if a bit slower than usual. The golden chain with a dog pendant was missing—a dog pendant that looked a lot like the charm on Nadeem's bracelet. Nadeem's words drifted through the blood rush pounding in my ears, *my new master*.

"It's the necklace, isn't it? That's how you control him?"

The fury on Craig's face cooled slightly as an eyebrow rose doubtfully. "Shit, you don't have it, do you?"

I tried to cage my own emotions, though sarcasm still dripped heavily from my lips. "No, I like being mentally pistol-whipped by a genie. It's loads of fun; you should try it sometime." My tone changed from mocking levity to condescending anger. "Don't be stupid, Craig. You've been acting like that long enough."

The last remnants of anger faded beneath a cloud of hopeless anxiety drifting across his face like a dense fog. "You'd never understand."

His forlorn expression pulled at my heart. I took a half-step in his direction, but the pain in my wounded leg thrummed anew, and my aggravation twisted it together with Craig's pitiful expression, kneading it into a high-octane fuel for my anger. *Oh, he doesn't get to act all pathetic after the bullshit he's put me through.*

My brows scrunched incredulously as my voice took on a low heated quality, like boiling water about to burst free of a tea kettle. "You're right. I don't understand. I don't understand why my best friend would set me up for a bar fight with an army of gorillas. And I don't understand why you would try to ruin my career.

"Sure, life put you through a shit-storm when your father died, but that's fuckin' life, and I don't understand why you think I had anything to do with it. I have always, and I mean *always,* had your back, even when I knew you were wrong. Even when it cost me a knife to the guts for defending you. Damnit, brother, I don't understand what I ever did to make you hate me so much."

I delivered each statement like a hammer blow. Each one driving his eyes toward the ground in flinching jerks until even his shoulders slumped in penitent defeat. I didn't stop, though, despite having said more than enough. In my righteous anger, I swung that hammer one more time. "And I definitely don't understand what would make you think you have any right to treat Teressa like you do. She deserves so much better."

Craig's back stiffened at Teressa's name, and his head snapped up with a renewed jealous fire burning in his eyes. He worked his hands into fists until his knuckles popped. His reaction didn't make the statement any less true, and it was too late to put the cat back into the bag. Besides, I was tired of watching him treat her like he did. If it's going to come to blows to straighten him out, then so be it. I slid a foot back to widen my stance, readying myself for Craig's temper.

He lifted one of his fists. The forefinger uncurled to point at my chest like a dagger. "You best leave her out of this," he growled. "I know how you feel about her."

My dander was up; I wasn't about to back down now. I leaned into his

LES GOULD

finger. "You've always known how I felt about her, even when you took her away from me!"

Hot spittle flew from his lips as he jabbed a thumb into his chest. "She —chose—me."

My jaw muscles spasmed at how hard I clenched my teeth, and my eyes moistened with tears I couldn't keep from forming. "And I buried my feelings for her the moment she did." He didn't need to know how shallow I kept that grave or how often those feelings clawed their way out of the dirt like a zombie trying to eat my soul. "I stood by you at your wedding and watched you say your vows. Brother, I love you too much to do anything to come between the two of you, but I love HER too much to let you keep treating her like shit. If you're having any marital issues, it's not because of me."

His mouth worked, but the noises coming out sounded like the snorts and growls of an enraged bull. His eyes flared, and I braced myself for the first blow, but he abruptly turned and stomped away, back around the corner.

I watched his back disappear, my breath coming in bulky adrenaline-fueled gasps, which faded into guilt. *I should have never brought up Teressa.* At the thought, my chest ached in a confusing mix of longing and worry.

Mentally, I brought out the shovel and started digging a new grave for old emotions. As the hole grew, Nadeem's words drifted into thoughts once more, *my new master.*

My heart leapt before I could even get my feet moving. I sprinted around the corner after Craig, willfully ignoring the jolts of pain in my leg. I heard the door to Craig's truck slam close and the engine roar to life. "Wait!" I yelled.

The truck pulled away. I kept sprinting after him, following the taillights out into the street. "Craig, wait!"

The brake lights grew bright well before the vehicle reached the stop sign at the end of the street. His truck rolled to a stop, and I could see Craig slam his hand repeatedly against the steering column as I closed the distance.

"Craig, wait, I know where it is!" I yelled again, and this time his head came up, and his eyes found me in the rearview mirror. I charged up the side of the truck to the passenger side door and pounded on the glass until he rolled the window down.

"Let me in…I know…where it is!" I managed between huffs of air that burned my throat.

He gave me a confused, angry frown. "Where what is?"

"Your necklace."

Craig's left hand hit the controls on his armrest, and the door locks popped up. I pulled the door open and jumped into the seat. "Teressa has it."

The truck squealed into motion before I got the door closed.

15

I struggled to get my seat belt latched as Craig blew through a stop sign and turned the corner like a NASCAR driver on a time trial. After missing the receiver twice, the latch clicked into place, and I grabbed the oh-shit handle with one hand for a bit more stability.

"I need to borrow your phone," I said, reaching over to pull the device from its cradle.

Craig didn't respond. He stared out the windshield, mumbling in a panicked mantra, "She doesn't know what she's doing. She doesn't know what she's doing. She doesn't know what she's doing."

"Craig, I need you to unlock your phone." I held his phone out with the finger sensor up.

Craig jerked the wheel to the left, rounding the next curve with a fishtail that slammed me into the passenger door. My exposed Goliath-bruised ribs found the door's armrest, and the shock of pain made me drop the phone. It bounced off the seat, did a somersault with a half twist, and dove straight into the driver's side footwell.

Unbuckling, I bent over the center console and searched for the phone, trying to keep my hand from tangling up Craig's feet as he haphazardly navigated the city streets. I chased the phone around, eventually pinning it down with an extended finger, and pulled it back into reach. As I sat up with my prize in hand, Craig's mindless chanting finally worked its way under my skin.

"Will you please stop saying that," I growled. "She'll be fine."

His horror-struck face turned to me. "No. You don't understand what he's like."

"Who, Nadeem?"

Craig glanced back at the road and jerked the wheel. We swerved across the double yellow, narrowly missing the vehicle in front of us by less than the hair on a gnat's ass. "Yes, Nadeem. Look, man, I was in a bad place when I found him. I'd just gotten back to the Sandbox, and I was mad at the world, mad at my dad for his heart attack, mad at the bank for taking the farm. But more than all that..." He let out a deep, aggravated sigh as he barreled past a Cadillac doing ten under the speed limit. "I was mad at you for getting a promotion after I got busted back to private with a ticket back to the Sandbox." He shot me a glance, but I could still see the streamers of hate beneath the regret in his eyes.

I didn't know how to respond. All I remembered was the sharp pain of the knife slipping between my ribs after I jumped in to defend Craig in some bar fight he started. I couldn't refuse the fast-tracked E-5 promotion any more than I could have intervened in his court-martial for instigating the whole thing. I knew they knocked him all the way back to private, but I honestly thought he volunteered for the transfer.

"I'm sorry," I volunteered, but even I could hear the lack of sincerity in the words.

"Anyways, Nadeem took all my anger and balled it up into one steaming pile of shit, pointing back to you. Then he finagled me an early release from the army with a promise to help me get my revenge on you if I'd only set him free."

Gracie's warning resounded in my ears. "You didn't free him, did you?"

"No. I wouldn't be looking for the necklace if I had, but Teressa will. And when she does, he'll kill me."

While the statement agreed with Gracie's warning, it seemed a bit insightful for Craig. "What makes you say that?"

"He's angry. A thousand years of playing bitch to whoever holds that damn dog medallion has made him—so very angry. I didn't realize how much until last night. I was supposed to free him after..." he peered guiltily at me from the corner of his eye.

"After arranging to have the shit beat out of me," I finished for him.

"Yeah, well, he didn't deliver, so neither did I." His voice carried a considerable amount of spite, considering he just confessed to trying to put me in the hospital.

I pushed the surge of rage welling up inside me to the side. I could deal with Craig later. At the moment, I had more pressing matters to contend with. "Well, since you're so tight with Nadeem, how do we get it back from Teressa?"

"I'm just going to take it," he said as matter-of-fact as the sky was blue.

"Right? Just take it. From someone who has control of a djinn? Who had already used that djinn to make you invite me home?" I watched his hard look melt into something of surprise, with grim satisfaction. "Not so fun to realize someone's been fucking with your brain, now is it?"

I held the phone out to him again. "Here, unlock your phone."

He gave me a skeptical glance. "Why?"

"Because I need to call someone who might actually know what to do." Doubt plowed furrows into his forehead, but he pressed a finger to the sensor.

I opened a web browser and logged into my Google account. It took a moment, but I found Gracie's name in my contact list. *God bless her hacker heart.*

"Pull into McDonald's while I make this call," I said, pointing to a pair of golden arches about a mile up the road. When he didn't immediately slow down, I lowered my voice into that flat no-nonsense monotone that makes insolent children and privates obey without question and repeated myself.

When the truck came to a rest in a parking spot, I said in the same commanding tone, "Go get us a couple of burgers. I'm not sure how long this will take, and I don't plan on going there starving."

I waited for the door to close before touching the series of hashtags opposite Gracie's name. The phone app opened, and I pressed send.

The phone rang once before Gracie's sleepy voice answered. She sounded like I just woke her up from a nap. "Hello?"

"Hey, Gracie, it's Matthew."

A yawn like a creaking door filled the earpiece. "Who?"

"Matthew Peterson."

"Oh, sorry. What's up?"

"You know that thing you said I shouldn't do? What if someone else does it?"

"Huh? Sorry, I only just got to sleep, you're going to have to be a bit more specific." Another yawn dragged at her last few words.

"Yeah, sorry. It's the djinn I've been dealing with. It's changed hands, and I'm not sure I can get its necklace away from the new owner before she frees him."

"Oh..." The drop in her tone sent an involuntary shiver up my spine. "That would be problematic."

"You don't say. I just ran across him a half-hour ago, and he put me on my knees without even touching me. It's like he pushed his way into my head and just willed the pain into me."

An exasperated sigh filled the earpiece. "It's called psychic projection, and it's pretty much his mind against yours. And I'm sorry to say; he's likely got centuries more experience than you."

"Okay, so in other words, it ain't real unless I think it's real."

"More or less, but I think you already know there's a bit more to it than that."

I rubbed my temples at the fresh memory of the pain and sighed heavily. "Yeah, I do. All right then, how do I harm him? Can I shoot him?"

"Sure, but if you're using lead bullets, he'll heal about as fast as you can wound him. Iron, on the other hand, does a little more lasting damage. If you can manage to find any iron loads."

Iron loads? I had no idea where to find iron loads. What I wouldn't have given to have access to Jacob's monster-hunter weapons stash. My chin dropped to my chest, and I ran my free hand through my hair, flinching as the gesture pulled at my bruised face. *This was looking about as promising as I did at the moment.* I disregarded the unhelpful thought and asked, "Will anything made of iron hurt it? Like a crowbar?"

"I guess you could beat him with it, but it'd be better if you could find an iron stake or something to stab him in the heart with. Or better yet, decapitate him."

The haunting memory of Jacob hacking off the head of a werebear, to make sure it stayed dead, flashed through my mind. I had even done the same thing to the one that killed Jonny with a silver-plated Bowie the old hunter had given me. I wished I wore that knife now and even briefly considered running back to barracks for it. "What about silver? I have that knife Jacob gave me."

"Djinn aren't particularly susceptible to silver, so it's not any better than a regular knife. And neither is stainless steel before you ask."

The driver's side door creaked opened, and Craig climbed in with a brown paper bag and a couple of drinks in his hands. I held up a hushing finger before he could speak.

"Thanks, Gracie. If you know of any help in the area, I could use it. Otherwise, I'll give you a call later and let you know how it goes."

"Matthew, take care of yourself," she said with a voice thickened by worry.

I pressed the end-call button and traded the phone for the drinks in Craig's hands. He quirked a questioning eyebrow to which I only answered, "Iron. We need iron."

Over burgers and fries, we debated the best place to find weapons made of iron and decided on stopping by the local home improvement store on our way to his apartment.

Without sufficient credit remaining on my card to buy my own cordless nail gun, I felt a bit guilty for jamming the safety on the rental, but that's what the security deposit is for. It took a bit of jury-rigging, but I eventually got it to where it would fire without having to jam the tip against the djinn's skull. I loaded a sleeve of nails and took a couple of test shots. The motor whined and then spat the nails into a tree a dozen paces away with a thud. They stuck firm, though they didn't sink in as far as I would have liked.

"It'll have to do," I said over my shoulder. Then placed the improvised weapon in the bed of the truck next to a digging bar, claw hammer, pickaxe, and an industrial-looking fireplace poker. They were the closest thing to iron we could find, but I doubted any of them were pure iron. I blew out my cheeks and said, "Heaven help us if we have to use any of these."

Craig gave the pile a dubious once over and shook his head. "We're so fucked."

I clapped him on the shoulder. "Couldn't agree with you more. Now let's get going."

By the time we pulled up in front of Craig's apartment, a bright orange sunset bloomed across the sky. It cast the row of townhomes in an ominous blood-drenched hue, which made our battle preparations seem that much more surreal. I draped a small section of chain over my neck, slipped the handle of an Eastwing hammer through my belt loop, and lifted the nail gun. Craig hefted the digging bar in one hand like a six-foot iron spear and shouldered the pickaxe with the other.

He led the way up the sidewalk with a slight swaying bounce to his step. I watched him for a moment then matched his step, whistling "Heigh Ho." Craig stopped midstep and shot me an incredulous glare. I gave him a wink and kept on whistling. The corner of his mouth curled up with a shrug of his shoulders as he resumed moving in the waddling march of one of Snow White's dwarves.

I managed to carry the tune for another measure or two before the stoop light flipped on. The townhome's beat-up front door opened, and the soft glow of light framed Teressa with Annabelle on her hip. "You two are lay…What the hell are you two doing?"

That did it; I couldn't keep my lips pursed together any longer and broke down laughing. Craig took another step then bent over in an echoing laugh of his own.

"And what are you doing with those tools?" she asked, sounding considerably less amused, which only made us laugh harder. "Tsk. Dinner's getting cold." She turned back into the house. "Let's go, Annabelle. Daddy and Uncle Matthew are acting like idiots."

Craig swallowed his laughter and gave me a nod toward the door. "Come on. She's pissed enough already, and I'd rather not have her sick Nadeem on us for dawdling."

Nadeem's name killed the mood faster than a firecracker in a cow pie. Don't ask. It's all fun and games until you're the one volunteered to see if the firecracker's a dud. Of course, that's why you let your best friend talk your younger brothers into it—only after you lengthened the fuse, of course. Though, following Craig into the apartment felt as if I'd just volunteered to check that firecracker, knowing it should detonate at any moment.

Last in, I turned to close the door. Long shadows cast counter to the setting sun crept ominously across the parking lot like the fingers of death himself reaching for my soul. The sick sensation of walking into a trap intensified between my shoulder blades. When my eyes landed on a pair of glowing orbs over a wolfish snarl watching from the depths of the shadows, I slammed the door shut and threw the deadbolt. It latched with a click that started the time bomb in my head ticking away.

Tick, tick, tick, tick.

A boom of crashing pots and pans came from the kitchen, and I practically jumped out of my skin. I spun and raced toward the sound with the nail gun raised.

The chain around my neck bounced off my chest as I stutter-stepped to a stop at the kitchen door. Craig stood on the other side of a stockpot, drenched in an explosion of chili. He stripped out of his shirt and used it as best he could to wipe away bits of meat and beans from his face and arms.

I swallowed the wisecrack comment forming on my tongue as my eyes found Teressa standing by the stove with a face redder than a ripe tomato and steam coming from her ears. She held the necklace in one hand and a meat tenderizer in the other.

"Whoa, Tee, wait a minute," I said, raising my hands in a cautionary gesture spoiled by the electric nail gun.

She pointed the tenderizer at me like a judge waiving his gavel at an unruly courtroom. "You...you stay out of this. And you better watch where you point that thing."

I placed the nail gun on the counter to my right, keeping the open palm of my left facing her. My mind raced as I scanned the room, trying to figure out how to diffuse the situation.

Annabelle sat beside the pool of chili splashing in the sauce. She grabbed beans by the handful and shoved them into her mouth completely oblivious to the parental standoff above her. Seeing her playing with chili dripping from her face and hair gave me an idea, not a particularly good idea, but better than anything else I had at the moment, so I went with it.

"Look, Tee, why don't you give Annabelle a bath while Craig and I clean this up."

"I said, stay out of this. Do you realize what he's been up to?" Teressa asked, shaking the tenderizer at Craig as if she'd rather beat him with it. "With this?" She thrust her other hand in my direction, sending the dog pendant swinging back and forth on its golden tether.

I nearly choked seeing the amulet so close, but still out of reach. "Yeah, actually, I do."

Craig balled up his shirt and threw it to the side. It bounced off the wall and landed on a pile of broken wood that used to be the kitchen table. "Give it back," he growled.

Teressa pulled the pendant back to her chest, protectively. "Nadeem's told me everything, Craig. You need help." Her voice broke painfully, and tears welled up in her eyes.

The patio door shattered in a shower of broken glass, drawing the alarmed attention of everyone in the room, even little Annabelle. Nadeem strode into the room, walking on the fragments of glass without making a sound. His linen pants disappeared into a bluish light that never quite touched the floor where his feet should have been. An emerald fire burned in his eyes, and his skin shown in a luminescent silver through his half-open shirt. The air in the room changed with his presence. It turned colder and became charged with an unnatural electricity.

Craig was the first to react. He shifted back on his feet, shying away from the djinn as if his mere touch would burn him.

While Craig slunk away, every muscle in my body tensed in a feral reaction to Nadeem's presence. My hands balled into fists, tightening until my knuckles popped. I wanted nothing more than to take him down and tenderize his face in a UFC worthy ground and pound, but seeing as our last run in left me incapacitated before I could even reach him, I held my ground and waited for the right opportunity.

I watched Nadeem slither closer with one wary eye while I kept the other on the nail gun resting on the countertop beside me. Uncurling my fists, I flexed my fingers, getting ready to snatch up the gun like Wyatt Earp at the djinn's first hostile move.

Teressa, on the other hand, relaxed. The tension left her face as she lowered her arms to her side. "Nadeem," she greeted in a voice devoid of any sincere emotion.

"Mistress," He replied in an equally flat tone thick with a middle-eastern accent. He took another step into the room, and Annabelle crawled away from him, backing toward her mother. The little girl never took her eyes off of the djinn.

I itched to do something, but with Annabelle and Teressa so close to him, I hesitated. While I waited, I felt him enter my mind. He slipped into my thoughts like quicksilver, slick and heavy. He pressed himself against my will, and my muscles loosened ever so slightly, just enough that they weren't ready to spring anymore.

Craig stopped retreating, and while his body took on a posture more at ease, his eyes shown with fear.

"Mistress, I have performed the tasks you have given me," Nadeem spoke hypnotically. "It is time for you to do the same. To fulfill your husband's promise to me."

Teressa shot a disappointed glare at Craig, a wordless look that spoke volumes of regret and shame. She placed the necklace on the counter and raised the meat tenderizer, spikes forward, above her head.

"Wait!" I shouted.

Teressa turned a startled expression, troubling the placid calm on her face.

Nadeem's presence in my mind exerted itself, and my mouth snapped shut as if sprung like a bear trap. I struggled to speak, to force words past Nadeem's influence, except every muscle in my jaw remained slack and unresponsive.

Teressa raised a questioning eyebrow, waiting for me to speak. I glanced as best I could from her to Nadeem and back again, hoping she could read in my eyes what I couldn't say with my mouth.

She turned to Nadeem. "Let him speak."

"Mistress, he'll speak only lies. Fulfill your promise, and I'll release them both."

Teressa lowered the tenderizer and laid her free palm over the begemmed medallion, hiding it from Nadeem's view. "I want to hear what he has to say first."

Nadeem's eyes turned a hair duller, and his presence in my mind relaxed, letting me move my jaw again. I worked my chin side to side, exploring my full range of motion, but when I tried lifting a hand to massage my jaw muscles, neither of them would move. Nadeem rocked his head side to side, sending his braided beard swaying with the gentle motion.

Teressa waved the mallet at me in a *get-on-with-it* gesture, "Well?"

"Don't do it. If you release him, he will kill Craig."

She turned to her husband, whose posture at the other end of the room was all casual disinterest, but I could see the sheer terror in his eyes. Teressa's face turned hard, and her brows drew down angrily.

"It's nothing more than a bed of his own making," she snarled.

"Then think of Annabelle," I pleaded.

We both looked to where her daughter had been playing. My heart leapt into my throat. Nadeem's silver hands held the girl close to his chest. His manicured fingers slid through her hair, pulling out bits of chili that had already begun to dry.

"Now, now," he whispered. "I would never harm such a pretty, innocent, little face. No, I would never—unless," the cold fire of his green eyes turned up to stare into Teressa's. "Unless I had to. Promises have been made, and promises shall be *kept*." He stressed the last word, and Annabelle stiffened abruptly.

I reached for the nail gun, but my hands still wouldn't move. Nadeem had reasserted himself, coiling his presence around my mind and squeezing like an anaconda. The world around me turned white in agony as pain blossomed in my skull. He then twisted a knife of red-hot iron into my leg wound. My knees gave out in the shock, sending me crashing to the floor like a toppled statue. Unable to brace myself, my face bounced off the linoleum.

A very real physical pain sung through my broken nose at a slightly different key than the djinn's psychic projection. The difference was subtle, but enough for me to remember, *it's not real unless I believe it is.* I struggled to hold on to the thought. The djinn induced pain faltered, flickered like a faulty fluorescent lamp, but then slammed back into me with renewed vengeance. I doubled in half; a whimpering scream escaped my lips.

Craig let out his own renewed cries of torment, but I registered it as something remote. Something that didn't have any immediate bearing on me. I heard Teressa's feet patter through the pool of chili in a rush of motion. I envisioned her coming to my aid. I waited for her gentle touch on my shoulder, but when she spoke, her voice came from the same direction as Craig's cries.

"Stop. Please stop!" she pleaded.

In the midst of the fury of pain, Nadeem's taunting laugh echoed inside my head. It hammered like a battering ram into the fortress at the back of my mind, where I kept my feelings for Teressa walled away. The barrier shattered into a million pieces as if made from tempered glass, releasing a flood of anger, frustration, jealousy, longing, and loneliness. The torrent of emotions pressed against Nadeem's influence and drowned his manufactured feelings in pain more real than anything he could inflict. I mentally picked myself up and wrapped myself in those emotions, then shoved Nadeem out of my mind.

"Release me," Nadeem growled.

Teressa rushed back to the necklace on the counter by the stove.

I pressed myself up to my knees and tried to speak, but my screams had worked my throat raw, and it came out as a croak.

She raised the mallet above her head, and I could see the tears dripping from her chin.

I managed to get to my feet and fumbled along the counter beside me for the nail gun.

Teressa brought the tenderizer down. It crashed into the jeweled medallion pointy side first, and the fragile stone shattered. It exploded outward in a crash of thunder. The sound concussed through my body with enough physical force to knock me off balance, but not before I slipped my fingers around the nail gun's grip.

The releasing energy shuddered through Nadeem as he drank in his freedom. His arms loosened their hold of Annabelle, and the girl fell to the floor with a shriek. Teressa dove toward the ground, unable to catch her daughter, but fast enough to get a hand under her head and cushion it from the impact.

I swung the nail gun up in front of me and pulled the trigger as fast as the gun could cycle. Sixteen-penny nails flew from the end of the modified gun. They bit into Nadeem's flesh as it changed from silver to the living fire of lava.

He snarled in pain and turned blazing eyes of sapphire blue on me. "Fool," he said, raising a hand in my direction. The presence I ejected earlier shouldered its way past my defenses. Unbridled, his renewed attack carried the momentum of an eighteen-wheeler and dropped me howling to the floor once more.

Nadeem reached down to Teressa, where she clutched her startled two-year-old tight to her chest, and placed a blackened finger against her forehead. Teressa's head snapped back with enough speed to give her whiplash as she screamed in agony.

"You petty mortals don't deserve to live." He sounded like a kennel master talking to worthless dogs. "But I did promise. Release your daughter before she gets hurt."

Teressa's arms opened, but Annabelle clung to her mother, crying at the top of her lungs.

Nadeem sighed impatiently and bent over to pry the little girl's arms free from Teressa. At his touch, Annabelle let go and her wails stopped.

The press of the djinn's presence in my mind pulled back as he dealt with Annabelle and her mother. With Nadeem distracted, I drew upon my very real pain, my broken nose, my bruised ribs, the ache of the dart wounds in my leg, and wrapped my mind in a shield of physical hurt. Behind that protection, I forged the tempest of emotions boiling inside of me into a sledgehammer. Then I went after the djinn like a SWAT team battering down a secure door. I pummeled Nadeem, striking him again and again until I beat him from my mind. The effort left my head splitting as if he'd taken a bit of me with him.

I carved a small void in the midst of the pain—an eye in the hurricane where neither Nadeem nor the hurt could touch me. From there, I summoned just enough clarity of thought to make decisions.

I rolled over, rising onto all fours. My hand hit something hard and heavy—the cold steel of Craig's digging bar. I curled my fingers around it and lifted my head to match eyes with the djinn. Surprise flared in his sapphire gaze as I worked my feet back under me.

Nadeem placed Annabelle to the side with a gentleness that contradicted the look of wanton violence he never diverted from me.

I watched him from a kneeling crouch, readying my feet for Annabelle to be clear of danger. When he stood, I sprung. The sixteen-pounds of metal pulled on my arm and slowed my rise. With a surge of adrenaline, I pushed through the resistance, straining my arm, and felt something give in my bicep, but I got my other hand on the bar and forced it up in front of me.

The wound in my leg burned as I exploded through my first step. My second step, however, splashed in the pool of chili. Beans and meat squished and slid beneath my foot, and I struggled to keep my balance. Nadeem used the misstep to renew his mental assault, but I was ready. I let the void collapse and allowed the surge of real pain and emotions to fill my mind once again. It left Nadeem no room, and the shock of it showed in the cracks of his lava face.

I advanced with animalistic rage, holding the point of the digging bar in front of me like a lance.

Nadeem recovered, sidestepping my charge and sweeping the point past him with a hand that sizzled as it contacted the iron bar.

The mass of the bar carried me past him. I tucked and rolled on the way to the wall beyond, absorbing the brunt of the impact on my shoulder with a grunt. The weight of the bar threatened to pull it out of my fingers, but I kept my grip. The heavy bar turned slowly, but I got it pointed at Nadeem, who took on a fighting stance with the practiced ease of a millennium of experience.

With my surprise spent, I didn't stand a chance with the albatross of a weapon against the agility of the djinn. Still, I readied my feet for another charge. I shifted my balance forward, and an electric whine accompanied my war cry.

The telltale thump, thump, thump of the nail gun drew a half-glance from Nadeem as the nails found their mark in his shoulder. Teressa held the gun in both hands, squeezing the trigger as fast as she could. The gun jammed after the fifth nail, but it gave me the chance I needed to close the distance.

Nadeem grabbed the bar with both hands, trying to wrestle it from my grasp, and let out a scream of pain that sounded like the mad howl of a wounded wolf. With supernatural strength, the djinn wrenched the bar to left and then back to the right. I hung onto the implement for dear life, not daring to let go.

As he pulled me back the other way, Nadeem stiffened. His back arched and he let go, sending me and the bar flying into the broken glass of the patio door. The bits of glass cut into the flesh of my hands as I tried to catch myself. The bar danced along the floor with a metallic ring.

I hustled back to my feet and wearily hefted the bar in front of me, readying myself for another attack.

Nadeem flailed his arms, trying to reach behind him, while out of the center of his chest, I could see the bloody point of the pickaxe.

I rushed in and drove the point of the digging bar into the djinn's chest. The mass of the bar pushed the point through him. He let out a wounded hiss and collapsed to his knees. Still holding the bar with both hands, I fell to the ground with him. Face to face, I watched the fire in his sapphire eyes dim until only black obsidian remained.

I levered the djinn onto its back, careful not to remove the heavy bar, then exhaustion eked out the last of my strength, and I sagged onto my back.

"Is he dead?" asked Craig weakly.

"I think so," I said, prying my eyes open. I looked past Craig, who was bracing himself with his hands on his knees and panting heavily, to Teressa. She rocked back and forth on her knees, clutching Annabelle to her chest and smothering the little girl with kisses. I rolled over and crawled back to my feet. "But let's make sure."

The sound of glass being ground into the floor by very heavy feet made my heart leap into my throat before I could take more than a step toward the knife block next to the stove. I turned my head and followed a pair of combat boots up an off-the-rack black suit hugging a dark man much too large to shop off-the-rack.

He slipped his drawn pistol into his shoulder holster. "We'll take care of that," he said as two more suits stepped up beside him.

17

C raig stepped protectively between Teressa and the suits. "Who the hell are you?"

"The Calvary," I said dryly while I found a chair to sit in.

"Sergeant Peterson, I presume," said the first suit.

"DEMON," I said with a dip of my head. "I see you got my smoke signal. Punctual as always."

"Wait. You know who these people are?" asked Craig.

"Yeah, they're the government's version of the good guys—for things like this." I nodded to the still cooling body of the djinn.

The lead suit gave a flick of his hand, and the two behind him began examining the djinn's body. "It was my understanding, Sergeant, that Senior Agent Stewart instructed you to contact us the next time you ran into something within our jurisdiction."

"Thanks, I never did get her name. And you know what, she completely forgot to give me her number, too."

The man's stoic expression faltered for a moment before muscle memory kicked in, and it slipped back to a resting bitch face. "Yes—well, regardless, we cannot condone citizens taking the supernatural into their own hands. In the future, Sergeant Peterson, we would appreciate it if you would contact us should you encounter the supernatural again. As a soldier, I'm certain you can appreciate the importance of letting the professionals take care of things like this." The man gave the dead djinn the same disinterested pissed-off flat look he'd given me since he stepped into Craig and Teressa's house.

"For someone who's always late to the party, I must admit, y'all do have a knack for showing up for the cleanup, but I'll keep you in mind the next time."

"Sir, we're packed and ready for transport," one of the smaller suits said.

The big suit turned to Craig, who still stood defensively in front of his wife and daughter. "Private Flannigan, Missus Flannigan, we'll dispose of this for you," he said, scooping up the remnants of the necklace in his meaty hands. The pair of smaller suits carried the djinn's body out the patio door. As they walked past him, he added, "We'll dispose of that, too. Have a good night."

He spun on his heel to face me, then reached into his inner jacket pocket before extending the hand to me. "Sergeant Peterson, we wouldn't want you to have an excuse next time."

I plucked the plain white business card from between his forefinger and thumb with a sardonic smile. "I'll do my best."

He harrumphed and strode out the way he came in. At the broken door frame, he turned back one last time. His face relaxed, and he scoffed, "You took on a djinn with nothing but gardening tools. I'm not sure if you're a genius or just one hell of a lucky fool." He pointed at the card in my hand. "If you want to find out, give that number a call." He withdrew his hand and disappeared into the night.

Craig and I stared out after him, unsure of what to do next. Teressa, however, stood and disappeared upstairs with Annabelle. She came back down a few minutes later with a duffle and diaper bag in her hands.

Craig took one look and popped up to his feet. He rushed to relieve her of the bags. "Where are we going?"

The simple, inclusive question put a weary smile on Teressa's face. "A hotel. I can't stay here."

I followed them out the door to Teressa's car and watched as they loaded it like a family for the first time in a long time. A smile touched my lips, and I mentally started rebuilding my fortress for all my Teressa feelings.

Without a word, I left them to each other and went to Craig's truck to fetch my bag. It was a long walk back to post, and I didn't dare risk showing up late to morning formation. As I climbed back down from the truck bed with my bag in hand, Craig stepped up behind me and placed a hand on my shoulder. I never heard him approach, and his sudden touch nearly made me jump out of my skin.

"Sorry about that, brother." It had been ages since Craig called me brother. The simple term of endearment softened the burr between us. He then did something else he hadn't done in an equally long time; he wrapped his arms around me in a hug. It took me an awkward moment before my arms rose to return the embrace. With a clap on each other's back, we pulled apart.

"Um...I'm going to go to the hotel with Tee and my Annabee," Craig said, stuffing a hand into one of his pockets. When it came back out, his keys jangled from his fingers. "Take the truck; I'll come get it tomorrow."

Some element of stupid pride wanted me to reject the offer, but my bone-weary legs overcame it, and I took the keys. "Thanks."

Craig clapped me on the arm and then jogged back to Teressa's car. She started the engine as he got in, and I watched them pull away.

After the taillights faded from view, I opened the door to the truck cab and tossed my bag into the passenger seat. I climbed into the cab and noticed the corners of Jonny's journal pressing against the thin plastic of the bag. Pulling it out, I flipped it open and placed the DEMON business card into a spare slot in the cover, between the pen and the card that read *Jacob McGinnis, M.H.*

I flipped through the journal's pages, passing sections with little more than a name on them; there were so many incomplete sections. So many monsters that Jonny had only heard of and so much I still didn't know. When I finally reached the page I was looking for, I reached for the pen and came to a decision at the same time. One way or another, I was going to complete Jonny's journal.

With the driver's side door propped open to keep the lights on, I filled out the page with everything I now knew about the djinn.

THE END

III

POLAR PROTOCOL

1

I stepped off the bus in Amsterdam, NY, disappointed with the lack of snow this close to Christmas until Old Man Winter wrapped his cold gnarly fingers around my balls and reintroduced them to my abdomen before my heel hit the pavement. The shock drove thought from my mind and sent a gasp of frigid air whistling past my clenched teeth.

"Ho...ho-oly cra-ap it's cold!" I stammered, rubbing my arms through the long sleeves of my combats with enough vigor to start a friction fire. It did little to settle the gooseflesh, but at least it kept the blood from congealing in my shrinking veins.

"Damn straight, it is," called a familiar voice.

Turning toward the voice, I found a snowman dressed as a cowboy sitting on the concrete barrier and smoking a cigar. A weathered hand plucked the cigar from his lips with a puff of smoke. The gray smoke curled around the brim of a broad hat pressed low over white hair. He wore the collar of his heavy duster popped up to protect his ears, and his face hid behind a healthy start to a winter beard. The long tails of his duster parted over thick canvas pants that I'd wager ten to one had a nice thick fleece lining keeping him warm.

He kept one hand buried in the pocket of his duster while the other lifted the cigar back to his lips. The cigar's tip flared to bright red, and a moment later, his lips curled back in a smile that released another gust of smoke.

I started toward him, shaking my head with a broad smile. "Jacob, wha...what are you doing here?"

He took another puff on his cigar, before grinding it out on the concrete block and flicking the stem into the parking lot. He stood, blowing the cherry-scented cloud of his Black and Mild in my direction. "Enjoying this fine winter day and waiting for you. Though you look like you forgot how cold it can get up here."

I slid my bag off my shoulders and pulled out the heavy jacket that went with my combat uniform. "It's not like I needed this in Georgia." The thick material cut off the bitter breeze as I slid my arms through the sleeves. "It was sixty-degrees when I left."

A glint of laughter touched Jacob's eyes as the corners of his mouth curled into a smirk. "You grunts are all alike, won't even put your pants on unless you're told to do so." He bent over, choking on the last couple words as a sudden bout of coughing erupted from deep in his chest. He spat the wad of phlegm dislodged from his lungs into a handkerchief and braced himself on his knees, keeping his breaths shallow.

Worry knitted my eyebrows together. "Are you going to be all right?"

"I'll be fine. The cold's just catching up to me is all. Come on, let's go warm up." Jacob pulled a key fob from one of his pockets and, after a few clicks, an F-150 in the neighboring parking lot honked its horn then roared to life.

We climbed into the cab, and I cranked my seat heater to the max. The warmth soon drove Jack Frost back outside, and I melted into my seat with a sigh. "God bless seat heaters."

Jacob made an agreeable noise. "I'll second that. Seat heaters and coffee...and hotcakes." Jacob closed his eyes and licked his lips. "And bacon. God bless bacon. You know, I think I could go for a nice hot breakfast."

"It's nearly twenty-hundred hours."

His right eyebrow quirked up skeptically. "It's never too late for breakfast. Come on. You know you want some."

My stomach growled eagerly. "I would, but Mark should be getting here any minute to give me a ride home."

"Oh yeah, about that. Uh, he's not coming." He raised a pacifying hand at my sudden alarm. "Now, don't you worry. Everything is fine. Your family has been through a lot this year, so I swung by the farm a few days ago, just to check in."

Been through a lot? More like been through hell, and we're still trying to find our way out. This past spring, a werebear had killed my old man and Jonny, my youngest brother, and I spent the last six months in therapy trying to come to terms with it. The fact that I no longer considered Jonny's death a suicide spoke volumes to the effectiveness of the kind of help I'd been getting. Help my mother and siblings couldn't afford. I couldn't begin to imagine how hard it'd been for them without it.

I sat back into my seat and gave Jacob a rueful grin. "Thanks." The word came out heavy, carrying more than simple gratefulness for his recent visitation. Without Jacob, the monster hunter, we never would have avenged Jonny's death. No, more than likely, I, along with my brothers, Mark and Luke, would have been the bear's next meal. I owed the man a debt of gratitude I could never repay.

Jacob grunted something of an uncomfortable acknowledgment and moved the conversation along. "Anyways, your mother mentioned you were on your way home, and Mark has his hands full managing things on the farm. Since I was in the area and had some spare time, I offered to give you a ride home." His eyes lit as a devilish grin creased his lips. "Unless you'd rather walk."

I glanced out the windshield and watched the leafless limbs of the trees sway in Old Jack Frost's taunting sigh. I shook my head and warmed my hands over the truck's vents. "No. I think I'd rather ride."

Jacob unleashed a burst of laughter that degraded into another coughing fit until his hacking managed to shake something loose. He cracked the window and spat into the street then gave his chest a few thumps with his fist as the window rolled back up. He tipped a silver traveling mug up to his lips, swished the contents around in his mouth, and then swallowed. "Ack, sorry about that," he said, stuffing the base of the mug into the cup holder and dropping the gear shifter into reverse.

The tires hummed on the pavement, and the Ace hardware store marking the bus stop soon disappeared from view. "So, I've been meaning to ask," Jacob said with a quick peek into the review mirror. "Why the bus? Flying would be much faster."

"Yeah, the fastest way to the bottom of a six-foot hole. The bus may be slower, but I prefer staying on the ground."

Jacob shot me an incredulous look. "Then how the hell did you get over to Afghanistan?"

I shrugged my shoulders. "With a shot of whiskey and a healthy dose of Dramamine. I slept like a baby through the whole flight."

Jacob scoffed. "Of course, you did." He turned on the highway and accelerated. "How about that meal? My treat?"

"I'm a farm kid and a grunt, you sure you can afford to feed me?" I asked with a smirk.

"I'm sure. I'm starving, and I really don't want to eat my meal with you drooling into your lap."

"Fair enough, what did you have in mind?"

"Miss Johnstown Diner. Like there's another option?"

"Nope. I was just checking," I replied, enjoying the views of the countryside speeding past.

We rode the rest of the way to the diner in pleasant silence. There was just something about a couple of military men alone in a truck. We could enjoy each other's company over the hum of the tires without saying a word or looking anywhere other than out our windows.

Jacob's F-150 rolled to a stop outside the diner. The narrow red building stuck out like a sore thumb between a blocky two-story building dating back to the early twentieth century and another, judging by the peeling paint, that hadn't seen the wet side of a paintbrush in more than a decade. The lighted sign dangling from a simple pole declared the place as our destination, even before my nose picked up the fragrant aromas that set my stomach begging for food.

Jacob got out of the truck and sucked in a huge breath of air through his nose despite the cold. "Ah," he sighed. "I'll never get tired of that smell."

I inhaled my own draft of the savory fragrance and couldn't disagree. It smelled of all the good things I could remember from my childhood, not that there were many of them.

The man attending to an assortment of short-order items sizzling away on the grill popped his head up at the sound of the opening door. "Seat yourselves, guys."

Customers filled the stools lining the service bar behind the cook. Their faces bore the familiar look of Upstate New Yorkers who favored places like this more for the warmth of company amidst the bitter start of winter than to enjoy a good meal. Having endured my fair share of northeastern winters, I knew the feeling.

Jacob and I worked our way toward the back of the room and sat at a table beneath a curio cabinet of miniature racecars heralding back to the origins of stock car racing.

The cook plated and served the food from the griddle to customers waiting eagerly at the bar with silverware in hand. He wiped his hands on a cloth tucked into his apron then made his way around the counter with menus in hand to greet us.

"Welcome to the Miss Johnstown Diner, I'm Georgie. Can I get you something to drink?"

"What, no Sophie tonight?" I asked more earnestly than I intended.

"Nah, I'm on my own. Sophie only works when her brother Keith is on the grill."

"Oh," I said, trying to not sound too disappointed, but by the humor lighting Jacob's eyes, I failed miserably. I examined the menu, flipping back and forth as if I could hide the scarlet flushing my face in the laminated page.

"I'll take coffee, please," Jacob said, bailing me out.

"Yeah," I began, then cleared the frog from my throat. "Coffee sounds great."

Georgie reached over the counter and grabbed a couple of mugs. After a quick splash from the coffee pot, he pushed full mugs in front of each of us. "I'll give you two a moment to look over the menu." The door opened, and Georgie drifted away to greet the new customer.

"So, Sophie?" The teasing tone to Jacob's voice grated as if my younger brother, Luke, had asked the question. The fact that Luke decided to go skiing with his college roommate this year, instead of coming home for Christmas, made the comment sting a bit more than it should.

I took a couple slow breaths to flush away the anger replacing the heat of embarrassment in my cheeks. Once calmed, I answered the question. "After the werebears, I completely forgot to give her a call, and by the time I remembered, I was on the bus heading back to Georgia. Kinda' hoped I'd get the chance to explain myself today, though."

"Somehow, I don't think she lost much time waiting by the phone," Jacob said in an ambiguous tone somewhere between chiding and consoling.

"You're probably right," I conceded, pushing the menu to the edge of the table. I folded my hands in front of me and put on my best poker face before meeting Jacob's blue eyes. "So, are you ready to tell me the real reason you're going so far out of your way to buy me dinner?"

Jacob opened his mouth then closed it as Georgie stepped back up to the table. "What can I get you?"

I stuck with the classic breakfast for dinner while Jacob ordered a sunrise burger, blackened all around. How he could eat charcoal for dinner baffled me. Once Georgie collected the menus and left with our order, I raised a quizzical eyebrow at Jacob.

"I have to admit you're smarter than the average grunt."

I clapped a hand to my chest in a mocking pained gesture. "That almost hurt," I said, then narrowed my eyes. "Now talk, Squid."

He sucked in a deep nasally breath and blew it out through pursed lips. "Fine. Gracie told me you handled that djinn in Georgia well enough that DEMON matched my offer."

"How the...nevermind," I sighed and waved off the rest of the statement. With Gracie, Jacob's technical wiz of a granddaughter, I probably didn't want to know. "The guy only gave me his card. It's not like he meant it as a real offer."

Jacob took a sip of his coffee then put the mug back onto the table without breaking eye contact. "Son, that's about as real as DEMON gets."

I scowled back at him. Jacob calling me son dredged up deep-rooted emotions of my no-good old man that six months of intensive therapy couldn't free me from. "Be that as it may, *Gramps*," I stressed the word somewhere between teasing and mockery. "It wasn't the most cordial invite. But if you keep calling me son, I may reconsider."

"Ah, sorry about that. At my age...well, some habits are hard to break. Anyways, what I meant to say is, I'm on a case, and I could use some help, especially from someone willing to take on a djinn with nothing but garden tools."

I shook my head. "Jacob, I haven't been home for Christmas in four years. Besides, I'm not even sure how I survived the djinn."

"Matthew, I promise to keep you properly armed and to have you home for Christmas." Jacob sighed heavily. "Look, I'm not trying to humor you. There're a bunch of kids missing, and I need all the help I can get."

A very real need filled his hard, blue eyes. I lowered my gaze and stared into the black of my coffee, selfishly trying to lose myself, but instead, my mind focused on the man I owed for saving my family. I didn't have the right to refuse him, no matter the danger, no matter my longing to just stay home. With a nod of decision to the table, I picked up my cup and drained it, feeling the warmth spread down my chest as I swallowed both the coffee and the fear which were keeping my tongue tied. I lifted my eyes to meet his. "I'm in. Whatever you need. But just so you know, I was in before you mentioned the kids."

2

The crunch of frozen gravel crumbling beneath the weight of Jacob's F-150 announced our arrival to my family's farm. The truck's headlights swept across the Dutch Colonial barn at the end of the long drive. Rusted roof tin met weathered wood in streaks of oranges and grays that gave the building a depressed, beaten-down look. It brought back memories of a childhood I'd rather forget. At least this time, my old man wasn't here to greet me with the business end of his Winchester.

Jacob turned the wheel and parked next to the old Cape Cod farm-house. The spotty fur of peeling paint sent oblong shadows along the siding under the spotlight of the truck's lights. Through the living room window, I could see a Charlie Brown Christmas tree, dressed in lights and garland that twinkled in the soft flickering light of the only TV my family owned.

Slapping the shifter into park, Jacob pressed the ignition button, killing the seat heaters along with the engine. The oppressive cold wormed its way into the cab, chilling the air until my breath came out in billowing clouds of foggy mist while I stared out the windshield like a deer caught in the headlights of an oncoming semi. My mind worked through the freight train of dredged up memories and emotions until finally it dawned on me that this place no longer felt like home.

"Everything all right?" Jacob's voice drew my attention, breaking the hypnotic pull of forgotten memories. The dashboard lights cast dark shadows across his face, but I could see the concern in his eyes.

I smoothed the frown creasing my lips and shook my head before glancing back out the windshield. "No. It's the same as I remember, but somehow…" I shrugged, "I don't recognize it anymore."

Jacob clapped an encouraging hand onto my shoulder, jostling me back to reality as much as it lent his strength. "When you've been gone for a while, home can be like that, and the longer you're gone, the more it loosens its hold on you. Especially when you lose someone who made it home in the first place." His fingers squeezed my shoulder before he let go. "Come on, your family is waiting for us."

We kicked our boots off in the vestibule, and Jacob let me go through the kitchen door first. My mother stood at the refrigerator door, rearranging the plates of leftovers cluttering the shelves. The gray outnumbered the black in her hair and her shoulders slumped beneath the burden of an unseen weight. She looked decades older than the last time I saw her and well beyond her fifty-some years. The door clicked closed behind us, drawing my mother from the fridge. When her eyes took in her new guests, her back straightened and a warmth brightened her face with a broad smile.

She spread her arms wide and shuffled across the tile floor in slippers old enough to have the imitation fur worn off. "Matthew, oh thank God you made it home safe."

In two long strides, I closed the gap between us and engulfed her in my own embrace, squeezing her into me. I couldn't remember the last time I received a hug as my first greeting in this house. Not that my mother ever withheld affection from her children, just that my old man, Paul, would normally spoil the mood before she got the chance.

The place may not have felt like home, but in my mother's arms, it was the closest I've come to home in a long time.

"Well it's about time you showed up," said a high pitch voice with all the sass of an annoyed cat.

My mother tensed beneath my arms, and her head leaned hard into my shoulder as she blew out a sigh before letting me go and moving to greet Jacob. My sister, Mary, swooped in and gave me her customary slug to the shoulder in greeting. At nearly fifteen and a body toned by slinging hay bales and keeping the cows in line, it knocked me off balance and revived the pain of a gunshot wound I had thought healed.

I rubbed the developing bruise in my bicep. "Hey, easy there. That actually hurts. You're not as small as you used to be."

"Mary, be nice to your brother," my mother said, reaching into the cupboard for a coffee mug. Mary shot her a hurt glare with a *harrumph* before she spun on her heel and stormed back upstairs without a word. The mug in my mother's hand hit the countertop with an echoing thump of ceramic on Formica, and she shook her head with a growl at the sound of stomping feet coming from the floor above.

I quirked an uncertain eyebrow at Jacob, who shrugged his shoulders in a *don't-ask-me* gesture.

The kitchen door opened behind us, and Mark stepped in, bringing the aromas of a working dairy farm with him. He glanced from me, to our mom, to the heavy steps echoing through the ceiling, and then back to me. In a gasp that rivaled a semi's airbrakes, he closed his eyes and hung his head. "For heaven's sake, please give me one night. Just one night of peace. That's all I want. Is it really that much to ask for?"

Jacob glanced at my mother, still filling coffee cups at the other end of the kitchen before lowering his voice to a barely audible whisper. "Son, in my experience, when there's more than one woman in the house, it usually is."

Mark's eyes opened in an unappreciative glare. "Not that I was asking you, but if you have something more constructive than antiquated wisdom to offer, I'd appreciate it."

"That's why I brought him home," Jacob said, jabbing a thumb in my direction.

I brought my hands up defensively. "Whoa, don't throw me to the wolves."

"They're more like mountain lions," Mark said. "They hiss and growl at each other non-stop and if I try to say anything, they both eat you alive. I've even considered spending a night or two curled up in the barn with the cows for safety."

My mother's head snapped up from fixing the coffee to shoot us a cold glare from across the room. "I think the barn might be warmer," I added under my breath.

The look she gave us through the steam drifting off the cups in her hands dropped the temperature in the room another degree or two. "You boys seem to forget I can hear like a cat, too."

"Sorry, Momma," Mark and I said together.

She handed one of the cups to me and gave the other to Jacob, not letting it go until he met her eyes. "Do you have anything you want to add on the subject?"

"Uh, no, ma'am." Jacob accepted the cup and pressed it to his lips. He flinched at the temperature but didn't lower the cup until my mother turned her narrow eyes back on her sons.

Her glower settled on Mark and his barn clothes. "Go get washed up and changed. I'll warm you up some leftovers for dinner." Mark squeezed by me without another word. "What about the two of you? Have you eaten yet?"

Jacob tilted back the coffee cup, finishing it without ever taking a breath. He handed her the empty cup with a smile. "I'm sorry to say that we have. It's my fault really, I didn't give Matthew much of a choice. Besides, I'd hate to impose. Thank you for the coffee. It was lovely, but I best be going."

"Well, thank you for giving him a ride home," my mother said, then shot me a reproachful look before I could get a word in edgewise.

Rolling my eyes, I reached out a hand to pump Jacob's. "Thanks, *again*, for the ride home and for dinner." I stressed the word, "again," so that my mother wouldn't feel she raised a completely ungrateful dolt.

"Ah, no problem. Happy to help. I'll pick you up at eight then?"

"Sure."

"Ma'am," Jacob said, tilting his head goodbye.

My mother placed her hands on her hips as the door closed behind Jacob. "And where will you be going tomorrow?"

"Jacob needs some help with something. I figured it's the least I could do for the ride home."

"Uh-huh. Just make sure you make some time for family."

"I will, I promise."

She nodded smartly. "Well, since you've already eaten, you best go upstairs and let your sister welcome you home without my interference." In a thready whisper, she added, "I don't know what got into her, she's been so excited that you were coming home."

I reached out and pulled my mother into my chest with a hug. "Mom, I'm glad to be home. Merry Christmas."

She resisted with the stiffness of habit then melted against me with a weak smile creasing her lips. "Welcome home and Merry Christmas, Matthew. Now let me go so I can get your brother's dinner ready."

I picked up my bag and charged up the stairs. Turning at the top landing, I collided with Mark on his way to the shower. I bounced off him, stumbling backward and losing my balance as my foot missed the top step. Mark reached out and grabbed a handful of my shirt, arresting my fall before I took the express to the bottom of the stairs.

"Whoa, take it easy there."

I clutched at his hand as my heart leapt into my throat and gave the stairs an uneasy glance. "Yeah, thanks. That's a long way down."

Mark pulled me up to the landing next to him. "Yeah, don't mention it." He let my shirt go but stood there wringing the clean clothes in his hands, putting wrinkles into them that even a steamroller couldn't smooth out.

"Is there something else on your mind?"

Mark glanced around to make sure we were alone, then threw his arms around me and pulled me in for a hug. I returned it awkwardly, not necessarily for the *odeur-de-barn* fragrance emanating from his work clothes but because, aside from our mother, my family's not usually the hug and hold type. He gave my back a clap that I felt reverberate through my chest before releasing me.

"Matt, thanks for the loan. I'm not sure how we could have survived this fall without it."

I gulped, uncomfortable with his gratitude. It was quite literally the least I could do. Our old man ran the family farm in the red for years and after he died Mark had the good graces to take it over, along with all its debts. So, when the bankers came circling like vultures to pick the carcass clean, I sent Mark most of my life savings as a stopgap. Which made a sizable dent seeing as I had spent the last four years living on Uncle Sam's dime, though I did have to kiss my dream of paying for my first truck in cash goodbye.

"Don't mention it. And it wasn't a loan." I couldn't see how the farm would ever manage to pay me back, and I'd rather not have that kind of thing hanging over our heads for the rest of our lives.

Mark thumbed away a tear, playing it off as cleaning dirt from his eyes, which, considering his unwashed state, he probably just put dirt in his eyes. "I'll pay you back as soon as I can."

I shook my head. "No, you won't. If it makes you feel any better, we'll call it an investment and we'll split the profits. If we ever have any," I added, unable to contain the eye roll.

He reached out, grabbed my hand, and pumped it. "Fine then, partner. Welcome to the Peterson Farm Shit Show."

"Silent partner," I amended. "And don't go expecting me to chip in with the labor, too."

"Wouldn't imagine it; I've seen you work."

"Yeah, well, F-you too, partner. Now can you please take a shower before your stench ruins the moment."

Mark barked a grunt of a laugh and descended the stairs.

Partner? Now what the hell did I just get myself into, I wondered as he turned the corner at the bottom and disappeared toward the bathroom. I let the thought fade and knocked on Mary and Jonny's door at the end of the short hallway. *Mary's door*, I amended, feeling the pang of Jonny's death bite into my heart once more. The double-tap I gave the door with the back of my knuckles echoed off the hollow wood.

"What do you want?" Mary snapped angrily.

"Mary, it's me."

The timbre of her voice eased as she responded, "One sec." A scuffling sound came from inside the room, followed by the familiar heavy thuds of shoes being tossed out of the way. A moment later, the door cracked open and Mary peered out as if verifying my identity before she'd let me in.

Piles of clothes circled a clear patch of floor in the middle of the room as if a whirlwind had set down and blew the clutter to the walls in small drifts like snow. Long runs of pulled yarn ran through the exposed orange carpet. In the center of the clearing, the remnants of a failed magnifying glass experiment left a fist-size hole with scorched and melted edges in the polyester rug. It brought back fond memories of the years Jonny and I shared the room before I graduated high school and Mary moved in. The memories soured as the wound of his loss opened again. I barricaded the pain in the part of my mind marked *I'll-deal-with-it-later*, knowing I just fueled another month of appointments with Dr. Swartz when I got back to Georgia.

Mary shuffled back to her bed, kicking clear a path along the way. The cheap dye in her hair needed to be redone and her face shown with a few more pimples than last time I saw her, but it was the shadows in her eyes that troubled me the most.

"How have you been, sis?"

She flopped onto her bed and propped her feet against the sloped ceiling above the headboard where the repetition of habit and dirty feet left a stain in the white paint. "I'm fine," she muttered without looking at me. Her eyes glassed over with restrained tears.

I considered my lack of seating options and settled for leaning against her dresser. "Liar."

She rolled her head in my direction, her face screwed up in an annoyed, if pained, grimace. "What do you care?" Teenage angst flowed thick in her voice.

Oh, this is going to be fun. "Sis, you know I do. Now come on. Tell me about it."

She scoffed, turned her attention back to her feet, and worked them against the ceiling as if she could grind her emotions to pulp like a bug. "You wouldn't understand."

"You might be surprised by what I understand."

Her fists slammed mutely into the rumpled bed covers. "I have no one." Tears rolled down the side of her face in a wet stream that connected the corner of her eye to her ear.

"You have me," I said softly, not sure what else to say.

With a loud sucking snort, she cleared her nose then pulled the sleeve of her shirt over her palm and mopped away the track of tears, though new ones found their way back through the missing hair on the shaved side of her head. When she spoke, her voice cracked. "Beth's family moved to Jersey."

Jersey? I'd feel sorry for Beth too, I thought but I swallowed back the comment before it made it to my lips, nearly choking on it. At least I have enough tact for that and besides my heart ached for her. Beth had always been a big part of Mary's life. A childhood friend, who may have grown into something more—I never was quite sure. But when Jonny and Paul died, she did for Mary what I, in my anger and rage, never could. She carried her through, gave her a rock to hold on to, and now that rock was gone. At least Beth only moved a state away, but at fifteen, it might as well have been the other side of the world.

I crossed the room, and Mary sat up, swinging her legs over the side of the bed to give me a spot to sit down. The bed sank with my weight and tipped Mary into me. "I'm sorry," I said, then wrapped my arms around her and let her cry into my shoulder.

3

The following morning, I woke in the black of our windowless dungeon of a basement unable to sleep a minute longer. Rolling over, I snickered at the dim numbers on my phone, oh-seven-thirty on the farm meant I got to sleep in. I unplugged my phone, flipped it over to not blind myself, then activated the screen to use it as a light to navigate to the stairs.

The door at the top of the stairs opened to the sound of forks hitting plates and the aroma of pancakes and coffee. My stomach growled in longing anticipation of my mom's home-cooking as the smell pulled me in a euphoric haze to an empty seat at the table.

"Mmm," I moaned, stabbing my fork into the stack of cakes cooling on the serving plate, but before I could retrieve my prize, a second fork joined mine.

"Oh, I'm sorry, Matt," drawled Mark with a smirk. "Don't you have someplace you need to be?"

I tore the stack in half and stuffed my share of the pancakes between my teeth along with a shot of syrup straight from the Aunt Jemima bottle. Syrup oozed out the corner of my mouth and down my chin as I chewed the oversized bite. I gave Mark a victorious grin and wiped my mouth with a paper towel. In a large farm family, you learn to eat fast at a young age, and I was still king.

My mother stacked up the pancakes on the griddle and carried them to the table balanced on the end of her spatula. I waved her down with my fork and guided the load to their proper place on my plate like marshaling in a jumbo jet.

Properly dressing my lumberjack breakfast with butter and more Aunt Jemima, I finally addressed Mark's question. "Not that I know of."

Mark tipped his head toward the kitchen door as he made room on his plate for another helping of pancakes. "Jacob's in the drive waiting for you."

My eyes grew wide as I remembered my appointment and decided to quarter my pancakes rather than cut them into more modest bitesize pieces. "Why didn't you wake me up?"

"Mom said you were on vacation, and we didn't need to go spoiling your sleep." By the annoyance in Mark's voice, I suspected he wanted to wake me up long before Jacob arrived.

"Well, did you at least invite him in?"

"No. I'm an ass like that." Mark flinched as our mother swatted him with the spatula she just used to deposit another tower of pancakes on his plate. "Sorry, Mom."

Our mother grunted dismissively. "Matthew, would you like some eggs?"

I glanced longingly at the stove but shook my head. "No, I better not. I don't think I have the time."

The door creaked open and Jacob walked in, blowing warmth into his hands. "Mrs. Peterson, may I say, I could smell your cooking from my truck—and I kind of hoped you might take a little compassion on an old man."

An incorrigible expression twisted the features of my mother's face, and she waved her spatula at the table. "Have a seat, Mr. McGinnis. I'll have some hot ones for you in just a minute."

"Oh, thank you." He reached for the chair at the head of the table but as his fingers touched the carved wood, the table fell suddenly silent. Despite my recent progress in therapy, my shoulders tensed irrationally at the thought of seeing anyone else sit in my old man's chair. Jacob glanced from my siblings to me and he pulled back his hand, electing to sit in the spare chair on the side of the table next to Mary instead.

Jacob and I hit the road about a half hour later with our bellies full and hot joe steaming from the pair of travel mugs sitting in the cup holders between us. We jumped across the Mohawk River and headed up Route 5S away from the morning sun. We followed the river and passed through small villages with the hard resiliency of towns too stubborn to succumb to the blight of abandoned industry. Towns that somehow survived on the shoulders of the surrounding farms and the growing influx of Amish migrating to upstate New York for cheap land.

We veered off the main road and followed the maze of rural roads winding through the gentle barren hills of the valley. Nearly an hour and a half later we arrived at our destination in the middle of Amish country as evidenced by the half-dozen horse and buggies we passed in the last ten miles.

The farm we pulled into looked just like my family's backcountry farm except in lieu of rust dulling the barn's metal roof, their tin shone in the late morning sun and the wood siding still completely hid the summer harvest of hay waiting in the loft. The place oozed idyllic success from the green tractors parked neatly beneath shelters built for them to the two-story colonial home with a columned porch decked out in lights and garland. The seasonally jolly red paint coating the outbuildings instead of weather-battered wood only seemed to show how poor a farmer my old man had made.

Resentment bubbled inside my chest as I wondered if farming really could be profitable or if I only saw makeup over the abscess of failure.

Jacob pushed the shifter into park and shot me a glance before following my gaze. He let out a derisive snort, but it ended in a hacking cough he hid behind a handkerchief he fished out of his back pocket. The coughing ended, and he folded the red fabric over whatever he hacked loose from his throat. "Ack, winter," he said as if the word dismissed the demonic coughing fit I had just witnessed.

I stared back out the window, ignoring the grimace distorting his face, and tried to convince myself the darker stain seeping through the cloth was a wad of phlegm and nothing more. When he wanted me to know, he would tell me. For now, I ignored the facts and honored his illusion like us soldiers always did, but it didn't lessen my concern.

Jacob released his seatbelt, leaned forward, and stuffed the handkerchief back into his rear pocket. "You going to be ok?"

I turned back to him, scowling at the question. "What?"

"Nothing, you just looked a bit green with envy when we pulled in." He put a hand on the door. "Forget it. Just keep your perspective, their son is missing, so no matter how things might appear on the outside, they're hurting on the inside."

"Right." I nodded with one last glance over the perfect farm before pushing those feelings back into the pit I kept them in. "They're grieving. I'll put on my kid gloves." He raised an eyebrow that said he doubted I had the necessary tenderness required. *Well, if he didn't think I could behave myself, then why the hell did he bring me?*

The crashing of the truck doors swinging closed echoed in the cold morning air and a matched set of hunter-orange beanies popped up over the back of the rear tires of the largest tractor in the shed. They swiveled back and forth, investigating the noise much like curious groundhogs peeking out of their holes, that is, if groundhogs made homes in black rubber boulders and used winter chains as climbing ropes.

Jacob lifted a friendly hand, but the orange groundhogs ducked back behind the tires with a squeak. He let out a grandfatherly chuckle and retrieved a thin cigar and a cheap lighter from his shirt pocket. After a few clicks of the lighter, cherry-scented smoke puffed from his mouth.

"You two, get the hell down from there before your mother has your hides," growled a gruff voice. A stocky man stepped out from behind the neighboring tractor, wiping his hands on a shop rag. He wore heavy winter overalls and a matching canvas jacket that made him seem nearly as wide as he was tall. His dark eyes narrowed at us as he hollered, "Whatever the hell you're selling, I don't want it."

Confused, I looked Jacob and myself over, trying to figure out what gave the man the impression we had anything to sell. I wore an old pair of barn-jeans with holes in the knees big enough to show off my thermals, and three layers of shirts and jackets that didn't quite keep the cold at bay. Not my best attire, but Jacob said he wanted me to connect with the farmer and I didn't think showing up dressed for bear would send the right message. Besides, I hadn't known a farmer yet that turned away a helping hand, so I came dressed to work. Jacob, on the other hand, resembled a smaller version of John Wayne, dressed in his usual duster and hat while he chewed on the end of a long cigar.

My eyes slid to the truck Jacob leaned against. It still wore the shine of a new vehicle beneath the coating of winter road-shit covering the grill and collecting in the wheel wells. In the country, people who drove new trucks and showed up on your doorstep unannounced tended to have something to sell, the only question was what: equipment, feed, Jesus, or lies.

He took one more tug on his cigar before putting it out against his tire. "Then I suppose it's a good thing I ain't got nothing to sell. Are you Mr. Andrews?"

"Yeah, that's me. Who the hell are you?" Mr. Andrews's tone carried that frustrated, pissed-off edge that farmers get at ten a.m. when the morning hasn't been going particularly well.

Jacob shifted his feet, taking a stance that while still relaxed, no longer leaned on the truck. Between Mr. Andrews's tone and the way his dark face glared at us, I followed Jacob's lead and shifted my feet. Typically, it's safer to not venture too far onto someone's property without a welcome invitation, and at the moment, the need for a swift retreat seemed more likely.

"I'm Jacob McGinnis. I work for the Church. Father Hastings asked me to help look into Steven's disappearance."

Mr. Andrews spat into the gravel beneath his feet and grumbled something under his breath. I caught the stray words of "wife" and "church," but neither sounded complimentary. "Why? Are you some sort of P.I.?"

"Something like that. Do you and the missus have a moment to talk?"

Mr. Andrews peered back at the tractor and the pile of parts beneath it. "Not really, but she'd have my ass," he growled, then tossed the rag behind the tractor and pointed a thick finger at the children peeking out from their hiding place. "You two stay out of trouble, and I better not find you climbing on the tires again." Clearing the contents of his pockets, he dropped a few more tools on the ground then pulled his knit cap a little lower over his ears and trudged across the frozen ground toward us.

He strode straight past us with a grunt, which we took as encouragement to follow him up the brick walk. Barn muck shook loose from his boots as he stomped up the half-dozen front steps and went straight in the house, ignoring the boot brush by the front door.

Jacob, however, pushed his boots through the brush, doing more to ruin their shine than to remove the driveway dust. I shrugged my shoulders and ran my own barn-shoes through the brush before going inside.

The tapping of boots on the tile floor called Mrs. Andrews from the kitchen. She rounded the corner with a kitchen knife in hand, the edge still wet with the juices of trimming meat as if straight from the set of Friday the Umpteenth. "Joseph Allen Andrews, if you don't take your boots off at the door, I'm going to…"

"Emily." Mr. Andrews raised his voice to cut her off. "Emily!" She snapped her mouth shut at his bark and lifted teary, swollen, dark eyes that spoke of hours of weeping to meet his. Mr. Andrews's shoulders sagged and a tenderness slipped into his voice. "We have company. Father Hastings sent them to help find Steven."

"He did?" Hope widened her eyes as she pulled up the hem of her apron to wipe free her tears with her free hand. "Please come in, come in. Let me get you gentlemen a cup of coffee." She spun on her heel and fled back into the kitchen without waiting for an answer.

Within moments, I heard the clatter of the knife being tossed in the kitchen sink followed by the jingle of mugs. Mr. Andrews tipped his head in a gesture toward the kitchen. "Come on."

We took places around the small kitchen table tucked away in a bay window overlooking the barren backyard. Then we waited in awkward silence for Mrs. Andrews to join us a few minutes later with a steaming percolator and four rattling cups in her nervous hands.

Jacob stood, his lips drawing back in a comforting smile. "Please, allow me," he said relieving her of her burden.

She let him take the cups from her hands, her anxious eyes never leaving his. "Can you really help us find Steven?"

4

J acob managed to keep his smile steady, but I saw the flicker in his eyes. *The truth or the lie?* Based on my brief experience and the catalog of horror Jonny collected in his journal, either answer would hurt her in the end. Jacob elected to go with something between the two.

"Ma'am, I can't make any promises, but I am here to help figure out what happened to Steven."

The renewed light in Mrs. Andrews's eyes didn't falter, but her husband's deepening frown said he didn't miss the evasive answer. "You can't? Then why the hell are you here? What makes you think you can find the boy when the police and the FBI can't?"

Jacob placed his cup down on the table with deliberate slow attention, letting the heat of the question simmer in the air. When he spoke, his eyes met Mr. Andrews's and delivered each word in a measured level tone. "Because, Mr. Andrews, I'm going to look in places they won't." Jacob's assurance did nothing to cool Mr. Andrews's temper.

"Bah, I don't have time for this." Mr. Andrews pushed himself back from the table with the loud screech as his chair scraped across the wooden floor. "I've got work to do. Look, the boy ran away like he said he would. He'll come back when he finally gets cold or hungry enough."

"Joe..." Mrs. Andrews's hand reached for her husband's, but he pulled it out of her reach and stormed out of the house. The sound of the slamming door echoed back down the entry hall and started Mrs. Andrews's tears flowing again. "I'm sorry," she said, her voice cracking.

Jacob laid a hand on Mrs. Andrews's. "It's fine, Mrs. Andrews, everyone worries in their own way."

She wiped at her eyes with her apron again. "They had words, Joe and Steven. The night before he went missing. It was hardly the first time. They were out in one of the sheds, but I could hear them shouting at each other from inside the house."

"Do you know what they were arguing about?"

"No, and he won't tell me. But you know how fathers and sons can be."

I snorted unintentionally. "Yeah, I do."

Mrs. Andrews' teary face turned toward me. She sniffed back her runny nose. "Did you two ever come to see eye to eye?"

I swallowed the *Hell-no* response in my throat and opted for something I hoped sounded a bit more tactful. "No, unfortunately, he passed before I got the chance."

She gave me a sympathetic smile. "I'm sorry."

I grimaced awkwardly. "Thank you, ma'am." With effort, I pushed the phantom of my old man away and twisted my face into the most encouraging expression I could muster. "Hopefully, we can find Steven in time to give him that chance though."

Jacob pulled out a small notepad and pen like a sleuth ready to interrogate a witness. "Yes, to that matter, what else can you tell us about the night he disappeared?"

She sobered up, wrapping her thin fingers around her cup of coffee, but she didn't take a drink. "That night after Joe and Steven had their fight, Joe sent Steven to bed right after dinner. Steven said some...um... hateful things and well, Joe did too if I'm being honest." A troubled, nervous expression filled her eyes. One my mom used to get when talking with friends about how Paul and I got along. One that worried they might take it the wrong way and call child protective services; sometimes I wish one of them had.

Mrs. Andrews raised her mug to her lips in a rote mechanical motion. She took a sip and placed it back on the table, engulfing it in her fingers again. "We had some trouble with the older four when they were teenagers too, but they eventually grew out of it. Steven though—he has been the hardest. Him and Joe are a lot alike. Tempers as quick as firecrackers and twice as mean, though they don't usually mean what they say. Not really."

Memories of Paul and the fights we used to have flowed through my mind, especially how they used to end. I could feel my hackles rise, and I couldn't keep the gruffness from my voice. "Ma'am, did your husband ever hit Steven?"

The corner of one of her eyes twitched as if the question was exactly what she feared. I know my mom always feared it. "We're good Christian folk, so yes we spank our children when they're young, but we don't abuse them. And spankings never did Steven any good, the boy had a hide thicker than tanned leather. It's part of the reason we've had so much trouble with him, we never could figure out how to properly discipline him. That's why Joe sent him to his room early that night."

"But does..." I began, but Jacob cut me off.

"Ma'am, we're not here to judge how you discipline your kids. We're just trying to gather all the facts we can."

Her eyes shifted to Jacob where they locked onto his for a moment before she relaxed into the general worry for the welfare of her son. Her gaze slowly drifted back to the inky blackness of the coffee in her hands.

"Ma'am, what happened after Steven went to bed?" Jacob asked to get her talking again.

She shrugged her shoulders. "Nothing. The twins share the room with Steven, and he was asleep when I put them to bed around nine. Then the next morning Joe wakes up an hour after the morning milking should have started, but he didn't hear the vacuum pump running. So, he went upstairs, madder than a hornet to wake Steven up, only he wasn't there and the window was wide open."

"Any chance your husband's right and Steven just ran away?"

Her head snapped up, panic-stricken. "No. No. I know that's what Joe and the police think but I know he didn't. Mothers just know. And besides, he couldn't have, it was ten below that night."

Jacob took a long sip of coffee. "Ma'am, I have to ask. Considering the temperature, did the police conduct a search?"

"They didn't find anything. But I know he's still out there."

Jacob closed the notebook and slipped it back into his duster. "I'm sure he is. Would you mind if we took a look at his room?"

"Sure." Her hands unfolded from the cup, and she got up stiffly. "It's this way."

She led us back through the kitchen, passed the pile of half-trimmed stew meat, and up the back stairs. She stopped at the top and pointed to a room halfway down the hall. "That one. It's still the way Joe found it. The twins have been sleeping on the floor with their older brothers."

"Ma'am, how many children do you have?" I asked, the curiosity getting the better of me.

"Nine. Five boys and four girls. The two youngest girls share the room next to ours, and the older girls sleep in this room," She said, pointing to the door behind her. Pointing the room opposite Steven's, she added, "The older boys share that room."

Jacob started down the hall. "Thank you, Mrs. Andrews. I'll let you know if we need anything else."

I hesitated a moment trying to figure out how one boy would be taken, but not his younger brothers in the same room. Especially without them hearing or seeing anything. "Mrs. Andrews, are the twins in school today?"

"No, none of the kids are. We haven't sent them to school since…" She waved a hand at Steven's door, but couldn't say it.

"Do you know where they are now?"

"They're supposed to be helping their father fix the tractor."

I let a genuine smile touch my lips for the first time since I got here. "So that's who those two little groundhogs were. Cute kids, what's their names?"

"Timmy and Noah."

"Matthew?" Jacob called from the end room.

"I…uh…need to go. Don't worry, we'll find him," I said before I could stop myself from making a promise I had no way of keeping.

"Thank you," she said.

I gave her a weak nod then jogged down the hall to the small bedroom Steven shared with his little brothers. A twin bed mirrored the bunk bed on the opposite wall and a dresser flanked either side of the only window in the room. The crowded room left little space for two grown men to go snooping around.

I worked my way into the room, kicking free a path through the childish clutter. "Damn, and I thought my parents shoehorned us in. You couldn't force my brothers in here with a tub of lard and a cattle prod. Though I wouldn't mind trying."

Jacob stood staring out the window without offering my offhanded comment the appreciative chuckle I expected. Instead, he leaned out the window far enough that his toes lifted off the floor.

Shaking off my disappointment, I rushed over and grabbed his duster by the belt to make sure he didn't fall out. "Need some help?"

Jacob grunted and leaned a bit further out the window. "No, I just wanted you to leave that poor woman alone."

"Oh. Well, if you don't need me then." I let him go, and he tipped precariously forward.

"Hey. Whoa," he croaked, flinging a hand for the window sill as his boots drifted up off the floor. I reached out, grabbed his duster, and hauled him back before he actually fell out.

His feet hit the floor, and I couldn't help but break out laughing. "I didn't realize you could sing so high. Your voice must have jumped two octaves."

Jacob climbed the rest of the way back in and braced himself on his knees. "You son of a bitch, that wasn't funny."

"I think that all depends on which side of the window you're hanging out of." Jacob scowled at me through his bushy eyebrows, and I gave him a *not-my-fault* shrug. "I'm not the one who didn't want my help."

He scoffed with a gentle shake of his head. "Maybe the next time, you don't take me quite so literally."

"Sure, and maybe next time you won't assume I'm bothering someone when I ain't."

Jacob's face hardened. "Perhaps, but I saw that look in your eye when she mentioned spanking the kids. Mr. Andrews isn't your father."

I locked eyes with Jacob, mine becoming as hard as his. "Maybe he's not, but if I find out he's been abusing his kids..." The flush of anger burning in my chest choked off the rest of the threat.

"If he is, I'll call CPS myself."

The muscles in my forearm ached, and I unclenched the fists I hadn't realized I made. My fingernails left a quartet of painful crescents in each of my palms. I rubbed my hands together as much to keep them from curling again as to soothe the pain. "If he's abusing his kids, it's not CPS he'll need to worry about."

Jacob stood and took me by the shoulders. "Son, there is evil in this world that we take care of because no one else will and then there is evil in this world that we must allow the authorities to handle. You can't do this job if you can't keep the two separate. Do you understand me?"

"Yes," I grumbled, unable to completely temper my righteous fire.

"Good," he said, clapping me on the shoulder and turning back to the window. "Because I'm pretty sure this is one of those things that we handle, and I'm going to need your help on this one." He groaned the last word trying unsuccessfully to choke back a coughing fit. This time, I didn't miss the smear of red he folded away in his handkerchief.

"Is that something I need to worry about?"

He waved it off with a wrinkled hand. "Bah, I'm just getting old. What you need to worry about are those scrape marks on the garage roof right there." He pointed a gnarled finger out the window.

I squeezed past Jacob and maneuvered into the small space between the dressers to get a better view. A worn field of green asphalt shingles covered the garage roof less than a half-dozen feet away. A handful of bare spots showed where the wind had torn some of them free, or at least that's what I thought until I realized that all the missing shingles formed a drunken line from the edge nearest the window to the one furthest away.

"Drag marks?" I ventured, following the line across the frozen drive to a pasture with a handful of cows munching away at a feeder loaded with hay. The drag line pointed like an arrow to the branchless remnant of a tree standing tall above the long hedgerow defining the far side of the pasture like a bony finger.

Jacob sat on the edge of the bed, careful not to disturb the sheets half-falling off the side where Steven had tossed them. He pulled his hat off with one hand and ran the other through the graying threads of his hair. "Yep, just like all the others."

I shut the window and faced him. "Yeah, about that. How many others?"

5

J acob donned his hat with a sigh. "According to the police reports, there's been three other disappearances this December. It started with Ethan Daniels. His parents reported him missing from their farm just south of Little Falls. Then a few miles east of there, Christina Smith vanished in the middle of the night from her rural country home. Ben Harris lived only ten miles up the road from here. He disappeared last week. And now Steven has been gone for three days. Whatever is taking these kids, it's smart enough to move around and doesn't have any plans to stop."

His gaze drifted out the window, across the farm and roaming cows to the tree on the other side of the pasture. "The FBI can't even see how these cases are frick'n linked. They're too far apart with nothing to connect them except rotten attitudes. Only one of the police reports mention drag marks, but there're signs at each one, if you know what to look for. Instead, those dolts at the Bureau write these kids off as runaways and call it a night. As if they aren't worth more than a weekend search party and a handful of fliers with aging dates and crappy pictures."

The timbre of Jacob's voice carried more than the rasp of his cigars or the wheeze of phlegm in his lungs. I found a spot to sit on the bottom bunk and watched Jacob's eyes grow distant and haunted. Weariness dragged at his shoulders, and I no longer saw the strong, confident, bull of a man that helped me tackle werebears last spring. The missing kids were eating at him in a way I would never have expected. *But then again, how well did I really know him?* Somehow right then didn't seem like the right time for the deep dive into the man's past.

I did, however, recognize that all too familiar acquiescence to fatigue. That beating a man takes over weeks of late nights and early mornings, especially when he feels like he's all alone. "What about DEMON? Shouldn't they be out here riding this case to ground like the bulldog they pretend to be?"

Jacob snorted his disdain, and his gaze retreated to his lap. "From my experience, DEMON's not the greatest at picking out patterns until someone points it out to them. So, unless the folks at the FBI can find enough brain cells to put two and two together, we're on our own."

"All right, as long as you understand, it's *we* and not just *you*. We'll get them back."

His head rose slowly and his eyes, glassy with tears, turned hard as they met mine. "At this point, I don't think there's much hope for recovery, only vengeance."

I gave him a muted, level look. I knew the need for bitter revenge, or at least how it burned and ate away at your soul. I spent years resenting my abusive old man, dreaming of the day karma would finally see him get his, but it all felt hollow when we buried him last spring. Jacob was on the verge of falling into that all-consuming fire of rage, and if I wasn't careful, he'd drag me into that furnace with him.

"I've been down the road to vengeance before, and when the dirt settled, I didn't like the payoff. But if it's justice you're aiming for, I won't back down from that fight."

A dimpled grin ruffled the scruff of Jacob's beard in the smallest of resigned smiles. "I can settle for justice."

I clapped my hands together with exaggerated bravado. "Good, then why the hell are you still sitting down? Moping around up here isn't going to show us where those tracks lead. Let's get going." I bounced to my feet, ready to get some real work done.

Jacob rolled his eyes as he pushed himself upright, stretching his back against sore muscles and old bones that popped and cracked like a string of firecrackers. "Just try to remember, I'm still an old man."

"How could I forget when every time you move, I hear the chorus to *Snap, Crackle, Pop*."

The blackness of his dour mood lifted along with one of his eyebrows. "Yeah, well let's see how well you move when you reach my age."

"Damn, Jacob, I don't think I can even count that high."

He scowled at me. "Now listen here, son…"

Satisfied to see him on his feet and in a better disposition, I ignored him calling me son along with whatever spewed out of his mouth and led the way out of the room.

At the bottom of the stairs, Mrs. Andrews busied herself with straightening up a knick-knack table, her hands adjusting and readjusting the same little pieces. The last few steps emitted a series of squeaks as I made my way to the bottom of the stairs and her red-shot eyes snapped in my direction and widened hopefully, as if we had divined her son's location from our brief scouring of his room and all we needed to do now was tell her.

I didn't know what to say to her and glanced up the stairs to Jacob for help. He stood at the top of the steps, massaging his back and rolling his head, deliberately ignoring me. He knew what would happen when we came back down and he'd set me up. Not that I didn't deserve it. I had called him old, but I should have recognized the tricks of an old fox.

I schooled my face into something I hoped looked encouraging or at least neutral, and in the handful of strides it took to cross the room a question occurred to me. "Mrs. Andrews, do Steven and the twins sleep with the window open?" While it's not the most energy-efficient way to regulate the temperature in your room, it was often the easiest in an old farmhouse with a single source of heat.

Beneath eyes that flashed with the heat of an old argument, Mrs. Andrews bit at a lower lip chapped from worry and the remarkably cold start to winter. "I've told him he'd give his brothers pneumonia if he kept it up, but the boy likes to sleep half-frozen."

An empathetic noise grunted in my throat. "Yeah, I know what it's like. Our wood furnace roasts me out most nights. If I don't crack a window, I can't get comfortable enough to sleep. Though I will admit, I usually wake up curled in a ball between frozen sheets." My weak attempt at a connection didn't alter the pained look on her face. "Ma'am, I'm sorry. We'll do our best to find him."

"That's what the police said, too."

Jacob laid a hand on my shoulder. "Emily," he said gently. "It would be extremely helpful if you would pray for our guidance and your son's protection. With the Lord's intervention, there's still time for a Christmas miracle."

Somehow that lightened the weight pulling at her shoulders, and her hand drifted to the crucifix dangling from the chain around her neck. "I will, and God bless you."

"And your family as well, ma'am." Jacob steered me toward the front door, and we left Mrs. Andrews in the kitchen with her head bowed.

We stepped out into the bitter cold, which had only gotten colder while we were inside. A sudden gust of wind shot a painful batch of bitter air into my lungs that made my chest convulse involuntarily. In a panic, I tried to breathe through my nose only to have the moisture instantly freeze my nostrils together. Short on air, I popped the collars of all three shirts I wore and drew the sweatshirt hoodie up over my head, mouth, and nose until the wind only cut at my eyes. My trapped body heat thawed my nose, and I began breathing the body-warmed air, trying to ignore the rancid smell of my old barn clothes.

Hunkered down behind his own popped collar, Jacob missed the miserable frostbitten glare I shot him as he strode past me. He stalked to the truck with purpose, and I rushed to catch up. We hopped in the cab to the echoing bang of slamming doors.

"Shit, I think the temperature dropped another ten degrees," I grumbled, waiting for him to start the truck.

He didn't though. Instead, he rummaged around through a collection of duffle bags in the backseat until he pulled out a scarf, thick gloves, and a half-dozen warmers, the kind you snap in your hands and stuff in your boots to keep your toes the flesh-colored side of black.

"Here," he said, dumping the load in my lap and returning to the bags.

I wrapped the scarf around my neck then held the warmers dumbly in my hands. "You can't be serious? We're not walking, are we?"

"That boy has been out in the cold for three days now, and we ain't going to be able to follow the tracks bouncing around in this truck."

I looked at the bleak sky clouding over with the promise of a brewing snowstorm and sighed. "You know..." My tongue suddenly went dry, and I worked my mouth mutely trying to find the right words.

Jacob made a resigned noise. "You don't need to say it. After three days, I'm well aware of what Steven's chances are against exposure alone, not to mention whatever took him. But whatever has been snatching kids will grab another one soon if we don't find it first."

The wind howled across the windshield in a taunting sound that sent a cold shiver down my spine. I'd been out in worse weather; not much worse mind you, but Jacob had a point I couldn't ignore. Cracking a pair of chemical heaters, I massaged the packs in my hands until they warmed, then unlaced my boots and stuffed them in as close to my toes as I could.

"Fine, but I'm not going out there with only a Bowie knife." The handle of the large silver-plated knife he'd given me last spring dug into the soft flesh of my right side just above my belt. I'd strapped it on this morning just in case, but underneath all the layers I wore, I doubted I'd be able to draw it with any kind of speed if I needed to. "You promised to keep me well-armed."

Jacob paused in winding his plaid scarf around his neck to reach into the backseat of the cab once more. He retrieved a military grade handgun case and placed it on the seat between us. "So I did."

I spun the case around and flipped back the latches. Even the cold couldn't keep my lips from curling back in a smile at the Smith and Wesson 327 TRR8 revolver I used last spring. It sat in a perfectly cut hole in the foam padding that filled the box, along with three already loaded moon clips. Dull rust coated the iron tips of .357 magnum loads in the first clip, silver rounds filled the second, and the third held conventional hollow points. I pulled out the pistol and wrapped my fingers around the familiar grip. "Now that's what I'm talking about."

"Thought you might miss her." Jacob handed me a black bundle of woven nylon straps.

"What's this?"

"A shoulder harness. Now quit gawking at the thing and suit up."

The bulk of my multiple layers of shirts and coats made wrangling into the harness considerably harder in the confines of the truck's front seat, but hell if I was going to take a single layer off. The TRR8 slipped comfortably into its holster, and I practiced drawing the pistol a few times before adjusting the holster position to make the draw smoother.

Satisfied, I reached for the moon clips. My hand hovered above the circular loads. "Um, which one should I take?"

Jacob finished tucking the ends of his scarf into his duster and looked over. "I'm still not sure what we're up against, so you better take them all, but load the hollow points. They've been blessed and soaked in holy water." He reached through a slot on either side of his duster and pulled out his matched pair of 1911s. "Besides, I've got silver and iron covered." The pistols disappeared back through the same slots.

"Man, I've got to get me one of those."

Jacob patted the duster with a reminiscent smile. "Good luck with that. Gracie's mom custom-made this one for me."

It was the first time I'd ever heard him speak about his granddaughter's mother. Questions flooded my mind, but I hesitated to ask, hoping he would share more. Instead, he reached into the backseat one more time and pulled out a black backpack.

"Here. New guy gets to carry the food and supplies," he said, shoving the pack at me.

I held up a hand. "Hey, I ain't no FNG."

"Fine, then the young buck carries."

The corner of my mouth quirked up in a smirk as I took the pack and slid my arms through the straps. "That sounds better, old man."

He raised an eyebrow. "The young buck better shut his trap before the wiser, older, buck teaches him his place."

I snorted a laugh then enjoyed one more breath of air that wouldn't turn my lungs to ice before opening the door. The wind nearly ripped the door from my hand. I slid off my seat and slammed closed the door to warmth and safety. *It could be worse. I could be thirteen, alone, frozen, and scared,* I reminded myself as I followed Jacob trudging across the frozen terrain toward the barren tree.

6

The wind didn't get any warmer between the truck and the pasture fence. If anything, the temperature dropped a few more degrees despite the sun having only just crept past noon, or at least I thought it had, judging from the slightly brighter nimbus in the thickening cloud cover. I scaled the strands of barbed wire, snagging only the tattered edge of a pant leg on the upper wire. The fabric tore away, adding yet another hole to my jeans.

Jacob followed me over the fence but before his second foot reached for the ground, a gust of wind wrapped the tail of his duster around the top wire and the toes of his boot scraped ineffectually across the top of a frozen cow pie. "Shit," he said, reaching out blind to catch himself on a knotty fence post, but grabbed the barbed wire instead. He snatched his hand back with a yelp, and the barb refused to let go of his glove. "Son of a bitch!"

"I don't know about the son of a bitch part, but yes, that is shit," I said in a burst of laughter.

He gave me a cross look as he hung tethered to the fence and massaging his wounded hand. "Ha. Ha. Don't suppose you could help?"

I pulled off my gloves to work the tangled fabric from the barbs. By the time I got him free, I could barely feel my numb fingers when I stuffed them back into the gloves. Jacob handed me a pair of hand warmers. The heat soaked through my thin gloves and began to thaw my hands as I stuffed them into my pockets to help contain their warmth. "Thanks."

"Likewise."

Windswept and beaten down by cattle, the pasture grasses didn't yield much by way of useful tracks. However, several trampled pathways cut through the bramble hedge at the far end of the pasture beneath the silver tree.

"Looks like they really did send out a search party," I shouted into the increasing howl of the wind.

Jacob grunted something, but it got carried away in the advancing storm front. He stared back at the farm, squinting into the wind like a sniper sighting in his target, and raised an arm to point at the garage standing between us and the house. Then peering the other way, he pointed his other hand through the branchless tree and across the barren field to a wood that rose up a gentle hill on the opposite side.

I followed his finger to where it roughly pointed at a cluster of pine trees. The swell of the plowed field hid the tree bottoms, making it impossible to tell if we would have any better luck there than we did here. The brooding, thickening sky and continuing drop in temperature threatened a storm that would put the icing on this bitter start to winter. It worried me. I didn't relish the thought of getting caught in a whiteout.

I took out my phone to consult the weather app. "Bullshit."

"What's that?"

"According to my phone, we're supposed to have a high of thirty-eight today." I stuffed the phone back into my pocket.

He raised an eyebrow. "Any chance you still have your location set to Georgia?" He gathered the tail of his coat in his hands and scaled the fence with a bit more skill than last time.

"No," I scoffed but pulled my phone back out. "Well, maybe," I conceded grudgingly as I revised the location setting to *current location*. The screen flashed and then resolved to show a plummeting temperature and forecasted snowfall to make Buffalo proud. "Fuck." I scampered over the fence and ran to catch up with Jacob.

The plow furrows broke under my feet, and I stumbled in the dirt to bash my knee on an overturned rock. My scream of pain was lost on the wind. I pushed myself up and hobbled forward, watching my footing. I came alongside Jacob about halfway across the field.

"There's practically a blizzard moving in."

"I know." The way he said it, like he knew all along, pissed me off.

Everyone raised in upstate New York knew better than to get caught out in a blizzard.

"We need to head back."

He stopped to glare at me, the humor and softness I'd come to expect missing from his face. "If we head back, we'll lose the trail. I can't lose it now." I couldn't see any trail in the barren dirt, but I could see steel in his blue eyes. He blinked against the wind then kept walking. "Go on back if you have to."

I watched him trudge on for a few steps more as I debated internally. The smart thing to do would be to head back before I couldn't find my way, but the only thing worse than getting stuck outside in a blizzard is to be stuck in one alone. I sighed heavily and followed him into the woods as the first snowflakes started to fall.

Trampled paths matted down the brush that lined the edge of the woods at regular intervals like slots in a very large comb. The search party had certainly come this way. I didn't see how we would find anything they missed before the snow started flying. I was just about to drag Jacob back to the truck when he proved me wrong.

Caught on the sharp thorns of a crabapple tree about fifteen feet from the cluster of pines was a patch of wiry hair and a torn bit of burlap. Jacob pulled them free and held them up in his fingers. "This is it."

I looked at the brown tuft of fur. "So, it is a were?"

He rubbed his fingers together, a few of the hairs blowing away in the wind. "I don't think so, it's too coarse. Feels more like boar or goat hair, but I haven't run across many were versions of those two. Besides, weres don't usually use burlap sacks." He held up the bit of fabric in his other hand. The wind made it hard for me to hear every word, but I grasped his point.

"Any idea what it is, then?"

"Not at the moment." He stuffed the bits of hair and fabric into his pocket then worked his way along the track through the brush. "Come on."

"Great," I grumbled soft enough that the wind blew my words away without Jacob hearing. I ducked under the thorny branches of the crabapple and followed Jacob further into the woods.

The trees bent and swayed in the wind, but void of their leaves they did nothing to lessen its fury. I tucked my hands up into my armpits, hugging myself as best I could to keep warm. Jacob found more markers of the abductor's passage in turned leaves and broken branches.

Assuming of course we were on the abductor's path and not one of the searchers'.

Snow began to fall, whipping around the trees and biting into my exposed skin like wind-driven needles. After half an hour or so, a light dusting covered the ground, making it hard to find the patches of disturbed leaves marking the trail. The wind blew the light snow into serpentine snakes winding their way around the tree trunks and our feet, but Jacob pressed on. So far, the path from the farm had been straight as an arrow, and with that assumption, he kept moving.

At least finding our way back won't be that hard. I regretted the thought as soon as it formed. The path led to the steep embankment of a ravine with water moving swiftly through patches of ice at the bottom.

Jacob stood on the edge of the bank and squinted into the snow. He raised an arm and pointed to the far bank, where a small bush took advantage of the break in the tree canopy to grow. "There. It climbed out there."

I squinted and tried to make out enough detail in the far bank to verify what he saw, but the wind and snow stung at my eyes. "I can't see it. And there's no way we're going to be able to cross here."

Jacob glanced up and down the ravine searching for options. "I'm going to try to find a place to cross further uphill. Stay here so I don't lose the track." He went off along the ravine edge without waiting for me to acknowledge him, not that I had a better idea.

The wind cutting through the ravine whispered to me as if calling for help. I stepped to the edge and followed the valley until it disappeared into the haze of white. The storm was growing worse, cutting through my barn clothes and numbing my skin. Retreating from the ravine and its haunting call, I moved to the leeward side of a thick oak tree and squatted down to hide from the frigid wind.

"Fuck this cold and give me a Georgian winter," I grumbled, shrinking into my clothing as much as possible. "Christmas snow ain't worth freezing my dick off."

The minutes ticked by slowly, and I could feel my eyes getting heavy until a high-pitched whistle woke me back up. The whistle sounded again followed by, "Matthew, where are you?"

I rose to my feet, losing the little reserve of heat I had stored, and hollered back. "Jacob. Here." I waved an arm. Jacob waved back from a few yards further up the hill.

He worked his way across the ravine edge until he stood more or less directly across from me. After a minute or two of searching, he gave me a wave beckoning me to come over. "I found it. Hurry up and get over here. There's a place to cross up the hill."

I started up the hill at a jog, following Jacob's footprints in the fresh snow as the wind tried to erase them. By the time I found the fallen pine tree bridging the ravine, my lungs burned from gulping in raw, frozen air. The scarf wrapped around my head no longer helped as a circle of frost iced over the fabric, covering my mouth. I pulled the layers of my shirts up over my nose and breathed the air warmed by my body to catch my breath. Once I stopped panting, I balance-beam walked across the tree, then picked up my pace after Jacob's tracks again.

Something tugged at the hood of my sweatshirt, but with my eyes down watching my footing, I didn't catch what it was. Figuring I dodged too close to a low hanging branch, I ignored it and charged on. A dozen steps later, in the middle of a break in the trees, something else pulled at the tail of my outer jacket. I twisted to see what it could be. Distracted, my foot found a frozen puddle and slipped out from under me. I fell to the ground, tumbling in the leaves and snow. Something thudded into the ground in front of me and I rolled onto it, breaking it beneath my weight with the crack of a snapping branch.

My momentum carried me halfway over my backpack before rocking me back the other way. Something jabbed me in the side, and I lurched away with a cry of pain. The jagged edges of a broken stick about as thick as my index finger stuck up out of the earth, fletched with turkey feathers. I almost missed the other half of the shaft in the jumble of leaves and snow. I stared at it dumbfounded. "What the hell?"

An uneasiness I recognized all too well crept between my shoulder blades, and I snapped my head up, searching the trees through the blowing snow. I couldn't see more than a dozen yards or so, and through the howling wind, I couldn't hear anything.

Pressing myself up off the ground, I sprinted to the nearest tree, hoping to put the bulk of it between myself and whoever shot drumsticks like arrows. I fumbled the restraining loop off the pistol as I ran, pulling out the TRR8, but with my thick gloves on, I couldn't fit my finger through the trigger guard. Ripping my glove off, I tossed it to the ground and held the pistol close to my chest in a ready position.

Rotating to the left, I took a three-second look. *No target.* I twisted to the other side of the tree. *No target.* Not that I could see much farther than

I could throw a rock. *Time to move.* I sprinted in a random direction, counting the movement in my head. *I'm up. They see me. I'm down.*

The birch tree I dove behind barely covered me standing sideways. I repeated the scanning procedure again and still couldn't find any targets. At the edge of my visibility, I could just make out an old hickory tree more than up to the challenge of hiding my frame. It stood well beyond my three-count combat movement range, but I didn't like the idea of dropping knee first into the frozen ground. Sucking in a large breath, I took one more quick glance around the side of the birch tree toward the hickory but didn't see anything through the snow.

Something thudded into the other side of my tree with a *thunk* and like the sound of a starter's gun, I ran for it. I made it behind the hickory in time to hear the impact of another arrow. At least now I knew which side of the tree to hide behind.

7

I n an effort to keep my head free of additional holes, I crouched low, hoping the shooter wouldn't expect to find my face waist-high, and peeked around the base of the tree. Beyond the few trees closest to me, the howling wind blended the falling snow with what it picked up off the ground into a maelstrom of white noise incarnate. Blinking through the biting bits of ice, I saw tall slender shapes move through the wall of white. *No, they're not moving, they're trees. Damn, and to think I actually wished for snow on the bus ride north.*

Adrenaline-infused blood pounded audibly in my ears over the wind. I needed to move, to fight back, but to do that I needed my shooter ducking for cover and I'd be shooting blind. The voice of my very politically minded butter-bar lieutenant giving his *Welcome to Afghanistan* speech filled my mind. "Know what's downrange. You don't want to be the one who puts us on the news for a friendly fire incident." Ideals like his rarely survived first contact, and with the thought of getting an arrow through the chest, today was no exception.

Using the tree as a body shield, I raised my pistol in a one-handed Dirty Harry hold then took a glance at the arrow protruding from the tree for direction and adjusted my aim. The gun barked over the wind as I pulled the trigger.

I rolled along the ground away from my cover, jumped, and raced to another tree a few yards away. While I assumed my adversary knew better than to remain in one place, my shift in position should have brought me closer to my target. I glanced left then right, then fired a covering round before bolting once again, hoping to keep the archer's head down as I ran in their direction.

Another tree and another round gained me ten more yards. The wind carried a hollow call I couldn't quite make out. It sounded like Jacob, though I couldn't be sure which direction it came from. *Time to listen to old butter-bars and make sure of my shots,* I admonished myself.

To my left, I saw something shift in the snow. A solid white form moved, unaffected by the whipping wind. It slunk from one tree to the next trying to maneuver around behind me. I slipped from my tree to another, tracking and closing in on it.

Midway between two trees, Jacob called again and the hunched form turned to face away from me. With Jacob in the background, I couldn't risk a shot. Instead, I holstered the pistol and drew the Bowie in a reverse grip. With the knife came the haunting memory of foolishly charging a werebear. I dashed forward praying, *Please, for the love of God, I don't care what the damn fox says.*

I dove, arms out wide like a defensive end tackling a quarterback. My shoulder hit something hard, but as I attempted to wrap my arms around it, the bulk I thought I'd find collapsed under me like a tented sheet, and I sailed past my target with nothing more than a white tarp in my hands.

I stomped on the tarp as I sprung back to my feet, but my knife caught in the fabric and ripped out of my hands. Knifeless, I whirled on my opponent. Not a beast, but a man with shaggy dark hair and a full beard that left his upper lip bare. Without the tarp, he stood out against the snow in a nearly black jacket and pants that moved with the stiffness of thick fabric. He reached toward the ground and the crossbow collecting snow.

I pulled out the pistol and leveled at him. "Leave it!" I shouted into the wind. His hand froze a foot above the crossbow. "Stand up. Get over there." I pointed to a thick tree with my gloved free hand, never taking the dangerous end of the pistol off of him.

He obliged my commands and as his back hit the tree, he spoke in an odd thick accent like he didn't like to move his tongue when he spoke. "What now, you foul beastie."

"Beast? You're the one trying to skewer me with a crossbow."

"Ack." He spat onto the ground. "I know not what manner of creature you be, but you will take no more of our children."

It took me a moment to work out what he said through his accent. But, once I got the gist of it, I had to give the man props, it takes guts to be that ballsy with a pistol pointed at your chest; that— or a friend.

The realization hit me about the same time I felt the point of knife press against my ribs. Having been stabbed before, I can tell you I really didn't want it to happen all over again; it's not pleasant.

"Put your pistol down now, English." The voice behind me said.

I lifted my empty left hand over my shoulder and spread the fingers wide. Likewise, I showed the pistol in my nearly frozen right hand and worked the hammer down to a safe position before I lowered it to my waist and dropped b it. I used the movement to take a fading step away from the knife while sweeping my left hand down to catch his outstretched arm.

The man behind me pulled his knife hand out of the way and danced away to a fighting position. He looked much like the other man, except with more gray in his hair and he still wore the thin white tarp over his shoulders.

I spread my feet and lifted my hands for a fight as the first man pushed himself off the tree and drew out his own knife. The older man held out his free hand to the first in a halting gesture. The younger man ignored the signal and tested a fainting lunge. I shuffled my feet, retreating out of his reach.

"Beheef dich!" shouted the older man. The younger man shot him a sullen glare but halted his advance.

A crack of gunfire snapped all our attention to behind my attackers, where Jacob leveled his 1911s, pointing one at each of them.

"All right boys, let's put down the blades, and we can talk this through."

The older man nodded and sheathed his knife beneath his coat. After a rough hand gesture, the younger did the same. With the knives away, Jacob waited for me to collect my pistol before holstering his. I followed his lead, though my bare gun hand itched for the grip despite being unable to feel my fingers.

"Now, who would like to tell me what the hell is going on?" Jacob asked.

I slipped my gloveless hand in my pocket and cracked a hand warmer. "Don't ask me, I was just trying to avoid getting turned into a pin cushion." I tried to work feeling back into my fingers as the chemical heater converted my pocket into a miniature sauna. I wanted to be ready in case things went sideways—again.

"Samuel mistook your friend for what we hunt." The older man said thickly.

Jacob made a show of sizing me up. "I know the boy can be a bit boorish, but he hardly looks like game to me."

The younger man, Samuel, sized me up as if he still needed convincing. The older man simply tipped his head in acknowledgment. "My apologies, English. The prey we hunt runs on two feet like a man, but it is not. The snow made it hard to see your son clearly."

I opened my mouth to object to being Jacob's son, but Jacob spoke first, his tone serious and formal. "And what is it you hunt, sir?"

"English do not believe in such things as we hunt. If I told you, you would not either."

Jacob's eyes narrowed. "Oh, I don't know about that. I have a fairly open mind. If it's the same thing we're hunting, I'm thinking it's either a vampire, a Lamia, or maybe even the Boogeyman."

The older man's eyes widened then his whole posture relaxed as did Jacob's, like two old men coming to the realization that they actually knew each other. Samuel and I shared a confused look.

"You are monsterjäger, English," The older man said with a nod of respect. "I know not this Lamia you speak of, but we hunt Krampus."

Jacob hung his head. "Shit. Do you know if it's the eating kind or the beating kind?"

"When they are hungry, they are one in the same. As much as I wish we may, we have found none beaten."

"Wait, hold on? What the hell is a Krampus?" I asked.

Jacob pulled out a Black and Mild and placed it between his teeth. He flipped the top of his lighter open and slapped at the striker several times. Each time the flame caught, the wind stole it before he could touch it to the cigar's tip.

The older man cast me an exasperated *don't-interrupt-the-grownups* glower. "It is a goat demon."

Well that cleared it up about as much as the sky overhead, which, by the way, I could no longer see through the snow. Cold sliced its way through my clothes, and my arms started shivering.

Jacob abandoned his attempts to light the cigar and stuffed both it and the lighter back into his pocket. "Krampus is like the opposite of Santa Claus. Instead of rewarding the good kids, it punishes the bad ones. That is, until one gets hungry, then it eats them instead." He nodded toward our new companions. "And it appears this one is hungry."

"Not only one." The old man said. "We have lost too many for only one."

"You mean there's more than one Krampus?"

This time Jacob shot me a *don't-ask-dumb-questions* glare. "Of course there are. You can't possibly think there's only one Santa Claus, do you?"

More than one? If he had asked me two minutes ago, I would have said none. Considering the condescending tone in his voice, I chose to keep my mouth closed rather than voice that particular thought. Though, if we ever managed to get out of this cold, I certainly had a lot to unpack as well, as a pair of new journal entries for Jonny's monster manual that no one would believe, not even Mary.

I decided to voice a more helpful suggestion as I began to dance in a vain attempt to warm my toes. "Don't suppose we could get moving? You know, before I become a human popsicle."

Jacob scanned the ground. The once autumn blanket of leaves now lay beneath several inches of undulating snowdrifts. The wind had blown away our footprints in the few minutes we spent working things out. He let out a disappointed growl. "There's no chance I'm going to find those tracks again. I'm not even sure I can find my way back to the truck."

"It's about two hundred meters to the log bridge, another five hundred to where the trail met the ravine and then about three and a half clicks due east to the farm," I said, mentally retracing the path in my head.

"How the hell do you know that?"

"I'm an army grunt. Counting paces and land-nav is kinda built-in."

"So, somewhere in the neighborhood of three miles?"

My eyes rolled as I tried to do the math through the ice clogging my brain. "Something like that," I stammered as the shivering reached my mouth.

"You best come with us," The old man said and started walking the other way. "Levi Miller's farm is much closer this way."

Jacob dropped in behind him without a word and so I followed along. Samuel managed to find his crossbow and the edge of his white tarp where it still poked out above the snow. He handed me my knife before balling up the tarp under an arm and bringing up the rear.

8

I followed Jacob close enough to hold on to his duster with my still gloved hand to keep from losing him while he did the same to the older gentleman in front of him. Our intrepid leader guided us out of the woods and into a field, where the storm swallowed all the landmarks from view. He walked with the purpose of a bloodhound on a trail, but I began to wonder if he knew where he was going until the bleak light from a two-story farmhouse broke through the haze like a lighthouse on the bay.

We clambered out of the snow into a small vestibule lit by the hissing glow of a kerosene lantern hanging from the ceiling. With everyone inside, I helped Samuel push the door closed, cutting off the wind and improving the temperature in the room considerably, though my entire body continued to shiver uncontrollably.

We stomped the snow from our feet then took turns on a three-legged stool to pull off our shoes. I pulled off my boots, but feeling refused to return to my numb toes. In a panic, I ripped my socks off half-expecting to find my toes blackened with frostbite, but beneath the thick wool, they hadn't gone past the inflamed red stage. I gave them a testing, painful wiggle and breathed a sigh of relief as they moved. They needed to be thawed, but wrapping them in my chilled hands did nothing to warm them. Slipping the backpack off my shoulders, I rummaged through the pockets until I found a few more warmers. Activating the heaters, I dropped one in each sock before sliding them on, wishing for the hundredth time I had doubled up on the socks today.

The door opened and a tall dark-haired man with a severe, troubled look over his chin-strap beard surveyed the group until his eyes met the elder man who brought us here. They widened a moment and then dropped in disappointment, a whole conversation said without a word. "Eli, kumme esse," he said, stepping back from the door.

We filed into the kitchen where another kerosene lamp filled the room with a cozy yellow light. A long table with the better part of a dozen chairs sat opposite a cast iron woodstove where a short woman in a dark dress and bonnet bounced a baby on her hip as she stirred a pot of stew and let two young girls use her skirt as a playhouse.

The smell of fresh bread baking in the oven blended with the stew and set my mouth watering worse than Scooby-Doo. I managed to keep my tongue from licking my chops but couldn't silence the growl of hunger.

The door clicked closed behind Samuel, and the woman turned to consider her guests with the wet eyes of a worried mother. When they landed on Eli, they narrowed painfully and lingered only a moment before moving to her husband. "Levi, shall I put on a pot of kaffi?"

Our host led us past the enticing food to the table where he pulled out the captain's chair at the head and sat down. "Please, Sarah." The rest of us filed into our seats in something resembling order of seniority with Jacob and Eli flanking Levi and me staring across the table at Samuel.

"It is getting to be a mighty storm, Eli, it's good you came back when you did."

"Aye, Levi. Once the schnee clears, we will continue to look for young David."

Levi's mouth tightened at the name, and he bobbed his head as if not knowing what else to do. "So, Gott will, it does not snow all night."

"Aye, so Gott will," Eli said.

Sarah brought a stack of bowls to the table and began to place one in front of each of us while her two little helpers brought us utensils and enameled coffee mugs. My "thank you" received meager polite nods from Sarah and the kids. Except for leaning back in their chairs to be out of the way, the Amish men did not help to arrange the place settings.

Levi waited for Sarah to finish and return to the stove before he asked, "So, who be these English?"

"I'm Jacob and this is Matthew," Jacob answered. My name caught in his throat as he broke down in a coughing fit, barely able to fish his hand-kerchief out of his pocket in time to catch what came up.

"Gesundheit," our host said then as if realizing Jacob might not under-stand him, he added, "God bless you."

Jacob folded the red fabric and slipped it back into his pocket. "Thank you."

"They are monsterjäger," Eli added.

Levi sized Jacob up with a renewed measure of respect. "English monsterjäger? I would not believe it."

Sarah placed a loaf of bread with a knife and crock of butter in front of Levi. Steam wafted into the air as Levi sliced the bread and served it first to Jacob, then to Eli and Samuel. Finally, he passed me a thick slice smothered with butter. I lifted the plate to my nose, relishing the smell and eager to push the whole slice into my mouth before I realized that the table had gone quiet with everyone else's head bowed. Sheepishly, I placed my plate on the table and bowed my head in something resembling a praying posture.

I hadn't spoken with God since Jonny died, and I still hadn't recovered from that disappointing conversation, so I waited in silence for heads to rise and Jacob to finish crossing himself.

The bread melted in my mouth and slid down my throat thanks to the hardy helping of butter. I had never tasted anything so good, not that I would ever let my mother know. My stomach growled longingly at the empty plate, but Levi and the others had only eaten a small piece of theirs as if breaking the bread completed some kind of ceremony I wasn't aware of. The thought brought back scripture verses from a forgotten childhood and the crumbs littering my plate became silent accusations that I had, once again, ignorantly overstepped the bounds of custom. One of these days, I was going to remember to follow my host's lead and not come out looking like an ass.

Sarah brought over the pot of stew and a tall metal pot of coffee. She spooned out bowls of stew while the girls worked together to pour coffee in our mugs. Once she finished serving us, Sarah took the girls by the hand and led them to another room. I watched them leave, wondering why they didn't join us, but the thought evaporated as the men at the head of the table began comparing notes over bowls of stew.

Jacob began, laying out the facts as best he'd been able to piece together.

I listened for any details he hadn't mentioned before while doing my best to not shovel the stew down my throat. The thick slices of meat and potatoes nearly burned my mouth as they sated the hollow noises coming from my stomach. In a satisfying conjunction of heat from the woodstove meeting that of the stew, I began to thaw.

Finding the bottom of my bowl much sooner than I liked, I made a hand gesture in Levi's direction, trying to get his attention without interrupting Jacob. However, instead of getting a nod from our host, Jacob waved me off with the barest shake of his head as he finished telling our Amish friends about Steven.

Levi's eyes narrowed at the mention of Steven Andrews. "Verglinselder." While I didn't know what the word meant, the way he spat it out made the meaning clear.

"Schtillschweige, Levi. You know well, David is not innocent either." The scolding tone in Eli's voice did little to assuage the anger in Levi's face.

"I take it there's a bit of bad blood between the boys?" Jacob asked.

"Aye, more than a little. Buweschtreech that have gotten out of hand."

Eli's accent made him hard enough to understand without the random Amish phrases he threw in, but Jacob appeared to be following along without the need of a translator. I would have to get the finer points from him later. From what I gathered, though, Steven had started the feud almost a year ago when he decided to douse David in a bucket of water after he lost Steven's ice-fishing pole while they fished together on the pond between their properties. From there, things continued to escalate all year.

Eli laid out the highlight reel for us, and I couldn't help but snicker at some of the cleverer pranks. Samuel shot me an evil glare, but I could hardly be blamed for boys' imaginations. David had spooked a heifer Steven was trying to ride bareback to impress a couple of his *English* friends, and it bucked him off into the barnyard slush. Steven then set off a string of fireworks in the pigsty as David dumped in the morning slop, setting off a shower of flying *scheisse* and a minor stampede. David retaliated by letting a skunk he trapped loose in the Andrews's bus shelter and Steven got sprayed on the first day of school. Then, just last month, Steven dug a pit in the Miller's haymow, tied strings across the top tier of bales, and concealed the hole with loose hay. Unfortunately, Levi found it when he fell ten feet, dragging the top row of bales onto himself. Having fallen victim to that particular prank myself, courtesy of my younger brothers, I burst out in a snort of laughter that thankfully the group took as derisive condemnation.

"Yes, well, boys be boys," Eli said.

"You don't think the boys drew the Krampus, do you?" asked Jacob.

Eli considered and then let out a heavy sigh from his nose that ruffled his long beard. "No, but it certainly did not help. Krampus live on Keffer."

Jacob raised his eyebrows and gave an affirming shrug. "You said before that you have lost too many for there to be only one Krampus. How many have you lost?"

Eli slumped in his chair. "Ten, this Dezember plus yours. Five the year before, if it is the same family we chased out of Pennsylfaani."

"You chased them out of Pennsylvania?" Jacob asked.

A haunted look drifted across Eli's deep-set eyes. "Ya. We could not catch them all before the hibernation."

"And how many Krampus—uh, Krampi do you think there are now?"

When Eli didn't immediately answer the question, Samuel spoke for the first time since sitting down. "We found two different sets of hoof prints outside David's room, and another set at Aaron's house down the road. Both boys were taken on the same night, so no less than three, but there may be more."

"Three?" Jacob mouthed the word, chewing on it like a tough piece of meat too big to swallow.

"I take it that's a lot?" I asked, unable to stay quiet.

Jacob turned his head in my direction, but his eyes never really focused on me, they seemed lost in consideration. "Son, I thought I needed your help when I believed there was only one."

"Oh," I said with dumbfounded clarity.

Jacob's eyes recovered their focus as he regarded the men across the table. "This may be too much for either of us alone. Would you be willing to accept some English help?"

A half-smile slipped up from Eli's white beard. "Many hands make the work light."

Jacob glanced out the window, where the snow had stopped falling, though the wind continued to howl, whipping up little dust devils of snow. The failing light of the setting sun cast long shadows across the ground. "It's getting late and it'll be near impossible to find, let alone follow any tracks in the blowing snow. I suggest we get a good night's rest and start fresh in the morning."

Eli nodded his agreement. "Samuel and I will give you a ride back to

259

the Andrews's farm. Then tomorrow, we meet here when the sun rises and we can see."

I moved to push back my chair, but then stopped as the Amish bowed their heads once more. Jacob also paused halfway through the motion of getting up. At least this time I wasn't the only one caught off guard by their unexpected show of supplication. Once finished, Samuel went to hitch up the monsterjäger's wagon while I stole a little more heat from the woodstove before putting my boots one with a fresh set of warmers in my socks.

Samuel led a team of muscular draft horses out of Levi's barn. Behind them, they pulled a boxy wagon whose wheels cut into the snow. Brass hinges and latches covered the black paneling, revealing more doors and drawers than a furniture store.

With the wagon's bench seat only able to fit two, Samuel and I climbed into the wagon's hold. The inside of the wagon stretched further than it looked from the outside, with even more doors and compartments. In the center of the space, the gentle glow of a coal fire flickered behind the vented door of the small potbelly stove, chasing away the winter chill. I ducked my head beneath the low roof and warmed my hands over the stove with a smile. *As long as there's a fire in here, Jacob can have the front seat, even if I have to sit on the floor.*

Samuel turned a few latches and the small table at the back of the wagon folded itself away and a pair of built-in cots dropped from the sidewall like bunk beds with just enough space between them for a man to lay on his side. Samuel cranked another lever and the top cot returned to its stowed position. I sat in the middle of the remaining cot, still warming my hands on the stove. Samuel tucked his bare hands into his armpits and sat at the far end of the cot, where he leaned against the back wall. A draft crept in through the joints of the wagon and tossed the ends of the longish hair sticking out from beneath his hat. The hard level stare he shot me as the wagon lurched forward made me wonder if he really had mistaken me for a Krampus in the woods.

9

Horse and wagon meant taking the long way around the country block, giving the sun plenty of time to set before Jacob and I climbed into the cab of his truck. The engine rumbled to life with a touch of Jacob's finger, and we watched the wagon's taillights disappear into the night while we waited for the heat to kick in.

"Well, they're an odd sort of people," I said in an effort to hear something other than the howl of the wind.

Jacob's shoulders bobbed in a shrug. "To each their own. I can't say that I understand the Amish way, but you have to appreciate their dedication."

I made a half-hearted derisive noise in my throat. Anyone who willingly choose to live that hard of a life certainly had something I didn't, but I don't know if I would call it dedication.

The seat heaters kicked in before the vents started to spew lukewarm air, and Jacob dropped it into drive while simultaneously thumbing the phone button. The snow crunched beneath the tires as the phone rang.

"What'cha need, Gramps?" Gracie's voice came over the speaker punctuated by loud smacks.

"I need you to keep me on the road. I'm looking at a solid sheet of white out here."

"You didn't get caught out in that storm, did you? I sent you a bunch of texts about it. It came in faster and harder than anyone would have thought." Gracie finished with a noise that sounded like she reached the bottom of a Slurpee. My teeth chattered just thinking about drinking something cold while I watched the gates of Hell freeze over out my window.

"Shit, ringer must be off. Check my messages." Jacob tossed me his phone then toggled the four-wheel drive on.

I powered on the screen, but only a number pad showed on the black surface. "It's locked."

"Eleven—oh-four—nineteen—seventy-three." I punched in the code and the screen came to life.

"You're still using Mom's birthday?" Gracie said, her voice tightening slightly. "I thought I told you to change it?"

"I'd rather not discuss this now, Gracie." Jacob's voice carried the impatient tone of a worn-out discussion.

"Fine," she said, but I heard *this-isn't-over* in her undertone, and by the annoyed expression on Jacob's face, he didn't miss it either.

"Yep. Your ringer was off," I said, checking the settings and turning it back on. "And you have six texts from Gracie, two from Father Hastings, and another from a Bishop Mueller."

"Thank you, Matthew. He never does believe me." Gracie's voice remained firm and friendly, unlike the first time she heard me on the phone, where it became shy and nearly inaudible. I guess walking me through my run-in with a djinn this past summer upgraded our relationship. I liked hearing the more confident Gracie.

Jacob, however, growled in frustration as he stopped the truck in the middle of the road; at least I hoped it was the middle of the road, I really couldn't tell through the fresh coating of snow. "You're going to have to drive while I deal with the bishop."

I swallowed hard. Personally, I hated driving in a fresh blanket of snow. The ditches look just like the road, especially at night. In these conditions, I'm about as good at staying out of the trenches as I am at staying out of the gutter when I'm bowling, and I really didn't want to spend the night in a ditch.

I turned my head at the sound of the seatbelt alarm going off and found Jacob staring at me. It didn't take me long to figure out which one of us he expected to walk around the truck and which one got to slide across the warm seats. With nothing for it, I unbuckled and hopped out the truck straight into a two-foot deep snow drift. By the time I high-stepped it around the truck, snow worked its way into my right boot and the wind stripped away what little heat my multiple layers of shirts held. I hopped into the truck and slammed the door.

Wrapping my fingers around the warmed steering wheel, I glared out the windshield at the headlight's beams stretching out from the truck across the flat plane of snow. "Gracie, I don't have any gutter-rail snow-banks to bounce off of, please tell me you have a way of keeping me on the road."

"Keep? No, but I can show you where it is." A head's up display projected itself onto the windshield in front of me. Long thin red lines illuminated the edges of the road ahead, bending slightly to the left at the edge of the headlights.

My jaw bounced off the bottom of the steering wheel. "That's so cool."

"Well thank you. I added it this past summer," Gracie said with only a hint of smug satisfaction.

Jacob smirked in the seat beside me. "Yeah, it's easily my favorite thing she tweaked this summer."

"Wait, there's more?" I asked, surveying the assortment of toggles and buttons decorating the lower part of the dash.

"Of course there is, but Gracie will have to walk you through those later. Right now, you need to start driving while I call the Bishop."

"Just one more question?"

"What?" Strained patience ate away at Jacob's voice.

"Which way's home?"

"I've got you covered," Gracie said with a snicker. A small screen slid up from the center of the dash and blinked to life with a road map and a highlighted route home complete with turn-by-turn directions.

"You've made your own mapping service?"

"Uh, no. That's Google. I make things better; I don't re-invent the wheel—unless it's an idiot who invented it in the first place."

I chuckled, almost forgetting the snow melting in my boot. "Thanks, Gracie."

"Nothing to it, Matthew. Goodbye, Gramps."

"Oh, Gracie, wait," Jacob said.

"Yeah?"

"I need you to dig up everything you can on Krampus."

"Okay. When do you need it by?"

"Daybreak."

"Of course you do. Why do I even ask?"

"Thanks, Gracie. Gotta go," Jacob said, then ended the call. He disconnected the phone's Bluetooth, dialed another number, and pressed the phone to his ear. Apparently, I didn't need to hear what he discussed with the bishop.

I drop the shifter into drive and trudged home through the snow-blown roads in four-wheel drive. By the time we pulled into the driveway a few hours later, only the wind remained of the storm, leaving the sky clear to reveal a bright starry night with the promise of record lows. The barn sat dark at the end of the drive with the evening milking complete. We pulled in beside Mark's beat-up Bronco and watched silvery gray smoke drift up from the home's chimney in an invitation that Jacob and I didn't refuse.

Tired of the cold and snow, I rushed ahead of Jacob, pounding foot-size holes into the drifts. Swinging the vestibule door in, I kicked my way through the two-foot-high wall of white that leaned against it, deliberately obliterating the door's imprint with satisfaction. Jacob stomped his way in a moment later, and we took turns batting the snow off each other's pant legs with the old broom before taking off our boots and retreating to the warmth of the kitchen.

My mother sat at the kitchen table, a steaming cup of tea in one hand and the cordless house phone in the other. She gave a relieved sigh as the door squeaked closed, but her brows knitted together angrily. "Couldn't give your mother a call and let her know you're all right. I've been worried for hours."

"I'm sorry, Momma, but I thought you knew I would be out late."

"Out late? In a blizzard? Why would you be out late in this?"

By the look in my mother's eyes, I couldn't invent a rational explanation she would find acceptable. "I...uh..."

Jacob spoke up to save me the trouble. "It's my fault, Mrs. Peterson. The snowstorm blew in a bit sooner than I thought it would, and we had to hunker down for a few hours to wait it out."

"And your phones didn't work?" The accusation in her eyes cut like daggers.

Even Jacob got tongue-tied under her stare. "Um, to be honest, ma'am, in the midst of the storm, I didn't think about it."

Her glare shifted to me. I shrugged my shoulders and opted for a simple, "I'm sorry. It won't happen again."

I suffered under her smoldering stare a moment longer before she finally said, "You best see that it doesn't."

"Yes, ma'am," Jacob and I said together.

Now that we'd been properly scolded for our transgressions, my mother let a smile creep across the stern features of her face. "Now, have you two eaten?"

The hours spent getting home turned my single bowl of stew and slice of bread into faint memories, and my stomach rumbled in response before either of us could voice an answer. Not that my mother waited for one. She busied herself putting together plates of leftovers from the fridge. All the while she never let her eyes drift far from the phone on the table.

"Momma, you expecting a phone call?"

"Luke hasn't called yet. His connecting flight from Philly got canceled and he's supposed to let me know when his new flight will be arriving tomorrow."

"I thought Luke was going skiing with his roommate's family in Vermont." My voice heated with residual anger from when Luke told me about the trip. Granted, I didn't handle it with the big brother positivity I should have. I'd been hoping to fill the Jonny-sized hole in my heart with my first family Christmas in years, but Luke bailed on me to go skiing. I knew we both had a childhood full of less than pleasant memories that we needed to balance out, but instead of being excited for him, I was pissed. Now that he changed his plans though, I felt a bit guilty about giving him a hard time. "I hope he didn't change his plans on my account."

"Luke wanted to surprise you." My mom said, placing a mountain of reheated spaghetti with her homemade sauce in front of me.

I licked my lips in anticipation of my favorite meal and plunged my fork into the hill of spaghetti. With a twirl, I pulled out a ball of noodles almost too big to stretch my mouth over, but I managed. Forget everything I said about Sarah's cooking, nothing could beat my momma's. Jacob skewered the sausage sitting on top of his own heaping plate, and my mother beamed at the contented noises we both made as we ate.

Momma handed Jacob and me a tall glass of milk then sat in her usual chair beside the head of the table. She picked up the phone in one hand and sipped from her mug of hot tea in the other. Two sips later, she jumped at the ringing phone and nearly sloshed her tea over the rim of her cup. Placing the mug on the table, she tugged the antenna out of the antique handset with a practiced hand and put the phone to her ear without checking the caller ID.

"Hello. Peterson Dairy Farm, Lisa Peterson speaking, how may I help you?" My mother answered the phone in the same rote greeting she taught all of us to use. Come to think of it, I never heard her use a different one even when she did check the caller ID.

The Charlie Brown teacher squawk on the other end sounded like Luke, but I couldn't understand him any more than I did the cartoon.

Summoned by the ringing phone, a herd of elephants charged across the floor above and rolled down the stairs like an avalanche that materialized into my little sister. At five-three and a little more than a buck-ten, she walked like a pro wrestler on a rampage.

She strode up and slugged me in the shoulder hard enough to hurt. "When did you get home?"

I grunted and swayed dramatically at the impact. Righting myself, I stuffed a forkful of spaghetti in my mouth and waved a hand over my half-eaten plate. She accepted the gesture as all the explanation she needed and then proceeded to drain my glass of milk without asking.

With the back of her hand, she wiped away her milk mustache then thumped the empty glass down onto the table like the victor of a drinking contest no one else entered. She flashed me an evil smile then spun and gave Jacob a small wave. "Oh. Hi, Mr. McGinnis."

Jacob washed down his latest bite with a gulp of milk. "Good evening, Miss Peterson." Mary's face twisted in disgust; she liked being called miss about as much as I liked being called son.

I swallowed the half-chewed wad of food then tapped the empty glass with my fork. "I think you forgot something."

She lifted her hands innocently. "What?"

"You know the rules. You kill it, you fill it."

Momma hung up the phone and pressed the antenna back into place, the disappointment clear on her face. "Well, that's just fine. Luke can't get a flight home until the day after tomorrow."

"I'm sorry, Momma," Mary said, stepping around me to give her a hug. The sudden show of affection caught my mother by surprise, but she accepted it gratefully.

Jacob looked over to my mother in that comforting grandfatherly way of his. "At least he'll be home for Christmas, Mrs. Peterson."

"Yeah, but he's stuck in Philly and has to fly on Christmas Eve, and you wonder why I take the bus," I added with a rueful shake of the head.

Mom shot me scolding scowl but spoke to Jacob. "Yes, he will, and I'll thank you to make sure this one is here for Christmas as well."

"You have my word, Mrs. Peterson."

My mother's mouth narrowed into a tight line of consideration then quirked up slightly at the edge. "At this point, Mr. McGinnis, you may as well call me Lisa."

"As long as you call me Jacob, ma'am." Jacob waited for my mom's acquiescent nod then continued, "Well then, Lisa, thank you for a wonderful dinner, but Matthew and I have an early morning appointment and I dread to think how long it will take me to get to my motel in these road conditions." He pulled a sheet from the paper towel roll in the center of the table and wiped his mouth before pushing back his chair.

"Nonsense, we have an extra bed, you can stay here for the night." She tapped Mary's arm still wrapped around her. "Mary, please put clean sheets on the bed downstairs for Jacob."

Mary stood up sharply with a *tsk*. "Fine," she spat before spinning on her heels and stomping to the basement.

"I don't want to be a bother, Lisa."

Mom gave Jacob a friendly smile. "You're not. She's been a mix of sweet and sassy ever since spring." Neither Jacob nor I missed how Mom deliberately didn't mention the deaths of Jonny and Paul or the hurt look that threatened tears in her eyes.

Jacob laid a hand on her arm. "She'll grow out of it—eventually. They all do."

10

With Jacob sleeping in the basement, I got the privilege of sleeping in Luke's bed listening to Mark, the human sawmill, snore his way through the night. I had never suffered a worse night of sleep and when the stabbing pain of his bleating alarm clock went off at five in the morning, I prayed I might actually get some real shuteye. My eyes closed and I slowly slipped into the beginnings of an ethereal dream when a pair of rough hands shook me back to the less than pleasant fragrance of my brother's room.

I seriously debated beating my brother back into unconsciousness but as that would only resume the non-stop sawmill, I growled hoarsely, "What the hell, Mark? Just let me sleep."

"Sorry, can't do that. We have an appointment to keep," said a voice much older and raspier than my brother's.

I pried an eye open to shoot him a devastating scowl, but Jacob stood up and the light from the ceiling fixture ruined the effect as it blinded me. The grit in the corners of my eyes bit into my eyelids as I scrunched them closed against the light. After another moment I tossed back the covers, sat up, and worked at dislodging the gunk with a fingernail. "Give me a minute. I'll meet you downstairs."

"I'll give you five," Jacob said in a voice much too cheery for this early in the morning.

I took ten, but only because I had to wait for Mark to finish up in the bathroom before I could use it, plus all my clothes were in the basement. Eventually, I emerged from the basement in enough layers to make me move like Ralphie's little brother in that Christmas movie Mark always makes us watch.

"Good morning, Michelin-Man. Or should I call you Stay-Puft?" Mark teased as he tied his barn boots.

"You can keep your damn mouth shut if you know what's good for you. I didn't get near enough sleep last night to deal with your bullshit."

"You will watch your language in this house, if YOU know what's good for you," my mother said from the stove where I could hear the sizzle of frying bacon.

"I'm sorry, Momma," I apologized then swatted the back of my brother's head to remove the arrogant smirk from his face. He ducked and I only managed to flip a bit of his hair into the air.

"Hey, take it easy on the hair." Mark finished with his boots and stood to start putting on his own layers. "Don't suppose you're going to be around today to help, eh, partner?"

"Nah, I have to help Jacob with something." I raised a meaningful eyebrow, but he didn't care. "Besides, it's silent partner."

"Whatever," he said sullenly. He snatched the tall thermos of coffee off the counter and left for the morning milking, pulling hard on the kitchen door. It didn't exactly slam closed behind him, but it came close.

Momma shot a look at the banging door then placed a plate of bacon and eggs on the table. "Here, I'm going back to bed." Dark bags hung below her eyes and she moved slower than usual, but I got the feeling it was something more than lack of sleep that dragged at her.

I wrapped my arms around her before she could pass and pulled her close. "Thanks, Mom. I love you."

She smiled up at me through the tiredness and pecked me on the cheek. "Please. Be safe."

"I'll do what I can," I promised and watched her shuffle to her bedroom.

Jacob got up from the table and took his own empty plate to the sink. He rinsed it off then turned to me. "Perhaps you should stay here today. I've taken enough of your vacation already, and besides, I have the Amish monsterjäger team to back me up."

I picked up a piece of bacon and chomped off half of it in a single bite. "You already woke me up, and I'd rather hunt this Krampus thing than shovel shit or milk cows. Besides, I get the impression that even with the four of us, these Krampi thingies are going to be tough to handle."

Jacob gave a snort of appreciation and topped off his mug of coffee from the pot. "You have a point, but please tell me you have something a bit more um...tactical to wear."

I surveyed the bulky layers I wore and all the stains, tears, and threadbare spots that earned the garments the category of barn clothes. "I thought you wanted me dressed for farm work?"

"Not today. Today we're hunting, and you need to be able to move. I've never dealt with a Krampus before let alone multiples, and I'm not exactly sure what they can do. So, the more tactical the better."

"Yeah, I've got some surplus cold-weather gear downstairs. I sent it home a few years ago for my brothers to use when they go hunting. Give me a minute to get this down, and I'll go change."

A few minutes later, I climbed into the cab of Jacob's truck feeling considerably nimbler in only three layers: long johns, winter weight ACUs, and a water-resistant outer layer in winter camo broken only by the black straps of my pistol harness. I also borrowed Luke's balaclava, making me look like an armed albino gorilla with a huge black zit for a head, but at least I was a very warm gorilla.

The wind died overnight, and our headlights panned over the static winter wonderland left behind. The barren farmland now hid beneath a picturesque whitewash of pristine snow. We followed our half-filled tire tracks back out to the main road where the diligent efforts of New York's fleet of snowplows had cleared a recognizable path.

Unlike the secondary roads with their crust of snow and splattering of sand, only random splotches of dirty slush covered the blacktop of the main thoroughfares. With the clearer roads and the orange glow of dawn lightening the skies behind us, we picked up speed. Jacob soon relaxed, trading his two-handed iron grip for an easy one-handed hold on the steering wheel, and thumbed the call button.

Within moments, Gracie's sleepy voice answered with a yawn that stretched out her words. "Good mor-ning, Gra-amps."

"Morning, Angel. Did I wake you up?"

"No. I've been up all night doing YOU a favor." The heavy sarcasm in her tone carried just a hint of affection.

"I'm sorry, dear. Were you able to get what I needed?"

"More or less." Gracie yawned and I felt my own mouth stretch wide sympathetically.

"Jeez, the two of you need to get more sleep," Jacob said then took a sip of coffee from his travel mug.

"I don't want to hear it. You got to sleep in my bed. I had to share a room with Mark, and let me tell you, I've heard more tolerable noise coming from mating cats." The illustration received a very satisfying snort of coffee straight out of Jacob's nose.

Jacob put his mug back in the cup holder delicately, trying to not make the coffee mess any worse. "Ugh, hand me a napkin from the glove box, will ya?"

I barked a laugh and handed him a small stack.

"Thanks," he said, cleaning up as best he could one-handed. "Back to the question at hand. Gracie, what can you tell us about Krampus?"

"Not much you don't already know. Half-demon half-goat. Literally the opposite of Santa Claus. Has supernatural powers. Can be a real problem to try to get rid of. Oh, and it either beats or eats children, depending on the source material."

"Our Amish friends think we have the eating kind. They also seem to think we have a pack."

"Amish friends?" Gracie's voice dropped to just over a whisper as if she thought they may be in the car with us.

"Yeah, sorry. We're working with a pair of Amish monster hunters on this one. We're on our way to meet them now."

"Well. That's new."

"I take the Lord's help where I can get it. Did you find anything on how to kill one?"

"Mixed reviews on that one. There's your usual: impaling and burning. Some sources say it has to be wood, others aren't all that clear. I suggest you take the usual tact."

"Punch it full of holes and then remove its head?" I offered, trying to be helpful.

"Pretty much. Being that it's supposed to be a demon, I'd start with blessed iron rounds and hope that does the trick."

"Thanks, Gracie. How's the weather today?" Jacob turned left and rolled across the bridge spanning the Mohawk River and into Canajoharie. The river below looked eerily solid, not that I would chance walking across it.

"Forecast is clean and clear. I should be able to keep tabs on you today."

"Thank you. We have about another hour or so, if you want to catch a few z's before I need you again." Jacob clicked the phone off and the radio crackled to life, playing a country song older than me through the static of poor reception.

"An hour? Can we stop someplace where I can pee?"

I jumped at the sight of a ghostly figure rising in the backseat under the woolen blanket Jacob kept there.

Jacob jerked the wheel at the sudden voice, narrowly missing the bridge's guardrail, then swerved across the other lane as he over-corrected. The truck fishtailed on a patch of snow left behind by the snowplow. Another near miss with the other rail as we finished crossing the bridge and skidded to a stop beneath the I-90 overpass.

Jacob reached back and ripped the blanket back. A half-mop of unruly black hair flopped over the other, half-shaved, side of my sister's head. She pushed it back to the proper side of her head.

"Mary, what the hell?" I gasped, trying to keep my heart from beating its way out of my chest.

"Miss Peterson," Jacob said in a tight voice with a measure more civility than I could have managed. "Why, may I ask, are you in my truck?"

My sister didn't even have the decency to look abashed. "I'm coming along this time."

I twisted in my seat; just the thought of what could happen to her made my voice jump a dozen decibels and half an octave, or maybe I was just afraid of what our mother would do to me. "Oh, no, you're not!"

Her eyes held a fierceness that only made my hackles rise more. "I most certainly am."

Jacob glanced from my sister to me, then stepped on the gas and spun the truck around. I shot Mary a smug look.

Mary's face fell as we rolled back across the bridge. "Wait, you're not taking me home?"

Jacob peeked at Mary in the review mirror. "I should. The things we're going after..."

My jaw dropped and I cleared my ear with a pinky finger, I couldn't possibly have heard him correctly. "Should? What do you mean *should*? We're taking her back home." Jacob drove through the light at the other end of the bridge and up the hill. I watched Route 5 East and the way back home zoom pass my window.

"We don't have time to take her back home."

"Then where..." I let the question die as we crested the hill and I saw the red roof and golden arches.

"Bathroom break," Jacob said, pushing the shifter into park. He turned to Mary. "Please hurry, we are already late."

Mary hopped out of the truck and dashed into Micky-D's. The door no sooner closed behind her when I heard Jacob grumble, "Oh, hell, now I have to go."

I scoffed until the power of suggestion hit me full on in the bladder, then unbuckled and followed everyone else into the building. Saddling up to the urinal next to Jacob, I tried voicing my objection once again. "You know, we can't take her along with us."

"We don't have time to run her all the way back home. She'll have to stay at the Miller's while we're hunting. She can help Sarah around the house and maybe she'll learn a touch of respect for your mother while we're gone."

His criticism of my sister, though not wrong, crossed a line, and I wasted a glare over the partition as Jacob concentrated on coercing his bladder into action. "Watch what you say about my sister, she's been through a lot."

Jacob gave up on relieving himself and zipped up his pants. "Your whole family's been through hell this year, and none of you have climbed out of it yet. That doesn't give your sister the right to treat your mother like she does."

I finished up and joined him at the sink to wash my hands. The water flowing from the tap felt cool compared to the anger burning inside me. "Just shut it. There's a lot going on with her, and you don't know what you're talking about."

"Don't I? I lost my daughter and her husband to a vamp years ago and raised Gracie as best I could without her. I know what you all are going through, and I know how the holidays amplify the pain. It's been sixteen years and they still do it to me." Jacob hammered the towel dispenser a half-dozen times then ripped off the three-foot sheet to dry his hands. His blue eyes rose to meet mine with tears threatening to fall from their corners. "Look, I don't mean to judge. We all grieve in our own way, but if your sister and mother don't find some solid ground between them, their grief will tear them apart and I know you don't want to see that."

He balled up the paper towel and tossed it into the wastebasket before leaving the bathroom. The water continued to run uselessly over my hands as I watched him leave. He had a point and I knew it. After months of therapy, I still struggled every time we pulled up to the farmhouse. Mom and Mary saw Jonny's empty seat at the kitchen table every day.

Combine that with Mary's best friend, Beth, moving away, then toss in your usual teenage bullshit and you got the perfect hormonal shit-storm. It had been brewing for months and Christmas would only throw gasoline on the fire.

"Fuck," I muttered, drying my hands. Now I had something else to worry about.

11

When Mary returned to the truck, I made her call Mom. I should have known better when she rolled her eyes, because the conversation never got past hello before they both raised their voices. I looked at Jacob uncomfortably. He quirked an eyebrow and tilted his head in an *I-told-you-so* gesture before turning his concentration back out the front window.

I twisted in my seat and made my first mistake of the day. "Mary, watch your tone, you're talking to Mom."

The phone drifted away from Mary's ear, and our mother's voice continued to screech through the phone. "Here, you talk to her then, she ain't listening to me anyways," she said, throwing the phone at me.

I reached for it instinctively, but it bounced off my fingertips and I dropped it. Sweeping my hand blindly across the floor a few times, I eventually managed to get a finger on it. I picked it up to my mother's continued rant about how she had never known a child as foolish, irresponsible, and selfish as Mary. She would have made an impressive drill sergeant, the way she could go on without ever uttering a single curse word.

"Mom," I said into the phone, making my second mistake of the day before the sun even crested the trees.

"Matthew?"

"Yeah, Mom, it's me."

"You bring your sister home this instant."

"Mom, we can't ,we're already..." The next word never made it to my lips as my mother cut me off and proceeded to remind me of my own long list of flaws. I tipped the phone away from my ear to preserve my hearing and let the beratement continue uninterrupted. I tuned her out and let the bulk of her remarks wash off of me like water from a duck's back. Between the army and my old man, I certainly had plenty of practice.

Jacob mutely drove on to the Millers, unable to outrun the rising sun. Mary sat in the backseat with her arms folded over her chest refusing to look at me or the phone in my hand. I stared out the window at the beauty of fresh snow sparkling in the light of dawn, but between reasoning out how best to protect my sulking sister and my mother's verbal assault, it passed by my window unnoticed.

My mother did give my ear a rest and hung up about ten minutes before we rolled up the Miller's drive. The door to the farmhouse opened, and Levi stepped out slapping a broad-brimmed hat onto his head.

"Shit, they already left," Jacob said, watching Levi trudge through the snow toward us.

"Who?" Mary asked her eyes wide.

It took me a moment to notice the missing hunting wagon as well. "The Amish monsterjägers. Maybe their wagon is still in the barn?"

Jacob shifted the truck into park and shook his head. "No, the wagon tracks lead off that way." He pointed to the deep ruts cutting through the fresh snow and leading off around the side of the house opposite of the barn. "I'll be right back." Jacob unbuckled and met Levi half way.

Mary leaned forward over the back of the front seat. "Who are these people?"

"You mean the Amish?"

"No, I get the Amish." She heaved a sigh. "Or at least I as much as anyone else gets them. I mean who are the monsterjägers?"

"Oh. Well, I only met them last night, but I think monsterjäger means monster hunter. So, they're kind of like—the Amish version of Jacob."

"Okay then. Who exactly is Jacob?"

I waved a hand in the man's general direction. "Jacob. He's a monster hunter. You know, the werebear last spring."

"Wait, you guys were serious about that?" She gave me a look like she expected a punchline, but I didn't have one to hit her with. It never occurred to me that she didn't believe Mark, Luke, and me when we told her about it. Though to be honest, I doubted I would have believed my brothers if I hadn't been there myself.

"Yes, werebears are real and one really did kill Jonny and Paul. Djinn— uh, genies are also real, I had to deal with one of those this past summer. I wrote you about it."

The expression on her face wavered from pure disbelief to wondering if I should be admitted to a mental hospital. "I thought you were just making up stories, like Jonny always did."

I swallowed hard, remembering Jonny's monster journal hiding in my bag back home. "I don't think he was making them up. It's kinda' how I met Jacob."

"So, we're actually out here hunting for another werebear or something?"

"*We* aren't hunting for anything," I said, stressing the *we*. "*You* are staying here with the Millers, while Jacob and I go after the Krampuses or Krampi or whatever it is you call more than one."

"Oh, hell no I'm not!"

Jacob pulled open his door. "Levi says Eli and Samuel left about a half hour ago. He also said Mary can stay here so long as she helps out."

Mary scrunched her face up in outrage. "I'm not staying here."

"Oh, yes you are," I said hotly, matching the tone my mother used when one of us was being particularly obstinate. It had about as much effect as I should have expected.

Jacob gave me a flat, exacerbated look. "Matthew, you're not helping." He closed the front door and opened the back, driver's-side door of the king cab. "Miss Peterson, please get out of the truck." His voice carried a lack of inflection that made it sound more severe in the way a drill sergeant's did right before smoking the shit out of a company or the way Paul's would get right before he took off his belt. Mary's eyes widened and she shuffled across the seat to the open door. "Now, please go with Levi and help his wife Sarah with whatever she needs doing. We'll be back to take you home later." Mary swallowed hard and gave Jacob a shocked nod, before shuffling off in the snow after Levi.

Jacob watched her go until she disappeared into the house. "Shit," he muttered slamming the backdoor. He got into the driver's seat and buckled, but his finger hovered over the start button and his head dropped against the steering wheel. "I think I just fucked up with her."

"I...uh...yeah. It's kind of how Paul used to speak right before the shit would hit the fan."

His head turned to me with a pained expression. "I'm sorry. I didn't mean it that way."

I mustered a forgiving smile. "I know. I'll try to explain it to her later."

Jacob pushed the button and the truck roared to life. "Thanks."

Uncertain of what lay beneath the snow, Jacob followed the wagon tracks at a crawl until, at the far end of the field, they squeezed through a gap in the trees too small for the truck to fit. We didn't see any F-150 sized holes in the dense wood for as far as we could see to either side.

Jacob put the truck in park, and with a last throaty rumble, the engine cut out. "I guess we walk from here." He leaned over the center console and flipped up the backseat, revealing a cache of ammo cans nestled in the hold. Grunting, he hefted out one of the cans and placed it on my lap.

"What's this?"

He reached for another can. "I'm too old to climb into the back in this kind of weather, so I keep the essentials in the winter stash."

I popped the top on my can. Inside sat boxes of .357 rounds. Following Gracie's suggestion, I fished out the boxes labeled blessed iron and changed the load in all three of my moon clips as well as the load in my pistol.

Jacob handed me the remnants of his blessed-ammo box and a black backpack. "Put the spares in here. Just don't crush the protein bars, they're nasty enough when they aren't mush."

I reached into the bag and pulled out a chocolate-peanut butter bar. They didn't make a better flavor, but not even chocolate and peanut butter could make a protein bar more than tolerable. "Agreed," I said, tossing the bar back in the bag. I added Jacob's box of .45 and my half box of .357 magnum to the bag then slipped the pair of water bottles he handed me into the elastic nets on the sides. Throwing my arms through the pack's straps, I opened the door and hopped out into a knee-deep snowdrift. "Ugh, I don't suppose you have snowshoes in that toolbox of yours, do you?"

"Ahh, and there it is," Jacob said with a half-cocked smile and a raised forefinger.

"There what is?"

He slung a belt of shotgun shells over his chest and shouldered a short double-barreled shotgun with a pistol grip. He looked up with a grin. "That one thing I need on a hunt that I don't have." He hopped out of the truck and the door banged closed behind him, echoing in the frosty air.

I barked a grim laugh. "Right, I almost forgot." I pushed the door closed then nodded at the shotgun. "Should I get something with a bit more punching power, too?"

"I doubt we're going to catch these things out in the open, and I don't have any blessed iron for the rifles. These are only buck-shot." He waved a hand over his belt of shells.

"A hole's a hole and a rifle can make a pretty damn big hole, iron or not."

"You got a point. They're in the back. Help yourself."

My eyes drifted to the trees as I debated whether I wanted to carry the extra weight of a rifle. The barren trees swayed in a gentle breeze, the snow drifting off their branches like powdered sugar from a shaker. The sparkling illusion of fairy dust didn't change the necessities of war, and I'd never been in an engagement when I didn't want more weapons.

I held my hand out, and Jacob tossed me his keys. Snatching them out of the air, I placed a foot on the rear tire and sprung up into the truck bed like an action hero until I found as much snow in the bed as on the ground and my foot slipped out from beneath me. At least it provided a soft pillowy landing. With a chagrined grimace at Jacob's laughter, I dug myself out of the snow and opened the large diamond plated tool chest. I pushed the trays of stakes, knives, machetes, and spare ammunition to the side and considered the rifles at the bottom.

The Ruger Hawkeye Alaskan had better punching power, but the Browning BAR was a semiautomatic. I went with shooting speed over punching power and picked up the BAR. I checked the loaded magazine, then added a spare box of .308 ammo to the backpack. Adjusting the shoulder strap, I slipped it over my head and carried the rifle crossbody over my backpack, careful to make sure the strap didn't impede my pistol draw. If I needed to react fast, the pistol would be my better option.

Armed for bear, I hopped down and high-kneed it into the woods. The snow crust partially supported my weight before crumbling and dropping me back to the ground. It made walking in the stuff something like scaling a StairMaster with a trick belt and twice as exhausting. I shifted to the already broken path cut by the monsterjäger's team of horses. At least that only felt like walking in sand.

Fifty feet into the woods Jacob broke down into a coughing fit so violent he braced himself on his knees, unable to fish his handkerchief out. When it ended, he spat a bloody wad of phlegm into the snow then pulled out his handkerchief and wiped his mouth clean with it instead. He folded the fabric and tucked it away before continuing after the horses without a word.

I watched the blood melt into the snow for a moment then jogged to catch up to him. "Okay, out with it."

Tired misery stretched his face thin as he kept walking without even a glance in my direction. "It's nothing."

"Don't do that. Don't go playing it off, you've been coughing up blood ever since I got home. What is it? Emphysema, pneumonia, bronchitis, the flu? Whatever it is, let me know so I can help. Hell, you probably shouldn't even be out here in the cold with it."

Jacob continued to plod one foot in front of the other. "Hell sounds about right." He cleared his throat and spat out whatever came up behind a maple tree. "I don't know what it is. It started right after I caught this case, and I can't seem to shake it. And I haven't had the chance to go to the doctor yet." He pulled out a Black and Mild and lit it relaxing into the inhale of smoke.

"You know those probably aren't helping any."

He examined the offending cigar between his fingers then took another drag before blowing out cherry-scented gray smoke. "I've been smoking since I was fifteen. What's done is done. It doesn't make any sense worrying about damage control now."

He trudged on, and I followed in silence accompanied only by the sound of snow crunching beneath our feet. I could tell by the way he savored his cigar, like this one could be his last, it scared him to think about what rattled around in his chest. The thought of what that blood could mean worried me too. I'd only known the man for less than a year, but he was more of a father to me than Paul had ever been.

In time, he finished his cigar and flicked the plastic mouthpiece out into the snow. "I'd appreciate it if you didn't mention this to Gracie. Not until I know what it is."

"I won't," I agreed. Old men, farmers, and soldiers, none of us liked showing our weaknesses, and we were all stubborn enough to take them to our graves if we could. By the way Jacob looked, that day may be coming sooner rather than later if he didn't get help but he already knew that. "So long as you find time to see a doctor."

He nodded, accepting my terms. "Tomorrow, then. We've got hunting to do today." Another coughing fit threatened to turn his lungs inside out. "Tomorrow," he wheezed. The neighing of horses ahead answered his cough, and we quickened our steps.

Around the next copse of trees, we found the black monsterjäger wagon and their team of monstrous horses tied off to a fallen pine tree.

"Eli?" Jacob said. "Sorry we're late."

"Hey, Samuel, it's us," I said, peeking around the trees. "Don't shoot me," I added under my breath.

Jacob's hand clapped me on the back, and he tugged me onward. "Come on. Quit screwing around." I stumbled forward, but I would hardly call a little caution within range of Samuel's crossbow *screwing around*. Except, neither Eli nor Samuel came out to greet us.

One of the horses whinnied as Jacob passed a hand over its flanks. "Easy boy. Don't suppose you can tell me which way Eli and Samuel went?"

"They went that way." I pointed to a trail of trampled snow diving deeper into the woods.

12

The soft dawn light filtering through the leafless canopy above cast eerie shadows across the broken path where it disappeared into a gully. A chill ran down my spine that had little to do with the frigid temperature, and my hand drifted automatically to the pistol strapped to my chest.

Jacob followed my gaze, and his hands slid into the slits in his duster as if heading for the warmth of his armpits, but they stopped short at his concealed 1911s. A moment later, he withdrew his hands still empty. "Just checking," he said, eyeing the TRR8 I held in my hands. "You better put that away, we don't want to startle the monsterjägers when we find them."

I eyed the woods warily but slid the pistol back into its holster. "To be honest, I'm more worried about them startling me with a crossbow bolt through my ass."

"Yeah, well, just keep your eyes open." Jacob coughed and spat the phlegm into a bush, then led the way, adjusting the weight of the shotgun hanging from his shoulder.

The path wound its way deep into the gully where the shear earthen walls stretched high enough into the air to cast the ravine in dark shade. Feeling tactically disadvantaged, I let the distance between us grow to more than a dozen strides to be sure we both couldn't be jumped at the same time. Remarkably, Jacob moved with an infantryman's discipline despite being ex-navy. One of these days, I'd have to ask him what he did in the navy, but for now, I trusted him to guard our front while my own head swiveled about trying to watch our flanks and rear.

Jacob stumbled to a stop, choking through another coughing fit until it bent him over double, and he had to brace himself with his hands on his knees. With a fit every few hundred steps, we didn't need to worry about surprising the monsterjägers or the Krampi, they'd hear us long before we ever got close. I became very aware that it didn't mean they couldn't surprise us.

Turning slowly, I scanned the banks above us for the ambush I feared and not watching where I put my feet. The ground beneath me let out a muted crack and I froze. Sweeping my foot side to side, I cleared a small patch of snow to reveal an ice-covered stream. Spider web cracks radiated out from beneath my feet, and I shuffled back to the beaten-down path.

Jacob glanced up at me, misery glistening in his eyes as he wiped at his mouth.

"Jacob, you're not going to do these kids any good if you die of pneumonia before you get to them."

He shot me an evil glare before grunting and walking onward.

"At least watch your step. I'm not sure the ice over the creek is safe."

We both shifted closer to the near bank hoping that at least there, the snow only hid solid ground. "Why the hell did they come this way?" I asked, ducking under a tree root sticking out of the ground at chest height. It snagged my rifle and choked me with the strap. I lurched forward and ripped the weapon free, breaking the root in the process and pulled a dusting of snow and icy dirt on top of my head. Annoyed, I brushed the dirt from my collar. "It would have been easier going up on the bank."

Jacob paused and stifled another cough before pointing at a long mark in the side of the bank. It wasn't deep, just enough to make it out. I looked back the way we came. The mark left a steady scar in the wall just a little more than four feet above the ground, like a kid had passed by with a big stick or—like someone carrying a sack over their shoulder.

"They're following the Krampus's trail?"

"Got it right in one." He cleared his throat, but nothing new came up. "Come on."

I glanced up to gauge the sunlight cutting through the trees, but the top of the ravine obscured the sun's position, so I pulled my phone out to check the time instead. Quarter till ten. I slipped the phone back into my pocket, but not before noticing how few bars I had. Hopefully I'd get a few of them back once we crawled out of this canyon.

The trail eventually left the ravine and skirted along another field, though I didn't see any more Krampus signs, only the same trodden path that we'd been following for what felt like hours. I checked my phone. Two hours to be exact and that would also explain the growl in my stomach. At least I had full bars now.

I slid the pack off my back and fished out a bag of trail mix and a couple protein bars. Catching up to Jacob, I placed one of the bars in his hand. "Here."

He ripped the package open with his teeth and chomped off more than half of it in one bite. "Thanks."

"Yeah, you're welcome," I said, swallowing the second half of my own bar and washing it down with a gulp from my water bottle. "I thought we would have caught up to them by now."

Worry flashed across Jacob's face as he swallowed. "Me too."

A faint echo of a howl or screech drifted through the trees. Both of our heads snapped up, unsure of what we heard. It didn't sound right, not like an animal. We stopped, straining to hear through the gentle creaking of trees moving in the wind. The noise bounced off the trees again, and this time I could hear the scream for what it was. Jacob threw the remnants of his protein bar to the side and broke out in a run.

I chased after the screams myself, unslinging my rifle as I passed Jacob. My boots pulled like ankle weights as the snow shifted and moved beneath my feet. The frigid air scoured my throat and burned its way into my lungs with each laboring breath. Another scream for help drifted on the wind. I pressed through the pain and ache and forced my legs to move faster.

Suddenly the mature trees zipping past thinned to younger, spindlier trunks. The new growth forced its way through the rusting hulls of a hillbilly junkyard as if the forest was trying to reclaim the land robbed from it years ago. Snowdrifts transformed the shattered remains of American muscle cars and trucks into blinds perfect for an ambush that made my hackles rise.

I slowed to a walk, trying to look a hundred different directions at the same time. The trail swept around a VW bus that only needed a better paintjob to double for the mystery machine. My imagination turned the white snow into yellow sand, and I began to see landmines and men with knives and guns behind every hollowed-out carcass. I bit back the fear and swallowed it whole before it could take me completely back to the Sandbox. The snow and cold returned and I held onto it, forcing my mind to remain in the present.

Another round of screams came from further ahead, though the metal jungle made it difficult to pinpoint an exact direction. I glanced over my shoulder hoping for support but couldn't see any sign of Jacob. Waiting would be the smart thing to do. I couldn't have out-paced him by that much, but then again, I didn't have to stop and collect my lungs every other step.

The scream croaked again as if the person's voice was about to give out, and I decided I couldn't wait for the man that actually knew what to do. Snugging the butt of the BAR against my shoulder, I slipped the safety off and readied my finger alongside the trigger guard. I crouched down until only my eyes showed above the tops of the cars then made my feet move, still following the path in front of me.

I crouched down behind the back end of a nineteen-fifty something pickup. Across a clearing in front of me sat a school bus. The blown-out tires along one side caused it to lean heavily against the cedar tree sprouting from the cheese-wagon's engine compartment. Through the broken windows, I could see someone or something struggling furiously against whatever held its arms to the ceiling.

Fresh wrecking-ball-sized dents decorated the ruined cars to either side of the clearing, collapsing the drifts of snow on top and revealing small bare patches of earth as if a rampaging bull had decided to test the limits of his pen. Fletchings of crossbow bolts sprouted from sheet steel still solid enough to hold them and bright red splotches stained the churned snow between me and the bus.

I could hear nothing over the screams for help coming from the prisoner on the bus, but I also couldn't see anything from my current position. Crouching down, I rushed across the clearing, taking cover behind the front end of a Chevy Nova. The rusted fender gave in as I collapsed into it to stop my momentum, and I cringed at the noise. A puff of snow wafted into the air, making it difficult to see until the breeze pushed it away.

Nothing moved outside of the bus. A dark, almost black splotchy trail of stained snow led off around its near side and disappeared behind an El Camino. In the other direction, a bright red trail of blood turned from spots to a smear as it squeezed between a tree and the bus's backend. I pressed my rifle's scope to my eye, following the bloody tracks past the edge of the bus to a heavy boot and dark blue trousers.

"Eli?" I called out, watching the foot beneath the bus. It didn't move. "Samuel?" It still didn't move, but over the howls from the bus, they probably couldn't hear me.

Trudging through the deeper snow around the back of the Nova, I kept low and concealed. I'd been suckered into a wounded warrior trap before and didn't care to repeat the experience. I worked my way toward the bus the long way, bounding from car-cover to car-cover to avoid the clearing.

Hunkering down behind the tail end of an old station wagon plagued by peeling wood paneling, I reassessed the situation. Between me and the bus, one of the Amish monsterjägers leaned against a tree. His head lulled to the side, making it difficult to tell if he was conscious, but his hands clung to the crossbow in his lap.

Having been shot at only the day before, I watched the crossbow as much as for anything else that might jump out and kill me. "Eli? Samuel? It's Matthew Peterson." The crossbow didn't move and neither did their head.

Holding my breath, I scuttled forward and placed a hand on their shoulder. Eli's head snapped up in a sneer, and I jumped back just in time to avoid the sharp end of his meat clever of a knife. He fell over in the snow and struggled to push himself back upright while keeping the knife pointed at me. More blood than snow puddled under his legs.

I ripped off my balaclava so he could see my face. "Eli, whoa. It's me, Matthew." The fog of exhaustion and blood loss cleared momentarily, and he lowered his knife to lean back against the tree. Blood oozed from a pair of wide slits in the thigh of his pant leg. "Where's Samuel?" I asked dropping down beside him to examine his leg wounds.

"Gone after the Krampus." Eli's voice sounded hoarse.

Drawing my bowie knife, I cut away the fabric to reveal two stab wounds about four inches apart and perfectly inline. "What the hell did this?"

Eli crushed his eyes closed and sucked in a sharp gasp of air. "Barbed hoigawwel." he swallowed dryly. "Uh, pitchfork."

"That's one hell of a nasty pitchfork," I muttered, pulling off my belt. I wrapped it around his leg a few inches up from the wound and cinched it as tight as I could, letting the teeth of the buckle bite into the webbing.

Eli groaned through gritted teeth. The blood slowed but it didn't stop.

Needing a windlass to tighten the tourniquet, I ripped the heavy bolt from the loaded crossbow. As thick as my forefinger, the thing looked more like a feathered stake with a wicked broadhead than a crossbow bolt. After several hacks with my bowie, I knocked off the head and stripped off the fletching then loosened the belt enough to work the shaft of the bolt through.

I met Eli's eyes. "I have to tighten the tourniquet. It's going to hurt."

He put the wooden handle of his knife in his mouth and nodded. I twisted the bolt. Eli's face paled, and his eyes rolled into his head. A couple more turns and the blood finally stopped flowing. Eli fainted from the pain as I panted with the effort of tying off the windlass.

Metal crunched and I snatched out my pistol as I spun only to find Jacob leaning on the station wagon's hood coughing up a lung.

13

J acob's coughing became a wheeze, and he spat his own contribution to the bloodstained snow. "Is he dead?"

I placed a couple fingers to Eli's neck to check for a pulse. The artery thumped softly beneath my fingers. "Still alive, but he lost a lot of blood."

"Where's..." Jacob huffed "Where's the other one?"

Before I could answer, someone screamed, "Help!" Somehow, I had forgotten all about whoever was in the bus.

I left the rifle on the ground next to Eli and stood with my TRR8 in hand. With a quick hand gesture, I mimed for Jacob to watch the backdoor while I worked my way to the front. He nodded and leveled the business end of his shotgun at the door.

Bringing my pistol up to my chest in a close ready position, I crept along the side of the bus. The folding passenger door stood open, and I peeked around the edge. Snow laid on the driver's seat, blown in through the broken door glass, but no Krampus. I climbed the steps and popped my head past the bottom of the front bulkhead down low where it shouldn't be expected. A boy stood on the edge of one of the seats about halfway down. He pulled frantically at the ropes holding him to the luggage rack above the seat. Blood dripped down his arms from where the ropes cut into his wrists. More frayed ropes dangled from the luggage racks.

I stood, keeping my pistol ready but away from the boy. "Easy there. Is anyone else in here?"

The boy jumped at the sound of my voice, his eyes widening at the sight of my pistol. He cowered back from me as far as his restraints would allow and shook his head. Still, I checked each seat as I passed. My stomach churned violently at the litter of bones and discarded clothing littering the floor. The anger burning inside of me helped me keep my lunch as I worked down the length of the bus, edging past the boy without a word. I needed to clear any threats before I could worry about freeing him, but there was no way to relay that to a traumatized child, let alone explain the carnage.

I got to the back of the bus and tapped on the glass with my pistol. "Jacob, all clear."

Once he lowered his shotgun, I worked the emergency release lever and swung the door open despite the objections of its creaky hinges. "There's a boy in here. He's really shook up, but I think he's the one the monsterjäger's were searching for. He's looking at me like I'm about to cut him open or something."

The boy yelped behind me. *Damn, I didn't realize he could hear me.* "You better get up here and use your grandfatherly charms on him." I stepped back from the doorway to make room for Jacob, but he shot me an incredulous glare.

"Son, what makes you think I'm in any shape to climb in that way?"

"Fine, then go around, gramps." I hopped spryly out the backdoor and landed in the snow with a grin. "I'll check on Eli."

Jacob muttered, "show off," as he took the long way around to the boy.

I knelt by Eli and checked on his leg wound. The tourniquet still held the bleeding at bay. His pulse felt weaker though, and I shook him awake. "Eli? Eli, wake up."

The man's eyes fluttered open. "Eh," he said then groaned in pain.

I fished out one of the water bottles and held it to his lips. "Here, drink some water."

He managed to swallow a couple mouthfuls before pushing the bottle away. "Where's Samuel?" he croaked.

"He's not here. You said he went after the Krampus."

His eyes narrowed, and he nodded to himself. "Dummkopp, I told him not to chase it."

"The Krampus? How many of them were there?"

He licked his lips. I offered him the water bottle again, and he took a few more gulps. "Just the one. What about the boy?"

"The boy's right here, Eli," Jacob said, escorting the scared child closer. At the sight of Eli's familiar Amish beard, the boy rushed to his side and clung to him.

The boy refused to take the water bottle from me, so I handed it to Eli who forced another gulp down his throat before passing it to the boy who finally took it. Rummaging through my backpack, I pulled out a handful of protein bars and put them in Eli's lap. "He needs to eat something."

Eli nodded and began talking softly to the boy in that half English, half Pennsylvania Dutch dialect all Amish seemed to use. The boy took one of the bars and tore it open. After a hesitant bite, he devoured the entire bar and ripped open a second one.

I stood and nodded to the side for a quiet word with Jacob. He followed me to the front of the station wagon, trying to stifle another coughing fit, but only managed to turn it into a wheeze. The run had done him in, and his coughing was getting worse; he could barely walk a handful of steps before doubling over. I glanced over to the boy clinging to Eli for dear life while he shoved another protein bar in his mouth. Eli's complexion had grown a ghostly pale; he wouldn't be walking out of these woods, not on that leg.

"We need to get them back to the farm," I whispered. "If we don't, Eli's going to die from blood loss and the boy will probably die from exposure. I don't know how he survived this long. And Samuel has gone after the Krampus all on his own."

Jacob's blue eyes studied Eli and the boy over the crook of his elbow as he barked another cough. "I don't think I can carry him."

"Do you think you and the boy can manage a litter? I hate wasting the time to make one, but I need to go help Samuel if you think the two of you can haul it."

He sighed heavily. "I'm not too keen on letting another fool go after these Krampi without help either."

"I'm just going to get Samuel and hustle back so we can regroup."

"All right. But let's make it quick, it'll take a lot longer to get out than it did coming in."

The bowie knife didn't make the best axe, and it took more than a few minutes to cut down a couple saplings and sling some vinyl bus seat covers between them. I helped Jacob load Eli onto the litter and then before we could ask, the boy, David, picked up one end of the litter and started dragging it out of the junkyard.

"Damn, that's one tough kid," I muttered.

"Amish tough," Jacob agreed before jogging to catch up to him.

I didn't waste time considering the hardships that made Amish tough or in watching them leave. Instead, I hefted up the Browning BAR and raced down the path, following the droplets of blackened blood, trying to make up time. My long strides chewed up the ground, though the snow slipped and shifted beneath my feet.

Winded and sucking in frozen air, I slipped at the distinctive twang of a snapping bowstring and slid to a stop in the snow. A bestial howl erupted from further ahead. I struggled back to my feet and charged on, rifle ready.

A handful of strides later, I broke through the tangling underbrush at the edge of the woods and stepped out onto a field. Only a few yards in front of me, a hellish creature towered over Samuel. Stout horns sprouted from the thing's head, curved backward then flared to the sides over its wide oval ears. Coarse thick hair as black as a moonless night swept down from its head to powerful legs that bent the wrong way at the knees. Its long tail whipped the air as it squared off with Samuel. With one hand, it swept a silver trident high over its head, caught the pommeled end of the shaft with the other, then gave it a two-handed swing at Samuel's waist.

Samuel jumped back. The barbed prongs sliced through his coat, leaving a shallow trail of blood in its wake. Samuel ignored the wound and lunged in, brandishing a pair of knives that could double as daggers.

The Krampus brought the heavy pommeled end of its pitchfork into the side of Samuel's extended arm. The force of the blow sent Samuel careening harmlessly past the beast. The creature spun the fork in its hands, bringing the points to bear on the young monsterjäger.

Samuel scrambled to get out of reach but lost his footing and fell onto the snow as the prongs of the fork lanced through the air where he used to be.

I dropped to a knee and raised the rifle to my shoulder. The shot echoed in the cold winter air as I pulled the trigger.

The Krampus jerked with the impact but shook it off undaunted and stepped closer to Samuel, raising his fork in a two-handed grip, ready to skewer him to the earth.

Samuel crab-crawled backward, but the depth of the snow kept him from making much progress.

"Fucking wrong rounds," I muttered at the memories of a werebear ignoring similar wounds. I rose back to my feet and screamed my best war cry as I charged. At the sound, the Krampus shot me a quick glance, but it was too smart to not eliminate a threat while it had the chance. It turned back to Samuel, ready to skewer him like a shish kebab. I pulled the trigger as I ran. Four of the remaining nine rounds I fired found their mark.

The Krampus staggered off balance from the successive impacts and rammed its fork into the ground to catch itself, missing Samuel.

Samuel rolled to his hands and feet and scrambled out of the way.

The Krampus bellowed its own war cry and raised its fork like a javelin thrower and launched the trident into the air before I even realized what it was doing.

I dove to the side as one of the barbed prongs sliced through my jacket, but only grazed my arm. My combat roll came up short in the knee-deep snow, and I lost my grip on the rifle in the process. The beast charged as I struggled to right myself and draw my pistol, but the weapon caught in my chest holster. I jostled it around trying to work it out, but the Krampus lowered its head and rammed me before it came free.

The freight-train collision lifted me off my feet and drove the breath from my lungs as I sailed through the air. Thankfully, the snow cushioned my fall, though my aching ribs made me wish for all the layers I had on yesterday.

The Krampus stalked over to where its trident stood in the ground like a frozen lightning bolt and yanked it free before twisting to face me.

Samuel howled as he charged it from behind.

A club of woven branches materialized in the beast's offhand, and it swung it backhanded without looking. The club connected with Samuel's head and sent him sprawling into the snow.

I tried for the pistol again, and it came free.

The Krampus released the club, and it disappeared before it hit the ground. Its lips pulled back in a goat-faced grin as it took its trident in two hands.

"Oh God," I prayed, pulling the trigger and sending blessed iron into the creature. I placed a tight grouping of three where a man's heart would be then put a double-tap between eyes growing large with shock.

The Krampus took one more step before crumbling to the ground like a cow trying to sit on its haunches. Black smoke drifted up from its now empty eye sockets.

"Thank you, Jesus," I said, keeping the barrel pointed at the corpse while I caught my breath. Once I could breathe normal again and the thing still hadn't moved, I got close enough to kick it with the toe of my boot.

"Es dot," Samuel said, holding a hand to his head and stumbling closer. "Eh, dead," he added at my bewildered expression.

I shoved the TRR8 back into its holster and drew my bowie knife. Kneeling beside the thing I set to removing its head.

"Rug! No, stop!" Samuel yelled, pulling me back from the Krampus. "What are you doing?"

"I'm making sure it stays dead," I said.

"Then burn it and send it back to hell."

I liked his idea better, but I didn't have any matches. "How?"

Samuel pulled out a pack of cigarettes and put one between his lips then took out a box of matches. He struck one on the side of the box, lit his cigarette, then tossed the still burning stick onto the Krampus' body. The hair caught fire like tinder sending up black inky smoke, and I backed away from the sudden intense heat.

He took a drag on the cigarette then blew out a puff of white smoke and shot me a toothy grin. "That is how."

The fire consumed most of the body in the time it took us to find our discarded weapons in the snow. I reloaded the Browning BAR and my pistol before hoisting the pack onto my back and slinging the rifle over a shoulder. With one last look at the burnt remains of the Krampus, I let out a sigh of relief as we headed back. *This one hadn't been nearly as bad as I thought it would be.*

14

S amuel insisted on running back after I told him about Eli. My legs didn't like it, but I managed to keep up. *The Army could learn a thing or two about Amish tough.* By the time we made it back to where the monsterjägers had left their wagon, the fingers of the skeletal trees tickled the sinking sun. Except the wagon wasn't there.

"At least they made it this far," I said, bending over and catching my breath.

"Praise Gott," Samuel said, pacing in the broken snow.

"Yeah, thank the Lord." I pressed myself back upright, still breathing hard, and started walking again. "Jacob's truck should be this way."

We rounded the copse of trees and my phone rang. I pulled it out of my pocket. Jacob McGinnis showed on the caller ID. I swiped the answer button. "Hello."

"Matthew, it's Jacob."

I snickered to myself. "Yeah, I know. I saw it on caller ID."

"Easy now, I'm just being polite."

"Fine. How's Eli doing?"

"He's holding in there. I'm on my way to meet up with an ambulance now."

"Wait, you took the wagon and the truck?" I asked, my legs screaming at the idea of walking all the way back to the farm.

Jacob laughed. "No, we left the wagon when we took the truck. Eli needed faster wheels." Relief I couldn't begin to describe seeped through my weary muscles and bruised ribs. It vanished the instant I heard Jacob's voice turn serious. "You haven't seen Mary, have you?"

I stopped dead in my tracks. "Why would I have seen Mary? She's supposed to be safe and sound at the farmhouse with Sarah."

Jacob grumbled something I couldn't make out. "When I dropped the boy off, Sarah said Mary ran off right after lunch. She figured she'd gone after us."

I growled in frustration.

"What is wrong?" Samuel asked in alarm.

"My sister has gone off on her own," I said through gritted teeth.

"Matthew, I'm sorry. I would have gone out looking for her, but I already called the ambulance for Eli and..." He broke off in a coughing fit. When he finished he said, "Sorry about that. I'll hurry back as soon as I can."

"No, you did the right thing. Besides, we already killed the Krampus. Get Eli to the hospital and while you're there, get the doc to check you out, too. You're sounding worse."

While his voice remained cordial, I could hear his annoyed undertone. "I'll be back as soon as I can." With that, the phone fell silent.

"We will find your sister," Samuel said as I pulled the phone away from my ear.

I gave him a half-smile, unable to muster anything more than appreciative thanks to my sister's stupidity. *What was she thinking running off on her own like that? What I wouldn't give to have a tracking app on her phone.* My smile broadened at the thought and I called the one person who could keep it there.

"What'cha need, Matthew?" Gracie asked after the first ring.

"A Hail Mary. My sister wandered off and I need to find her pronto. I was hoping you could hack her phone's GPS and help me out."

"Are you sure she wants to be found?" She asked in a curiously protective tone. "Sometimes a teenager just needs a little fresh air to think things through."

"She's had plenty of time for that, she's been gone since lunch. Look, I'm tired, sore, and cold. It's practically zero out, the sun's about to set, and we're a hundred miles from home. I don't want to spend half the night trying to find her." I knew I let too much of the annoyance I felt for my sister bleed into my voice, but damn, I really was tired.

"Wait, you took her on the Krampus hunt." Disapproval rang heavy in her voice.

"No, I didn't." My voice rose defensively. "She snuck along, in the backseat of your grandfather's truck. We left her at the Amish farm to help the Mrs. Millers, but she ran off."

"So, you left a twenty-first-century teenager in the care of a seventeenth-century farmer's wife while you went off hunting the devil of Christmas, and you thought everything would be okay? I thought you were smarter than that."

I felt more like a fool with every word, so I took a fool's defense. "It was Jacob's idea."

"And that makes it better how?" She let me stew on that for a minute while I heard the click and clatter of fingernails on a keyboard in the background. "What's her number?"

"Uh—give me a sec."

I started to pull the phone from my ear to find her number in my contacts, but stopped as Gracie scoffed, "Forget it. I'll get it through the backdoor."

"Wait, I thought I told you not to do that anymore."

"Here it is," she said, ignoring me. "Give me a few minutes. I'll call you back." The line cut out before I could even respond.

Frustration, anger, and worry boiled together inside me as I glared at the phone in my hand. "It's not my fault."

Samuel shook his head with a smirk and started walking after the wagon tracks. I slid the phone back into my pocket and followed.

We found the team of horses tied to a small tree at the edge of the field a little while later, but Gracie still hadn't called me back and I didn't know where to look for Mary. Samuel used the delay to care for the horses. He retrieved a couple feed sacks from one to the compartments on the wagon and tossed in a few scoops of grain from a barrel strapped to the side. The horses nuzzled him then greedily ate the grain as he checked their harnesses. I felt absurd, watching him care for the horses without knowing how to help. My old man never let us have one since you couldn't milk a horse or otherwise make money off it.

When Samuel finished checking the tack, he folded down one of the wagon's many doors. Brass chains held it level, turning it into a makeshift work shelf. The compartment beyond was divided into three cubbies, each filled with neat stacks of crossbow bolts. Samuel pulled out a handful and refilled his quiver on his hip.

I picked up one of the bolts with a shaft twice as thick as a regular arrow, just like the one I used as a windlass for Eli's tourniquet. Orange rust covered the broadhead, but silver gleamed amongst the stacks in the neighboring cubby. In the glint of silver heads, I could see a cross etched on the side of each. Even the head of the bolt in my hand bore the holy cross beneath a coarse coating of rust. "What are you doing? We just killed the Krampus."

Samuel snatched the bolt out of my hand and added to his quiver. "We killed one Krampus. Not all the Krampi."

"But what's with the cross? Did you get a priest to bless these?"

He scoffed. "Pfft. You English. You think only your priests know Got. Yet we Amish know him. We dedicate our lives to becoming closer to Got. We beseech the Holy One, and He blesses our weapons in His name."

He stowed one of his long knives into another drawer with a dozen other similar blades. Then with a twist and a pop, a long panel running the length of the wagon fell away, and he took out a heavy two-handed axe with a spike on the end.

"What is that?" I asked, dumbfounded.

Samuel turned the long axe in his hands. His eyes alight with awe as the curved edge of the blade gleamed in the last light of the setting sun. "Die gsegent schpiess," he said in a revered whisper though I didn't have a clue what it meant. His mouth moved in more silent words as he ran a finger along the lines of scrollwork surrounding the unmistakable shape of a cross etched deep into the blade. While I didn't understand the words, I recognized a prayer.

I waited for him to finish but before I could ask what the hell *die gsegent schpiess* meant, my phone bayed like a hound dog on a coon trail. It made me nearly jump out of my skin and the horses pranced uneasily. I fumbled it out of my pocket and practically dropped it as the hound dog sounded off again. My heart raced as I swiped the answer button before it could bellow again.

"Son of a bitch. What," I cursed into the phone.

"Hey, I'm sorry. I thought you might appreciate a little hound to go with your fox," Gracie said with the touch of a laugh ringing in her otherwise serious voice. I rolled my eyes, but silently thanked God she didn't set my ringtone to "What Does a Fox Say" again. Thanks to my brother Luke, I don't think I'd ever find that particular song funny again.

"Please don't bring up that other song."

297

"Oh, I..." Gracie snorted a laugh, "I meant a bloodhound to help you find your runaway fox. You know? Your sister."

Sheepishly I hung my head and rubbed at the frustration out of my forehead. "Sorry. So, did my hound track down my sister?"

"Oh, I ain't your hound, honey," Gracie said and I felt my cheeks turn hot beneath the balaclava. "I put the hound on your phone. It should lead you right to...Hold on a sec. That can't be right."

My heart started beating hard like the bass drum in a heavy metal band. "What?"

"She's moving again. Moving fast!"

"Shit, there really is more than one!" I ran to the wagon and jumped up into the front seat. "Come on, Samuel, we gotta move."

Samuel quickly removed the feed sacks from the horses and shut the open compartments with practiced efficiency while I sat on the wagon seat feeling stupid watching him. Finished, he hoisted himself up into the driver's seat and slipped the great polearm into a slot in the floor of the wagon. The butt of the weapon dropped a few inches into the floor then Samuel wrapped a bit of rope around the haft to secure it against the front rail. He collected the reins and shot me an expectant look.

"Gracie, which way?"

"East. About two miles, but she's moving away fast. Three miles."

"East," I passed on. "Three miles. Now four."

"Scheisse," Samuel said, snapping the reins and making the horse bolt forward in a run. I couldn't be sure but I thought Samuel just swore.

"Gracie, where's she at now?"

"Matthew, I'm not your..." her voice drifted off distractedly, not finishing the sentence.

"Gracie, where is she?"

"Use the app," she said curtly before cutting off the call.

The wagon lurched as the wheel rose and fell over something buried in the snow. It bounced me on the seat sending a jolt up my spine that jarred my teeth.

Samuel reached down to the side and flipped a switch. A bright light sliced through the darkness of the new moon. He pointed down by my shin. "Get the other one."

I reached down and found the switch. The new light blazed a path for the horses and Samuel swerved around the remnants of a tree stump. "I thought you didn't use electricity?"

"They are battery powered. It is allowed," Samuel said with the touch of annoyance at answering a question asked too many times. "Where are we going?"

Unlocking my phone, I found a new app with a basset hound icon on the home screen. I opened the app. A compass emerged on the top half of the screen with a small map below. The compass needle pointed slightly to the right. I gestured with my hand in the general direction of the compass needle and conferred with the little text box just above the map. "That way. Three miles."

I clutched the side of my seat with one hand to keep from bouncing out of the wagon. With my other hand, I clung to the compass and signaled course corrections to Samuel. Which only got harder when hedges and fences made us leave the fields for the country roads. My heart pounded faster than the beating hooves of the horses kicking up snow as the wagon skated down the partially plowed road. Eventually, the distance meter started to count down.

Less than a quarter-mile away from Mary, we turned left down a road that the local municipality felt only warranted a single plow-truck pass. The snowbanks rose on either side of the wagon with no room to pass should another vehicle come the other way. The compass needle gently swung to the left of the road as the horses trotted onward. We stopped when the needle pointed just past a mailbox to a gap in the trees that could only have been a driveway if someone had bothered to push the snow.

Samuel pulled the left headlight free and shone it in the direction the needle pointed. A single footpath disturbed the otherwise pristine sheet of snow. Out beyond the reach of the lamp, I could make out the silhouette of an abandoned house in the starlight.

The light glistened off the damp flanks of the horses as Samuel placed the headlight back in its mount. At the sight of his sweating animals, I could see a debate brewing behind his eyes. Between the cloudless night sky and temperatures already kissing Frosty's nether regions, I didn't need to be a horseman to know the dangers of leaving the animals to cool in their sweat.

I followed the compass needle, weighing the intervening darkness between me and the house, then let out a resigned sigh. "Catch up with me after you take care of the horses." With a touch of a button, I killed my phone's screen and slipped it into my pocket.

"Ya," Samuel said with a solemn nod I could barely see in the radiant edges of the wagon's headlights. He wrapped the reins around the wagon brake and leapt out of sight.

Unslinging the rifle from my shoulder, I propped it against the bench then wriggled out of the straps of my backpack. It hit the floor between my feet with a solid thump. Ripping the zipper open, I rummaged blindly though protein bars, spare bullets, and hand warmers, until I eventually dug out the flashlight hiding at the bottom. Clicking it on, I surveyed the remaining contents of the sack for anything else of immediate need, but after a moment's consideration, I tactically opted for mobility and decided to leave the bag of supplies at the foot of the driving bench. Instead, I snatched up the rifle and pulled back the action to make sure it hadn't frozen solid. I let the receiver go. It slid forward, ramming a round into the chamber.

The heavy breathing of the horses and Samuel's soft whispers were soon lost to the crunch of snow beneath my feet as I stalked toward the house. Despite minimizing the beam from the flashlight as best I could, the circle of light leading the way made me feel exposed. I kept a watchful eye on the night in front of me and prayed the Krampus didn't have the sense of mind to look out the front window. I never wanted my military-issue night-vision goggles more. The critical voice of a drill sergeant from my past whispered in the back of my mind, *Soldier, if we could fight with wishes, we wouldn't need you. Now get your mind out of the fucking clouds.*

15

I stopped and crouched low in the snow where the light of my flashlight barely reached the abandoned farmhouse. Paint peeled from the lap siding, and jagged edges of broken glass jutted into the otherwise black holes.

I clicked off the flashlight, the snow making light-discipline nearly impossible, then closed my eyes, trying to night-adapt them as fast as I could. The small noises of the monsterjäger's impatient horses seemed to echo in the otherwise soundless winter night. When I opened my eyes, the stars did little to help my night vision. The blotchy mess of shadows in front of me only seemed to vary in their degree of blackness like a poor grayscale picture with the contrast turned all the way down. If I stared hard enough, I could almost see the outline of the house, but I thought that came more from memory than actual sight.

With a resigned sigh, I flicked the flashlight back on, better to see and be seen than to fight a Krampus blind. The light reflected harshly off the snow, and I had to wait for my eyes to readjust. Once the ghost image faded, I adjusted my grip on the rifle, searching for a way to comfortably hold the flashlight and the stock of the gun in one hand. I gave up after fishing my dropped light out of the snow for the second time. Slipping the strap over my head in a crossbody sling, I drew my pistol. Besides, the pistol proved more effective against the other Krampus, and it would be easier to wield in the house's smaller spaces.

I followed the furrow of footprints up to the front door. With the flashlight on, I went for shock and awe over surprise and kicked the door in. The door latch ripped through the rotted out old jamb and the door slammed into the interior wall with a thud and a shower of plaster. I swept left, right and then up the staircase in front of me. "Clear," I muttered more out of habit than for any other purpose.

Sidestepping one foot over the other, I made my way to the room on the left and poked the pistol through the door. Wallpaper peeled from walls and more of the ceiling lay on the floor than where it should have been, but nothing moved in the room. "Clear," I said, spinning around to the room on the opposite side of the hallway.

A drift of snow blown in through a broken window reached a long white tentacle into the room. Rot ate away at the floorboards edging the hearth of a deteriorating fireplace at the far end of the room. I took a cautionary step backward, questioning the solidity of the floor on which I stood. Neither the snow nor the heavy layer of dust my flashlight panned over showed signs of anyone besides me setting foot in the room in the past decade.

Dust? I shook my head at my own stupidity and flashed the light at the front door swaying loosely on its hinges then dropped the light to the floor. Shuffled footprints swirled in the dust and grime, making a mess of any tracks that used to be there. Beyond my careless footsteps, hooved prints led past the staircase, deeper into the house. Leading with my pistol stretched out, I stalked after them.

I followed the prints down the hall and through the kitchen doorway. They wove around a ragged hole in the floor to a freshly swept arc of missing dust at the backdoor. The floor creaked as I danced along the edge of the opening, avoiding the broken joist hanging from a matching hole in the ceiling as if the second-floor bath had dropped through the ceiling and floor all at once like an ACME safe in a Looney Tunes cartoon. Keeping my pistol pointed at the backdoor, I shined my light into the remnants of the bath above then followed the trajectory of chaos to the basement below.

A pair of animal-like eyes between curling horns reflected the light back at me. The creature snarled at the light and my body froze, my pistol still pointed at the backdoor.

The beast leapt into the air and rammed into my side, knocking the flashlight from my hands and me into the neighboring dining room. I fell to the floor, plowing dust as I slid along the hardwood.

The floor echoed with the hard tap of heavy, solid feet.

I rolled over to my back, staring up at the horned beast in front of me. Backlit by the flashlight laying on the floor by the door, it stood a foot taller than the Krampus from the field. Its horns were thicker and bare patches in the fur covering its broad shoulders revealed skin with more wrinkles than an old folks' home. This creature carried a look of age that made the rotting house around me seem new.

It held a hand out to the side, and a heartbeat later a pitchfork materialized in its palm. A long, snakelike tongue lapped hungrily at its lips. "You're a bit older and tougher than I care for, but seeing as how the season is almost over, I'm willing to make an exception."

Swallowing, I dislodged my heart from my throat. Suddenly I could move again as if I had just pulled the lock pin from my joints. I rolled away as the prongs of the Krampus' pitchfork buried themselves into the floor. I brought my pistol up, but before I could get it pointed at the thing's chest, a club of birch twigs appeared in the Krampus' offhand midswing and smashed into the back of my hand. My finger fell onto the trigger and the gun went off. Between the impact of the club and the recoil of the gun, I lost my grip on the pistol, and it slid along the floor to crash into the wall.

"Son of a bitch," I said, wriggling away from the beast before scrambling to my feet.

The Krampus let the club vanish and held a hand to its hip. Black sludge for blood oozed between its fingers. It sneered and hissed at me then wrenched the pitchfork free, pulling up several floorboards with it.

I reached a hand to my belt and drew my bowie knife. The silver-plated blade gleamed in the flashlight, the wrong metal for the job but the only weapon I had left.

The Krampus took a step toward me, licking its lips again. "You are a fighter and a sinner. Oh, you will be tasty even if you are a bit tough." The rotting floor boards creaked dangerously under the creature's advance.

I retreated, backing away and holding my knife out before me. My eyes searched the dark, looking for a way out or at the very least my pistol with its blessed iron rounds.

It took another step then swung the pitchfork with its barbed prongs at my chest. I pushed off the floor to jump back but the heel of my boot pressed through a rotten board and I fell backward instead. The fork whistled in the air as passed inches over my chest and crashed through the dividing wall between the dining room and the front room with the chimney. Plaster, lathe, and studs all broke free, scarcely slowing the weapon down as if they were only waiting for a reason to crumble. Considering my foot currently trying to make its way to the basement the hard way, perhaps they were.

My foot came free with a yank, and I somersaulted backward, breaking the rifle strap in the process. I stumbled into the far end of the room, unable to fall back any further. For as rotten as the rest of the house was, the wall at my back seemed remarkably sound, with neither a door nor a window for me to escape through.

The Krampus recovered from its overswing and whirled the trident in its hands for a better thrusting grip.

With no other options available, I set my feet, waiting for an opportunity and praying for deliverance. Earnest, actual prayer to the God who robbed me of my youngest brother this past spring. To the God my bastard of an old man claimed to worship. To the God my mother still believed in. To the God that I knew in the depths of my heart *I* still believed in.

The words formed on my tongue without much thought, not the rote words of a memorized prayer but those of a man of conviction. "My God, as I face the demon before me, bless the weapon in my hand and deliver my sister safe from harm."

Bracing a foot back against the wall for leverage, I feinted left as the last word faded from my lips and the Krampus thrust with its fork. I pushed off the wall, lunging the other way and hacked at its thighs with my knife. The blade cut through the coarse hair and meat with ease, showering me in a spray of black blood.

I danced under the club forming in its outstretched hand and sprung up behind the beast. Its horns carved away at the ceiling as it turned with a backhanded swing of the birch club. I stepped in and blocked with the knife blade. It bit deep into the Krampus' forearm, ricocheting off the bone. The club fell from fingers unable to hold it.

The Krampus bellowed with pain like a wounded animal. Its good hand twirled the fork around like a majorette with a baton. When the points settled to bear at me, devilish blue flames danced along the prongs as they struck at my chest.

I stepped to the side, parrying with my knife, but one of the prongs still found the bicep of my right arm. The knife slipped from my fingers and clattered uselessly to the floor. Hot searing pain radiated from the wound as if the trident caught my whole arm on fire. After a quick panicked glance, I realized it had. I tried to pat out the flames with my other hand, but the Krampus swung its wounded arm into me like a club. With the mass and strength of a creature born in the fires of hell, it threw me through the dining room wall. I rolled across the broken bricks from the fireplace and thudded into the far wall. Powdered snow from the drift slid down the neck of my jacket and snuffed out the flames on my burning arm.

The Krampus sliced at the wall one-handed with its blazing pitchfork, working the hole wider. The trident's blue flames licked at the tattered wallpaper, singeing the edges and lighting small pieces of it on fire, but they failed to remain lit. It kicked a cloven hoof through the wall and in the flickering bluish light, I could see the outline of my pistol.

Struggling to my feet, I evaluated my options. Freedom lay through either the front door or the broken window behind me. With the Krampus' wounded leg, I could possibly outrun it, but with the pistol full of blessed iron rounds, I could kill it here and now. I just needed to reach it. In the end, the thought of my sister made my decision for me. Besides, I never was much of a runner.

I took two lumbering steps forward then dove.

The Krampus struck with its trident. The barbs pierced through my calf and pinned me to the floor halfway through the opening. Pain and fire erupted in my leg. The Krampus roared a guttural laugh of victory that cut off abruptly at the punctuated report of my revolver as I unloaded the remaining seven rounds into it from underneath.

Black blood fell on me as the creature wavered on its feet. I feared for a moment that with my leg pinned to the ground, the beast would fall on me, but as it teetered forward, the pitchfork dematerialized and freed my leg. I scampered the rest of the way through the opening. The beast collapsed, crashing through the wall. The rotted floor around the fireplace broke and the Krampus plummeted into the basement.

My heart racing with spent adrenaline, I gazed down into the blackness of the pit, unable to see anything. After a moment, the thought of my sister still out there somewhere in the night drove me back up to my feet. I limped to my rifle and then used it like a cane to collect my flashlight.

The front door burst open and banged off the wall, making me jump. I fumbled with the revolver's cylinder release and dumped the spent shells onto the floor before I realized it was Samuel filling the doorway to the kitchen from the hall. The head of his *gsegent schpiess* stuck out over his head, and he held his bulky crossbow to his shoulder ready to fire.

He saw me and partially lowered his crossbow. "Where is it?"

I limped forward and nodded to the hole in the kitchen floor. "Down there. Or rather over there," I said pointing toward the front room with my empty pistol. "It fell through the floor, but it's dead."

He looked at my wounded leg and then my arm and his eyes grew wide. Before I knew it, he raised his crossbow at my head and pulled the trigger. At this range, I couldn't move in time, and the edge of the broadhead nicked my ear as it flew by.

I reached for a loaded moon clip on my chest holster as Samuel dropped the crossbow to the floor. I got the moon clip inserted and the cylinder back in place about the same time he freed the *schpiess* from his back. Before I could get the pistol raised, the backdoor crashed open clipping me in the back and knocking me forward. I pushed off my bad leg and managed to dive to the side and avoid falling down into the basement but landed on my wounded arm.

Samuel jumped over the hole with a roar and swung the *schpiess* with both hands. The Krampus got its trident up in time to block the brunt of the blow, but the axe's razor edge still sliced a considerable chunk of meat from the creature's arm.

The floor broke away from Samuel's feet as he crashed into an old cabinet. He lost his hold on the *schpiess* and clung to the counter to keep from falling into the basement.

The Krampus snarled, blood oozing from the crossbow bolt buried into the meat of its chest. I got my pistol around before the creature could reorient its trident and skewer Samuel to the counter. Time stilled as I unloaded all eight shots into the beast, zippering it from center mass to between its eyes. The Krampus staggered one more step into the room then fell into the depths of the basement.

Samuel glanced over to me, relief flooding his face. "Thank you."

"Don't mention it." I sat up and peered with my flashlight into the hole. The Krampus lay broken over a cast iron tub, its black blood pooling on the white surface. "That makes three. Please tell me there aren't any more."

Samuel worked his way off the cabinet and collected his *schpiess*. He leaned on the long haft as he stared down at the body. "This one is small, like a baby Krampus, what about the other?"

The corner of my mouth turned up in a smirk. "Big and scary," I said quickly, then more seriously added, "Bigger than the one in the field and it certainly looked old, but then again, I've never seen one before."

"Most likely we killed them all." Samuel's words didn't fill me with much confidence as he walked over to his crossbow and reloaded it.

I pushed myself back up to my feet, wincing as fresh pain shot through my leg. "Right," I said then reloaded my pistol with my last moon clip, found my knife and hobbled to the door leaning on my rifle. "We better go find Mary."

16

I let Samuel go out the door before me with his crossbow raised and ready while I followed behind, hobbling on my rifle-crutch. A trail of broken snow led from the house to an old barn whose sagging roof only needed a reason to cave in. The structure leaned distinctively to one side and many of the side boards were missing. How it had remained vertical through the blustery storm the day before amazed me.

On two good legs, Samuel reached the barn before I even made it halfway across the yard. He waited for me to limp closer, dragging my bum leg through the snow. Each step came with a new shard of pain I felt down to my bones and a fresh trickle of blood oozing down my leg to soak into my sock.

He placed a hand on the handle of the massive sliding barn door and shot me a look over his shoulder. I stopped still a dozen yards from the barn and hefted the rifle to my shoulder then gave him a nod. Tucking the butt of the crossbow under one armpit, he yanked the door open. It screeched along the track but only moved a foot or so. Samuel raised his crossbow and shined the small light attached at the end into the dark. He checked left, then right, then disappeared behind the door.

I kept the muzzle of my rifle aimed at the breach, straining my ears against the cold of night, listening for a fight, but only small indiscernible noises drifted back to me. My leg ached, my shoulder burned, but I didn't dare lower the rifle. Time ebbed by slowly, and the rifle grew heavy. I struggled to hold the muzzle steady. Finally, a hand appeared. Long fingers wrapped around the edge of the door and pulled Samuel back out through the opening. Relief flooded my bruised body as I pressed on the safety then pushed the butt of the rifle into the ground to keep from teetering over.

Samuel slipped out of the barn with his crossbow lowered at the ground. Once outside he reached back in and led my sister out of the darkness. She looked rattled. Her eyes flicked back and forth in wide shock. When they landed on me, she raced across the snow and wrapped her arms around my neck, carrying us both to the ground. Fortunately, the carpet of snow softened the blow, though I think I would have preferred her customary punch in the arm to the shock of fresh pain coming from my wounds.

"She said you would come," Mary said breathlessly, "but they overheard. They set a trap." Her voice rose steadily in panic. She pushed off of me and scanned the night worriedly.

I extricated myself from the snow sitting up as best I could with one good arm and one good leg. "They're gone now. We got them."

"But how? There was two of them and they were so...so..."

I pushed the half mop of hair back from her face and cut her off. "I know. I know. Samuel helped." I nodded to the man holding a hand out to us.

Mary took his hand and let him pull her back to her feet, then they both reached down and helped me to mine. "Thanks—Ow!" I yelped as Mary slugged me, thankfully, in my good arm.

"What took you so long? She said you would be right there."

"I got here as fast as I could and who is *she*?"

Mary held up her cell phone. "She did."

I picked up the phone with realization and smiled as I placed it to my ear. "Gracie, thank you."

"Oh, good. Matthew, you found Mary. Now, tell me: why has my grandfather just been admitted to the Bassett Medical Center?"

"Um, the medical center?" My head suddenly felt light like all the blood drained from my skull and spilled down my arm. My grip slipped from my makeshift cane, and I lost my balance.

Mary caught me by my arm and kept me from falling. She got me steady then pulled her hand back, alarm spreading across her face as she thrust it beneath the light of Samuel's crossbow.

Samuel picked the rifle up out of the snow. "I will carry this. Get him to the wagon. It is in the road."

Mary struggled to turn me around and get me walking back around the house. "Can you help me?"

I couldn't tell if she was speaking to me or Samuel, but thankfully Samuel answered her. "I must see to something first." He unstrapped the *gsegent schpiess* from his back and handed it to me. "Use this. I will meet you at the wagon."

"Matthew," a faint voice called. The phone vibrated in my hand. "Matthew!" The voice came from the phone, but it sounded so much further away.

Mary took the phone from me. "Gracie, Matthew's hurt real bad. Please send help." I didn't hear Gracie's response, but Mary pushed the phone in her back pocket and tried to get me to walk faster.

Halfway back up the drive, the path erupted in light from behind us and the night lost its bitter cold bite. I leaned on the haft of Samuel's massive axe and peered over my shoulder. Bright yellow flames flickered out of the old farmhouse's windows and licked their way up to the roof. Within moments, fire engulfed the tinderbox of a building in an inferno that hurt my eyes.

A shadowy form in a broad hat strode up the drive to meet us.

"Making sure they stay dead?" I asked as Samuel relieved me of the axe and draped my good arm over his shoulder.

"Ya. I return them to Hell. Saint Nicholas will never know. Come now. We take care of your wounds."

Mary and I shared a bewildered look but said nothing as we let Samuel half-carry me back to the wagon. The two of them eventually got me hoisted up through the wagon's backdoor and situated onto the cot. After rummaging through a handful of compartments, the Amish monsterjäger set to work on my wounds with the practiced speed of a battlefield medic. Moments later he had managed the flow of blood and wrapped my cuts in fresh bandages.

Samuel's eyes narrowed at my astonished expression. "We choose to live a simple life; it would behoove you to remember that does not make us simple."

Embarrassed and lightheaded, I apologized. "Sorry."

He reached out, pressed my eyelids open, and stared into my eyes. His expression became grim, and he let my eyelids go. My eyes became heavy, sinking closed on their own as Samuel's voice grew distant.

"Your brother has lost a lot of blood. He needs more than I can do for him. Can your friend get us an ambulance?"

"Already on the way," I heard Gracie say through the speaker on the phone. "I'll guide you to them."

"Good. Sit here behind me and tell me which way to go." His rough hands shook me, and I reopened my eyes. "You do not sleep."

I did my best to not sleep—much. I can remember when the medics moved me to the ambulance, it's hard to sleep through that much pain. Then they wouldn't let me sleep the whole rocking ride to the hospital, where the doctor examined my arm and leg with a *tsk* at how much blood I lost. That dissolved into a whole hubbub about the right blood type for a transfusion, which quieted down once I pulled out my dog tags. Then, thank God, they finally let me sleep.

S ometime around mid-morning, I woke to the gentle shake of someone fooling with my arm. My eyes drifted slowly open, adjusting to the sunlight streaming in through the window and falling across Mary's slouched form in the armchair by my bed. Her soft snores were a welcome sound after the night we had. The nurse fiddling with my arm pinched me. "Ow. Do you mind?" I asked, turning an angry scowl on the nurse, but instead of scrubs, I found an unshaven gray face staring back at me. "Jacob, what the hell?"

"Oh good, you're awake."

"Well, it's not easy sleeping through someone jabbing you in the arm you just got a dozen stitches in."

"Sorry," he said then tapped my wounded leg. "Scooch over, will ya'. This stuff they have me on is making me a bit woozy." He gestured up at the bag hanging from an IV tree as he pulled it closer.

I sucked in a sharp breath and moved my leg out of his reach. "I just got thirty stitches in that leg."

He looked apologetic, but then he sat on the edge of my bed in the spot I vacated with a moan of relief.

"So, what did the doc say is wrong with you?" I asked.

"Bah, just a bit of pneumonia."

"Pneumonia? Should you even be walking around?"

"No. That's why I asked you to move your leg. Now, tell me about the Krampi."

311

I glanced over at Mary still curled up and sleeping under a blanket and swallowed dryly. Jacob handed me a cup of water, and I drained it in one go. "They took her. After Samuel and I killed the one from the junkyard, two others took Mary." Anger turned my expression and voice hard, but Jacob didn't react to it. "We killed them all and Samuel set their bodies on fire. He said it returns them to Hell."

Jacob put a comforting hand on my shoulder and glanced at Mary. "I'm sorry." This time he swallowed stiffly, like a boulder had caught in his throat. When his gaze came back to me, restrained tears shown in his eyes. "Did you find any of the other children?"

"No, but on the bus, there was plenty of..." At the moment I didn't know how to finish the sentence as the horror of the bus scene filled my memory.

Jacob wiped the unfallen tears from his eyes and gave me a resolute smile with a comforting pat on my good leg. "That's all right. We saved the Miller boy and got Mary back. I should have known better than to expect more. I'll have Father Hastings notify the families. Some will refuse to believe it, but it'll give others some closure. I'll have to make sure DEMON finds the remains first. The FBI will only make a bigger mess of things."

Mary jerked awake in her chair with a yelp. The blanket tangled around her arms and legs before she clawed her way out of it and jumped to her feet. The chair skated back across the polished floor with a screech. I sat up in my bed, but Jacob rolled his IV tree to Mary before I could scramble out from beneath my covers.

"Easy there," Jacob whispered, extending a hand to Mary. "You're all right, sweetie. You're safe here. I've got you."

The unfocused, panicked look in her eyes eased as Jacob continued to speak softly to her in that grandfatherly way of his. She drifted forward and sagged into his arms.

I finally disentangled the set of wires and tubes caught on the rail of my bed and slid my own IV tree over to Mary and Jacob. Jacob passed Mary into my arms and sat in her chair.

Mary held me for a while longer then pushed back, wiping away the streaks of tears down her face. "I'll be fine," she said, slugging me softly in my good arm. "Um, Momma called while you were asleep. She's coming over after she picks up Luke from the airport. Um..." She looked around, at Jacob sitting the armchair with his IV next to him and at me propping myself up on my own IV tree, before patting her back pocket for her phone. "I think I'm going to go for a walk and…uh…wait for Momma downstairs. Call me if you need me." Jacob and I watched her leave with similarly concerned expressions.

The door closed and I returned to my bed. "How's Eli doing?" I asked, not wanting to let the silence consume me.

"He'll recover. Doc says you saved his leg with the tourniquet."

"Good, Samuel will be glad. I still can't believe there are Amish monsterjägers."

Jacob shrugged. "Why not, considering what's out there? It's more than any one group can handle. Besides, a little interreligious cooperation every now and then can be fun."

I gave him a smirk. "I'll give it different. I'm not sure I'm ready to call any of this fun. But, speaking of fun, what are your plans for Christmas? We'd love to have you over."

Jacob pressed himself up out of his chair. "Unfortunately, I'm on bed rest for at least a few weeks. Gracie's coming by tomorrow to take me home to convalesce."

"Convalesce? Just when I forget how old you are, you go and use a word like that."

He let out a less than patient sigh that became more of a wheeze. "Right, and just when I think you are a mature young man—you open your mouth and remind me, you're just young." As he waddled past my bed, he gently patted my good leg. "Thanks for the help, but you need to get some rest before your family gets here."

I flashed him a grin. "You too, old man."

Jacob rolled his eyes and dragged his IV tree to the door, but before he could pull it open, I asked, "Any suggestions on how to explain my injuries to my CO, *this* time?"

Jacob smiled and pulled the door open. "I've heard farming is the most hazardous profession in the world."

I rubbed my forehead with a cheeky laugh. "Farm accident it is. Hey, what's the deal with Krampus and Santa? Samuel said something about how Santa will never know?"

"Did he now?" Jacob laughed and stepped through the door. "That's probably for the best. I'll see you this spring," He called through the closing door.

I shook my head at his evasive answer and hollered back, "Thanks. See you in the spring."

The door clicked closed, leaving me alone with my thoughts. *Spring?*

My term with the Army would be up this spring. And that means choices, DEMON, Jacob, the farm? What the hell am I going to do? Weariness dragged my eyelids closed as I tumbled the question in my mind. I fell into dreams, that while they weren't plagued with monsters, didn't have any answers either.

H ey there, big bro. Wakey, wakey," called a very annoying voice from the hospital room door, drawing me out of a very satisfying sleep.

"Huh." I licked my chapped lips to get some saliva flowing. Parting my eyes, I peeked at the speaker then closed them again with a moan. "Luke, what the hell are you doing here?"

"It's Christmas Eve and I wanted to see my big bro. It's hardly my fault the only place I can do that is in a hospital. You seem to like these places. What is it? The smell of antiseptic or..." He took a peek down the hall then ducked back into the room with an evil grin. "Or is it the nurses?" He stumbled forward, massaging his shoulder. "Ow!"

Mary squeezed past him rubbing the knuckles of her right hand.

Our mother pushed passed him next. "Luke Daniel Peterson, you best keep your eyes to yourself."

Luke wiped the mischievous grin from his face. "Yes, ma'am." He let the door close behind him and joined Momma and Mary at the side of my bed.

Mary slugged me gently on the good shoulder, but it held none of her usual tomboy charm. Her cheek bore a dark purple bruise as did her wrists. Anger flared in my gut, but I had dealt with the bastards that did that to her. The anger melted into pity that I couldn't keep from touching my eyes. Mary saw it and her own expression became a mixture of guilt, shame, and anger as she pulled her sleeves lower on her arms.

Momma wore a weak smile as she placed a hand on Mary's wrist then wrapped her other arm around her daughter and pulled her head closer for a hug. Mary didn't back away but wrapped her own arms tightly around Momma.

Luke shook his head. "Mary told us all about the—uh, Krampuses."

"Uh, I think the plural is Krampi, or at least that's what Jacob used."

"Right. Well, I wish I'd been there. I'd have helped you kick their asses."

Momma shot him a scowl over Mary's head. "Luke, I can't keep you from using that language at school, but you will watch your tongue at home."

He sighed resignedly. "Yes, ma'am,"

Her glare then fell on me. "That goes for you, too."

"Yes, ma'am."

"Now, about these Krampi." Momma held up a quieting hand when I opened my mouth to defend myself. "After last spring, I didn't know what to believe or think about what took your brother and your daddy from me. But after last night," she hugged Mary a bit tighter. "After what those demons did." Her voice caught and tears threatened her eyes, but beneath it all, I saw that stout determination, that strength, that fortitude that always made me respect my mother even when Paul was at his worst. "Son, you and Jacob did a good thing. You keep doing what you've been doing."

Luke slapped playfully at my foot tented beneath the blanket. "Only, maybe next time, try doing it without ending up in the hospital."

I rolled my eyes and gave him a *you've-got-to-be-kidding-me* look. "I'll do my best."

"Great, then get dressed. I want to be home for Christmas Eve." Luke retrieved my clothes from the closet and tossed them at me. "Momma, we still get to open a gift on Christmas Eve, right?"

She smiled at the pure childish glee on Luke's face. He always loved Christmas more than any other holiday. "Of course."

THE END

ACKNOWLEDGMENTS

This book has been a whirlwind, from the first word of *The Lost Peterson Apostle* to the last of *Polar Protocol*. To say I am amazed and overwhelmed would be an understatement. To every one of you who helped put this together, thank you. To everyone who has enjoyed reading Matthew's story, thank you. To my wife and kids, thank you.

If you're reading this, thank you.

ABOUT THE AUTHOR

Les Gould grew up in upstate New York where a childhood on a working dairy farm provided fertile soil for a rich imagination. He migrated to Virginia where he graduated from the Virginia Military Institute. He currently works as a mechanical engineer and uses his spare time to spin stories.

Les lives in Virginia with his wife, two kids, and one itchy cockapoo.

You can reach Les at any of the following:

Web: http://www.lesgould.com/
Facebook: https://www.facebook.com/LesGouldWrites/
Twitter: https://mobile.twitter.com/lesgouldwrites
Instagram: https://www.instagram.com/lesgouldwrites/

ALSO BY LES GOULD

Gen-Ship Endurance

The Adam Initiative

Peterson Apostle Monster Hunter

The Lost Peterson Apostle

Solo Op

Polar Protocol

FRIENDS OF FALSTAFF

Thank You to All our Falstaff Books Patrons, who get extra digital content each month! To be featured here and see what other great rewards we offer, go to www.patreon.com/falstaffbooks.

PATRONS

Dino Hicks
John Hooks
John Kilgallon
Larissa Lichty
Travis & Casey Schilling
Staci-Leigh Santore
Sheryl R. Hayes
Scott Norris
Samuel Montgomery-Blinn
Junkle

Made in the USA
Columbia, SC
19 January 2021